CHRONICLES OF CURSES

BOOKS 1-3:
BIG, BAD MISTER WOLFE
SNOWSTORM KING
THE TOWER WITHOUT A DOOR

H. L. Macfarlane

For everyone who loves a good fairy tale.

BIG, BAD MISTER WOLFE

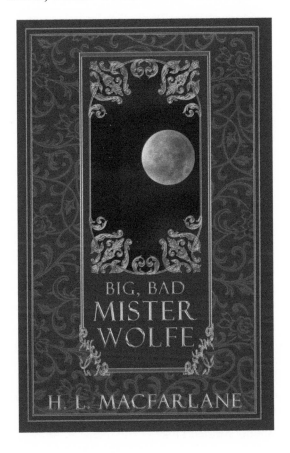

PROLOGUE

Scarlett

There were wolves in the woods. Everyone knew it. You could hear them, howling mournfully in the distance, and then you'd know to keep away from the trees. When they were quiet the people of Rowan could venture through, though they rarely dared to go alone.

But the townsfolk were fearful of travelling too deeply into the woods regardless of whether they could hear the howls or not. The mere thought that just one hungry, smiling, loping wolf might be out to get them was enough to stop most folk from straying off the beaten path that wound through the trees.

But not Scarlett Duke.

For Scarlett's grandmother lived deep in the woods, at least an hour from the outskirts of Rowan. Nobody knew why the kindly old lady chose to live so far from the town and her wealthy son's family. There were rumours that she had fought with her daughter-in-law and that she was kicked out of the house as a result.

But that was only a rumour.

Scarlett loved visiting her grandmother and was often sent to her little house in the woods laden with supplies for the woman. Her mother, Frances, never let her take her younger twin brothers with her, though they longed to explore with their older sister, who doted upon them. Her mother said it was because it was too dangerous, though Scarlett had been travelling through the woods since she was younger than her brothers were now.

Sometimes Scarlett wondered why her mother treated her differently than her two brothers. Where she was warm and generous with Rudy and Elias, she was cold and distant with Scarlett. But she was never cruel, and Scarlett wanted for nothing, so she loved her mother deeply anyway.

Her father, on the other hand, lavished attention on his only daughter, though not in front of his wife. He spoiled Scarlett, sneaking her extra dessert after dinner, taking her out riding on weekends and buying her new dresses when she didn't need them.

Richard Duke was the wealthiest man in town and respected by many. But by virtue of being the wealthiest man in town, and having a daughter who was fast approaching womanhood, many men had begun approaching Scarlett's father vying to marry her to their sons, in the hopes of joining their families together. Scarlett didn't like this...not least because her mother's face twisted into a scowl whenever someone brought it up.

Scarlett sighed heavily in front of the mirror that adorned her dressing table. She didn't look much like her mother, instead inheriting the pale skin, dark hair and blue eyes of her father, whilst Rudy and Elias both had burnished copper curls and green eyes. Frances Duke didn't seem to appreciate that only Scarlett looked like her father, though it wasn't as if her daughter could do anything about this.

And now she was sixteen. Scarlett could see the last vestiges of her childhood disappearing from her face. Her cheeks had lost their baby fat. The Cupid's bow of her lips had become more pronounced. Her lashes had grown in thick and long and fluttering. Her chest and hips were filling out whilst her waist stayed small, and her dark, wavy hair grew long and shiny. She knew, objectively, that she was a pretty girl, but all she yearned for was the tall, willowy frame, golden hair and green eyes of her mother.

Thinking that some fresh air would help her feel better, Scarlett laced up a deep red dress over her white petticoat, sliding on a pair of delicate slippers before casting one final glance at her own reflection. She opened her door as quietly as possible and crept past her brothers' bedroom, since they were both long-since asleep. But just as she reached the bottom of the stairs and made to enter the kitchen to inform her parents that she was going to step outside for a while, the sound of her mother's voice gave her pause.

"Richard, you promised! You swore and you swore that you would send her away, and now you say you won't?"

"My love, Scarlett's done nothing wrong! Why must you punish her for my mistake?"

"She doesn't need to have done anything wrong," her mother scoffed. "Have you seen the men lining up for her hand? I won't have our sons' inheritance put at risk because that whore you slept with gifted you with a beautiful daughter!"

Scarlett froze. What on earth were they talking about?

Her father sounded pained as he said, "Frances, she wasn't a whore. You know that. She –"

"But she wasn't me, was she? I wasn't enough for you back then, and you took it out on me by taking that woman's daughter in."

"It wasn't like that, Frances. Our parents knew I never wanted an arranged marriage. I was acting out. But I love you. I came to love you and that's all that should matter."

"If you loved me you wouldn't have taken Scarlett in."

Scarlett didn't know what to think. Her mother's aloof attitude towards her made far more sense to her now, though.

That didn't make her feel any better.

"What was I supposed to do? Her mother disappeared. She had no-one else."

"So you give her to another family! You don't shame me by bringing her here."

Her father sighed heavily. "She's my daughter, Frances. I love her, and she's dear to Rudy and Elias. I cannot throw her out."

"I'm not asking you to! I'm asking you to send her to her grandmother's. I want her out of sight, and not in line to inherit what are rightfully your sons' fortunes. Lord knows the woman will be happy to have her; she's always been her favourite."

"If you'd let my mother see Rudy and Elias more often –"

"What, in that wolf-infested forest? I think not."

"Frances –"

"Please, Richard," she pleaded. "Just send Scarlett away. I can't bear watching her grow up to look more like you than our sons ever will. Just send her away."

There was a long, conflicted pause, during which Scarlett hardly dared to breathe.

"...as you wish," her father said eventually, his voice sad and resigned. "But let me have one more day with her. I shall send her away after that."

Scarlett didn't hear the rest of the conversation. She fled the corridor, opening the door with trembling hands as she flung herself into the cold, spring evening.

She didn't know where she was going at first, her manic feet scrabbling across the dark, empty road through Rowan. Scarlett's brain was numb; she didn't have the capacity to process what had just occurred. What she had heard. What she had learned.

Her entire life had been a lie.

Before she knew it Scarlett had reached the woods, her breath coming out in little puffs as she shivered slightly. It was only early April, after all, and the night air stung her face. But Scarlett couldn't turn back now. She couldn't face her father – let alone the woman who had always been her mother – when she felt like this.

No. She'd go precisely where they had intended to send her, anyway.

To her grandmother's.

Sincerely wishing she had thought to wrap herself up in one of her expensive cloaks before leaving, Scarlett steeled herself for the hour-long walk along the winding road that eventually led to her grandmother's lonely house.

But Scarlett had never walked through the woods at night before. The place she loved so much felt unfamiliar and eerie, as if one of the long, slender shadows created by the trees might reach out and grab her.

And then she heard it.

The howling.

The wolves, Scarlett thought in sudden, abject terror. She had forgotten the one and only rule even her 'mother' had insisted upon her following – do not enter the woods when the wolves are heard. For the first time in her short life, Scarlett thought that she might die. That this would be her end, pitiful and tragic though it was.

But Scarlett didn't want this to be her end. Hitching up the skirt of her dress, and ignoring the blisters beginning to form on her feet from wearing such insubstantial shoes for a hike through the woods, Scarlett picked up her pace and began to jog along the road.

The howls only grew more and more frequent as she headed deeper into the forest. And they were louder, too, echoing all around until the only sound Scarlett could hear were the soulful, eerie cries of the wolves pacing in the darkness. When she was just ten minutes away from her grandmother's house she was sure she could pick out the tell-tale yellow eyes of the creatures, stalking her every footstep through the woods. Their woods.

"I don't want to die," she cried out silently, the words barely creating a cloud of chilly air in front of Scarlett's face.

When she ran straight into someone her scream was not-so-silent, but a hand was quick to cover her mouth and quell the noise just as she felt another on her back, keeping her from falling.

14

"You have a funny way of showing you don't want to die, little miss," a man growled softly. "What are you doing out here?"

Scarlett hardly dared to look at the man currently holding her up. But she had to; she knew she did. It was too dark to see him properly, though even if it had been bright as day Scarlett would only have taken notice of his eyes.

Amber, like the wolves.

Scarlett fought against him, desperate to pull away for some innate, visceral reason. But the man only held her tighter; then, when the wolves howled once more, pulled her against his chest. Scarlett's heart was hammering so painfully the stranger was bound to feel it. She was too frightened to care.

"Best get you to your grandmother's, Miss Scarlett," he murmured, his voice low and melodic as his strange eyes bored into her own, "else you're liable to get eaten."

Blindly Scarlett allowed the man who somehow knew her to pull her along by the hand, ripping through the trees instead of taking the road without sparing another glance Scarlett's way.

She dared not let go. She knew that if she did it would be the end of her.

When finally she spied the silhouette of her grandmother's house Scarlett could barely breathe, her vision as red as her dress whilst her lungs felt like they were being torn apart. As soon as the pair of them reached the front door the howling of the wolves abated, many of them whining in disappointment. They would not risk getting so close to Scarlett's grandmother's house. They never had.

In the warm light of the lantern hanging above the

15

door Scarlett could finally look at her saviour. He wore a dark cloak over equally dark clothes which matched the ebony of his hair, though a solitary streak of white had broken through the black. But despite that the man could not have been much older than his mid-twenties, going by his relatively unlined face. A small scar split his left eyebrow in two.

And those eyes. In the light those deep amber eyes looked no less unnatural. And they were staring at Scarlett as intently as she was staring at the man they belonged to.

It was only then that Scarlett realised she recognised him as a travelling merchant from the market and clearly why, in turn, he had known who she was. But then the door of her grandmother's house was thrown open, and the woman herself stared at the pair of them with surprise written all over her face.

"Adrian Wolfe, what are you doing on my doorstep with – Red, my goodness! My love, what are you doing here so late?"

Scarlett still hadn't caught her breath. She found her eyes flailing wildly from Adrian's face to her grandmother's as she struggled to vocalise her thoughts.

"I found her close by," Adrian explained, sounding as if he hadn't just run full-pelt through the forest with a young woman in tow. "Someone ought to tell her it's dangerous out here."

"And they have. Get in here, Red! You're freezing – what were you doing out here in clothes like that? You're barely dressed! And Mr Wolfe –"

But the man had disappeared in the time it had taken her to usher Scarlett inside.

"Typical merchant, travelling here and there without so much as a warning," her grandmother tutted. "I should ask him what he was doing out here, this close to my house. We're so far from Rowan! You'd think he'd have learned his lesson about how dangerous the woods are by now."

But Scarlett could barely take in anything her grandmother was saying, numb and shocked as she was. A wave of exhaustion quite suddenly washed over her and so, without saying a word, Scarlett retired to bed and fell into a troubled, dark and fitful sleep.

That night she dreamed of wolves, amber eyes, and a woman who left a baby and ran away.

CHAPTER ONE

Scarlett

Scarlett reached her eighteenth birthday faster than she could have ever thought possible. Two years spent living in the woods with her grandmother after her brush with the wolves had been easy and peaceful and happy...so long as she didn't think about the rest of her family.

For although Scarlett had seen and even conversed with her father and 'mother' since she had run away in the dead of night, and had played with her little brothers on the occasions they were brought along to market at the same time as her, Scarlett was very much separated from the rest of the Dukes. It was a miserable feeling, especially when her father failed to elaborate any further on the nature of Scarlett's existence. She knew he was doing this to spare his wife's feelings, and though often Scarlett resented the way the woman was acting she could hardly blame her.

I'm a threat to her sons and to her marriage, Scarlett reminded herself on a regular basis. *Frances is not wrong to want me out of the picture.*

And it was hardly as if she had been kicked out onto the streets. Heidi Duke – Scarlett's grandmother – was a warm and generous person. And though her house was small and isolated it was by no means impoverished. It was...ordinary. Grounded. Safe.

Which was exactly what Scarlett needed to forget about the circumstances of her birth.

"Are you planning to sleep all morning, Red?" her grandmother called out, startling Scarlett. She had always called her Red, ever since Scarlett was a little girl. She loved the nickname, though thinking about how Rudy and Elias also called her by the moniker made her sad, since she rarely heard their voices now.

"One moment, Nana!" Scarlett replied, hurrying with the laces on her boots before bolting through to the kitchen. When her grandmother saw her generally dishevelled appearance she smiled kindly whilst rolling her eyes.

"You can't go into town looking like that, my love. Have you even combed your hair?"

Scarlett shrugged. Most of the time she kept her hair tied back and out of the way. It served no purpose for her to have it down. And besides, she wanted to draw as little attention to herself as possible, and if that meant keeping up a plain appearance then so be it.

"Come now, Scarlett, you're eighteen now. *Eighteen!* You can't be looking like this now you're a woman."

"What does it matter, Nana?" she replied as she was motioned to sit in a chair. Her grandmother got out a comb and began to run it through Scarlett's long, wavy hair. "If any man were to find out they don't *actually* get a portion of the Duke fortune then they'd turn tail and run away from me as fast as wolves!"

"I somehow doubt that, dear," her grandmother murmured. And then, in exasperation, "Do you take no pride in yourself at all? You still have all those beautiful dresses your father sent over for you."

Scarlett winced as her grandmother worked out a knot in her hair.

"They're not practical for working in, are they?"

"Ah, because I get you to help with such strenuous manual labour, of course."

From the window the two of them heard a snort of laughter.

Her grandmother raised an eyebrow. "Is that you, Samuel?"

The man popped his head up, cheeks red with embarrassment. "Yes, ma'am. My apologies; I didn't mean to sneak about. Ah – morning, Miss Scarlett. Happy birthday!"

"Morning, Sam."

Samuel Birch's family ran a mill; Scarlett's grandmother had hired him to do all of her heavy lifting, such as wood cutting, gardening, repairing the roof and helping Scarlett carry supplies back from the market. Scarlett was fond of the young man, whose sandy hair, green eyes and tanned skin reminded her of her little brothers.

There was nothing *little* about Sam, though. He had

grown big and well-built like his father; Scarlett had once witnessed him carry three sacks of flour over his shoulders like they were nothing.

"Right, my love, head back through to your bedroom and put on that red dress you used to love so much. Yes, the one with the white petticoat. And put some colour on your lips! I have a present for you when you're ready."

Scarlett knew there was no arguing with her grandmother on the subject so she gave Sam one, final smile before retreating back through to her room to change. But she didn't want to unlace her boots, nor remove the thick, woollen tights she was wearing. Rowan had been hit by a bout of cold, nasty weather that was only just beginning to dissipate. Though it was a gloriously sunny, early April day today, snow still lay on the ground and the air bit at Scarlett's cheeks.

Thinking that her grandmother would simply have to accept a compromise, Scarlett shirked out of everything but her tights and boots and carefully redressed in the petticoat and red dress she had originally worn two years ago when she'd been saved by Adrian Wolfe.

Scarlett hadn't thought about the man for a while. Or, at least, she had tried not to. The merchant was only in Rowan once a month so Scarlett found it fairly easy to avoid him. She didn't know *why* she was avoiding him – she still hadn't even thanked him for saving her life, which Scarlett knew was desperately rude.

But there was something about Adrian Wolfe that scared her. Perhaps it was his eyes. Or maybe it was the fact that he'd been prowling through the woods at night, just like the wolves had been doing, and had caught her.

But if he hadn't I'd be dead, Scarlett thought as she finished lacing up her dress and moved to her dressing table. She picked up a pot of red pigment and a tiny brush – a previous gift from her grandmother – and proceeded to carefully paint her lips. Though her grandmother continually insisted upon it Scarlett rarely wore the stuff; there was an association between painted lips and witchcraft amongst the townspeople that she'd rather avoid.

The thought used to scare her, and painting her lips certainly didn't help Scarlett to blend into the crowd, but for some reason now she was beginning to feel bold. Her grandmother had told her to take greater care of her appearance because she was of marrying age. Scarlett didn't care for that but, perhaps now that she was an adult, she could be free to be whomever she pleased for *herself*. And maybe who she wanted to be was a woman who dressed in the colour of her name and wore her hair down her back and smiled mysteriously at strangers.

But Scarlett couldn't help but laugh at the notion, watching as her red-lipped reflection did the same. She certainly looked the part for the fantasy. She merely lacked the confidence and backbone to do it. And, at the end of the day, she didn't care for being a beautiful, mysterious woman. All she wanted was to be accepted back into her family.

"I guess one day as someone different needn't hurt," she mumbled as she ran her fingers through her long, soft hair. With her dark lashes, pale skin and red lips, Scarlett had to admit that she liked her reflection, even though it still pained her to look nothing like her brothers and Frances Duke.

With a swish of her skirts she headed back through to the kitchen where Sam, who was currently leaning on the windowsill drinking a cup of tea prepared for him by her grandmother, gawked at the sight of her.

"Miss – Miss Scarlett, you look –"

"Beautiful," her grandmother beamed, though she frowned when she saw Scarlett's boots.

"There's still snow on the ground, Nana," Scarlett reasoned. "Boots make sense."

"I suppose I can let you off with that *today*. But from now on I want to see you put this much effort into your appearance every day, Red. You have a family name to uphold, whether that wife of my useless son wants to acknowledge you or not."

Scarlett smiled softly as she watched the lined, aged face of her grandmother grow harsh with contempt. When Scarlett had finally explained to her why she had run off at night two years ago, her grandmother had wanted to march over to the Duke household the very next day to shout at her son. But Scarlett had begged her not to – not for her sake but for her brothers.

"If it will make you happy then I'll try to look a little better, Nana," Scarlett said.

The woman's dark expression finally disappeared, and she smiled. "Come over here, Red," she murmured, gesturing for Scarlett to follow her over to the chest she kept by the front door. Inside was lying a large pile of thick, deep crimson fabric.

Scarlett stared at her grandmother. "What is this?"

"Pick it up and see."

With delicate hands Scarlett picked up the fabric, discovering that it was a cloak complete with a white, fur-lined hood.

"I've never seen this before."

"That's because I haven't worn it since before I was married. Seems a shame to let it go to waste when I have such a beautiful grand-daughter who could use it."

"Nana, I can't!" Scarlett protested. "This is yours. I can't take it from you."

But her grandmother merely waved away her comments. "Nonsense! And you've needed a new cloak for a while, now. May as well have one of your own instead of relying on that useless father of yours, right? Come on, my love, try it on!"

She was wrapping Scarlett up in the fabric and tying it across her breastbone before Scarlett could protest further. The material was heavy; the fur that tickled her neck surprisingly soft.

"What's the fur from, Nana?" she asked curiously, twirling slightly to appreciate the way the cloak spun around her feet.

"It's the undercoat of a wolf. Softest fur you'll ever get around these parts."

"Oh." Something about literally wearing a wolf somewhat unsettled Scarlett but she pushed the feeling to the side for now. She smiled for her grandmother and curtsied slightly for Sam, who had watched her put on the cloak in numb silence, his tea long since forgotten. "How do I look?"

"Like a Duke," her grandmother said proudly. "Like a beautiful, confident woman. What do you think, Samuel?"

"Huh? Oh, I – Miss Scarlett, you look wonderful!"

Scarlett couldn't help but giggle at Sam's bumbling compliment. She had known him for two years and in that time she had never seen him struggle with his words *quite* as much as he currently was. There was something deeply satisfying about it.

She reached up to unhook a basket from the wall. "I best be off to market before Mr Beck is out of bread."

"Ah, Miss Scarlett, would you like a hand?"

Scarlett shook her head. "That's okay, Sam. And I'm sure my grandmother needs you here." She kissed the woman on her cheek as she opened the front door and felt the cold spring air hit her face. It was refreshing, and brought a flash of colour to Scarlett's face.

"Be sure to pick up some cake from Charles, too!" her grandmother called out after her. "It *is* your birthday, after all!"

Scarlett waved a hand in acknowledgement as she made her way down the winding, twisting road through the woods. On a beautiful, golden morning such as today, with the sun turning the frost dusting the trees to diamonds and birds filling the air with song, Scarlett could hardly believe how terrified she'd been of the very same place when she'd turned sixteen.

Unbidden she thought once more of Adrian Wolfe and his strange, strange eyes. They belonged in a dream, just like the night itself. He wasn't a man that Scarlett wanted to think about when the sun was out and she was dressed in red, informing the world that she was alive and she was there and she was grown.

And yet, even still, as Scarlett made her way into the town of Rowan, she couldn't help but secretly hope that the man would be there.

Secretly.

CHAPTER TWO

Adrian

"She's really grown up nicely, ain't she, Gerold?"

"And eighteen now, too! She'll be swarming in marriage requests soon, no doubt."

"But didn't she get sent to live with her grandmother instead of living in the main house? Why was that?"

"It don't matter - she's still his daughter!"

Adrian Wolfe had tried to avoid the inane chatter of the two merchants who'd travelled into town with him. Honestly, he had. But the men had been talking about the same person for over ten minutes now as they finished setting up their stalls, and even Adrian could admit he was curious.

"Who're you talking about?" he asked politely, keeping his face as blandly curious as possible.

Gerold Rogers stared at him in disbelief. "Why, Scarlett Duke, of course! I know you're only through here once a month but you can't have missed her, Wolfe!"

Of course Adrian knew Scarlett Duke. She had run into his arms in the dark of night, in the middle of the woods, just two years earlier. It had seemed like something out of a fairytale or a dream – a young, beautiful and terrified woman lost and alone at the mercy of wolves.

And more than one kind, at that, Adrian thought in amusement, though he kept his expression blank as he nodded at Gerold in acknowledgement.

"Ah, you're right. I know her. Does all the errands for Heidi."

"Didn't know you were on first name terms with the old lady, Wolfe," the other man, Frank Holt, replied.

"I've done business with her on more than a few occasions. She has a pretty great stock of rare herbs from the mountains that I like, though lord knows how she got them in the first place."

"She's a good girl through and through," Gerold continued on wistfully, talking about Scarlett once more. "I wish all the young folk looked after their elders like she does Old Lady Duke. I'd be content if I had a lovely girl like her looking after me when I grow old..."

"Come off it! You don't have a son to marry her to. Now if she likes her men a little older, then I'd –"

"A *little* older? You're almost old enough to be her father yourself, Frank! And ugly to boot."

"It's not like we can all look like Prince Charming

27

here," Frank muttered, gesturing towards Adrian.

Adrian chuckled in bemusement. "I'm too lowly and dishonest to be a prince."

Gerold slapped him on the back amiably. "You've got that right! Though anyone that falls for all those spells and potions of yours *deserves* to be conned."

"Most of them work, to be fair...if they were sold at the correct concentration," Adrian replied in an undertone.

"Oh, you're right. You're too sly to be Prince Charming. Best keep you well away from our Miss Scarlett."

"Keep who away from me?"

All three men turned in surprise to see who had spoken.

Of course it was Scarlett, but not a Scarlett whom Adrian had seen before, though he recognised her red dress immediately. This wasn't the girl with fear in her eyes, her feet bleeding and hair a tangled, wild mess as she fled the howling of the wolves.

No. This was a woman with gently curling, shining black hair framing her pale, heart-shaped face with the hint of a smile playing across her red, red lips. A crimson, fur-lined cloak cascaded down her shoulders, lending her the regal air of a queen. Her beauty had an unearthly quality to it that Adrian didn't quite understand, but it was clear that it wasn't just he who was enraptured by her.

Her smile disappeared when Scarlett realised that she had come face to face with Adrian. Her heavy lashes fluttered wide for a moment as she took a breath, then the smile reappeared, though it was altogether more formal.

"Mr Wolfe," she said, inclining her head slightly before turning to Frank. "Now what were you saying about me?"

"Miss Scarlett, happy birthday! You look breathtaking today."

She had the good sense to blush at the comment, though it was clear that Frank was trying to distract her. She glanced at Gerold. "Mr Rogers, my grandmother could do with some of that blue dye you said you were developing a few months ago. Do you have any?"

The man beamed as he slung an arm around Scarlett's shoulders and redirected her to his stall. "Anything for Old Lady Duke! As it happens, I made sure to bring extra just for her..."

Adrian turned back to his own stall to take note of what he was running low on. The long winter had depleted his stock of several herbs that should already be ripe for the picking, but were late to grow. He wondered if Heidi Duke had any, though he was loathe to ask.

After all, Adrian Wolfe detested the old woman down to his very soul, if indeed he had any soul left to hate a person with.

He glanced at Scarlett out of the corner of his eye, resplendent and glowing in red. When he had come across the young woman in the forest he had almost left her alone to die, simply to spite her grandmother. But Adrian was not a cold-blooded killer, and Scarlett held no responsibility for what Heidi had done to cause Adrian to hate her so much.

But now, looking at the woman's beloved grand-daughter, he had an idea.

When Scarlett had finished at Gerold's stall Adrian indicated for her to come over to his. In front of so many people she had no choice but to do as he wished, though she looked very much as if she wanted to run away.

He pretended to discuss a potion or two with her until both Gerold and Frank turned their attention to their other customers, then, when she was close enough to hear his voice, murmured, "You still haven't thanked me for saving your life, little miss."

Scarlett flinched. "You...disappeared."

"You saw me at the market just one month later."

"No I didn't."

"Liar."

She blushed furiously. "I didn't know what to say to you."

"What's so hard about 'thank you'?"

Scarlett hesitated. "...thank you."

"See, that wasn't difficult," he grinned, thoroughly enjoying the expression on Scarlett's face as he teased her. "What were you doing in the woods so late back then, anyway? And unsupervised! You could have run into *anyone*. Good thing I'm a gentleman."

"I highly doubt that," Scarlett bit out seemingly before she could stop herself, then covered her mouth with her hand as she realised what she'd just said.

"I highly doubt it, too," Adrian laughed, amused by her accidental candour, "though I must admit it stings to hear that from a young lady I most certainly *was* a gentleman to."

Scarlett's eyes darted up to his own and away again so quickly that Adrian almost imagined the action. "Really, thank you," she mumbled as she looked at her feet. "I didn't mean to insult you. I probably wouldn't be alive if not for you."

Oh, this is going to be fun, Adrian thought as he hooked a leather-gloved finger beneath Scarlett's chin and tilted her face up, only for her cheeks to burn in response. "No insult taken," he smiled. "Just so long as you stop so very clearly trying to ignore me from now on."

"I –"

But Scarlett didn't finish her sentence, instead breaking away from Adrian's touch in order to rush away towards the bakery across the street. A slew of people watched as her red cloak fluttered behind her, particularly the men, who couldn't take their eyes off her.

"Prince Charming, indeed," Gerold scoffed. "You've only gone and scared her off!"

Adrian shrugged. "I like a challenge."

"Don't you dare hurt Miss Scarlett's feelings."

"He'd have to be in with a chance with her to do that," Frank joked. "I have it on good authority that the baker's son's had his eyes on her for years."

"I thought it was the blacksmith? And Birch's boy?"

"So I have competition, it seems," Adrian murmured, not at all surprised. He knew the Dukes were the wealthiest family in town; it was natural that many of the single men in Rowan would be vying for Scarlett's affections. But she clearly wasn't used to the attention, given how she ran from Adrian merely touching her face. He had a sneaking suspicion that her confident, grown-up facade had been entirely her grandmother's doing.

That only works in my favour, Adrian thought wickedly as he spun a bottle full of turquoise liquid up into the air and expertly caught it to the delight and surprise of the group of young women currently passing by his stall. The liquid bubbled and fizzed for a few seconds and, once it had settled, the colour changed to a deep, inky purple. One of the women squealed in interest.

31

Women are so easy, Adrian thought with a grin as he sold the overly-diluted, useless potion to her as an attraction spell.

"I guess Miss Scarlett will be breaking several hearts over the next few weeks!" Gerold commented over on Adrian's left, the older man's eyes following the baker's son as he in turn followed Scarlett into his father's shop.

Adrian could only smirk. For whilst Scarlett broke the hearts of the simple boys in Rowan, he would work away at winning hers. It would be something Heidi Duke would be unable to abide. She'd beg for him to leave her precious grand-daughter alone.

And then, maybe then, Adrian could finally get back what she stole from him.

Yes, Scarlett's heart was the perfect bargaining chip. All Adrian had to do was make the shy, naive girl fall for him.

Something told him that it wouldn't be difficult at all.

CHAPTER THREE

Scarlett

"Miss Scarlett, might I – ah – have a word with you?"

Scarlett turned in surprise, her grandmother's cloak twirling around her as she did so. It was the baker's eldest son, Charlie. She gave him a gentle smile that belied the fact her heart was still battering in her ribcage after her unexpected encounter with Adrian Wolfe.

"Of course, Charlie. Is it alright if I finish paying your father first, though?"

Charlie's face grew red as a beet when he realised he had interrupted the transaction, though his father merely laughed.

"Overeager as usual, my boy. I've put in a few extra

buns for your birthday, Scarlett. Please wish Heidi well."

"Thank you kindly!" she beamed, before taking her basket now laden with baked goods from the counter and dutifully following Charlie back outside. He motioned towards the bench that sat outside the shop window, which an hour ago had been covered in frost. Now the sun had melted it away, leaving the grain of the carved wood littered with tiny droplets of water.

"Ah, let me dry that for you," Charlie said hurriedly, grabbing the cleaning rag he kept tucked underneath his belt and wiping away the moisture.

Scarlett motioned for him to stop before sitting down. "I'm fine, Charlie. My cloak will do more than a good enough job of keeping me dry."

He stared at the furred hood in barely-concealed envy. Scarlett had known the garment was expensive the moment she'd laid eyes on it, but she had grown up with expensive clothes all her life. She'd forgotten how such things looked to the other townspeople of Rowan.

"It's a hand-me-down," Scarlett found herself explaining, though in reality she had no need to defend herself for owning such a cloak. "My grandmother's. She gave me it today for my birthday."

"It's beautiful," Charlie replied, still eyeing the fur. "Is that – wolf fur – by any chance?"

"It is, actually," she replied in surprise. "How did you know? I had no idea until Nana told me."

Charlie held up his hand, waiting for permission to touch the cloak, so Scarlett gave the barest of nods before the young man gently ran his fingers over the soft, luxurious fur. "I used to go out hunting with my Da when he was a little younger. Not so much anymore. I was always surprised by how soft the underfur was on a wolf.

But usually the ones we caught weren't in the best shape so their fur was pretty useless. Not like this."

Despite the fact that the wolves had nearly killed Scarlett she somehow found herself not liking the idea of Charlie and his father venturing into the forest with the intention of hunting them down. It didn't seem...right, somehow.

"Nana said she's had this cloak since before she got married, so she must have taken especially good care of it for the fur to still be so soft," Scarlett murmured as she ran her fingers through it, then paused when Charlie's hand met hers. She glanced up through her lashes and saw that his face had grown red again, but it was resolute and determined.

"You're going to ask me to marry you, aren't you, Charlie?" she asked before she could stop herself. Scarlett had never been so bold before; clearly turning eighteen had allowed her to finally speak her mind.

Charlie looked taken aback by the question, though he kept his fingers intertwined through Scarlett's in the fur of her cloak. "I - yes. I was. I know I don't have much, but my father's bakery does well enough. But you would know that, since you're here most every day. And we have more than enough space in the house for you until we get a place of our own - which wouldn't be long because I've been saving, and -"

"Charlie, stop for a moment, please."

He looked at Scarlett in earnest, his blonde hair and freckled face dusted with flour.

Scarlett sighed. "Charlie, I'm not in line to inherit any of the Duke money. It's all going to my brothers."

"I...thought as much," he sighed, looking a little downcast. "I mean, why else would you be sent away from your father's house?"

"It's complicated. Let's just leave it at that."

But then Charlie grinned, his enthusiasm renewed. "I don't care about you not getting any of his money, Scarlett. You're the only girl in this whole town that I want to marry. You're well-spoken and pretty and helpful and my parents *love* you –"

"Miss Scarlett?"

Both Charlie and Scarlett frowned at each other at the interruption. They looked up in unison to see Jakob Schmidt, the blacksmith, standing in front of them, a very pretty bundle of snowdrops held between his burly hands.

Jakob was older than Scarlett by nearly ten years, and she had known him since she was very small. He dealt with all of her father's horses and so was often on the Duke property. Every spring he would gift Scarlett with a single snowdrop, which seemed so at odds with his rough demeanour that Scarlett at first found it amusing. But when she had reached twelve or so she had found the gesture very romantic and had even imagined herself marrying the man.

She couldn't imagine doing so now, though he was sweet, funny and hard-working. Which meant that Scarlett could only try her best to conceal her horror at the fact that Jakob might very well be intending to ask her the exact same question Charlie Beck had only just fumbled through.

"We were in the middle of something, Mr Schmidt," Charlie said, barely concealing his annoyance.

The older man shrugged. "Which was exactly why I interrupted. Can't have you jumping in before me, Beck." Jakob handed Scarlett the flowers, which she numbly accepted. "Miss Scarlett," he began as if Charlie wasn't there at all, "I have made no secret of my affection for you over the years. And now that you have grown into such a beautiful woman –"

Jakob paused, taking in Scarlett's appearance with deliberation, his eyes slightly wide as he realised how different she looked today. He took Scarlett's hands and motioned for her to stand up. Scarlett did so, feeling her face flush as Jakob took all of her in, focusing half a second too long on the curves of her breasts that could just barely be seen through the gap in her cloak. To her side Charlie also stood up, outraged into silence at Jakob's bold and blatant hijacking of his proposal.

"Beautiful doesn't even cover it," Jakob murmured. "Miss Scarlett, you are possibly the most lovely woman I have ever had the privilege of setting my eyes upon. You would honour me beyond belief in becoming my wife."

For a moment Scarlett didn't know what to say. It was easy to become swayed by Jakob's unexpectedly poetic words, especially after the over-eager, bumbling proposal Charlie had been in the middle of giving.

But then Scarlett cleared her throat and said, "Mr Schmidt, I shall say the same thing I said to Charlie – I do not stand to inherit any of my father's money."

Jakob merely waved a dismissive hand. "I do well enough. I don't care for your father's money – except what he spends on my services directly. Surely you must have known I'd intended to ask for your hand today, Scarlett?"

She shook her head. "I must profess to knowing nothing."

"Oh, your father is a crafty one," he laughed. "He was always so over-protective."

Scarlett frowned, as did Charlie beside her who had no

37

idea what was going on. "I don't understand, Mr. Schmidt. What are you trying to say?"

He squeezed her hands around the snowdrops he'd gifted her. "I asked your father to allow me to marry you two years ago, Scarlett. But he said you were too young, which of course was true. But now you're not, and I have no intention of losing you to anybody else."

"Ah – Miss Scarlett?"

"*She's busy!*" both Charlie and Jakob roared at the new-found interruption. For behind Jakob stood a young man Scarlett hadn't seen in four years.

Andreas Sommer, older brother of Scarlett's childhood friend Henrietta. Their father, Otto, was a prominent doctor in the area, and Andreas had been training as a physician abroad in order to take up his place when his father retired.

He had grown taller in his time away. Along with the high arch of his cheekbones, fine clothes and perfectly styled hair, he looked every inch the kind of man Scarlett imagined her father would have wanted her to marry. In any other situation Scarlett would have been very happy to see him after four years apart.

But not today.

"I – Andreas – I did not know you had returned," she said simply.

Jakob and Charlie glared at their new rival, but Andreas seemed immune to them. He smiled dashingly for Scarlett.

"It has been too long, Scarlett. Might I speak to you in private?"

"You may not!" Charlie exclaimed. "*I* was speaking to her before the both of you interrupted!"

"Oh please, boy," Jakob said, all his previously poetic words forgotten. "You were barely managing to vocalise your thoughts before –"

"I was doing just fine!"

Scarlett's eyes darted between all three of them, feeling very much like a cornered animal.

"Scarlett," Andreas continued on in earnest, "when we were children our fathers had plans to betroth us, but for whatever unfortunate reason this never came to be more than a discussion."

Now I know exactly *why that never came to be,* Scarlett mused, thinking of Frances and how distressed she must have been by such a betrothal. She felt a keening sense of regret; marrying Andreas seemed very much like the path Scarlett was *supposed* to have taken before she was kicked out. It was the right proposal for her, rather than her adolescent fancy for the blacksmith who gave her snowdrops.

"Well you've missed your chance, Andreas," Jakob said, surreptitiously trying to elbow the other man out of the way.

Behind them all Scarlett heard someone laughing raucously. For some reason she didn't need to see who it was to know that it was Adrian Wolfe. It made her feel angry. It made her feel small.

But above all, it dried up the last vestige of patience she had.

"Charlie, Mr Schmidt, Andreas – you must all realise your behaviour right now is entirely inappropriate," Scarlett said loudly, ensuring that many bystanders could hear her and help her escape if need be. The three men looked at her in surprise, perhaps shocked to realise that Scarlett was capable of raising her voice.

"Today is my birthday, and I came into town to fetch supplies to celebrate with my grandmother – not to listen to your proposals. Perhaps all three of you should take some time to rethink what it is you wish to say to me, and when it would actually be appropriate to say it. And perhaps..."

She rearranged her cloak over her shoulders, ran a hand through her hair and broke away from the three men, before turning back to look at them with a hint of a smile on her face.

"Perhaps you could all do with learning some manners. I'm a woman, not a horse up for auction. If you think I'd consider marrying *any* of you the way you are now, you are sadly mistaken."

And then she walked away with confidence, though it was all an act. In reality she was desperate to run away as fast as her legs could carry her, but that would only encourage them to run after her. No, she had to be strong and witty and opinionated, and maybe then they'd leave her be. She brought the snowdrops Jakob had given her up to her nose and smelled their crisp, gentle scent. She was allowed to keep them, even if she refused the man's proposal. They were a gift, after all, and she liked them.

When she walked by Adrian Wolfe and the rest of the travelling merchants she resisted the urge to look at her feet. Instead, she locked eyes with the man and nodded. His mouth quirked into a smile, the laughter from before still playing across his lips. Scarlett felt a heat coiling up inside her in response. It was like a snake, writhing around just below her stomach. She hadn't felt anything like it since the night he had saved her from the wolves. She had always thought it was because she was scared.

But she wasn't scared now, which meant it couldn't be because of fear.

She wasn't sure she wanted to know what it meant.

But, for now, Scarlett was going to return to her grandmother's and eat cake and regale her with the three disastrous proposals that had landed in her lap.

She could think about Mr Wolfe another day.

CHAPTER FOUR

Adrian

Adrian wasn't often in the town of Rowan just prior to the full moon. It involved him having to actually pay for room and board, which he had grown used to not paying whenever he was through. It was just about the only perk to what Heidi Duke had done to him.

"Sam, I don't know if you have a chance with her. She pretty much turned me down flat. Although it might have gone better if I hadn't been interrupted..."

Adrian had to resist the urge to laugh from his corner table in the local tavern. Charlie Beck, the baker's son, was drowning his sorrows in beer with the miller's son – the one Adrian knew worked for Heidi on occasion. He'd seen him help Scarlett with her shopping before, too.

From a stool by the bar the blacksmith choked on his drink. "You never stood a shadow of a chance, Beck! Now I, on the other hand, was actually getting somewhere before Prince Childhood Friend showed up."

But his friend, whom Adrian didn't recognise, shook his head. "Come off it, Jakob. You really think she would have accepted *your* hand when she could marry Otto's boy?"

"See, Sam, you don't stand a chance," Charlie said once more.

Sam stayed silent, fiddling with his tankard with large, clumsy fingers. "She *might* say yes to me, Charlie...I'm with her almost every day."

"And has she ever shown any romantic inclination towards you, boy?" Jakob hollered over.

Sam's ears seemed to burn as he shook his head slightly, but then he stared at the blacksmith in earnest. "But Scarlett hasn't shown *anyone* affection, has she? So maybe she's just really good at keeping her feelings to herself."

Adrian had to hand it to the boy; clearly he didn't want to give up. Well, it wasn't as if he'd built up the courage to propose to Scarlett Duke yet. For all Adrian knew she *would* accept his hand in marriage.

But I can't let that happen, he thought, immediately much more interested in the conversation the men were having. *I can't let Scarlett accept* any *of their proposals.* For if she did then Adrian wouldn't be able to use her to lift his damned curse.

"She's always been happy to accept flowers from me," Jakob said almost haughtily. "And at least I already know how to treat a woman right. The two of you are still wet

43

behind the ears."

"And what about me?"

Andreas glided into the tavern and interrupted the conversation as easily as he had interrupted Jakob's proposal. The older man rolled his eyes.

"I guess being a childhood friend counts for something," Charlie muttered reluctantly, "though Miss Scarlett wasn't exactly jumping straight into your arms, either."

The barkeep handed Andreas a tankard of ale and he sat himself down – unexpectedly – by Charlie and Sam, who both seemed rather surprised by the action.

"Where else do you expect me to sit?" Andreas asked, unperturbed. "I've been away for four years. Most of my friends are still abroad. How old are the two of you now, anyway?"

"Nineteen," Charlie replied defensively. "You're not going to spout all that 'wet behind the ears' nonsense too are you, Sommer? You're barely three years older than us."

Andreas chuckled. "Three years older but with a wealth of experience abroad. And I've known Scarlett since we were children. I'd say that puts me ahead of the two of you."

"Not ahead of Sam," Charlie said, willingly sacrificing his own claim in order to defend his friend against their rival. "He really does spend every day with Miss Scarlett. He's even seen her naked."

"*Charlie I told you that in private,*" Sam growled through gritted teeth in a monotone that barely hid his horror at being called out.

The comment garnered the attention of most all the

men in the tavern, particularly Jakob, who moved from the bar to squeeze in at the same table as his rivals. Even Gerold and Frank, who were sitting close to Adrian, moved their stools closer to listen into the conversation.

Of course Adrian was interested in what the boy had seen, but it wouldn't do to have everyone *know* that he was interested. He needed to keep a low profile and swoop in on Scarlett when the other men were all too busy trying to one-up each other. So he crossed his leather-clad legs, leaned back against the window and took a long draught of his beer, keeping his eyes half-closed as if he were sleeping, and listened carefully.

"You know, the past couple years she's clearly been trying to cover herself up but today she was dressed differently," Jakob said. "Now, that new cloak of hers was hiding most of her but my eyes don't lie – she's got some breasts on her, doesn't she, boy?"

Sam looked wildly discomfited by the question. But there were too many eyes on him, and the pressure was on. Something told Adrian he was incapable of lying.

"...yes," he mumbled. "They're, um, pretty perfect, like the rest of her."

"Outrageous!" Jakob protested, slamming his tankard down on the table to emphasise the word. "How is it that the miller's boy gets to see her naked *by accident* before me or even childhood friend over here? I'm beyond jealous."

"She was only fourteen when I left," Andreas murmured. "It wouldn't have been right for me to see her unclothed before now."

"Ah, I can't wait for the weather to get warmer," Charlie sighed wistfully. "We might see more of her, then. Has anyone seen Miss Scarlett swim in the lake or the river before?"

Even Sam shook his head. "She's fairly private."

"Do any of us even stand a chance? Miss Scarlett was pretty angry when she walked away this morning."

"Maybe you lads need some of Wolfe's love potions," Gerold suddenly chimed in. Adrian opened his eyes wide at the comment, throwing a proverbial dagger the man's way as all attention was suddenly on him.

Charlie moved over to his table eagerly. "Do you really have something that would help, Mr Wolfe?! Do you?"

Adrian quirked an eyebrow. "I do. I won't sell you it, though."

"And why not?!"

"I think the little miss should be allowed to make her own choice, should she not?"

"But that shouldn't matter to you. I want to buy your potion, Mr Wolfe."

He crossed his arms and kept up as serious a face as possible. "Absolutely not. You couldn't afford it, anyway."

Charlie's shoulders fell. "I guess not. I bet Andreas could, though."

"Love potions are nonsense."

Adrian couldn't help but laugh. "Think that at your own risk, doctor. I suppose it would make it all the more satisfying to watch you fall under the effects of one of them." He was thinking of the young woman he had sold the attraction potion to earlier that day, who had professed to having an eye on the man now that he was back. It was far too weak to work *properly,* but the look on Andreas' face as Adrian's words sunk in was priceless.

Jakob laughed loudly as he thumped Andreas on the

46

back. "That's what you get for insulting a merchant, Sommer. But I guess we should all just listen to what Scarlett actually said rather than trying to bewitch her."

Sam frowned. "What did she say?"

None of them expected Adrian to answer. "To paraphrase: don't corner her on the street and profess your undying love in front of the whole town one after the other and then get into a pissing contest that doesn't actually put her feelings into consideration whatsoever. Oh, and perhaps be a little more romantic."

The three men who had proposed to Scarlett had the sense to look abashed.

"I guess we *did* look like idiots," Jakob admitted.

"And now Sam has the advantage," Charlie said. "He can perfect his first proposal and not look like a damn fool."

I can't be having that, Adrian thought. He rummaged through the pockets in his cloak, where he stored small bottles of very concentrated potions that, for once, actually did what they were supposed to do. Locating the vial in question, which was half-full of colourless liquid, Adrian finished his beer, stood up and nodded good-bye to the men he'd been forced into conversation with.

When he moved past their table he slipped some of the vial's contents into Sam's tankard. Not a single person noticed.

"I'll have to speak to my father about organising a meeting with Mr Duke," Adrian heard Andreas say as he crossed the tavern floor for the stairs up to the bedrooms on the first floor.

"But she's been disinherited for some reason," Charlie said.

"Doesn't mean proper decorum shouldn't be followed."

"Show off..."

Adrian climbed the rickety stairs in silence up to his room. The substance he'd slipped Samuel Birch would cause him to forget about proposing to Scarlett for three days. That gave him three days to woo and impress Scarlett enough that she'd never consider accepting the boy's affections. By most anyone's standards that was barely any time at all. For Adrian, who wouldn't be able to do anything once the full moon rose, it was even less.

But that didn't matter. He would do it.

Three days was all Adrian Wolfe needed.

CHAPTER FIVE

Scarlett

"Nana, where's the sugar?"

"Where it always is, Red."

"It's not in the cupboard," Scarlett said in exasperation. "Where did you put it?"

"Oh, Miss Scarlett, that's my fault," Sam murmured from the parlour, where he was building a fire in preparation for the sun setting. He came through to the kitchen and reached up to one of the higher shelves that Scarlett couldn't reach and pulled down the jar of sugar she'd been looking for. "I was helping your grandmother tidy up yesterday and put it on the shelf."

Scarlett smiled warmly. "Thank you, Sam."

"No problem."

Sam scratched his head, then, and wrinkled his nose as if a fly had landed on it. It made Scarlett giggle.

"What's wrong, Sam?" she asked. "Seems like something's on your mind."

"There's nothing wrong. Well, at least I don't *think* there's something on my mind," he muttered as he fiddled with the ochre braces holding his trousers up.

"How can you not know whether something's on your mind or not?"

"He's probably hungover, the rate he was drinking last night."

Scarlett turned; by the open front door stood a grinning Adrian Wolfe. Her heart felt like it had jumped into her throat quite suddenly, which she didn't like in the slightest.

"Knock, knock," he chuckled, silently chapping his knuckles against the door.

"What are you doing here so late?" Scarlett's grandmother complained as she got up from the table, where she'd been knitting. "It's almost sunset! We were just about to retire to the parlour before the wolves started up their *dreadful* howling."

Adrian seemed amused by the comment, though Scarlett failed to see what was so funny.

"I was wondering if you still kept a stock of tansy and sweet violet?" he asked. "I'm all out."

Her grandmother frowned. "And why should I give any of it to you?"

"Because I'll pay?"

She sighed heavily; for a long moment Scarlett was

sure she would refuse, though she had no idea why her grandmother and Adrian Wolfe were on such bad terms. Scarlett had always thought her grandmother would be grateful to the man for saving her life.

But now, thinking about it, hadn't Nana initially been angry that Adrian was outside her house in the first place two years ago?

Now all Scarlett could wonder about was what Adrian had done to anger her grandmother so.

Eventually the old woman nodded and, with some reluctance, got up from her chair and beckoned for Sam to help her. "I keep my stocks in the attic these days. Come on, Samuel, I need you to pull the ladder down for me."

Sam looked very much like he didn't want to leave Scarlett alone in the kitchen with a man she barely knew, but then he frowned as if in confusion and ran a hand through his hair. He shook his head as he followed Scarlett's grandmother through to the corridor.

There were a few seconds of awkward silence as Scarlett moved about the kitchen making tea. She was very aware that Adrian's unsettling eyes followed her wherever she went.

"So where's the cloak, Red?"

She flinched. "Don't call me that."

"But that's what Heidi calls you. And it's what your name means."

"Even so."

"Red it is, then," he said, smirking when Scarlett finally looked away from her tea to glare at him.

"What were you talking about when you said Sam was hungover?"

Adrian moved from the doorway to settle into a chair before Scarlett could say anything about it, stretching out his long legs in front of him in satisfaction. He was dressed in black as usual, though the braces that held up the dark leggings largely hidden by his leather boots were silver. They matched the strange, white streak in his hair.

He shrugged. "He was drinking a lot in the tavern with those men who asked to marry you yesterday."

Scarlett bristled, turning away from Adrian in order to curl her hands into the wooden counter-top by the wash basin. The more she thought about what had happened the more annoyed she became, especially because Adrian had witnessed the entire thing.

"They were all talking about you," he continued jovially. "Apparently your Mr Birch has seen you naked before."

"He *what?*" Scarlett exclaimed, outraged and mortified. Her eyes darted to the corridor and back again to confirm that both Sam and her grandmother were out of earshot, then rounded on Adrian lounging by the kitchen table as if he owned the place. She narrowed her eyes. "You're only saying that to tease me."

"Oh, that's definitely so, but that doesn't mean it isn't true. They were all very enthusiastically discussing how you – ah – *measured up*, as it were. Now that I can see you without the cloak on I can ascertain that Samuel was telling the truth. Maybe you should wear a little more when he's around just so he doesn't get any ideas...or so your lack of attire doesn't excite unexpected guests."

Scarlett had no idea what Adrian was talking about at first, then felt her cheeks flush as she glanced downward. She was wearing the white smock she tended to wear to bed, though it was several years old and much too small for her now. The bodice barely held in her breasts and the skirt skimmed a few inches above her knees, something which Scarlett had never deemed an issue before given that nobody came out to visit her grandmother unexpectedly. And Sam was, well, Sam.

Clearly I need to rethink that last part, Scarlett thought, *though if he's already seen me naked then there's nothing else new for him to see.*

Shocked by her own obvious lack of modesty, she looked about for something to cover herself up.

Adrian merely laughed. "Good; be more aware of yourself. Never mind those wolves two years ago – a baker, a blacksmith and a doctor almost ate you whole yesterday morning. That sounds like the beginning of a joke."

"Do you take *nothing* seriously?"

Adrian stared at her. Scarlett had to fight the instinct to look away.

"Maybe. Maybe not. Why, are you interested?"

"No."

"Liar."

"Stop calling me a liar."

"I will when you stop lying."

"Who are you to tell me what to do?"

Adrian stood up and closed the gap between them, brushing a gloved hand against Scarlett's chin where he had touched her the day before. She couldn't believe he had the audacity to do such a thing in her grandmother's house.

"An interested party," he murmured, gently turning Scarlett's head left and right with his hand. She numbly allowed him to. "You really have grown up, little miss. Though I did enjoy the frightened look on your face when you were sixteen."

Disconcertingly close, a wolf howled, and Scarlett's eyes widened as her body twitched and her heart raced with the memory of the very night Adrian was talking about.

"Ah – that one. Beautiful."

He watched Scarlett intently, his amber eyes fiery in the bleeding light that filtered through the window as the sun began to die. The white in his hair flashed gold when he cocked his head to the side as if he were anticipating what Scarlett would do next.

The action didn't seem entirely human. Scarlett didn't know why.

"You're...very strange, Mr Wolfe."

It was an understatement, but it was all Scarlett could think to say without very obviously insulting the man. And then he grinned, drawing back his thin lips to reveal sharp, white canines. He moved away from Scarlett, retreating to the front door just as her grandmother and Sam returned to the kitchen.

"I found what you needed, Adrian," her grandmother said as she handed him a small, paper-wrapped packet, "but it could do with drying out by a fire. Be sure to do so before you use them for anything."

"Naturally. Many thanks, Heidi."

And then he was gone as quickly as he'd disappeared the night he'd saved Scarlett's life.

"Miss Scarlett?" Sam wondered aloud. "Are you okay?"

"Hmm?"

She turned to face Sam, though she barely saw him. Her hand had found its way to her chin, where Adrian had touched her. Part of her wished he hadn't been wearing gloves. Part of her was very, sincerely glad he had.

And then she came back to her senses and remembered what Adrian had said about Sam.

"I'm going to get changed. I'm cold," she muttered suddenly before rushing out of the kitchen.

In reality she was burning.

CHAPTER SIX

Adrian

Heidi Duke wasn't aware anyone was watching her. And, for all intents and purposes, nobody was. Unless one counted the animals, in which case there was a solitary pair of amber eyes shadowing her every move through the window.

Adrian prowled on silent paws, making sure not to be seen by the old woman responsible for his affliction. She seemed blissfully unaware of his presence, which was just as well. If she noticed then he'd likely suffer an even deeper curse than the one she had cast on him six years ago.

Because for the three nights surrounding the full

moon, each and every month of the year, Adrian's surname was *exactly* what he became.

And for selling the wretched woman fake potions, no less. Talk about grudges.

Adrian had been a fresh-faced twenty-year-old merchant at the time, setting off on his own after a plague had wiped out much of the village he had hailed from, including his parents. His father had been a professional con-man, whilst his mother was a healer. They'd always joked that opposites attract, and had been sickeningly in love for all of Adrian's life. The cumulative knowledge passed down from them to him had resulted in their son arrogantly assuming he could pass off diluted potions and spells even as he sold legitimate remedies for genuine ailments.

That had worked...for a while. It was, for the most part, fanciful, flighty young women who bought his potions, anyway. Nobody expected them to actually *work.* He made them just strong enough for the person who bought them to fleetingly capture the attention of their target before wearing off entirely. For most of them this was all they really desired – a fantasy.

Heidi Duke was not one of those young, flighty women. No, she had required something much stronger from him. Much darker. A poison of the soul, that slowly clawed away at the very edges of a person until there was nothing left inside of them. Adrian *had* possessed what she wanted to purchase.

He just hadn't wanted to give it away.

And so he'd sold the woman a version of the poison so weak that its effects were non-existent.

What he hadn't expected was for her to knock him over the head, tie him to a tree and feed him his own poison, thus demonstrating that Adrian had been trying to con her out of her money.

Heidi had been furious. Adrian was sure he was going to die, that day. It seemed as if she intended to keep him tied there at the mercy of the wolves. But then those wolves had given her an idea, and Heidi cruelly bewitched Adrian to turn into one of the very creatures that roamed the forest.

It was supposed to teach him a lesson. It was supposed to force Adrian to stop conning innocent townspeople with his diluted potions and feather-weak spells.

Adrian Wolfe, being Adrian Wolfe, had learned no such lesson, though he made sure to never sell Heidi Duke anything other than exactly what she asked for from then on. This seemed to sufficiently satisfy the woman, much to Adrian's relief.

To this day the two of them kept up some semblance of a truce, where the two of them traded and bartered and sold to each other as and when needed, but otherwise kept to their own devices. Adrian had been content with this for a while, but no more.

He wanted his whole life back.

Being a wolf was dangerous. He had to avoid other packs who viewed him as a threat. He had to avoid humans who would kill him if they could. To that end he couldn't risk travelling anywhere that wolves didn't exist when he was due to change. There would be nowhere to hide.

It was terrifying and stressful and, above all, limiting. All he could do was return to the same woods every month where the regular wolves just barely now accepted his presence.

He wanted free of it all. But for that he needed

something so important to Heidi Duke that she'd have no choice but to revoke the curse she'd placed upon Adrian.

He needed Scarlett.

Adrian was fairly certain the young woman had no idea what her precious *Nana* was capable of; he reasoned that nobody was.

If they only knew what she was doing when everyone was asleep at night, he thought as he dared stalk a little closer to the light pouring out of the kitchen window. Heidi was reading a book and preparing herbs. It was so innocuous that even if her precious grand-daughter or Samuel Birch were to suddenly appear they would have no idea what the old woman was doing.

But Adrian knew.

Atropa belladonna. Opium poppy. Water hemlock from the Americas. They were all on the table. But it wasn't poisonous plants that Adrian most feared her for. Anybody could poison a person if they got their hands on the plants and processed them correctly.

No, it was her curses. They were far stronger than anything Adrian had learned of or had indeed constructed himself. He'd seen his fair share of people afflicted by curses who had sought his mother for aid and yet, even still, Heidi's curses were stronger. It unnerved him to no end. Deep, deep down inside his heart, where nobody could see, Adrian knew she had to die.

She was too powerful to be walking the earth. The wolves seemed to innately understand this. They didn't dare come close to her accursed house. It was the only reason anybody could live out here in the first place.

Adrian wasn't even sure how old Heidi really was. She could be hundreds of years old for all anyone knew. Thousands.

Bored with watching the old woman through the limited colours his wolf eyes granted him, Adrian soundlessly padded his way around to the back of the house to the window overlooking Scarlett's bedroom. Dully he thought of Samuel Birch, and how it was through this very window that he must have spied the woman in a state of undress.

Scarlett wasn't asleep, as Adrian had expected. She was sitting up in bed with her back against the wall, clutching a pillow and...doing nothing. Thinking. Her face was red.

Stupidly – recklessly – Adrian prowled closer and closer to the window, bushy tail swinging softly behind him as he loped forwards. He needed only to reach up and place his front paws on the windowsill and his nose would hit the icy-cold glass separating him from the woman inside.

And so he did.

Scarlett was watching.

Adrian didn't dare move as she slowly edged towards him, which was the exact opposite of what a person was supposed to do when they saw a wolf outside their window. Perhaps it was because the glass was thick, and the fact that wolves didn't have the opposable thumbs required to unlock the latch, but Scarlett knelt in front of the window and pressed the very tip of her nose to the glass.

Her scent filled Adrian's nostrils through the smallest of cracks between the window and its frame, all vanilla and saffron and sandalwood. Even as a wolf it was enticing. As a man it might have driven him to break open the window and steal Scarlett into the darkness of the forest and do unspeakable things to her.

But Adrian wasn't a man right now. He could do

nothing but stare at her winter-blue eyes, until eventually Scarlett's perfectly-formed lips parted.

"Knock, knock, Mr Wolf," she whispered, gently rapping her knuckles against the glass as she spoke, though her eyes were wide in terror at what she was doing.

Adrian fled.

He didn't stop until he could no longer see nor smell Heidi's Duke's house, and the young woman lying within it.

CHAPTER SEVEN

Scarlett

The list of supplies Scarlett's grandmother needed from town was much longer – and far more bizarre – than usual.

"What in the world does she need concentrated hemlock for?" Scarlett muttered aloud as she reached the market. She knew it was a poison, and a strong one at that. She hadn't noticed any vermin eating the plants in the garden that would need getting rid of. But she knew her grandmother was far more knowledgeable about the natural world around them than Scarlett ever could be. She trusted that the old woman needed it for something Scarlett likely couldn't fathom.

A flash of copper hair at waist height caught her eye as she stopped by the fountain in the middle of the market square. For a moment Scarlett's spirits soared, thinking that it might be Rudy or Elias running rampant through the livestock auction, but a few seconds later she recognised the child as Charlie Beck's younger brother, David.

Scarlett's heart hurt at the sight of him. Maybe it was because of the slew of marriage proposals she had received causing her to think of her family but, whatever the reason, she wanted nothing more than to curl up by the fire in her father's study as she read a fairytale to her little brothers whilst her father finished with his accounting and her 'mother' fussed for her brothers to go to bed.

It will never be like that again, she thought sadly, just as little David ran full-pelt into Scarlett's skirt. She was dressed in dark grey beneath her red cloak, perhaps inspired by the wolf that had mysteriously appeared by her window the night before.

Scarlett nearly dropped her basket in surprise as the child extricated himself from her legs and looked up at her with a wide grin on his face. One of his front baby teeth had fallen out.

"Sorry, Miss Scarlett," he said, giggling when she ruffled his curly hair.

"I hope you're not causing your mother any mischief, little one."

"No..."

"David Beck, get back here this instant!" his mother, Brenda, bellowed across the crowd until she reached her son. She grimaced apologetically at Scarlett. "I'm so sorry about him. That's the last time I let him near the pastries for breakfast."

"Don't worry about it," Scarlett replied, smiling. "He's a charming boy."

"More charming than his older brother?"

It was Scarlett's turn to grimace. "I wasn't exactly in a position to respond to anything Charlie said properly."

Brenda snorted. "So I heard! You do right by yourself, Miss Scarlett. If my boy had any sense he'd have *prepared* for asking for your hand. Just know that I would consider it an honour and a gift from God to welcome you into the family. Heaven knows I could do with another woman around!"

"Thank you, Mrs Beck," Scarlett replied, genuinely moved by the woman's sentiments – especially considering she had only just been thinking miserably about her own, estranged family. "I *do* need to get going now, though. Nana gave me a long list to work through."

"Of course! Sorry about David being a nuisance again. Have a lovely day, Miss Scarlett!"

"And you."

Brenda dragged her youngest son along with her as he stared back longingly at Scarlett, whom he clearly thought he'd wrangled into playing with him.

Now in a somewhat better mood than she had been in, Scarlett swung her basket slightly as she made her rounds and collected the various supplies her grandmother needed. She was relieved not to run into Charlie, nor Jakob, nor Andreas, all three of whom Scarlett did not have the patience to deal with right now. Though she knew it was only pertinent to visit the Sommer family soon now that Andreas had returned – her father would be pleased by her doing so and Henrietta would no doubt be happy to see her.

My father hasn't even seen me to wish me a happy

birthday, Scarlett thought, unbidden, and she began to feel miserable again. So she forced herself to think about another matter. Anything would do.

Invariably she thought of the wolf.

Why had it come so close to the window? No wolves ever dared to step foot within the small clearing that enclosed her grandmother's house. Why had it watched her for so long? And why had *she* approached it?

She thought of its eyes, but then of course she thought of another wolf by name. For Adrian's eyes really were akin to a wolf's, as unlikely as it may have seemed. Considering the unnatural white streak in his hair, and the fact he sold potions and spells, Scarlett had to wonder whether he had taken something to change the colour of his irises for dramatic effect.

It was the only reasonable explanation she could come up with.

Nearly two hours later she had managed to purchase everything on her grandmother's list bar one item: the hemlock. The apothecary didn't stock it, neither did Rowan's two most prominent healers. Scarlett knew someone who would almost certainly have it, of course.

She simply didn't want to ask him for it.

But Scarlett didn't want to go back home without everything on the list and so, with some reluctance, she struggled over to Adrian Wolfe's stall, arms laden with her basket overflowing with everything else her grandmother had asked for.

Adrian's stall was swarming with the usual girls who fawned over the man and senselessly spent every coin they had on his ridiculous love potions and spells. Littered in amongst them were older folk looking for some of his far more respectable salves, which Scarlett knew from first-hand use actually worked when one was suffering from a fever or chills.

"Ex-excuse me," she mumbled as she tried to make her way though. When nobody moved, she called out in a firmer voice, "*Excuse me.*"

Finally some of the girls looked at her, distaste apparent on their faces, before returning their attention to Adrian without moving an inch.

Scarlett began to yell profanities inside her head when she heard a familiar chuckle. "Come on, ladies, I know you aren't buying anything today. Let Miss Scarlett through before she drops everything she's carrying."

That seemed to do the trick, though the girls kept looking back with wistful glances at Adrian as they stalked away. Scarlett didn't care; apart from Henrietta, she had never been popular with the other Rowan girls. She'd always had nicer dresses than them, and faster horses than them, and better marriage prospects than them. Even when Scarlett had moved to her grandmother's house their opinion of her hadn't changed, and that suited Scarlett just fine even as she admitted to herself, back when she was sixteen, that she was lonely.

"What on earth have you bought, Red?" Adrian asked as he deftly lifted the basket out of Scarlett's arms and placed it on an empty space behind his stall for safekeeping. "And where is that miller's son when you need him?"

"Working for his father," Scarlett replied. "I need hemlock."

Adrian's eyebrow – the one that was cut in half by a scar – quirked at the request. "Straight to business today, it seems."

"What else would you expect from a customer?"

"Small talk, maybe. 'What is all this cold weather about?' or, 'Oh, Mr Wolfe, don't you look dashing today!'"

Scarlett rolled her eyes, though in truth Adrian *did* look dashing today. He was dressed in, of all colours, red – red braces and red leggings and a white shirt with his usual leather boots and gloves. Slung over his stall lay a matching red waistcoat. It made a startling difference from his usual black.

"Hello Mr Wolfe, you finally look like you haven't just come from a funeral. Happy?"

He threw his head back and laughed heartily at Scarlett's comment. It was annoyingly infectious; she found her lips curling into a smile despite herself.

"My favourite colour seems to be brushing off on you, too," Adrian said when he finished laughing, reaching out to just barely touch the grey fabric of Scarlett's dress that was peeking out from her cloak. "It seems as if we've swapped."

"I was in a grey mood."

"Oh? And what's a grey mood, I wonder?"

"Do you have hemlock or not?"

He sighed dramatically. "I know you're capable of much better small talk than that, Red. I've seen you talk to every other merchant in this square."

Scarlett stayed silent.

"Okay, okay, you win," Adrian finally said in resignation, before disappearing behind his stall to rummage around in a locked box. "How is Heidi wanting this? Leaves? Powder? Concentrated?"

"Concentrated."

"Of course."

Scarlett hesitated for a moment, then asked, "Do you know why she needs something so dangerous?"

For the first time since the man had saved her life, Adrian's face was stony and serious as he placed a small vial into a straw-lined box. "Ask her yourself, Scarlett."

Scarlett was taken aback by the abruptness of the comment. She'd expected a joke or a lie or - something. It made her feel uneasy.

But then Adrian smiled, and he carefully stowed away the little box inside Scarlett's already overflowing basket of goods. When some of the items at the top began to tumble and fall, he disappeared beneath his stall and retrieved another basket, filling it up until both baskets evenly contained everything Scarlett had come into town to buy.

"I - thank you," she murmured. "How much for the hemlock?"

"For Heidi, no charge."

Scarlett stared at him in surprise. "Really? Why?"

"She never charged me for those herbs yesterday. Tell her I consider us even."

She nodded. "Will do."

Then she took both baskets, hanging one off each arm, and headed off without another word. She was barely out of the market square on her way back to the woods, however, when she heard the sound of someone running after her. Thinking that it was Charlie, or Jakob, or even Andreas, she sighed heavily before turning to face whoever it was with the intention of telling them to leave her alone.

But it was Adrian.

CHAPTER EIGHT

Adrian

"I'd say you need some help with those baskets, Red."

"Get back to your stall, Mr Wolfe. You have customers who no doubt miss you."

He waved a hand dismissively. "That's one of the perks of being a merchant; I can take a break whenever I want. And Gerold is watching it, anyway."

Scarlett frowned as she turned her back on him and continued towards the woods. "Thanks, but no thanks. I can handle the baskets myself."

"I'm sure you can," Adrian said as he quickened his pace to catch up with her, "but that doesn't mean you wouldn't benefit from some help."

"Again: thanks but no thanks."

But then Adrian stepped in front of Scarlett and placed his hands on her shoulders to stop her. He put the most serious expression he could muster on his face. "You and I both know the wolves are in the woods right now. It's safer not to travel alone."

"I came in on my own."

"Yes, and that was foolish."

Scarlett hesitated. "It'll still be light for hours. I'll be fine."

He smiled. "Humour me."

Scarlett eyed him critically. Adrian had put his red waistcoat on before going after her, completing his outfit for her benefit, though he had no cloak or coat to speak of. From the look on Scarlett's face Adrian knew she was wondering how he wasn't cold.

"You don't look like you'd be much help against the wolves dressed like that."

But Scarlett had barely completed her sentence before he gracefully slid a concealed blade from his right boot, then indicated another attached to his waist. He flashed her a grin. "I'm not so unprepared, Red. And you know yourself how quickly I can move through these woods."

Finally she relented, if only because it was clear that Adrian would not give up. "Fine," she grumbled, "*fine. Help me if you must*," before dumping the heavier of her two baskets into his arms.

Adrian laughed. "No need to be so graceless about it. I'm merely concerned for your safety."

"You're only out for yourself, Mr Wolfe," Scarlett called out as she marched ahead.

"So what do you call me leaving my place of work to

70

carry a basket for you?"

"Self-indulgence. You're getting a kick out of this. You enjoy teasing me, though Lord knows why."

"I told you why yesterday."

Scarlett briefly glanced at him out of the corner of her eye as the two of them reached the fringe of trees that marked the beginning of the woods. "And what did you tell me yesterday?"

"That I'm interested in you."

He watched her bite her lip slightly as her cheeks slowly flushed. Above them the sun filtered through the bare branches of the trees, alternately casting light then shadow across the two of them. The air grew colder as they moved deeper into the woods, though it was already unseasonably cold directly beneath the sun. If Adrian didn't know for a fact that it was early April he'd have sworn it was January.

"You have nothing to say in response?" he asked after a while, hanging back a few paces in order to watch Scarlett walk in from of him. A smile crossed his face as she neatly hopped up and over a creeping tree trunk that had grown across the path.

"I don't think it *warrants* a response. There's a difference."

"You responded to all of those proposals. What makes my interest any different?"

"You can't possibly believe that what Charlie, Jakob and Andreas said and what *you* said hold the same weight."

Adrian scoffed at her comment. "You never intended to marry any of them, anyway. Surely that means I actually have more of a chance than them?"

71

"And what made you arrive at that ridiculous conclusion?"

Adrian crept up silently behind Scarlett and slid an arm around her waist, snaking it beneath her cloak as she gasped in surprise.

"Because you don't react like this with anyone else," he murmured against her ear, tightening his grip a little on her waist as he did so.

"N-nobody dares touch me like this, that's why!"

"Maybe that's their problem. None of them are bold enough. *I* am, though."

"Clearly."

Adrian brushed his lips against Scarlett's neck, just above the fur of her cloak. Her skin was burning. "So is that a yes? Or a no?"

"...to what?"

"To whether I have a chance in hell with you."

Scarlett's eyes darted towards Adrian's for a moment. But when she tried to look away he let the basket he was holding drop in order to spin her around to face him. He ran a hand through Scarlett's hair and just barely brought her lips to his.

She was unfalteringly looking at him now, eyes wide and bright with the kind of fear brought about by being in an exciting, unfamiliar situation. Scarlett let the basket she was holding drop to the ground to join the other one, her hand now limp and useless at her side.

"Why did you do that?" she whispered in a wavering voice.

Adrian merely pressed his mouth against hers a little harder, biting down very gently on Scarlett's upper lip in the process. His hand on her waist slid around to the small of her back, urging her closer towards him little by little.

As if remembering that she had hands of her own, Scarlett raised her arms and splayed her fingers out across Adrian's chest. It seemed as if she was preparing to push him away but it never happened. Adrian could hear her heart thumping wildly; he was sure Scarlett could feel his own accelerated heart-rate against her palms.

"I seem to recall a meeting rather akin to this two years ago," Adrian said, voice low and silky as the words fell upon Scarlett's lips. "Your heart was like a drum back then, too."

Scarlett hardly seemed to dare to blink as Adrian kept his eyes on hers. "I was...terrified," she uttered.

"And now?"

"I think I am now, too."

He chuckled as he wound his hand further into Scarlett's hair. "Not necessarily a bad thing. Is that all you feel?"

"I – no."

"Excited?"

She just barely nodded.

"On fire?"

Her eyes closed for a moment. "...yes."

"See? That wasn't so hard to say."

She opened her eyes once more, frowning uncertainly. "What is it that you want from me?"

"Nothing not given willingly, Miss Scarlett."

And then, at the moment when it seemed as if she might finally kiss him back, Adrian pulled away from her. He bent down and reorganised the baskets, retrieving items that had rolled away before standing back up and placing both into Scarlett's arms.

"Your grandmother's house is only a few minutes away. I best be getting back to Rowan."

Scarlett watched him with a dazed expression on her face as if she couldn't quite believe what had just transpired. It was only after Adrian had turned from her and began to walk away that she shouted after him, in a querulous voice, "You're a sly one, Mr Wolfe!"

"So I've heard!" he called back, raising a hand in good-bye without looking back.

As he headed back into Rowan he felt like whooping.

Three days? Who ever thought I needed three days!

Adrian Wolfe needed only one.

CHAPTER NINE

Scarlett

"Little Red, oh little Red, time to wake up!"

"I'm already awake, Nana," Scarlett called back from her room. She was sitting in front of her mirror, carefully braiding her hair like a crown around her head. Though she was merely going to the market Scarlett wanted to look good. She knew it was because of Adrian Wolfe.

She hated that it was because of Adrian Wolfe.

To that end Scarlett had chosen to wear a low-cut, white blouse beneath a deep green dress; it fell to just below her knees and laced up tightly around the bodice, bringing in her waist and accentuating her breasts and hips. It was the first time she had knowingly dressed in such a manner.

Him seeing me in that too-small nightdress doesn't count, Scarlett thought, face flushing at the memory. It seemed as if she was doomed to be embarrassed by every encounter she had with the man. She knew it was because she lacked experience when it came to dealing with the opposite sex, whereas Adrian Wolfe had experience in abundance...if Scarlett used his manner when dealing with the women of Rowan as evidence.

It infuriated her that she still felt like that scared sixteen-year-old girl he had found running from the wolves in the woods. Scarlett had grown up, in more ways than one, and now that she was finally in a position to acknowledge that she had no idea what to do with herself.

I can't believe he kissed me. Twice! And then he walked away!

Scarlett was outraged by this. She felt very much as if Adrian was making fun of her, though he had professed to only doing so because he liked her. But he had waited for Scarlett to admit to being attracted to him before leaving, as if that was all he'd wanted to hear. Part of her was afraid that the man would lose interest in her now that she'd all but given in.

And so Scarlett was choosing to dress up as if to tell Adrian not to lose interest. It made Scarlett feel somewhat foolish, but she was going to do it anyway, even though there was no guarantee the merchant was even still in Rowan. He usually only stayed for three days – and he'd stayed for four already this month – so in all likelihood he really had already left.

Something told Scarlett this wasn't the case, however. She didn't know what.

Letting a few tendrils of hair loose from her braided

76

crown to frame her face, and staining her lips the barest red, Scarlett for once chose to wear low-heeled, black leather shoes with a silver buckle instead of her usual boots.

When she moved through to the kitchen her grandmother smiled in approval.

"Now *that's* more like the Scarlett Duke I want the world to see," she said. "Samuel, be a dear and escort my grand-daughter to market."

Sam – who was once more visible only through the open window as he tended to the garden – nodded immediately as he brushed himself off. He was dressed better than usual, Scarlett noted, in olive trousers, dark braces and a white shirt that complimented his permanently tanned skin. Her heart accelerated slightly even as Scarlett admonished herself for getting excited at the mere sight of a handsome man.

It finally seemed as if the weather had taken a turn for the better, and for the first time all year the air no longer held the chill of winter. With the pleasant sunshine and the warmth of the new southerly wind, Scarlett shook her head when her grandmother handed her the red cloak.

"I think I'll go without today, Nana," she said as she stepped outside where Sam stood waiting for her. "It would cover my outfit, anyway."

"Good to see you're learning," she grinned. "Now all you need is for a good, strong man to offer you *his* cloak when you pretend to shiver."

Scarlett rolled her eyes before setting off through the woods with Sam. Most of their journey passed by in a flurry of polite, easy conversation – the type of conversation she had come to expect them to have once Sam got over his usual, initial shyness.

77

But as they got closer and closer to Rowan the young man became somewhat fidgety. Whilst they passed through the permanent twilight beneath the trees Sam kept stealing glances at Scarlett, growing red in the face when she noticed him looking. Eventually she could take it no more.

"Just what is it you're looking at, Sam?" she demanded when they were but five minutes from the market square of Rowan.

Sam seemed somewhat taken aback by the question. He shoved his hands into the pockets of his trousers and stared at the earth beneath their feet for a few moments in silence, as if intending not to answer her. But then their eyes locked onto each other, whilst a nervously earnest look crossed Sam's face that confused Scarlett to no end.

"Sam...?"

"You know when you asked me the other day, Miss Scarlett," he said quickly, "whether I had something on my mind, and I said I wasn't sure?"

"Um, yes?" Scarlett replied uncertainly, wondering where Sam was taking the conversation.

"Well, I – ah – I don't really *know* why I wasn't sure at the time – maybe I really was hungover like Mr Wolfe said – but I know, very clearly, what's on my mind now. It's been all I can think about for a long time, after all."

"Sam, where is this going?"

His face grew even redder than Scarlett's namesake. He gestured towards the large, ornate fountain in the centre of the market square. "Can we sit down over there to talk?"

Scarlett nodded and followed him over, feeling altogether overcome by the unsettling sensation of déjà-vu. She delicately perched on the edge of the fountain as flecks of water momentarily darkened the fabric of her dress, only to disappear a second or two later.

The sun was shining directly in Sam's face; he held up a hand to shield his eyes as he stared, unsmiling and nervous, at Scarlett. She abruptly felt like she wanted to run away, though she steeled herself to the spot for Sam's sake.

He sucked in a deep breath. "Miss Scarlett, we've known each other for two years now. I know that isn't the longest time in the world, but I feel like at this point we both know each other rather well."

She smiled slightly at this. It was true, of course, and it filled her with affection for the sandy-haired young man still getting used to how broad and tall he now was.

He continued. "I was there when you first came to live with your grandmother. I know how complicated things are with your family. I know how much you miss them. I know how much you want to be with them again...for things to go back to the way they were."

Scarlett felt the corners of her eyes begin to sting at Sam's words. She knew he didn't mean them unkindly but the reminder of what Scarlett had lost was still as bitter as it had always been.

"But you and I both know that something like that won't happen overnight," Sam said. He finally lifted his hand away from his face when a cloud blessedly covered the sun, allowing him to see. He smiled gently at Scarlett. "It's something that has to be worked at. And I want to be by your side as you do that."

"I...what?" Scarlett uttered, not entirely sure if Sam meant what she thought he meant.

"Scarlett, marry me. I've never cared about your family name or inheritance or anything else – I only care about

79

you."

She frowned despite herself, resisting the urge to sigh in exasperation. "Sam, you *are* aware that I turned down Charlie and Mr Schmidt and Andreas three days ago, right? And I care deeply for all three of them – as I do you. So why do you think I would say yes to you?"

"Because, Miss Scarlett," Sam began, reaching out his hands to take one of hers. His fingers were large and rough and calloused; the hands of a hard-working, honest, down-to-earth young man who was currently wearing his heart on his sleeve. "Because, for me, there's only you. I don't want to marry you because you're the prettiest girl in town, or because my parents love you, or because I've known you the longest, or because I've been giving you flowers for years or I'm the perfect match to the Duke name. No, I...I just love *you,* Scarlett."

Scarlett stared at him, speechless. What was she supposed to say, anyway? That she didn't love Sam that way? That she had never viewed him as a 'man' before – because she'd never seriously viewed *anyone* like that before?

Except for Mr Wolfe, a small voice inside her head whispered, unbidden. *You've spent many a night thinking of him whether you want to admit it or not.*

"No, Sam," Scarlett eventually said in a small, small voice. His face fell immediately, hands slumping back to his side as his eyes filled with hurt and disappointment. "Sam, I – I'm not in love with you. I'm not in love with *anyone.* And I don't want to accept a proposal from a man I don't love. You must understand that."

Sam looked like he desperately wanted to argue. But he couldn't, for Scarlett was right. There must have always been a part of him that knew Scarlett did not feel for him the way he felt for her.

She touched his hand with gentle fingers for a moment, mouthed the word *sorry* and quickly hurried off, unsure what else to do in such a situation. She couldn't be angry at Sam's proposal; he had seriously thought about what to say and didn't force the conversation onto her. He had respected her. But that didn't make it any easier to respond to. If anything it made it even worse.

"How am I going to face him back at Nana's?" she said aloud as she escaped into a nearby side street, feeling mortified and terrible.

"Maybe you could feed him one of your grandmother's potions for a broken heart," an annoyingly familiar voice said from her right. "Telling him you don't love him and running off – what a cruel woman you are, Red."

She didn't have to turn her head to see who it belonged to.

CHAPTER TEN

Adrian

"I have to hand it to the Birch boy – he really tried hard with that proposal. Shame you turned him down flat."

"Go away, Mr Wolfe."

"Have I not earned being called by my first name yet, Red?" Adrian complained childishly. "I mean, we've already kissed and everything. I'd wager the only man who's gotten as close as that to you before is Mr Richard Duke himself."

"*You* kissed *me*," Scarlett bit back in a tone that very much suggested Adrian had done something far more disgusting to her. "And what are you doing eavesdropping anyway? Don't you have better things to do?"

"What, like listen to the same gaggle of young ladies unload all of their romantic woes on me? 'Mr Wolfe, how can I get him to notice me?' 'Mr Wolfe, do you have anything that would make me just a little curvier?' 'Mr Wolfe, Mr Wolfe, don't you have anything that will make him want to rip my –"

"I think I get it, *Mr Wolfe.*"

Adrian chuckled; clearly Scarlett hadn't taken him abandoning her in the woods after being kissed very well. Her cheeks were flushed in irritation; brows knitted together. But Adrian didn't pay attention to her expression for very much longer when he had the rest of her to take in. For Scarlett had foregone her cloak, allowing him a rare view of her figure in a very flattering green dress. She didn't even have boots on today. Adrian wondered if she had put this much effort into her appearance for him; it was a thought he revelled in.

He sidled closer to Scarlett, appreciating the view down her dress he was granted by virtue of being taller than her. She glanced up at him and scowled.

"Get away from me, Mr Wolfe."

"Did you dress up just to turn the poor boy down?" he teased, brushing a gloved hand against Scarlett's bare arm in the process. "Or was there somebody else whose attention you were hoping to attract? Because a certain somebody very much appreciates the absence of your cloak."

"I didn't even think you'd still *be* in Rowan, so how could I have dressed to attract your attention?" Scarlett said, rolling her eyes, though a subtle biting of her lower lip gave her away.

Adrian moved in even closer, resting an arm against

83

the stone wall above Scarlett's head in order to box her in. "But you were hoping I hadn't left yet."

"If only so I could punch you in the face for accosting me in the woods yesterday."

"Is that what that was?" he murmured, dancing his fingers up Scarlett's arm whilst he watched her nervously react to his touch. "I seem to recall the young woman who was accosted wanting me to continue with said accosting."

Scarlett hesitated. Then, curiosity clearly getting the better of her, asked, "So why didn't you? Why did you leave when you did?"

"So that you'd spend all night thinking about me," he replied smoothly, which had genuinely been his intention. "Did you?"

"You're despicable."

"And yet you didn't answer the question."

"I don't owe you an answer. I don't owe you *anything.*"

Adrian lifted a hand to Scarlett's hair, so perfectly wound around her head. He played with the loose strands and, when she brought her hand up to stop him, slid his fingers straight through the flawless braid until it uncoiled down her back.

"Why would you do that?!" Scarlett exclaimed in outrage, pushing Adrian away from her in order to pull the braid over her shoulder and secure the bottom of it.

"I like it like this," he said simply, picking up the braid and dropping it down her back to emphasise his point. "It's easier to mess up. It was too perfect before."

Scarlett glared at him for a moment. But then her expression grew uncertain, as if she'd taken Adrian's words at more than simply face-value...which had been his intention.

"You're just looking for someone to amuse you whilst you're in Rowan. I'd be a fool to fall for your tricks only for you to disappear the second you got what you wanted."

And with that she turned and walked away, leaving Adrian momentarily stunned. He had never expected Scarlett to get caught up in a whirlwind romance the way the girls who swarmed his stall were desperate to, but even so – her response sounded like it came from a woman who was already weary of the world around her.

It caused him to wonder why Scarlett had refused no fewer than four proposals in as many days. None of her suitors were hideous to look at; in reality they were all handsome in their own way. If Adrian was being honest the blacksmith, Jakob, threatened him the most. He seemed the most forthright and least traditional of the men who had proposed to Scarlett...and the one most likely to try and bed her before marrying her.

"Scarlett, wait –" Adrian called out before he could stop himself, stepping away from the alleyway in order to follow after her, but he paused when he saw that Samuel Birch was walking straight up to her. He glanced at Adrian for a second as if he was deeply suspicious of the two of them having appeared from the same side street, then reached out for Scarlett's hand. Adrian forced himself to hang back to listen to what Sam had to say to Scarlett.

"Miss Scarlett, I'm sorry for pushing all of that on you," Sam hurriedly told her before she could protest. "It wasn't fair of me. I knew you weren't in love with me but I thought it didn't hurt to ask, anyway. I was wrong."

Scarlett sighed, then closed her hand around Sam's and squeezed slightly. Adrian bristled at the action. "Sam, you don't have to be sorry," she said, "but you can't expect me to suddenly accept a proposal out of the blue, either."

"I know, I know!" he replied enthusiastically, his eyes bright with an intent that Adrian didn't like at all. "I realised I was doing everything backwards, because I was so worried about someone asking you to marry them first. And I *shouldn't* have been worried, because I knew there was nobody you held that kind of affection for. And yet still I panicked, because I..."

He shook his head as he laughed softly. "I'm an idiot, Miss Scarlett, and I make mistakes. But I learn from them. So let me learn from this one."

That seemed to pique Scarlett's interest. She cocked her head to one side. "And what do you mean by that, Sam?"

He moved in closer to her and took her other hand in his. Adrian had taken a step forwards in protest before he could stop himself, but then he felt a hand on his shoulder. Glancing behind him he saw Gerold and Frank, who were shaking their heads.

"Let the lad say his piece, you no-good Prince Charming."

Adrian rolled his eyes. "You're supporting *him*?"

"Over you? Any time."

"Thanks for the support."

And so Adrian stayed put with the other two merchants and continued to listen in on the conversation between Scarlett and Sam, whose blonde hair had turned to gold in the sun. It was almost too much to look at.

"If possible, Miss Scarlett," Sam explained, "could you maybe start looking at me as a man? You said before you'd never seen me that way. I'd very much like for that to change. And if, after you've gotten to know me like that, you still aren't interested in me, then I'll give up. I won't bother you on the matter, and we can remain as friends – if you want. I know I have no right to ask you to do this, but –"

"I think I can do that, Sam," Scarlett interrupted, smiling. Adrian almost thought he imagined it but he was certain she had glanced at him before replying to Sam's request. It was a glance that screamed *this is a man who won't run off.*

"Well if that's what you want, little miss, then that's what I'll be," Adrian muttered under his breath.

Without explaining himself to Gerold and Frank, and without so much as another look at the now-delighted Sam and lovely, smiling Scarlett, Adrian stalked over to the tavern and marched straight up to the barkeep, Mac.

"I'd like a room, please," he said, a determined grin on his face that Mac dutifully ignored as he wiped down the surface of the bar.

"For how long?"

"As long as necessary."

CHAPTER ELEVEN

Scarlett

"Here you go, Miss Scarlett."

"Thank you very much, Mr Macmillan."

"Call me Mac."

She smiled. "Thank you, Mac."

Scarlett rarely drank, having only ever indulged in warm, spiced wine in the depths of winter with her father and, later, her grandmother. Sometimes, when the weather was particularly lovely in the summer, her grandmother would serve her a lighter, paler wine diluted with freshly squeezed apples and berries.

Never had she touched beer, nor cider, nor spirits.

And yet here she was, in Gregor MacMillan's tavern, drinking her first tankard of ale by herself as if it wasn't the strangest thing anyone sitting at the bar had seen all day. For it was rare to have women in the tavern unaccompanied by male companions – let alone one young, lone woman such as Scarlett Duke. Many of the men in the tavern wanted to approach her.

Nobody had the courage to.

She had rejected four men since her eighteenth birthday, after all. *Four*! And all of various social standings. If money, family, status, looks or rogueish charm hadn't been enough for Miss Scarlett then the likelihood that any of the barflies had a chance with her was slim to none.

And so, even though many men wished to approach her or buy her a drink, Scarlett was left well alone. For that she was grateful.

She had broken away from Sam in the marketplace several hours prior and had spent much of her afternoon aimlessly wandering, for lack of anything better to do. Scarlett hadn't wanted to go back to her grandmother's, knowing that she'd have to tell the old woman about what Sam had said. She wasn't ready for that.

She wasn't sure she'd *ever* be ready for that.

For though Scarlett had agreed to Sam's second proposal – to start viewing him as a man instead of a friend – she had no idea how she was supposed to go about this. And she knew that her decision had been somewhat influenced by a desire to outwardly reject everything Adrian Wolfe stood for right in front of him. That part had been deeply satisfying, though when Scarlett had turned to see if the man was going to confront her he had gone.

She sighed. In all honesty Scarlett had absolutely no idea what she was doing. She had always thought life would somehow get easier when she reached adulthood – as if she'd innately know what to do in any given situation. But reaching an arbitrary age had, unsurprisingly, not granted her the experience and wisdom necessary to solve these situations.

Scarlett was on her own and she was hopelessly, dangerously clueless.

"Could I have another one, please, Mac?" she asked after a while. Though Scarlett couldn't profess to enjoying the taste of ale, the warm, buzzing feeling that was filling her from her head down to her toes was very enjoyable indeed. The barkeep nodded in acknowledgement as he poured her a new tankard and passed it over. She decided she liked Mac, who wasn't trying to impose on her solitude in the slightest.

Unlike Charlie Beck, who Scarlett caught out of the corner of her eye making a beeline for her the moment he entered the tavern.

"Hello, Miss Scarlett!" he exclaimed brightly as he sat by her side and then, to Mac, "I'll have what she's having." He turned on his stool to face Scarlett. "I've never seen you in here before."

"I figured it was worth seeing what all the fuss was about," she said politely, gesturing to her drink as she spoke.

He laughed. "All we do is waste our time and money and short-term memory in here. Best you stay out in the future."

Scarlett couldn't help but bristle at this. "I can do what I like, Charlie."

"Oh, I didn't mean it like that!" he quickly corrected,

looking horrified. "I didn't mean to...sorry. I didn't mean to tell you what to do."

She raised an eyebrow before returning to her drink without another word.

Charlie shifted in his seat somewhat uncomfortably. "I heard Sam proposed to you today."

"What of it?"

"You didn't flat-out turn him down."

Scarlett sighed heavily, resisting the urge to run a hand across her face. "And I didn't say yes, either. Charlie, I'm not ready to marry anyone. But I...do know it wouldn't be you. I don't say that to be rude. I just don't see you that way."

Charlie seemed a little put out. "You told Sam you'd try to see him as a man, though..."

"Sam is – different. I think. I don't know."

"If you don't know then how could you know about *me?*"

Just as Scarlett was beginning to feel like she might lose her temper at Charlie's incessant protests Mac came over and handed the young man his drink.

"Miss Scarlett," he said, "I don't suppose I could ask you to take a few things up to one of the guest rooms on the first floor? It's too busy for me to leave the bar and my wife has stepped out to the butcher's."

The slight smile on Mac's lips told Scarlett that this was a lie. But he was providing her with a much-needed escape from Charlie that she wasn't in her right mind going to turn down.

She returned the smile with a broad one of her own, getting off her stool and walking around the bar to retrieve a tray of food and drink from the man. "Of course, Mac.

91

Which room is it?"

"One-oh-three. It's at the end of the hallway once you climb the stairs. Thanks again."

Scarlett didn't bother to look back at Charlie or apologise for leaving the conversation so abruptly before she began her ascent. It was dreadfully rude of her, she knew, but then again – Charlie interrupting her obvious desire for solitude had been rude in the first place.

She reached the room in question frustratingly quickly. Knocking on the door once before swinging it open, she announced, "I'm just bringing up your meal from the – oh my *God*!"

For there, on the bed, lay a dishevelled Adrian Wolfe, his boots kicked to the floor, shirt undone and leggings unlaced. His hands were hidden somewhere beneath the waistband of the woollen drawers peeking out from beneath his leggings.

Scarlett turned around on the spot abruptly. She'd read enough books in her father's study – the ones she wasn't supposed to go near – to know what exactly Adrian had been doing.

Adrian stumbled off the bed until he reached Scarlett, pulling her back into the room as he simultaneously kicked the door closed.

"Seems like you caught me in a compromising position," he chuckled good-naturedly as he took the tray out of Scarlett's numb hands and placed it on a nearby dressing table. "Although, I have to wonder what kind of education you received to have known what I was about to do."

Scarlett was too mortified to look at him. "How do you even know that I knew what you were doing?"

"Your reaction speaks volumes, Red."

She took a step towards the door. "Well, you have your meal so I'll be -"

"Oh, I don't think you're going anywhere."

Scarlett frowned. "Who are you to tell me what to do?"

Adrian laughed, sliding a long-fingered hand up Scarlett's arm until he reached her shoulder. It sent her heart racing, especially when she realised he had no gloves on. It was the first time he'd ever touched her without them.

"I'm not telling you what to do; I'm merely stating what's invariably going to happen. I don't think you really *want* to go anywhere."

"And what makes you say that?" Scarlett asked uncertainly, achingly aware of every nerve Adrian's touch was setting on fire as his amber eyes scanned up and down her entire body.

"Why in the world would you willingly play the serving girl if not to get away from whatever - or whoever - is downstairs?" Adrian murmured. His fingers trailed up from Scarlett's shoulder along her collarbone, tilting her head to one side to follow the artery in her neck. Scarlett's whole body had gone numb; she couldn't move.

She didn't *want* to move.

"And what were you doing in Mac's tavern, anyway?" he continued, dropping his hand from Scarlett's neck to stalk around her slowly. She turned as he did, not daring to take her eyes off the man even for a second.

There was something different about Adrian that Scarlett couldn't quite place. Perhaps it was seeing him in a state of disorder, when usually he was immaculately dressed. Perhaps it was because he was a little drunk, if the empty tankards by his bedside were anything to go by.

Perhaps it was the setting sun flashing through the window, turning his eyes molten as he devoured Scarlett with them.

"I'm a grown woman," Scarlet finally replied after far too long. "I can do what I like."

"Are you drunk?"

"Nobody gets drunk from one tankard of ale."

Adrian threw back his head and genuinely roared with laughter. "How naive you are, little miss. I know plenty folk who can't handle their alcohol. The question is – can you?"

Scarlett's cheeks flushed despite herself. "Do I seem like I can't, Mr Wolfe?"

"Adrian. Call me Adrian."

"It wouldn't be proper for me to call you so informally."

"And I'm telling you I want you to. Can't you abide my request, Scarlett?"

Adrian had stopped circling now. He stood in front of Scarlett, reached out for her hand and edged backwards towards the bed. Just a little.

And then a little more.

Scarlett's eyes darted to the door and back again. "If I told you to let me go, would you?"

"If you meant it."

"...and what happens if I stay?"

A flicker of surprise crossed Adrian's expression, as if he hadn't entirely expected Scarlett to give in. With gentle, delicate fingers he began to unlace the bodice of Scarlett's dress. Slowly. Deliberately. Scarlett could only watch his face watching her as he did so.

"And what of your woodcutter, Red?" Adrian

murmured as he finished with the laces. He slid the straps of the dress off Scarlett's shoulders; the bodice fell down to her waist, leaving her top half covered only by her low-cut, white blouse. "What would Samuel Birch say if he knew you were here?"

Scarlett narrowed her eyes for a moment. "Why would you ask me that now?"

"Because he asked you to see him as a man. But I don't think you'll be able to do that when you're allowing another man to undress you."

"Are you trying to shame me?" She held up her hands against Adrian's chest as if to push him; he held onto them instead.

One by one he kissed Scarlett's fingers. His breath tickled across her knuckles. She inhaled deeply, wondering if she really *couldn't* handle her alcohol and that this was all one huge mistake.

"Absolutely not," Adrian murmured. Quite suddenly, he let go of Scarlett's hands in order to deftly pick her up and drop her onto the bed, climbing on top of her before she had an opportunity to protest. He grinned. "I'm merely relishing in the knowledge that you turned Sam down – and everyone else, too – and yet here you are, with me. It's very satisfying. I didn't want them to touch you."

Scarlett's eyes went wide at the comment. "How long have you...wanted to touch me, Mr Wolfe?"

"Adrian."

He pawed at Scarlett's blouse without quite removing it, then allowed one hand to wander down to roam underneath her skirt. His fingers danced against her skin as they travelled along the length of her thigh. Scarlett thought that her heart would surely burst at the rate it was throbbing in her chest.

She locked eyes with him.

"Adrian," she whispered, "how long have you wanted to touch me?"

"Too long."

And then his mouth was on hers, hot and wet and hungry for Scarlett even as she gave into the same urges for him. Her hands found their way into his hair, insistently pulling Adrian closer, closer, closer.

Scarlett had never so desperately wished to be naked before. Her dress was a nuisance; her blouse in the way. But Adrian easily pulled the white fabric down as he trailed kisses from Scarlett's lips down to her breasts, gently biting and sucking on her nipples when he reached them.

She gasped at the sensation. It wasn't a feeling she was familiar with, but she found one of her legs curling around Adrian's back and pushing him against her in response. She felt a very telling hardness rub against her, below her stomach.

Adrian's breathing quickened. He pinned Scarlett down, lips back on hers as his tongue found its way into her mouth, stealing her breath away.

But just when Scarlett thought he was going to rip away the rest of her clothes – just when she was about to succumb to the unbearable urge to do the same to him – Adrian stopped.

He stopped.

It was as if every muscle in his body had grown tense and taut; his grip tightened painfully around Scarlett's wrists. When she opened her eyes there was a vein throbbing in Adrian's temple. His strange eyes had gone glassy, only serving to further make him look like he wasn't quite human.

"...out," he muttered through gritted teeth.

Scarlett gulped uncertainly. "Adrian?"

But then he violently threw her from the bed, chest heaving as he pointed at the door. "Out. Get out. Just... please. Get out."

Scarlett took a step towards him, confused and concerned. "Adrian, what's -"

"*Get out!*"

And so Scarlett left, hurriedly pulling the bodice of her dress back up as she wrenched the door open and slammed it shut behind her. Her heart was hammering painfully, both from excitement and abject fear.

For there was no doubt that Adrian Wolfe had indeed looked terrifying as he screamed for her to leave, with his feral eyes and lips drawl back into a ferocious snarl. It left Scarlett shaking her head in disbelief as she choked back the threat of tears in her throat.

Just what on earth happened to Mr Wolfe? Scarlett thought as she laced herself back up, feeling somewhat humiliated as she rushed down the stairs and out of the tavern without so much as a glance at anyone inside.

Above her the sun had set, leaving only the fat, silver moon hanging in the sky. It was a few days past full, leaving it looking somewhat lopsided. It made her feel even more miserable; she shivered as the chilly night air bit at her arms where Adrian's fingers had been mere moments before.

"I should have brought my cloak," she said to the moon as she began the long journey back to her grandmother's house. "...I never should have left it behind."

CHAPTER TWELVE

Adrian

He shouldn't have changed into a wolf. He'd already had his three days. So how had it transpired that Adrian had to unceremoniously throw a half-undressed Scarlett Duke out of his room before locking the door and clawing at his throat – a tell-tale sign that he was about to transform?

Before he lost his human form Adrian struggled back to the window, unlatching the lock and throwing it wide open. He was only on the first floor; once darkness had fully settled across Rowan he could escape across nearby rooftops and into the forest without being noticed.

But, for now, Adrian had to strip himself of all

clothing and lie on the floor of the room he'd rented...and remain silent through the slow agony of losing his human form.

He clenched his teeth together as his bones cracked and split and stuck themselves back together in a disconcertingly familiar framework. His skull wasn't far behind the entire process; he bit back a yowl as his jaw broke apart only to grow longer and stronger before reattaching itself. His nails grew sharper and then his teeth did, too, filling out his muzzle. The hairs on his arms, then his legs, then the rest of his body, grew courser, thicker and darker.

When finally it was over Adrian was panting in dreadful pain. He thought one day he'd get over it. That he'd get used to it.

After six years he was certain that day would never come.

Jumping up onto the bed to poke his head out of the window, Adrian saw that the streets of Rowan were already quiet. He wasted no time in jumping to the nearest rooftop, clambering clumsily over the tiles before leaping over to the next roof, and then the next. He repeated this until he reached the very edge of the town, deftly dropped down to the ground and sprinted towards the forest.

The air whittled past his ears as he slalomed between trees and leapt over fallen trunks, racing towards Heidi Duke's house as fast as his legs would carry him.

He was furious.

He was humiliated.

He had probably ruined everything with Scarlett.

No, *he* hadn't ruined everything. Her witch of a grandmother had, and Adrian wanted to know why.

When he reached the old woman's front door Adrian knew he had beaten Scarlett there, even if she had gone straight home after he'd thrown her out. Heidi was standing outside her front door, her lined face accentuated by the light from the swinging lantern hanging above her.

Adrian stopped a few feet away from her and sat down on his haunches, staring at Heidi with a snarl on his face until her face broke out in a grin.

"What did you expect when you decided to stay here for another night, Adrian Wolfe?"

Adrian could do nothing but let a low growl simmer in his throat in response.

The old woman laughed. "I won't have that kind of attitude from you. So long as you choose to stay here longer than usual, I'll turn you into a wolf every night. I can't have you sticking your nose in where it doesn't belong – and don't think I don't know that you are."

For that moment he was glad he was a wolf and not a man, for if he were a man Adrian would have flinched. He wondered if Heidi had worked out he was trying to seduce Scarlett.

But how would she know? he wondered. *I doubt Scarlett would have told her anything.*

But then Adrian considered Heidi's accusation. It needn't be about Scarlett. It was more likely to do with the fact that Adrian knew what she was capable of as a witch. After selling her hemlock, perhaps Heidi was wary that Adrian was going to try and work out what she needed it for. This wariness wasn't unwarranted, of course; he *did* keep an eye on what she was working on when he was prowling about as a wolf.

But *she* couldn't know that.

He let out a whine.

"Don't give me that, you foolish man," Heidi said scornfully. "This was your own fault. I won't have you in my town longer than needs be. You'll be a wolf every additional night that you stay, you hear me? So why don't you do us both a favour and leave. I'm sure the young ladies in other towns are missing you dearly."

As she spoke, the tell-tale sounds of footsteps on the road not far from Heidi's front door caused Adrian's ears to stand up to attention.

Scarlett.

Her grandmother's face darkened immediately. "Get away from my house, Adrian Wolfe. Don't you dare let my grand-daughter see you or it'll be the end of you, I swear."

Letting out another low whine, Adrian turned tail and darted back into the darkness of the forest just as he was told. He didn't even turn back to look at Scarlett from the safety of the trees.

He couldn't. He would do something he'd later regret if he did.

With his tail thoroughly between his legs even as he gnashed his teeth in frustration, he thought bitterly about how difficult it was going to be to convince Scarlett to forgive his behaviour. Heidi Duke might have destroyed his ploy against her without even *knowing* she had. Adrian couldn't stand it.

I can't leave Rowan, he thought with grim determination. *I need to see this through to the end.*

And if that meant spending another few nights stuck in the body of a wolf then so be it.

CHAPTER THIRTEEN

Scarlett

Scarlett found herself standing outside the large, ornamental gates that opened onto the front gardens of the Sommer estate without really knowing how she had gotten there in the first place.

Why am I here? she wondered dolefully as the doorman led her through the gates, towards the entrance to the manor house. *It's not as if my father asked me to be here. There's nothing in it for me to act so polite on behalf of my family.*

Yet Scarlett knew she wouldn't turn back. It was the right thing to do, and the basket in her arms was laden with winter fruits, cured meats, wine and ale for the

Sommers. It would be a waste to turn back now.

And besides, Scarlett was willing to do just about anything to stop herself from thinking about Adrian Wolfe, even if it involved coming face-to-face with Andreas for the first time since he had proposed to her. For how was she supposed to process the way Adrian had so viciously thrown her out of his room when they had been mere seconds away from ripping each others' clothes off?

She shook her head, face flushing in shame as she was escorted through to a parlour room. Scarlett couldn't believe she had allowed herself to get so carried away. It was unbecoming and reckless of her. Unbidden, she thought of how her father had, in rebellion against his arranged marriage, sought out another woman's arms and left her pregnant. The woman had been lucky in that Richard Duke went on to raise the child for her, but if Scarlett had actually slept with Adrian and gotten pregnant...

I don't know what I would have done, she shuddered. In reality it was good for Scarlett that Adrian had kicked her out, though the look on his face as he had demanded she leave still haunted her. He'd looked more animal that human – feral and violent and out of control.

And in pain, Scarlett couldn't help but add on. She was deathly curious about what had happened to the man to cause him to act in such a way; however, dwelling on such a matter was pointless.

She had to get over him...even if part of her didn't want to. She had wasted too much of her time on the man already.

Sitting nervously in the parlour room with her basket of goods sitting on her knee, Scarlett wondered about what she was actually going to say to the Sommer family. *'Hello, I'm happy your son has returned in good health but perhaps you should teach him some manners'* seems a little inappropriate, she mused. *Just a little.*

But then the door to the parlour swung open and Otto Sommer, the ageing, most prestigious doctor in all of Rowan and its surrounding towns and villages, appeared, closely followed by –

"Scarlett?"

"Papa!" Scarlett exclaimed before she could stop herself, offloading her basket onto the nearest table in order to jump into his ecstatic arms. For Richard Duke was delighted to see his daughter in such an unexpected place; he hugged her tightly to his chest and kissed the top of her head as delicately as if she were a newborn babe.

"I'll give the two of you some privacy," Otto smiled. "Miss Scarlett, I'm afraid Henrietta and Andreas are out riding at the moment. I do apologise."

Scarlett curtsied deeply for the man after her father let her go. "It's my fault for arriving unannounced, Dr Sommer," she said politely. "I hope all is well with you."

"Very well now that my son has returned," he replied, "though I heard tale that he, ah, was a little *pre-emptive* in asking for your hand, my dear."

Scarlett blushed. "Perhaps a little. I admit I was more than a touch surprised."

Otto looked pointedly at her father. "Perhaps Andreas' proposal is something to discuss with your father. Heaven knows the boy has been badgering him for a meeting non-stop since his return!" He laughed good-naturedly before vacating the parlour room, leaving Scarlett and her father alone.

The pair embraced once more, Scarlett nuzzling her

face against her father's chest whilst he stroked her hair. "I never expected to see you here, Red," he murmured.

"It was the proper thing to do, now that Andreas has returned. I thought..."

Her father broke the embrace to hold Scarlett at arm's length to take a proper look at her, as if calculating how much she had grown. "You thought what, my love?"

She sighed. "I thought it was the kind of thing you would want me to do. I know I'm not *really* a Duke or – or whatever – but –"

"Scarlett you will *always* be a Duke, no matter what," he replied, gesturing for Scarlett to take a seat on the expensively embroidered sofa behind them. He followed suit once she was seated, then clasped both of her hands in his own. "I know things are...complicated. That's all my fault. But I'm working hard to rectify that. Oh, Scarlett, the boys miss you so."

She felt her eyes begin to sting with the threat of tears. "I miss them, too. They must be getting so big! And I miss mo – Frances, too, though I don't imagine she would appreciate hearing that."

Her father sighed heavily. "She *would* appreciate that, though she's too proud to say as much out loud. Despite everything that's happened, my love, I'm quite certain she sees you as her daughter, whether that's obvious or not. And she misses you, though she won't admit it."

Scarlett somehow found this hard to believe, and though she didn't say anything about it her father could read it plain as day on her face.

He laughed. "Of course I understand why you wouldn't believe me. I think you just need to give her a little more time, if you could find it in you to do that."

"It's not like I have many other choices, do I?" she

106

muttered, which only made her father laugh all the harder.

"You seem to have *many* choices, going by the number of proposals I've heard about over the last few days. How many is it now – three?"

"Four," she corrected, grimacing slightly. "Samuel Birch asked me, um, yesterday."

Her father nodded. "I should have seen that one coming a mile off. My mother has told me about the boy's affection for you on numerous occasions."

Scarlett was surprised by this. Of course her father and grandmother talked, but it was a bizarre feeling to think that the two of them would talk about Scarlett when she wasn't there.

"If I'm being sincerely honest though, Red," her father continued speculatively, "then I'll admit that I really would love to see you married to Otto's boy. He's made it clear he cares not for your inheritance, nor for any children you would bear having any claim, either. They're a wealthy enough family in their own right. And Andreas is fond of you and easy on your eye, I'm sure. I don't think you could ask for much more out of a prospective marriage."

Scarlett was silent for a moment, staring at their entwined fingers as she thought about how to reply. She had always figured her father had wanted her to marry Andreas, though she hadn't known about their potential betrothal.

"Was it because of Frances that you never accepted Dr Sommer's offer to betroth me to Andreas, Papa?" she asked quietly. "Was it because it was a threat to Rudy and Elias?"

"Scarlett –"

"It's fine if it was. I understand. I just want to know."

She glanced up and locked eyes with her father; the truth was clear on his lined face. Scarlett saw that grey had coloured his luxurious, dark hair around the edges and peppered his closely cropped beard. For the first time in her life she saw that he was getting *old*.

For half a second Adrian Wolfe passed through her head, who didn't look like he was getting old at all yet had that perfect, white streak of hair breaking up the black. Scarlett realised she'd never had the opportunity to ask him if he dyed it.

Well I won't be looking for him to ask now, she thought sullenly. *He can go to hell.*

"Scarlett...?"

"Ah, sorry, Papa," she said hurriedly. "I'm afraid I've grown tired, and I have a long walk back to Nana's. I guess I'll have to come back when Andreas is actually home."

Her father smiled sadly. "I am so proud of you, Red."

"Then will you tell me?"

"Tell you what?"

"About my mother. Not today," Scarlett added on when she saw a flash of panic cross her father's face, "but some day. It would mean a lot to me to learn about her... even if you don't know much."

He squeezed her hands. "Okay. One day. Let's repair our family and discuss it then. How does that sound?"

It sounded like more than Scarlett could have dared to hope for. It was everything she wanted.

Screw Adrian Wolfe, and all the other proposals I've had. They are nothing compared to getting my family back.

She grinned – a wide, infectious, genuine smile that her father eagerly returned.

"Like something I can agree to."

CHAPTER FOURTEEN

Adrian

Adrian had spent five days looking for Scarlett Duke. Five days with not a single sign of her dark hair or red cloak or wicker basket. He was beginning to wonder if he should simply visit her grandmother's house when, finally, Adrian spied her in Beck's bakery.

"Can you watch my stall for ten minutes, Frank?" he asked the man who was half dozing in a chair by his own stall. Not waiting for an answer, Adrian stalked purposefully over to the bakery and the promise of finally making up with the woman behind the window.

What he hadn't expected was getting waylaid by Samuel Birch.

"Leave her alone, Mr Wolfe."

Adrian blinked in surprise. Keeping his voice jovial and carefree he asked, "On whose authority should I leave her alone, Birch?"

But Sam was in no mood to deal with Adrian's mockery. He glared at him. "I know you're up to no good."

"And how would you know that?"

"You were eavesdropping when we were talking about Scarlett in Mac's tavern after her birthday. Everyone's seen you talking to her far more often since then. She seemed really bothered about something after you came by Old Lady Duke's house; she's not been herself since. And you cornered her in that alleyway a few days ago after I proposed to her. Whenever something's wrong with her you always seem to be involved."

Adrian quirked an eyebrow in amusement. "Is that all?"

Sam seemed angry beyond belief at Adrian's attitude. "Is that – is that *all?* Is everything a joke to you, Mr Wolfe?"

"Usually," he replied mildly. He ran a hand through his hair as he made to exit the conversation. "I don't see why me *talking* to a woman of age is so problematic, though. And it's not like Miss Scarlett and I are strangers."

He grinned wickedly as he said this, knowing exactly that it would have the intended effect of further infuriating Sam.

The other man grabbed onto the front of Adrian's shirt as he tried to walk away. "What have you done to Miss Scarlett?!"

Adrian held up his hands in mock surrender. "I didn't

do anything as bad as you're implying, Birch. Or bad at all, to be honest. I saved her life."

Sam paused for a few moments, confused beyond belief at the comment. He narrowed his eyes. "You saved her...? When?"

"On her sixteenth birthday. I could have let the wolves have her. I didn't."

"You actually considered letting her die before saving her?"

"Of course not," Adrian lied smoothly. "I was merely pointing out I *could* have."

"You're despicable."

"Probably."

Sam seemed to consider saying something more but ultimately decided against it. He let Adrian go, glowering at him one final time before saying, "Just leave her the hell alone."

As he began walking away, Adrian decided to bait the man for the sheer sake of it. "Well, we *did* kiss, actually," he remarked nonchalantly, as if what he was saying was nothing of importance. "More than once. Repeatedly, even. And –"

The rest of the sentence was lost to the sound of Sam's fist connecting with Adrian's face.

"You son of a – *leave her alone!*"

"Sam! Oh my God, Sam, what have you – Mr Wolfe?"

Adrian wiped at his nose, which was beginning to bleed in earnest. He winced at the pain spreading across his right cheekbone. *The bastard,* he thought. *That's going to bruise.*

But he smiled for Scarlett despite the pain. "Hello, Red. I've been looking for you. I'm sure you were aware."

Scarlett was frozen to the spot as her eyes darted from a furious, ruddy-faced Sam to a bleeding Adrian Wolfe. "What happened here?" she muttered, aware that the three of them were beginning to draw a crowd.

"Your boyfriend was merely telling me to stay away," Adrian said simply. "I retorted. He punched me. I deserved it."

"You admit that you deserved it?"

He laughed. "Naturally. It doesn't mean I'm sorry about what I said." Then his face grew a little more serious as he took half a step towards Scarlett. "Let me explain about what happened the other day. Please. I'm sorry."

"You're sorry for *what?*" Sam bit out, immediately suspicious.

Scarlett glanced at Sam one final time, then marched over to Adrian and ushered him away with her. Adrian couldn't quite believe it. Neither could Sam, who was shocked to speechlessness whilst he watched the pair of them walk away.

"I must admit I never expected you to speak to me again, Red," he said cheerily as they left Rowan behind, venturing towards the forest.

Scarlett scowled. "It's not what you think. I'm just... tying up loose ends. I'd keep wondering about what happened in Mac's tavern if I never asked you about it. But that's it. I have more important matters to concern myself with than you, Mr Wolfe."

"Are we really back to 'Mr Wolfe', Red?" Adrian sighed dramatically as they reached a small brook that ran along the fringe of the woods. Scarlett motioned for him to sit down on a fallen tree; he dutifully complied.

"It was a mistake to ever get on first-name terms with you," she murmured as she pulled a cloth out of a hidden pocket in her dress. She wet it in the brook then went to work cleaning up Adrian's face, though his nose was still bleeding.

"It wasn't a mistake," he protested, voice nasally as Scarlett held the cloth over his nostrils. "What happened before – really, I'm sorry. It was abysmal timing."

Scarlett frowned, her lovely eyes shadowed by her brows as she inspected the tender flesh of Adrian's cheek. "What do you mean, 'abysmal timing'? What happened to you?"

"I have a...condition. A chronic condition."

"What kind of condition?"

"A painful one."

Scarlett looked at him pointedly. "You'll have to give me more than that."

"I don't – ah, that smarts –I don't know exactly what it is. Sometimes I'm hit by convulsions. Like a seizure. It's not pleasant. And it's painful. I didn't want you to see me like that...it's humiliating."

The best lies were those rooted in truth, Adrian knew, and nothing was truer than that last sentence.

Scarlett seemed taken aback by his explanation. "You haven't – you never told me about them before."

"Why would I? Nobody knows. If I can help it I make sure no-one is around to see me when I feel the convulsions begin. It's not exactly something I would share."

"You could have told *me*..." Scarlett muttered.

Adrian felt a glimmer of amusement at the expression on her face. She seemed put out by the fact he hadn't told her. He set about using this to his advantage, raising his hand to cover the one Scarlett was using to clean his face. He squeezed it slightly, never taking his eyes off of hers.

"I know. And I should have. I could have done with the help, actually; I could barely eat afterwards." He chuckled darkly. "I'm just not all that great on the honesty front."

"I surmised as much."

"Ah, but what about you, Miss Scarlett?" Adrian pondered as he stood up, bringing Scarlett along with him by her hand.

She stumbled slightly in surprise as he took them away from the road and through the sun-lit, frostbitten trees. "Where are we going, Mr Wolfe?" she asked. "And what do you mean 'what about me'?"

"We're just going for a walk," he replied, which was the truth. He simply wanted to make sure Sam or anybody else using the road through the forest didn't follow the pair of them and ruin the mood. He raised an eyebrow at Scarlett over his shoulder. "You'll accept going on a walk with me?"

"It seems like I don't have a choice."

"You always have a choice, Red."

Scarlett's cheeks flushed prettily at the comment. If Adrian wasn't treading on such thin ice trying to repair their relationship then he would have kissed her.

"And what I meant," he continued as he wound them expertly through the forest, "is that I don't know anything about you, in truth. You're very private. So tell me about yourself."

Scarlett stopped abruptly, causing Adrian to trip over the rotting carcass of a tree. She giggled despite herself.

"How clumsy, Mr Wolfe."

"A moment I hope never to repeat," he muttered, feeling embarrassed despite himself. Falling over was *not* something Adrian Wolfe did...and certainly not when he was attempting to woo a woman.

"You say you know nothing about me," Scarlett mused, "but I know little and less about you."

"Your point being?"

Scarlett's lips curled up into the slightest of smiles. "Tell me about yourself first. Even the embarrassing things. Tell me it all."

Adrian couldn't help but laugh. "I'm a fairly boring person, really. I was hoping it would take a little longer for you to work that out."

"I think I'll decide that for myself. So...what makes you who you are, Adrian Wolfe? Will you tell me?"

He sighed for dramatic effect; Scarlett's smile grew wider.

"Fire away, Miss Scarlett."

CHAPTER FIFTEEN

Scarlett

"How long have you been working as a merchant, Mr Wolfe?"

"By myself? Since I turned twenty."

"Which was...?"

"Oh my, Red, are you so bold as to ask a man how old he is?"

"Only if the man is you...though I'd be inclined to believe you'd lie about it."

Adrian chuckled, letting go of Scarlett's hand in order to swing from a thick branch above their heads. He used the momentum to carry him over the stream they had been about to cross.

He flashed a grin as Scarlett rolled her eyes. "Show off," she murmured as she located a few rocks big enough to break the water's surface, nimbly jumping from one to the next until she reached Adrian's side.

"Nicely done, little miss. And I'm twenty-six. Twenty-seven in July."

"Huh."

"And what's that supposed to mean? I don't look older than that, do I? Is it the white in my hair?"

Scarlett's lips quirked as she took in Adrian's worried expression. "I knew you were a narcissistic man but I didn't realise you were *this* insecure, Mr Wolfe. And I assumed you dyed your hair, if I'm being honest. It's not artificial?"

He shook his head, fingering the white lock of his hair for a few seconds before pushing it back. "When my convulsions started the front of my hair just...lost its colour. I got quite depressed about it, actually."

"Strange that it stopped going white after just that one part, though," Scarlett said, eyeing up his hair curiously. "You sure you don't dye the *rest* of it to keep it black?"

"Now you're just being cruel. I don't need to do anything to look as handsome as this. It's all natural."

Scarlett swatted his arm. "You are *so* full of yourself."

"Says the woman who has deliberately been making herself up to look as appealing as possible to me, even as she refuses to speak to me."

"Can't I look good for myself?" she muttered, crossing her arms protectively over her chest as she did so. Scarlett knew it made her look altogether like a petulant child; she didn't care.

118

Adrian undid the clasp of his cloak and swung the garment over an arm. "Of course you can, Red. Who do you think *I* make myself look good for?"

"You're infuriatingly full of yourself." Adrian shrugged at the comment, because it was true. Then Scarlett asked, "Aren't you cold?"

He shook his head. "I tend to run a little hot. I feel like I'm about to overheat merely looking at you in that fur hood."

"But it's so cold! I thought the weather was getting better but it's slipped right back into winter again. It's mid-April! What's going on?"

"Are we really going to talk about the weather, Red?"

Scarlett glanced up at the sky where a cloud had only just covered the sun, casting the pair of them in shadow. "The weather is interesting, though," she murmured, almost to herself. "The woods completely change depending on the weather or the time of day. It's unsettling how comfortable I am here only to be terrified a few hours later. Do you not think so, too?"

Adrian seemed surprised by the comment. He scratched his eyebrow. "I guess I hadn't thought about it that way."

"How did you get that scar?"

Adrian paused before asking, "Which one?"

Scarlett raised her eyebrows. "You have more than one?"

"I have a few," he said, smiling mischievously. "If you ever feel inclined to undress me you'll see them all."

"You're...useless."

"It was a fair comment," Adrian laughed, "even if my *tone* was perhaps a little filthier than you wanted, Miss

Scarlett."

She merely stared at him, arms still crossed over her chest in disapproval.

"Fine," he sighed, "fine. The one across my eyebrow is from a wolf. Same as the rest of them, actually."

"I – what? Wolves? What happened?"

"I was attacked," Adrian replied simply. "It was quite vicious. But I got away."

Scarlett took a few steps towards him, eyes glittering with interest. "How did you get away? Did you kill the wolf?"

"No," Adrian replied softly. His expression seemed cagey to Scarlett, though she couldn't work out why. "I didn't kill the wolf. But I know the woods well. I got away."

Scarlett wasn't satisfied with his answer in the slightest. But there was something about the way Adrian was speaking to her that implied he wasn't going to elaborate. She decided to ask him about something else instead.

"Where are you from? Are your parents still alive?"

He shook his head. "Both dead. Most of the people in their village are dead, too. A plague," he explained, "though I survived. For a while afterwards I wished I hadn't. I didn't know what I was supposed to do on my own."

"Adrian, that's...awful," Scarlett said, at a loss for any other words. "I'm so sorry."

He waved a hand dismissively. "It's not like anyone could do anything about it. My mother was the healer for the village. As soon as she was hit by it we all knew the village was doomed. Sometimes I think my father only got sick because he had to watch her die."

"What did your father do for a living?"

"He was a con-man through and through," Adrian chuckled darkly. He moved through the trees in silence for a while, Scarlett meekly following behind him. She had no idea where they were; she was completely disoriented.

"Nobody expected them to fall in love," he eventually continued, pausing in his tracks for Scarlett to catch up. He smiled somewhat sadly, though there was a fondness in Adrian's amber eyes that Scarlett had never seen there before. "But they did. My mother kept him on the straight and narrow as much as anyone could hope for...which wasn't much. I guess it's no surprise I ended up the way I am with such miss-matched parents."

"Is that why you sell legitimate medicine alongside all your ridiculous potions?"

"They're not actually ridiculous, you know," Adrian said, which surprised Scarlett. "They'd all do their jobs properly if I sold them at the right concentration. But can you imagine – a whole town of men and women ensorcelled on the whims of those wealthy enough to put something in their drink or cast a spell on them? Lord help you all if I actually sold products that worked properly."

Scarlett raised an eyebrow. "Why not simply...not sell them any of these things? Why not focus on being a healer?"

"Oh, come now, Scarlett, you can't be serious."

"What do you mean?"

Adrian faced her, taking her hand before bowing deeply and kissing her fingers. His eyes flashed wickedly when he saw her blush. "Do you know how much money I make from women looking at men the way you're looking at me now? And the other way around?"

121

Scarlett tried to pull her hand away in retaliation; Adrian pulled it closer towards him instead. "And even more than that," he murmured when their faces were inches from one another, "do you know how much people will pay for *revenge?* To get back at a lover who spurned them? To make a person who wronged them suffer?"

"...I imagine people pay a lot," Scarlett admitted quietly, thinking about the number of times she had fallen into despair over her own circumstances and wished for a way out. "Desperate people will do anything."

Adrian grinned, all sharp canines and even sharper amusement. "Exactly. And they're *all* desperate." He let go of Scarlett. "And they keep my business afloat. Being a healer alone isn't enough – not for a travelling merchant."

"So why don't you settle somewhere instead?"

"As if," he snorted, rolling his eyes at the apparently ridiculous idea. "Can you see me ever settling down?"

"...I guess not."

"Okay, Red; your turn."

He glanced at her when she said nothing. Scarlett sighed. She ran a hand through her long hair and shook it out from underneath the fur hood draped around her shoulders.

"What do you want to know?"

"Why were you really kicked out of the Duke residence? I don't see you as someone who did anything scandalous."

"You would be correct. It was my father who did something scandalous."

"Which would be?"

"He had me."

122

That froze Adrian in his tracks. "...your mother?"

"Frances Duke isn't my mother. I don't know who my mother is."

"So...your step-mother didn't want you standing in the way of her sons' inheritance? I take it that's the gist of it."

"Yes. But..."

"But?"

"I saw my father a few days ago. He thinks we might be able to fix things – as a family."

Adrian smiled. "And that's all you want, isn't it?"

Scarlett's eyes were wide as she nodded. "More than anything else in the world."

"Oh, but...wait." Adrian scratched his head in confusion. "So when the blacksmith and the doctor and the baker all proposed to you, they didn't care that you weren't going to inherit your father's fortune nor his estate?"

"I told them and none of them rescinded their offers," Scarlett replied bashfully. "In truth I thought it would dissuade them. I thought wrong."

"I don't think you put enough stock in your individual worth, Scarlett Duke."

And then Adrian kissed her, but it wasn't rushed or forceful. It was soft, polite and chaste against her lips. It was a kiss Scarlett would never have thought he was capable of.

"We've reached your grandmother's house, Red," he murmured with a soft smile that genuinely reached his eyes. "Thank you for telling me about your family."

Scarlett hardly dared to breathe. Everything that she had decided merely days ago – that she was done with

Adrian Wolfe, that he wasn't worth her thoughts and attention – had been thrown out of the window. The man in front of her was...different. He was someone Scarlett very much wanted to spend time with. Someone she wanted to –

"Thank you for telling me about yours," she echoed back. Her fingers twitched with the desire to reach out and touch Adrian's face.

She resisted.

"I better be getting back to my stall," Adrian finally said. "Frank will be furious with me leaving for so long. And he'll be dying to know why I got punched in the face, too."

Scarlett chuckled despite herself. "It's going to bruise."

"I know."

"Your handsome face will be spoiled."

"Good to know you think me handsome, little miss."

Adrian grinned at the scowl on Scarlett's face – and then he was gone.

Scarlett held a hand up to her lips, fingers tracing where Adrian's mouth had been on hers. Her heart wouldn't slow down, thumping ever more painfully against her ribcage as she watched him walk further and further away.

I'm in deep trouble, she thought.

CHAPTER SIXTEEN

Adrian

Adrian was conflicted – a feeling he never thought he'd associate with himself. But here he was, conflicted, confused and capricious as hell.

I like her, he thought as he paced back and forth through the forest. *I genuinely, hopelessly like her.*

There was nothing else to it; Adrian Wolfe was more than merely physically attracted to Scarlett Duke, which threw a wrench in his plans he'd never had the foresight to consider.

And yet I'm a wolf! Adrian paced back and forth in the woods, bushy tail swinging behind him in frustration. *We're practically at a new moon and I'm still a wolf*

because of her grandmother. And I'll remain tied to this
curse for as long as the damn hag wishes.

Adrian wanted out. He was desperate for it. Though he was genuinely fond of Scarlett, escaping his damnable curse had to be his priority...even if he hurt Scarlett in the process.

A gnawing hunger ate at his stomach, causing Adrian to regret not having eaten before transforming. He didn't feel much up for hunting through the woods, though he had no patience for feeling hungry, either. And so, knowing that a few, errant deer could often be found close to Heidi's house by virtue of the other wolves being scared of the place, Adrian began to lope through the dark underbrush of the forest in the direction of her house.

If he were a man he would have laughed bitterly at the fact that a tiny, unassuming house in the middle of the woods of Rowan would be home to *both* of his tormentors. The one he couldn't stand had her nails digging ever more sharply into his soul; the other seemed to be stroking ever more insistently and distractingly at his heart...and somewhere else, too.

For Adrian knew that part of the hunger he was feeling had nothing to do with food. That feeling was only growing stronger every moment he spent with Scarlett, and getting worse every moment he spent *without* her.

It wasn't something Adrian was used to. Until recently if he felt an insatiable desire for a woman he'd simply... find one. It was easy to charm and seduce a woman into bed when he had entire towns full of them to choose from. But it was different now; if the woman wasn't Scarlett then Adrian didn't want her – even though he knew he was planning on discarding her in order to lift his curse.

He thought dolefully about how his situation would be so much better if he didn't actually hold Scarlett in any high regard. It made it even worse that she was painting her lips and braiding her hair and wearing low-cut dresses for the sole purpose of enticing Adrian, whilst at the same time (rightfully) keeping a wall up against him. It was infuriating. He wanted the woman and he wanted her *now*.

Well, not whilst I'm a wolf, Adrian thought as he reached his destination. *But if I don't get Scarlett into bed in the next day or so I might well go insane.*

The fact that he had to get her into bed during daylight hours made things even more difficult. People were far too proper during the day; it was much easier to entice and persuade and bewitch them under a murky, moonlit sky.

Adrian searched around the stone walls of Heidi Duke's house on soft, silent feet. The scents he picked up weren't promising – no deer had been close to her garden for hours. And yet he didn't want his search to have been in vain, so Adrian continued prowling around for another half an hour, nose swinging from the ground to the air in an attempt to pick up a promising scent.

All he could smell was Scarlett.

Don't go to her window, Adrian thought even as his wolf body ignored the command and stalked around to the back of the house, where Scarlett's bedroom was. Her window was ajar, which explained why Adrian could pick up the intoxicating smells of vanilla, saffron and sandalwood so strongly. There was a warm, soft light just barely shining through the glass, telling him that Scarlett was likely not yet asleep, which of course was even more reason for Adrian to retreat back into the shadows.

He didn't.

Padding over to the windowsill he stood up on his hind legs to place his front paws on the ledge in order to better see into Scarlett's room. The warm light Adrian had seen through the window was from her fireplace, where the roaring flames danced and crackled as if they were alive.

Adrian flinched despite himself; as a wolf he was instinctively, deathly afraid of fire. The feeling often seeped into his true form, causing him to shy away from fireplaces in taverns and inns even though he knew they posed him no harm. He had to wonder why Scarlett had her window slightly open when she had a fire going to keep the room warm in the first place.

The young woman in question wasn't actually *in* her room, sending a wave of disappointment over Adrian. But just as he wondered whether he should turn and leave she appeared, humming tunefully and wrapped in a robe as if she'd only just bathed.

He lowered himself from the ledge ever-so-slightly, reducing the risk of Scarlett spying him through the window. Adrian almost felt as though he was holding his breath when she disrobed, revealing that she was wearing nothing underneath. Thinking briefly of Sam Birch having witnessed a similar sight, Adrian happily agreed with what the man had said about Scarlett's body – it was perfect.

The warm glow from the fire cast her pale skin in amber light, revealing a fine mist of water still clinging to her from the bath. Scarlett's long, beautiful hair was tied back in messy disarray, but now that she had returned to the confines of her room she released it, sending it tumbling down her back. The action caused a fresh wave of her scent to roll over Adrian's nose; he found himself salivating and holding back a whine of longing as a result.

How can she be this unguarded when she knows Sam saw her through her window? Adrian thought, despite the fact he was thoroughly enjoying the view. But he didn't want anybody else to see Scarlett like this. To that end he wished he could cover up the glass and protect Scarlett's modesty on her behalf.

Scarlett rubbed at her shoulders as if working out a knot in her neck. Adrian watched her do so, transfixed by the way her breasts lifted when she raised her arms. She continued to hum some unknown tune as she turned to look in her mirror and inspect her face, giving Adrian full view of her body from behind. The shadows in the fire-lit room only served to accentuate each and every curve of her.

He dug his claws into the window-ledge.

If Adrian hadn't known any better he'd be convinced Scarlett knew she was being watched. He didn't see why, otherwise, she would masquerade around her room completely naked for so long and in such a sensual manner.

When finally she laid down on her bed Scarlett did so without putting on any clothes. She merely pulled back the sheets and snuggled beneath them, content in the warmth of the fire and the freshness of the low, icy breeze blowing through the gap in her window.

Adrian couldn't stand knowing that she was wearing nothing under the sheets. He thought of the morning, and the possibility of Sam Birch catching Scarlett, once more, completely naked and unaware. Sam had asked Scarlett to start viewing him as a man; perhaps he would use the opportunity to demonstrate just how *much* of a man he was.

Adrian let out a near-silent growl at the thought, the

vibrations of the noise running all the way along his spine. But it was loud enough to alert Scarlett to his presence. For the second time in his wolf form Adrian froze in place, eyes locked on Scarlett's as she watched him with an expressionless face.

He wondered what she would do. His behaviour was clearly unnatural for a wolf – Adrian had no idea how Scarlett would explain it away. He highly doubted her mind would immediately come to the conclusion that the wolf outside her window was actually a man, regardless of the fact that that was indeed the case.

To Adrian's surprise Scarlett's lips curled into the slightest of smiles as she sat up in bed. The sheets fell around her hips, exposing her body from her neck down to her waist. Adrian could do nothing but stare. Scarlett was *letting* him look.

What is wrong *with this woman?!* he thought, simultaneously confused and excited beyond belief. Nobody in their right mind undressed for a wild, vicious animal.

Nobody except Scarlett Duke.

"What is it that you want, Mr Wolf?" Scarlett murmured, just loud enough for Adrian to hear. She slid all of her hair over one shoulder and began to play with it, teasing out errant knots and tangles with quick, nimble fingers as she kept her beautiful eyes on Adrian.

He whined.

He licked his lips.

He ran away.

For what could Adrian do as a wolf? He darted back into the woods, never more frustrated not to be a man than he was now. Even after rutting against a fallen tree trunk he couldn't get rid of his dissatisfaction.

130

He couldn't bear to play the long game anymore. No longer could he toy with Scarlett's affections – having her give in and making her want more only to pull back for her to yearn for him all the harder. He was done. Adrian's body couldn't take it.

Tomorrow he'd properly seduce Scarlett once and for all.

CHAPTER SEVENTEEN

Scarlett

"Mr Schmidt?"

Jakob took a few seconds to realise somebody was calling his name over the sounds of his hammer. But when he eventually looked up and saw Scarlett his work was quickly abandoned.

"To what do I owe the pleasure?" he grinned, wiping away the fine layer of black soot that had accumulated on his brow before ushering Scarlett inside his workshop.

Scarlett smiled demurely. "I think it's about time we talked properly about your proposal, Mr Schmidt."

Outside the workshop the threat of rain hung ominously in the air. It was early morning – many of the streets of Rowan were still quiet – and Scarlett was keen to return to her grandmother's house before the clouds finally released the downpour they were carrying. But she was determined to tie up all the loose ends that were the proposals she'd been given so that, if and when Frances Duke was willing to welcome Scarlett back into the family, she brought no complications along with her.

And so here Scarlett was, in Jakob Schmidt's smithy, preparing to turn him down even as he realised that was exactly what she was doing.

"You turning me down flat, Miss Scarlett?" Jakob asked as Scarlett made her way around the workshop floor to where he stood.

She glanced at her feet when she reached him. "I... don't want to marry anyone right now."

Jakob chuckled. "So I might still have a chance?"

"Possibly. But – not likely."

"Ouch. That stings, Miss Scarlett. But this means you're turning down Andreas too, then?"

He didn't mention Charlie. He had never viewed the baker's boy as a threat.

Scarlett grimaced somewhat as she fiddled with the fastening of her red cloak. "I think my father would want me to marry him. But I barely know Andreas anymore. He's a fully-fledged adult now."

"But so are you."

"Which makes it all the more confusing. I don't really know who *I* am now. I'd like to take some time to find out, I think."

Jakob sighed magnanimously, then turned from Scarlett to rummage through a drawer for something. When he returned he was holding a perfect imitation of a

133

snowdrop, cast in silver and so achingly beautiful Scarlett almost cried.

"This is for you, Scarlett. I *had* meant it as a wedding gift, but...you turning down everyone to take care of yourself first is just as good a reason for me to give you it."

He proffered it to Scarlett, who didn't move at first. She eyed Jakob curiously. "This...for me? Truly? No strings attached?"

He laughed. "Maybe once you're done working out who you are you can entertain the idea of me taking you out for dinner. But no pressure – I was wrong to have sprung my proposal onto you in the first place. I'm a grown man; I should have known better."

"You've always been a competitive man, Mr Schmidt," Scarlett said, smiling slightly as she finally took the snowdrop. "It's not surprising that you fought hard to out-do Andreas and Charlie."

He chuckled at the comment, then asked, "Pray tell, Miss Scarlett – who out of all your suitors would you have been most inclined to choose, if you were going to choose one of us at all?"

Scarlett's mind flashed immediately to Adrian Wolfe, though he wasn't one of the suitors to which Jakob was referring. Her face flushed at the question. "I must admit...probably you. Although I don't see a marriage with you lasting all that long. You seem a little, um, *too* passionate for me to handle."

What Scarlett meant was that Jakob was known to have an insatiable appetite for women, and he knew this. For a few seconds he didn't respond but then he roared with laughter. Eyes glittering, he put both his hands around Scarlett's and squeezed slightly.

"Ah, you really are a keeper. A sharp tongue and

134

honest to a fault. Any man would be lucky to have your affections. So what about Samuel Birch?"

Scarlett blinked. "...what about Sam?"

"Come now, Scarlett. He follows you around like a lost puppy. You didn't even have the heart to properly reject him. Seems like he found the best way to try and win you over in the long-term."

She looked away uncomfortably. "I don't – that's not really what happened, Mr Schmidt. Regardless, when I say I'm not ready to marry anyone I mean it. With that in mind how I feel about Sam right now shouldn't really matter, should it?"

Jakob sighed as he let go of her hands. "You really have grown up. That was a more adult response than any I've heard from half the adults around here. I have no doubt you'll choose well if – and when – you do." He glanced outside when a gust of wind blew through the workshop. "I'd wager you should get back to your grandmother's before the weather gets worse, Miss Scarlett."

She nodded, carefully tucking the beautiful, silver snowdrop into the inside pocket of her cloak before pulling her fur-lined hood up and over her head. "Thank you for being so understanding, Mr Schmidt."

"Call me Jakob," he replied as Scarlett turned to leave.

She smiled. "Then have a good day, Jakob."

Jakob stared at her regretfully. "You really won't reconsider my proposal?"

"Good-bye, Jakob."

"You're a cruel one, Scarlett!"

The words followed Scarlett as she rushed back to her grandmother's as quickly as she could. It was something

Adrian had said to her, too, and made her wonder just how cruel she actually was.

I never mean to be, she thought, wincing when a few, icy drops of rain hit her face. Pulling her cloak around her a little tighter, Scarlett picked up her walking pace and powered through the unseasonably wintry weather until, with some relief, she spied her grandmother's house just as the rain truly began to fall.

"Nana, I'm back!" Scarlett called out after she struggled to close the heavy kitchen door against the wind. But nobody responded; the kitchen was dark and empty. No fire sat in the fireplace. Somewhat concerned, Scarlett moved through the house only to discover that her grandmother was nowhere to be seen. When she returned to the kitchen she realised there was a letter on the table. Frowning, Scarlett picked it up to see what it said.

It read: *Emergency supply run with Samuel to Burdich; your father kindly provided a horse and carriage. Won't be back before nightfall and may stay overnight so don't wait up. All my love, Nana.*

Scarlett was stunned. Her grandmother rarely travelled outside of Rowan and her beloved woods. Burdich was at least three hours away by horse and carriage – longer with the weather having taken such a bad turn.

What on earth was so important to buy that she had to travel in this rain? Scarlett worried. *She'll get sick.*

She felt a pang of frustration towards Sam, whom Scarlett should have been able to trust to dissuade her grandmother from going on such a journey.

"Men are useless..." she muttered as she shirked off her cloak, shivering at the chill in the air. Scarlett glanced at the empty fireplace in the kitchen, then, upon realising she was likely not to spend much time anywhere else but her bedroom for the rest of the day, took an armful of firewood and moved through to get the fireplace going in her own room, instead.

It took a long time for the air to finally warm up. Scarlett changed into a long, white, sleeveless nightgown that tied at her waist and huddled against the fire, feeling abruptly clueless about what to do until her grandmother's return.

Much of her time lately had been spent either thinking of, avoiding or interacting with Adrian Wolfe. She didn't much like acknowledging that fact especially because it was painfully true. And Scarlett was desperate to see him again – though she had to admit feeling somewhat apprehensive about what would happen when next they actually saw each other.

But she was excited, too. Her insides coiled up at the thought, a simultaneously pleasant and frustrating sensation that she couldn't get rid of. Determined to think about literally anything else Scarlett pondered the wolf that had been lurking outside her window the night before. It was the same wolf she had seen two weeks before, she was sure.

But as she remembered how brazen she had acted upon noticing its presence Scarlett's face only grew hotter.

"What's wrong with me these days!" she exclaimed, for nobody to hear but herself. "I must be going insane."

For she could find no explanation for her thoughts and behaviour other than madness. Scarlett wasn't acting like herself at all. She wondered if this was what it meant to be an adult.

As the wind and wild, torrential rain continued to roar outside her window, Scarlett huddled closer to the fire. Even if it was a sign of madness she still longed to see

Adrian, especially because she was alone.

Such things don't happen just because one wishes for them, she thought.

Then she heard a banging noise coming from the kitchen.

A knock on the door.

CHAPTER EIGHTEEN

Adrian

The storm had well and truly hit Rowan by the time Adrian finally made his way towards Heidi Duke's house in the woods. Though it was only early afternoon the thick, purple clouds and sheets of rain cast the woods in an eerie kind of twilight, which set Adrian's teeth on edge when he thought about having to transform in a few hours.

Adrian wasn't sure what he planned to do; it wasn't as if he could seduce Scarlett whilst her grandmother was there. He'd wanted to run into her in Rowan, of course, but Scarlett had already been and gone from the market square by the time Adrian had changed back into a human, emerged from the forest and made himself look presentable enough to see her.

But he needed to see her.

He was desperate to see her.

And so Adrian came upon the house sodden and frozen to the core, which was largely his own fault for not wearing a cloak. "So much for running hot," he muttered through gritted teeth. He guessed even the endurance his wolf form granted him had its limits – and pouring, bitter rain was it. His white shirt was translucent against his skin, his black waistcoat and leggings sticking to him in an uncomfortably thick, slimy manner. His leather boots had long-since soaked through.

It was only when he reached the front door that Adrian realised there was no fire going or lights on in the kitchen, though the lantern above the porch was lit. He became abruptly aware of the fact that there might be nobody in. He didn't know how he was supposed to cope with that, so Adrian ignored the growing feeling of dread and disappointment creeping up his spine as he knocked upon the heavy door.

He rapped his knuckles politely against the grain at first, then banged more insistently when even he couldn't hear the sound his hand made over the thunderous wind.

"Tonight is going to be so much fun," Adrian murmured humourlessly, thinking about how miserable being a wolf in such a storm would be. He only hated Heidi Duke all the more for her damnable, merciless curse because of it.

But all thoughts of the old woman were lost when the front door finally opened and Adrian came face-to-face with a very confused-looking, red-cheeked Scarlett.

Her eyes grew wide as she took in the sight of Adrian, shivering and dripping wet beneath the fluttering light from the lantern above him, which was swinging dangerously in the wind.

"Mr Wo – Adrian!" she exclaimed in disbelief. "What are you doing here? You're absolutely soaking! Have you taken leave of your senses altogether?"

He tried to smile in response; it came out as more of a grimace. "Quite possibly. Is your grandmother in? I wanted to raid her stores from the mountains."

Scarlett paused for a moment, eyebrow quirked at the explanation as if she wasn't sure whether to believe it or not. "She isn't here," she eventually said. "Nana and Sam took one of my father's carriages to travel through to Burdich for some essential supplies. They won't be back until after nightfall, she said."

Adrian flinched despite himself. Anything Heidi Duke would travel out of Rowan for in such horrendous weather couldn't be anything good. But when Scarlett looked at him in concern he shrugged off the flinch as a reaction to the howling wind.

"May I come in anyway?" he asked, gesturing around in the general direction of the storm. "It's not very pleasant out here."

Scarlett burst out laughing at the comment despite herself, then retreated from the doorway to let Adrian into the kitchen. It was only after she slammed the door shut behind him that she truly took in just how wretched the man looked.

"Why on earth were you travelling without a cloak on?" she demanded, hands on her hips as she scanned over his appearance with an affronted look on her face. "It's dangerously cold out there – you could have killed yourself!"

It made Adrian want to kiss her, to see her so concerned for his health. He tried to chuckle through

141

chattering teeth as he shook dripping wet hair out of his eyes like a dog. "I run –"

"Don't you dare say you run hot, Mr Wolfe. You're freezing."

Scarlett's fingers trailed along Adrian's arm just long enough to feel how truly cold he was before flinching away from the sodden material.

He glanced around the kitchen. "It's not much warmer in here, to be fair. How are your cheeks so rosy, Miss Scarlett? And I see you're once more not dressed appropriately for entertaining strange men – or the cold."

Scarlett only blushed harder at the comment. Though her night gown was certainly longer than the previous one Adrian had seen her in, the thin straps had fallen from her shoulders, giving him an enticing look at the curves of her breasts and the promise of the rest of her nakedness beneath the thin fabric.

When she realised Adrian's attention had very much diverted from the cold to her body she gulped slightly, then turned for the corridor. "I have a fire going in my bedroom. Come through and take your clothes off to dry by it."

"Well that is quite possibly the most wonderful invitation I've ever received," Adrian remarked, his tone filthy as he began to unlace his shirt with fingers made clumsy from the cold.

Scarlett threw an expensively-woven towel at Adrian's face. "You can make jokes when your teeth stop chattering, you idiot."

Adrian was thoroughly enjoying this version of Scarlett; he could only assume it was how she looked after her brothers. And so he complied, wincing as he struggled out of his sodden clothes and boots full of ice water. When

Scarlett finally turned to face him once more he was rubbing his hair dry with the towel whilst the rest of him was stark naked, revelling in the heat from the fire. She immediately looked away again.

"The towel was to cover your – you know."

Adrian could only laugh. "Are you embarrassed, little miss? You'd have seen a lot more back at Mac's tavern if I hadn't...had a fit."

She glanced at him for half a second before busying herself with picking up his discarded clothes, laying them over the metal grille that stood in front of the fire to protect the floor from getting scorched. Adrian followed suit and picked up his boots, resting them by the hearth before retreating from the flames as quickly as he could without raising any questions pertaining to his unreasonable fear of them.

"Your scars," Scarlett ended up saying, sparing another glance at Adrian's chest, and then another. "You weren't lying about them."

"Of course not," he replied, turning around to give Scarlett a full view of the ones on his back, too. Though most of his scars were now years old and well worn into his skin, there were a few from the turn of the year that were still shiny and new. "Do they make me less handsome?"

Scarlett snorted derisively. "You must know that they don't."

Adrian flung himself on top of Scarlett's bed before she could stop him, revelling in her scent even as she let out a noise of shock at his literal and figurative boldness.

"Don't lie on my bed when you have nothing on, Adrian!" she complained, rushing over as if to push him off before thinking better of it when she ended up staring

143

far too long at his entire body stretching out in front of her.

He could only grin. "I'm tired from my long journey through the storm. I need to rest, do I not? How do you smell so good, Scarlett? What is it that you use?"

Scarlett froze to the spot, shocked to speechlessness by the dramatic change of subject. She faltered for a moment before replying, "It's an oil that my mother – that Frances – has always used. Her grandfather was from somewhere abroad. I loved the way she smelled, so my father started importing more of the oil just for me to use years ago."

Adrian sighed contentedly as he closed his eyes and nuzzled into the sheets of her bed. Usually it was only as a wolf that he could fully appreciate the smell of her, but literally surrounded by objects belonging to Scarlett he could finally experience it as a human. The vanilla was so fragrant he could almost taste it.

"So good..."

"Adrian...?" Scarlett murmured uncertainly, for it very much seemed as if the man truly was intending to rest as he said. "Are you really just going to sleep on my bed?"

Half-opening his eyes he peered at Scarlett, the hint of a smirk playing across his lips as he said, "Am I really *just* going to sleep on your bed? What are you hoping for, Miss Scarlett?"

Scarlett ran a hand through her hair – a gesture that was simultaneously nervous and annoyed – before making to turn from Adrian. But he flung an arm out and grabbed her far more quickly than Scarlett could ever have imagined a human was capable of moving and, before she knew it, Adrian had pulled her onto the bed and held her in place above him. Scarlett's eyes grew wide for a moment, then her eyelashes fluttered down as Adrian

144

gently stroked the inside of her right wrist with his thumb.

"I'll be honest, Red," he purred, his eyes like fire in the warm glow of the room as he stared up at Scarlett's uncertain, excited face, "I have no intention of sleeping whatsoever. What about you?"

Her eyes grew heavy-lidded. She took a deep, shuddering breath. Then Scarlett reached down until she was almost close enough to touch Adrian's lips with her own. Tendrils of her dark, lustrous hair tickled the skin of his cheekbones.

"I don't feel much like sleeping, either."

Adrian's mouth was on hers before Scarlett even finished the sentence.

CHAPTER NINETEEN

Scarlett

Scarlett's body was tingling with fire and passion and heat, heat, heat. Her insubstantial nightgown was all but torn from her body before she had time to catch her breath from the first of many blisteringly demanding kisses Adrian landed on her lips. It was as if he would die if he let go of her for even a second.

It only made her want him all the more.

Adrian's hair was still wet from the storm which continued to batter on outside the window, turning the afternoon into twilight as Scarlett ran her fingers through the one, solitary streak of white in amongst the black. When she pulled on his hair, urging Adrian to deepen

146

their kiss, his tongue found his way into Scarlett's mouth even as his hands crawled all over her body pulling her towards *him*.

"You have no idea how long you tortured me, Scarlett," he growled in a fleeting moment between kisses, his words becoming a groan when Scarlett dared to brush a hand between his legs. Adrian squeezed his thighs around it, trapping her delicate fingers there. She gasped slightly when he toppled her beneath him on the bed.

"How was I to know?" Scarlett asked, breathless. Some animal instinct that had always known what to do from the moment she met Adrian caused her to dig her nails into his thigh and, when he let go of her hand in surprise, she grabbed hold of the length of his erection.

Adrian ran his lips down her neck, biting down against the artery there ever so slightly when Scarlett began stroking him. His fingers nimbly fondled her breasts before creeping down across her navel; her mouth formed a wordless *oh* when they travelled down even further.

"Surely you noticed me watching you over the last two years," Adrian whispered into Scarlett's ear. "For how could I not, after you ran into my arms the night you fled into the woods?"

Scarlett's breathing hitched as Adrian's fingers moved faster; more insistently. Her own hand matched his pacing until he reached for it and pulled her wrist up and over her head.

His eyes glowed dangerously in the firelight. "You're too good at that to be an innocent virgin, little miss. Do you know that?"

Scarlett laced her legs through Adrian's as she let a self-satisfied smirk cross her lips. "Maybe I'm just naturally talented."

"A talent I'd rather nobody else was aware of," he chuckled, kissing each of her breasts in turn before returning to her lips. It wasn't long before Scarlett's breathing became so fast that she was worried she would hyperventilate.

"Adrian –" she began, but he merely grinned wickedly before sliding his fingers inside of her. The rest of Scarlett's sentence was lost to pure shock and pleasure; a few, scant seconds later and she was moaning against Adrian's lips, struggling against his grip on her other hand to let her go. "Adrian," she cried out again, "let me touch you, let me –"

So Adrian let her go just as Scarlett climaxed, her fingers satisfyingly clinging into his back as her body was overwrought by wave after wave of tingling, ecstatic satisfaction. Scarlett felt like she could barely breathe because of it.

Adrian ran a hand through her hair, sliding his entire body against Scarlett until she bit back a cry.

"I'm – it's so sensitive. Adrian, be careful –"

"Careful is for later," he replied, eyes glittering. "It's my turn now."

And then the full length of him was inside Scarlett, and this time there was no biting back the noise that came from her throat. Her fingernails dug into his back, only digging deeper when Adrian began to grind against her.

"Oh God, oh –"

Adrian smothered her words with his mouth. "You're okay, Red," he murmured, the words tickling her lips as he spoke them. "Just trust me."

Scarlett didn't know what else she could do *but* trust Adrian Wolfe, given the situation. Though she gladly did so; now that the initial shock of pain was over her body was growing accustomed to the feeling of the man inside of her. A few more seconds passed and Scarlett began to crave more – for Adrian to hit harder, and faster, and deeper.

She ran her hands through his hair, pulling him closer against her. "More," she mouthed, being honest and clear about what she wanted, "give me more."

Adrian paused for but half a moment, gazing at Scarlett as if in wonder before giving her a hungry smile, all sharp, shining canines and flashing eyes. When he slammed into her Scarlett bit down on her lower lip in shock. When he did it again she reached up and bit into his shoulder, instead.

Adrian clung onto Scarlett even as she grabbed onto him, mercilessly kissing her with reckless abandon as he pounded into her. His breathing had grown even faster than Scarlett's.

When finally he let out a cry of pleasure, Adrian collapsed on top of Scarlett and buried his head against her neck, furling and unfurling his fingers through her hair as he kissed her skin.

"Thank you," he mumbled after a long moment, during which the only sounds had been the two of them regaining their breath and the ever-present crackle of the fire. "Thank you, thank you, thank you."

Scarlett glanced down at him, confused. "What for?"

"For letting this happen, of course," he laughed softly, somewhat incredulous. "That was...incredible. It shouldn't have been *that* good."

"Because I'm just an innocent little virgin, Mr Wolfe?"

Adrian bit into her neck before leaning up on his elbows to look at Scarlett. "Not anymore you're not, Red. Now you're mine."

149

She quirked an eyebrow. "Yours? I wasn't aware I was anyone's but my own."

"You can be both. Just not anybody else's."

"So you're not going to run off never to be seen again now you got me into bed?"

Adrian let out a bark of laughter. "Hardly. You don't fuck a girl like that and not come back for more."

Scarlett swatted his cheek with her left hand. "Such foul language. I'm a lady, I'll have you know."

"I'm aware of that," he said, running his mouth down along Scarlett's chest to her stomach. He glanced up at her, grinning mischievously. "Which is why it's all the more satisfying to defile you, language and all."

Scarlett couldn't help but return the grin. She darted her eyes over to Adrian's clothes, which were still dripping wet. "It may take a few hours for those to dry. Do you have to be anywhere else this afternoon?"

"Please tell me that's an invitation to stay."

For a moment Scarlett considered that allowing Adrian to stay was madness. But she had just given her virginity to him; a few more hours of lying in bed with him was never going to bring it back.

She didn't *want* it back.

She wanted more of him.

Reaching a hand over to stroke Adrian's broken eyebrow, Scarlett nodded.

"Yes. Stay until your clothes are dry."

"And then?" Adrian asked from his position over her stomach. "What of tomorrow?"

She laughed. "Tomorrow is tomorrow. Let's just live for today."

He flashed another of his brilliant, maddeningly wicked smiles.

"I think I can agree to that."

CHAPTER TWENTY

Adrian

Never had Adrian felt so supremely satisfied with himself, even though he had spent the night curled up inside the hollow of a dead oak tree, as a wolf, in the middle of a storm. But now the storm had passed and the sun was shining through thousands of water droplets hanging from the branches above him, turning them to priceless jewels that glittered impossibly bright.

It was still cold – unseasonably so – but for once Adrian didn't care.

For he had slept with Scarlett Duke.

He had slept with Scarlett Duke not once, nor twice, nor even three times.

I don't think I've ever *been insatiable enough to go for five rounds in as many hours,* he mused as he finally reached the room he was renting in Mac's tavern, stripping off his cold, weather-beaten clothes and collapsing onto the bed with a thump. *I couldn't even bring myself to leave. I was cutting it rather fine with transforming.*

But Adrian didn't care that he had only made it out of Scarlett's bedroom, his clothes still uncomfortably damp, with fewer than ten minutes to spare before he turned into a wolf. Those same clothes had lain abandoned by his side as he hid from the storm for the night, useless and wretched but for the lingering smell of Scarlett that clung to them. For that reason Adrian had buried his snout in amongst the wet fabric, not caring for how the fibres scratched at his nose.

He was also too pleased with himself to worry about the fact that, sooner or later, he'd have to use his new-found relationship with Scarlett to get rid of his curse. In his current mindset that could be later, later, later, though deep inside himself Adrian knew it had to be sooner.

But that was something to dwell upon after a few hours of well-earned, warm and comfortable sleep. Adrian was exhausted after having spent so many successive nights as a wolf, since he didn't often sleep when in his lupine form. Added onto that his really rather active afternoon with Scarlett and Adrian was left feeling drained and empty.

Just a few hours of sleep and he'd be back to normal.

Just a few.

*

Adrian woke with a start, surprised by the darkness in his bedroom. The sun was already low in the sky, hidden by cloud. By Adrian's calculation he had less than an hour before it was time for him to transform once more. His heart sank.

I've wasted the entire day. I slept away all my freedom.

His skin tingled and ached with the mere thought of transforming. For a moment he considered fleeing Rowan and its woods – to find the exact boundary where Heidi Duke's curse couldn't hurt him. But it was too late for that; with less than an hour until he transformed Adrian would never make it out of the woods in time.

He banged his head repeatedly against the headboard.

"Fuck this, fuck this, fuck this," he muttered, over and over again, as if his words were themselves a curse. The ecstatic mood he'd been in before sleeping had thoroughly dissipated, leaving only the absolute knowledge that Adrian couldn't bear to spend another night as a wolf.

It had to stop. He was going insane.

It wasn't just because of the lack of sleep, or the fear, or the constant obsessing over how to get his curse removed that Adrian felt like he was going mad. With every night spent as a wolf he felt more and more of his human self being overwritten by far more animalistic, lupine urges. In all honesty Adrian didn't know how he managed to stay in Scarlett's room with the fire so close. If it hadn't been for what the two of them had been doing he wouldn't have been able to handle it.

Adrian had never been scared of fire before. Rather, he loved it, for the way his parents had used it to kill sickness and make food safe to eat and keep predators at bay.

But now he *was* the predator to be kept at bay, and becoming less and less like a human because of it.

He chuckled wryly at the thought. For, with regards to Scarlett, he was a different kind of predator to be protected from entirely.

154

She will never trust men again after I break her heart, Adrian thought, somewhat arrogantly. *But at least I won't be around to see that. I'll be on the other side of the world, somewhere warm and exotic and entirely devoid of wolves.*

Adrian used his remaining time as a human as best he could. He had food and hot water sent up so that he could clean and eat. He shaved – for all the good that would do him as a wolf. He dressed in a finely made, loose white shirt with a forest green waistcoat delicately embroidered with gold. He paired them with green leggings so dark they were almost black, a supple pair of brown leather, thigh high boots and a jacket embroidered in much the same way as the waistcoat. He finished off the look with one, solitary gold earring in his left ear.

Even just for his remaining ten minutes Adrian wanted to look at himself in the mirror and see the man he could have been if not for the fact he turned into a wolf. The man he could still be, once the curse was lifted.

Except he would have little soul left to his name, and his heart would belong to Scarlett Duke.

My freedom for my heart is not too bad a price, Adrian thought bitterly as he watched his reflection frown, his split eyebrow appearing even more pronounced because of it. He ran a hand through his hair, pushing back the white. It was getting too long. Once he was free of Rowan – free of Heidi Duke – he'd have it cut.

And then he waited. Waited for the insufferable, agonising cracks of his bones that told Adrian he had to remove his clothes and prepare to transform.

The feeling never came.

For over an hour he waited. Two. For one wild moment he considered whether Heidi had simply given

155

up. But that didn't seem possible in the slightest; he knew her too well. He looked out of the window in his room, hoping for an explanation.

And then he saw it – or, rather, *didn't.*

There was no moon in the sky.

"The new moon," Adrian murmured, lips curling up into a delighted grin. He had never thought about the limitations of his curse, since Heidi could extend it past the full moon as and when she pleased.

Clearly he had found the limit.

Wasting no time, though he knew it was foolish, Adrian grabbed his cloak, since he had not been outside at night as a human for weeks and didn't want to be surprised by how cold the air could get. He raced down the stairs and out of Mac's tavern, making a beeline for the woods and the little house nestled inside where all his troubles lay. Even though Heidi Duke would be in – even though Samuel Birch might be there – Adrian didn't care.

If this was his only opportunity to have one night with Scarlett then he would take it. One whole night, to watch her under the light of the stars through human eyes. To touch her with human fingers. To speak to her with words understandable to human ears.

He would take it. It would be a memory he'd cling to after he destroyed one of the best things that had happened to him in a long, long time.

When he reached the edge of the trees surrounding the house Adrian slowed. He could see Heidi sitting in the kitchen, drinking tea and working with what looked like straw. On any other night he'd care about what the witch was up to, but not tonight.

He stalked carefully around to Scarlett's window, painfully aware of every noise he made that he could avoid making as a wolf. But he was much quieter than an ordinary human, and he knew where he was going.

Scarlett wasn't in her room, but Adrian didn't care. With skill he slipped a pin through the crack in her window and undid the latch from the outside. He manoeuvred through, landing on the floor with barely a sound at all. Closing the window behind him, Adrian considered what to do until Scarlett returned.

Outside the door, which lay ajar, Adrian could hear the woman in question talking to someone. Sam. He crept closer to eavesdrop.

"What do you mean there's something different about me, Sam? I'm exactly the same."

"But you're not! You're –"

"Happier?"

"I...yes. Sort of."

"And that's a bad thing?"

Sam sighed heavily; Adrian grinned.

You poor boy, he thought. *I know what it is you want to say. But will you say it?*

"You're distracted," Sam finally said. "And people have seen you conversing with Mister Wolfe far more often than you used to. Are the two of you –"

"Don't ask me about Adrian, Sam."

Adrian liked that she used his first name when talking about him to other people. It had taken him long enough to get her to use it, after all. With a pang he realised she would be loathe ever to think his name in a few days, much less utter it. He shook the thought away.

A glint of silver from Scarlett's dressing table caught his eye. Distracted, Adrian wandered away from the conversation to inspect it. It was a snowdrop, perfectly recreated in pure, solid silver. It was impossibly delicate. It was beautiful.

Adrian knew who had made it. After watching the man hand over real snowdrops to Scarlett when he proposed, it was obvious. He had to hand it to Jakob Schmidt – he was certainly a master of his craft. Picking the flower up Adrian thought that, maybe once Scarlett had gotten over his betrayal, she might find happiness with the blacksmith. He didn't seem like a bad man, and was certainly far more Scarlett's type than Sam was.

A few more seconds of staring at the entrancing piece of craft work in his hands and Adrian had an idea. Glancing at the door to ensure nobody was coming through, he pulled out a tiny vial of startlingly blue, viscous liquid. Adrian unstoppered it, tilting the bottle until three individual drops of the stuff fell onto the head of the snowdrop.

"Let no curse nor spell nor potion ever affect the person to whom this was gifted," Adrian whispered, very careful with his words. For a person could steal the snowdrop, or break it into pieces, or throw it away, but that could never change the fact that Jakob had given it to Scarlett. So long as even a piece of it existed on this earth then Scarlett would be protected.

From her grandmother, Adrian thought. *From me. Let this be my own gift to you, Scarlett.*

Adrian replaced the snowdrop onto the dressing table when he heard a creak at the door. Hiding behind her wardrobe he waited until Scarlett appeared, closing the door behind her. Then he crept up on her, holding a hand over her mouth when she gasped in shock.

"Shh," he murmured into her ear. "It's me. It's

Adrian."

Scarlett's eyes went wide as Adrian let go of her mouth and allowed her to turn around.

"What are you doing here?" she asked, keeping her voice quiet. Scarlett headed over to the window and closed the curtains, then slid a bolt across the door.

"Why else would I have crept into your room other than to see you, Scarlett?"

Adrian was satisfied to see a small, delighted smile curl her beautiful lips.

Face flushed, she whispered, "Would you like to spend the night, Adrian?"

His mouth on hers was all the answer Adrian needed to give.

One night, he thought. *We can have one whole night.*

For after that everything would change.

CHAPTER TWENTY-ONE

Scarlett

When Scarlett woke it was with shock and delight that she wasn't alone. Adrian was still asleep, softly breathing away his white lock of hair whenever it fell across his face. She glanced down; he was holding her hand.

When did that happen? Scarlett thought as she blushed. *Have we been holding hands the entire time we were asleep?*

Not that the two of them spent much of the night sleeping in the first place. Though they'd had to keep as silent as a wolf stalking through the night so that her grandmother wouldn't know Scarlett was anything but alone in her room, the act of keeping things secret only seemed to make them hungrier for each other.

Scarlett's body ached from it. But it was a satisfying ache – proof that what she and Adrian were doing was real. That they truly wanted each other.

She still struggled to believe it nonetheless.

Reaching out a hand, Scarlett dared to touch the gold earring Adrian was wearing on his left ear. It was the *only* thing he was wearing. Though the man was always vain and immaculately dressed to a fault, Scarlett had never seen him wear jewellery before. She wondered why.

The touch of his earring turned into Scarlett stroking back his soft, jet-black hair. It still surprised her how silky it was. She intertwined her fingers through it, revelling in the feeling of allowing herself to touch Adrian in the first place.

His amber eyes sprung open.

"Morning," he murmured sleepily. His mouth was curved into the laziest of smiles as he reached up a hand to envelop the one Scarlett had running through his hair. "Sleep well?"

"When I slept, yes."

He snickered. "Well put. I suppose I should run off before your grandmother checks to see if you're awake."

Scarlett couldn't help feeling crestfallen, though she knew Adrian was correct. With a sigh she tried to pull her hand away from his – the hands that had stayed clasped together all night – but Adrian merely held on tighter.

Pulling her against his chest, he sank his face into Scarlett's hair and hitched a leg around one of hers, only entangling them further.

"Adrian, what are you doing?" Scarlett whispered, though she didn't want him to stop. Before she found the

161

sense to resist the urge she planted kisses along his collarbone and up his neck, whilst running a gentle hand down his spine.

Adrian shivered contentedly like a cat getting stroked. He bent his head until his lips found Scarlett's; they were slightly chapped just as, Scarlett realised, her own were. She was parched. But to get a cup of water was to break the magic of being in bed with Adrian, so she ignored her thirst.

They kissed for as long as they dared – deep, lingering kisses that spoke of the night they'd just shared. But the sun was only creeping further and further across the floor of Scarlett's room through a gap in the curtain. Outside, the chatter of larks and wrens and thrushes was filling the morning air. They grew ever more insistent as the seconds passed.

Breathless and tingling, Scarlett forced herself to push Adrian away. "You need to go."

He kissed the tip of her nose. "I know. That doesn't mean either of us wants me to."

If their faces weren't a mere inch from each other Scarlett may well have looked away at the candid remark. It felt *wrong* to want to stay in bed all day, naked and hot and twisted around Adrian Wolfe.

But she wanted it. She wanted it more than anything.

"I'll see you when I come into market in a couple of hours," she said as Adrian finally, regretfully, rolled out of her bed.

"Would you like to eat with me at midday?"

Scarlett blinked in surprise. She sat up, clutching at the sheets to protect her modesty despite the fact Adrian had only just been in bed with her.

162

He laughed softly at the expression on her face. He pulled on his shirt and leggings, sliding into his boots before putting on his beautifully embroidered waistcoat. "Unless my lady doesn't have an appetite, or is trying to find a polite way to tell me to leave her alone."

"No, I'd love to!" Scarlett announced quickly, and possibly a little too loudly. "I was just...surprised, I suppose?"

Adrian raised an eyebrow. "How so?"

"It just seems like an altogether gentlemanly thing to do. Like you're courting me properly."

"I *am* a gentleman, and I *am* courting you properly."

She glanced at the bed pointedly. "Most courtships I know of don't involve climbing into bed together before at least a proposal for marriage is made."

"But I do not wish to be married, and neither do you. In which case surely I have courted you properly?"

Scarlett rolled her eyes, but she let out a small laugh. "Clearly I cannot hope to win against your infallible logic, Adrian."

He grinned. "Wonderful."

As he was reaching for his cloak, peeping out the window trying to determine if he would actually need to put it on, Scarlett couldn't help but appreciate how handsome the man was, especially in his green-and-gold attire.

"I can see you watching me in the window, Scarlett," Adrian said with a smirk.

She blushed. "I'm allowed to look, aren't I?"

"Far more than that, I should think."

"You look particularly dashing today. Those clothes –"

"Were the last gift my parents gave me. Or, rather, were planning to," Adrian explained. "They had them stored away for my twenty-first birthday. But then they died. I haven't worn them before."

"But you've carried them with you wherever you go since then?"

Adrian nodded. He continued to watch Scarlett watching him through the reflection on the window. It kept his own face somewhat obscured from Scarlett, so she couldn't see his expression properly. But the set of his shoulders seemed distant and deeply sad, so Scarlett crept out of bed despite her nakedness and went to him.

When she reached Adrian's side he turned to face her, though the look on his face was carefully crafted and neutral.

"You miss them," she said. It wasn't a question.

"Of course I do. But missing them won't bring them back."

It hurt Scarlett to hear this, though of course it was true. She wrapped her arms around Adrian and leant her head against his chest; his heart was beating quickly. Quicker than Scarlett's.

"You're not alone, you know," she mumbled. "Or, at least, you don't have to be."

Adrian was silent. When Scarlett looked up his eyes seemed just a little too glassy. But then he blinked, and they were fine.

He smiled at her. "I'll see you in a few hours, Miss Scarlett."

And then he kissed her lips, and then he was gone.

*

164

Adrian's idea of eating at midday was to not open his stall, sweep Scarlett onto his arm the moment she arrived at market and demand her attention for the entire day, under the gawking, disbelieving eyes of everyone in Rowan.

Scarlett saw Charlie, who realised there and then that he'd never be able to compete with a man like Adrian Wolfe. She saw Jakob, who roared with understanding laughter when he caught sight of the pair of them. He shook his head in amusement and despair. Scarlett stuck her tongue out at him.

She hoped he would take that as her way of saying: this isn't serious. I'm only having fun.

Scarlett didn't believe her own lie for a second.

For how could she? It had taken everything in her to resist Adrian's charms, and now she had given in and fallen for them. She was in too deep and she knew it. If the man asked her to run off with her in the dark of night she'd say yes in a heartbeat without even blinking.

It would be the wrong choice.

She'd make it anyway.

To that end she knew she had to be careful. But Adrian's arm was around her waist, or clasping her hand, or weaving flowers into her hair as he commented on the people watching them in typically witty, almost cruel fashion.

When finally the sun dipped low into the sky, Adrian settled her onto a bench whilst he entered Mac's tavern for food and drink. He didn't want to go inside with Scarlett, where everybody else was. He wanted her to himself.

Scarlett only felt herself falling even harder for Adrian with every passing moment. The last two days had been like a dream. She didn't want to wake up, though she knew at some point she needed to.

But not right now.

"Scarlett?"

Scarlett looked up at who had spoken; it wasn't Adrian.

Andreas Sommer stood there, a frown upon his perfectly elegant face. "Scarlett, what are you doing?" he asked when Scarlett continued to look at him instead of answering.

"I'm sitting on a bench, Andreas," she said, pointing out the obvious.

"You know what I mean. What are you doing with *him*?"

He gestured towards Adrian as he left the tavern and made a beeline towards Scarlett. The easy-going smile on his face immediately fell away when he saw Andreas.

Scarlett didn't like the way Andreas was talking to her, not at all. She stood up.

"What is that you're insinuating, Andreas? Is there something wrong with me enjoying Mr Wolfe's company?"

He grimaced when Adrian reached the two of them. "Can you leave us alone? I'm clearly speaking with Miss Scarlett in –"

"Whatever it is you want to say to me regarding Adrian Wolfe can be said in front of the man in question," Scarlett interrupted, ensuring that her face remained bland and genial even as her words were pointed and accusatory.

Andreas seemed to flounder. Adrian half-smirked at the look on the man's face.

"Go on, Andreas Sommer," he said. "What is so wrong with Miss Scarlett spending time with me that you felt it prudent to interrupt it?"

"You know fine well what's wrong with it!" Andreas finally exploded. He looked at Scarlett. "You're better than this. You're better than *him.* Don't damage your future more than you already have by wasting more time on him."

"Excuse me?" Scarlett spoke these words in a quiet, controlled rage. She took a step towards Andreas and pushed him away. "And who are you to tell me this? Nobody has the right to tell me what to do or who to see, Andreas. Especially not a classist, entitled man whose proposal to marry me merely involved the fact that our fathers would like it if we did. I'm not a chess piece, and I'm not your mild-natured future wife, either. So go away, and leave us alone."

Both Andreas and Adrian stared at her, stunned by the outburst. For a moment it looked as if Andreas might say something. But then, after spending far too long saying nothing, he scowled at the two of them and stalked away.

Scarlett let out a large *whoosh* of air. She laughed an uncertain laugh as she caught Adrian's eye. "I can't believe I just said that."

"Neither can I. Will there be repercussions for you saying that to him?"

"If there are, I don't care. Either I'm a nobody and it doesn't matter, or I'm a Duke and it matters even less."

Adrian's gazed at her in wonder. "That almost sounds arrogant enough that I would say it."

Scarlett shrugged, though in truth she was very pleased with Adrian saying that. "Is it arrogant if it's true? I suppose that doesn't matter, either."

He placed the food and drink he'd retrieved from the tavern down on the bench. Then, with an overwhelming tenderness that Scarlett had not yet experienced from the man, Adrian stroked the side of her cheek with an ungloved hand and just barely brushed his lips against hers.

But his expression was regretful. Scarlett didn't like that at all.

"Adrian –"

"You're going to hate me, but I have to go. Take the food back for your grandmother. Or Sam. I'm sure he'll see it as a peace offering after you told him off last night."

Scarlett's cheeks burned. "You heard all that?"

"Just a little. He's simply being jealous and protective. I would be, too, if I were pining for you and lost you to another man. I don't think there's any need to be so harsh with him."

She sighed, looking down at the ground before returning to stare into Adrian's sorrowful amber eyes. "I guess not," she mumbled. "Must you go *now*?"

He nodded. "You'll get home safe?"

"It's not time for the wolves to be in our neck of the woods yet. I'll be fine."

Adrian laughed at this. It was unexpected. It felt entirely out of place.

"I suppose they're *not* in the woods right now, are they? Of course they're not."

"Adrian?"

He kissed her again.

"Be off before it gets too dark. Give my regards to little Sam...I'm sure he'll appreciate it."

And then he left for Mac's tavern, where his room was. Scarlett picked up the basket laden with food and drink, numbly making her way out of Rowan and through the woods without really thinking about where she was going.

I have to go.

An uncomfortable feeling of dread washed over Scarlett when she realised Adrian did not say for how long.

CHAPTER TWENTY-TWO

Adrian

It took everything in Adrian's power to head to Heidi Duke's house when he was sure Scarlett was in Rowan. His night spent as a wolf had been exhausting. Even if he'd wanted to sleep he wouldn't have been able to.

All he could think of was Scarlett, and how he would betray her, and how much he didn't want to.

But it was taking him longer and longer to feel human again after transforming. If he took much more of this curse he'd lose himself altogether. He had to put himself first.

He *had* to.

Adrian glanced through the kitchen window of the

house first. Three straw dolls lay on the table, one larger than the other two. It seemed as if Heidi was beginning to give them features. Also on the table lay a few bottles. One of them Adrian recognised as the concentrated hemlock he'd handed over to Scarlett to give to the old woman. It didn't inspire in him much hope that what was in the other bottles was anything more pleasant than that.

He didn't like the look of what she was doing at all.

But it wasn't his problem anymore. A knock on the door, a threat and a bargain or two, and Adrian would be done. He'd be gone.

And he'd never see Scarlett again.

Adrian hated how torn he was on the matter. It wasn't like him at all. But when he thought about how Scarlett had defended him in front of Andreas - how she had spent all day with him under the judgemental scrutiny of the entire town of Rowan, and how her father must surely now know about what she was up to - all he wanted to do was find her and kiss her until she was aching for him.

He forced the painfully tantalising thought away. For his own good he buried it deep inside.

He knocked on the door.

"Who is it?" Heidi asked in a quavering, old lady voice that wasn't how she ever spoke to Adrian at all.

"Your grand-daughter," he joked humourlessly.

He knew she was frowning, trying to work out who it really was. "Is that you, Adrian Wolfe?" she eventually asked.

"A wolf indeed. May I come in?"

"Let yourself in," she said, irritated, reverting to her true, harsh voice in an instant.

When Adrian opened the door he saw that Heidi was

making tea over the fire. She glowered at Adrian. "What do you want? I'm busy."

"Clearly. I won't be long."

Adrian took in the contents on the table, eyeing them a little more suspiciously than before. But he didn't let on his misgivings.

He smiled easily. "Straw dolls. Working up a bit of long-distance magic, I see."

Heidi scowled. "My business is my own. What do you want?"

He resisted taking in a steady breath. "I slept with your grand-daughter. Many times. One might say I'm courting her. Doubtless word would have reached your ears eventually."

It felt as if the atmosphere in the room had frozen, though the fire Adrian kept well away from was roaring merrily.

"Leave her alone."

"Ah, see, that is why I am here. Lift my curse. Leave *me* alone, and I'll leave her alone."

"Give me one good reason why I shouldn't send your soul to hell and curse your useless corpse for a thousand years."

Adrian laughed at the threat, which he knew she could well make good on. "Come now, Heidi; no need to go to such extremes. And besides," Adrian put on his easiest smile, knowing he was lying, "if you do something to me Scarlett will know it was you."

Heidi looked torn between outrage and horror. "And what makes you say that? What have you told her?"

"Oh, nothing that would worry you...if you lift my curse. It will only matter if you don't."

Adrian was skilled with magic and curses and poisons too, of course, so Heidi daren't think his words an idle threat.

"She cares for you, doesn't she?" Heidi eventually said after a long silence. "Samuel was right; she's been different lately. It's because of you."

Adrian said nothing.

"Have you no heart?" the old lady continued, walking away from the fire to round on Adrian. "She is barely an adult. Just a child, really. Can you really be so cruel?"

"As I recall, I was *barely an adult* when you cursed me, witch. Now undo it, then you and Scarlett shall never see me again. If you don't then I'll keep courting her. I'll make her run off with me, until she's simply mad for me, and when she does I'll tell her all about you and she will believe every word I say. You will lose her. And then I'll break her heart, and you won't be able to comfort her."

Heidi seemed torn. To lift his curse would mean she lost to Adrian, but to do nothing would mean to lose Scarlett.

Adrian gave her the illusion of choice by granting her some time to think. He wandered over to the table, inspecting the straw dolls once more. It seemed as if the tallest was a woman, with a pretty, painted face; the other two, her children. The details – braces holding their trousers up, freckles, toothy grins – gave off the distinct impression that they were boys. They were identical. Twins.

Twins.

It took Adrian but a second to work out what was going on. The dolls were Scarlett's step-mother and her brothers.

What were their names? Rudy and…Elias. Rudy and

173

Elias. And their mother, Frances.

Adrian had never performed such magic before, but he knew how it went. Stab the dolls with pins, or break their legs, or set them on fire, and the same fate will be dealt to the individual whose likeness the maker has used. Soak the dolls in poison, and...

"You know what?" Adrian said, struggling to keep his voice calm. "You have until tomorrow to decide. I can see this is a tough decision you must make."

We'll run away, he thought, forming the best plan he could possibly think of on the spot. *Me and Scarlett. She'll come with me. She'll leave and she'll never know what her grandmother does to her family. It doesn't matter than I'm a wolf sometimes. I can live with that. I've lived with it for six years.*

Heidi seemed distracted. She scowled. "What, so you can crawl into my grand-daughter's bed? I think not."

"It's to pack my stall, actually. One way or another it won't be returning to Rowan. There are some things packed inside I'd rather the townspeople didn't get their hands on."

For a moment it looked like Heidi would refuse. But then she waved him off. "Fine. *Fine.* But you don't have until tomorrow. Come back just before sunset. We will make our deal then...one way or the other."

Adrian nodded, heart hammering in his chest as he headed for the open door and saw –

"Adrian?" Scarlett said in confusion. "Nana, what's going on?"

"*Run,*" was all Adrian said, making to grab Scarlett as he tried to flee. But Scarlett stood glued to the spot.

"What is going on?"

174

"Oh, Red, you must send this man away!" Heidi wailed, back to sounding old and defenceless and terrified. Adrian noticed that she'd swept the dolls and poisons away. "He has been threatening me, telling me the most awful things!"

Scarlett darted her eyes from Adrian to her grandmother, suspicious. She pulled her arm out of Adrian's grasp.

Oh, no.

"Scarlett, don't listen to her –"

"He told me he's planning on breaking your heart to get back at me! Oh, Red, he's awful!"

"I – what?"

"He tried to con me six years ago, and I caught him out on his lie, and he's been holding a grudge ever since! He was playing with you this whole time, intent on ruining you just to get back at me. A petty, selfish man if ever I saw one. I should have known."

Scarlett froze. Her face grew pale. She looked at Adrian.

"Tell me this isn't true."

"Scarlett, please, just get out of here and I'll explain. Your grandmother –"

"Is it true?!"

"Yes!" he cried out despite himself. He could feel bile and panic rising equally in his throat. Everything was going wrong. "Yes, but not really. Just let me –"

"Get out."

"Scarlett –"

"*Get out!*"

"But she's trying to –"

175

"I don't want to hear another word coming out of your mouth!" Scarlett howled, her face twisted in betrayal. "I don't want you near me. I was right to doubt you. I should have trusted my instincts. Look where ignoring them got me!"

He reached out for her; Scarlett backed away. Out of the corner of his eye Adrian saw Heidi grinning maliciously at him.

Adrian had lost. He had lost so much more than he thought he was capable of losing.

Scarlett's eyes were bright and shining with angry, vicious tears. "Get out," she uttered once more, her voice quiet and barely controlled. "Get out of this house. Get out of Rowan. Don't let me see you again."

He left.

On his way out he saw Sam, who had clearly been listening to everything from the garden. It looked like the man wanted to punch him.

"Look after her," Adrian muttered quickly, too quietly for Scarlett or her grandmother to hear. "Sam, *watch* out for her. In there."

His ambiguous warning left Sam too stunned to hit him, as he'd wanted.

Adrian ran off before he did something stupid, like heading back inside the house and trying to drag Scarlett out against her will. With Sam and Heidi there he'd never manage it.

But as he ran, numb and horrified on human legs, a thought that had never once crossed his mind before started screaming at him.

I wish I was a wolf, it said. *A thoughtless, unfeeling wolf who could tear an old woman to shreds and flee off*

176

into the darkness.

But Adrian was not a wolf.

He was merely a man.

CHAPTER TWENTY-THREE

Scarlett

Scarlett cried for a long time that afternoon. She cried for a long time that night. She cried for a long time the next morning and well past lunchtime even then.

It was only when evening fell the following day that Scarlett's tears finally dried up, leaving her head pounding, her eyes swollen and her heart crushed to a fine powder.

She should never have let this happen. She should never have taken a walk into the woods with a man like Mister Wolfe.

But Scarlett had, and now she didn't know what to do.

She was beyond furious with herself. *How many times did I try to stop myself? How many times did I say it wasn't a good idea? That I'd get hurt? And yet I didn't listen,* she thought, over and over again. She had shied away from everybody else's advice, thinking herself clever enough to make her own decisions.

But no, she wasn't clever. The only clever one was scheming, lying, heartbreaking Adrian Wolfe.

Her grandmother had called it correctly – he was petty. He'd clearly been thinking about using Scarlett to get back at her grandmother for a while. He had told Scarlett he'd been watching her since the fateful night he saved her in the woods. That he'd wanted her. She'd taken it as flattery. As desire.

And he had taken her for a fool.

Miserably she felt her eyes sting with new tears, though her eyes were too painful to bear them. She flung herself against the pillow, rubbing her face against the fabric even as she willed herself to stop existing entirely.

Scarlett's stomach grumbled and bit at her insides, reminding her that she hadn't eaten since the morning before and was starving. She felt too sick to eat. Too furious.

Too heartbroken.

For the only reason it hurt so much to have Adrian betray her like this was because Scarlett truly had fallen for him. She had known it for a while, from the moment she gave in and let him kiss her in the woods. She had known it, she had tried to ignore it, and then she gave in. It was all her own fault she had fallen for Adrian's con.

She wondered how much of his family history was true, if any. Were his parents even dead? Was his village overwrought by disease that only he survived? Thinking on it now it seemed so unlikely. Adrian had even told her his father was a con-man and that he'd taken that up.

Scarlett should have heeded that as the warning that it was: *do not trust this man. Ignore him. Push him away.*

"Miss Scarlett?" Sam's voice asked uncertainly, muffled by the heavy wood of the door as he knocked upon it.

"Go away," she tried to call back, but her voice was hoarse and cracked from disuse. She was so thirsty. It reminded her, unbidden, of how thirsty she'd been only two mornings before, when she was still in the arms of Adrian Wolfe. Thirsty for water and thirsty for him.

And now he was gone, and Scarlett felt like she was drowning in her own naivety.

"Miss Scarlett, you need to eat. At least let me bring you some water."

Scarlett saw the sense in this. She did not want to die, though she felt like she had died from shame a hundred times over already. So she nodded at the door on reflex before saying, "Fine."

Sam was carrying a tray laden with toasted bread and a selection of meats and cheeses. There was a bowl of broth, too, as well as a wooden cup filled with water and a steaming mug of tea. He brought it over and placed it on her bedside table; Scarlett picked up the water immediately, drank it in one go, then gingerly picked up the bowl of broth and cradled its warmth in her hands.

"Thank you," she eventually said to Sam, remembering her manners. He stared at her awkwardly, his shoulders stooped slightly despite the fact the ceiling was high enough for him to stand up straight. Scarlett couldn't bear to have him see her like this – not after Sam had tried to warn her away from the man responsible for causing her anguish.

"Miss Scarlett –"

"Please, Sam, I don't want to hear it," she interrupted, knowing that if she was forced to talk about what happened she'd start crying again.

"I – I didn't want to tell you I told you so or anything," he said, head drooping sadly. "I just wanted to ask how you are."

"I think that's fairly obvious."

"This isn't your fault, Scarlett."

"It is, and you know it," she snapped. "Don't you dare take away my responsibility for my own actions. I did what I did. I'll face up to it myself."

Sam seemed torn. He desperately wanted to comfort Scarlett but it was clear that she wasn't going to listen to anything he said.

He sighed heavily and headed for the door. "Okay, Miss Scarlett. Sorry to bother you."

"Oh Sam, no –" Scarlett called out, feeling immediately terrible about treating him so appallingly. "I'm the one who's sorry. I just need to wallow in it for a bit. Thank you for the food."

She managed just the barest of smiles in his direction. It didn't meet her red, teary eyes, but it was enough. Sam returned the smile, nodded his head, then left Scarlett's bedroom, closing the door behind him.

Scarlett collapsed against her pillow. She had no appetite for the soup in her hands but knew she had to drink it. And so slowly, agonisingly, she gulped the lot down, cleaning the sides of the bowl with a hunk of bread which she forced down her throat. She ignored the meat and cheese. By the time she was finished eating the tea had gone tepid, so she left it untouched, too.

Then she heard a noise outside, and Scarlett's head

snapped immediately to the window.

A pair of wolf eyes stared back, amber and gold and so infuriatingly like Adrian's that she couldn't bear it. The wolf whined when Scarlett's face twisted in fury.

"Go away!" she yelled, picking up the mug of tea and launching it at the window. It exploded against the glass, startling the wolf away with a swish of its tail and barely a look back over its shoulder at Scarlett.

But it didn't make her feel better.

No. All it left Scarlett was alone, with cold tea seeping into the floor like a poisonous curse.

She didn't care.

CHAPTER TWENTY-FOUR

Adrian

Close to two weeks had passed since Scarlett threw her tea at her window and chased away Adrian as a wolf. He had hoped she wouldn't. He had hoped that, even in the form he hated more than anything, he could stay close to her.

But she had yelled him away.

Adrian had packed up his stall and hidden all of his belongings deep in the woods, where Scarlett nor any other passerby would ever dare to tread. He had paid his bill for the room he'd barely used in Mac's tavern.

And then he'd left Rowan and its damnable forest until he could be sure he was out of reach of Heidi's curse.

The relief of seeing the moon with his own eyes was overwhelming, even though he had so desperately, viciously wished to be a wolf the day Heidi had outmanoeuvred him. He spent a few days in the nearest village, sleeping away most of his time in order to catch up on the hours he had lost. The rest of the time he merely lay there and mulled over what to do.

His original instinct to grab Scarlett and flee had been wrong. She would have found out what happened to her family and she would be distraught. She would hate him. She'd never want to see him again.

But most of all, Scarlett would lose her brothers and her step-mother, and Adrian wouldn't be able to live with that.

So it was without any sort of plan whatsoever that he warily crept back into the woods of Rowan. That night, however, he did not transform.

Good, he thought with some satisfaction. *Heidi has at least reverted my curse to what it was. Or is not aware that I am back.*

But the full moon was approaching; by his measure Adrian had just four days before he would have to transform for three nights, following the rules of his original curse. That didn't leave him much time at all, given that Scarlett would not listen to him if he were to approach her in public, and whilst she was in her grandmother's house or with Sam he couldn't speak to her, either.

Which left grabbing hold of her when she walked through the woods, alone.

Just like how we first met, he thought wryly.

And then...then he'd have to hope Scarlett believed him. He had no idea what to do.

It was with some surprise that Adrian found himself hiding in the tree-line by Heidi Duke's house. He knew he couldn't stop her right now, unprepared as he was. The best Adrian would be able to do is to try and prepare a curse or spell from what he had in his hidden, packed away stall, but until he was sure he had stopped what the woman was planning to do to Scarlett's family then Adrian's hand was stayed.

Adrian noticed, then, that he wasn't entirely alone. For Sam was in the garden, though he wasn't paying attention to what he was doing – he had been digging the same patch of earth over and over for at least five minutes. No, he was carefully watching Heidi Duke through the window, which was ajar.

Good on you, Sam! Adrian felt like whooping. Clearly the boy was smarter than Adrian had ever given him credit for.

It seemed as if Heidi was humming or singing or talking to herself, for Sam's face was scrunched up in concentration as he listened to what she said. Adrian couldn't hear, but by the growing horror creeping into Sam's face he realised it wasn't anything good. But it was what Adrian needed him to hear.

Sam's complexion had gone pale and sickly, as if he might throw up, when he spied Adrian in his hiding spot. He froze immediately; what would Sam do now? The young man mouthed silent, slow words at him, over and over again until Adrian worked out what he was trying to say.

What do we do?

Adrian ushered him over with a wave of his hand. But Sam was in such a rush to comply – so relieved to be told what to do – that he knocked over a bucket and tripped on the long handle of a shovel as he tried to exit the garden. He made it halfway to Adrian when Heidi appeared at the front door.

Adrian only just managed to conceal himself behind the trees, though he felt like a wretched coward leaving Sam alone.

"Samuel, I didn't realise you were here," Heidi said, her voice sickly sweet and sing-song.

Adrian didn't have to see Sam to know what kind of face he was making. "I was j-just finishing up, m-ma'am," he stuttered. "I'm going to head back to my father's mill, now. He needs me this afternoon."

But Sam knew he wasn't going to be leaving, just as surely as Adrian and Heidi knew. Adrian's stomach twisted in trepidation as Heidi laughed.

"Oh, I don't think so, dear," she said. "Going by your face you heard me singing to the dolls. Magic is such vocal work, you see. I can never do it when Red is around. Or you. I thought I had been so careful." She sighed heavily. "I was fond of you, Sam. But I won't let you tell Scarlett, and I know you will."

Sam bolted. In the opposite direction of Adrian he bolted, straight through the trees.

But Heidi was already weaving her words into a spell, and with a silvery pulse of light the hurried, frightened sound of Sam's footsteps disappeared without a trace.

Humming to herself in satisfaction, Heidi returned to her house without checking to see what had become of Sam. But Adrian wanted to know. He hadn't recognised her spell, after all. And if Sam were dead then Heidi would have taken care of the body, to ensure Scarlett didn't find him.

Which meant he was alive...in one form or another.

Adrian stalked through the trees until he reached where he'd seen the light originate from. He didn't need to search to find where Sam had gone or what had become of him.

For Sam stood in front of him, broad and tall and strong as he always had been.

Except, now, it wasn't just Adrian Wolfe who lived up to his namesake.

Heidi had turned Sam into a birch tree.

Adrian wanted to laugh in sickening, frightening glee, as if he had lost his wits entirely, but he held it back with a hand across his mouth as if keeping in bile.

We're doomed, he thought as he collapsed against the silver tree that was Sam, and cried. Adrian hadn't wept in years.

"I always thought I'd cry over a woman," he whispered to the tree, not knowing nor caring if it could hear him. "Not over a miller's boy. Though I guess I'm doing both."

He didn't know what to do. Adrian had no plan, no allies, and, increasingly, no time. He needed something – some irrefutable proof – to show Scarlett, to make her believe in everything Adrian told her. He glared up at the sun glaring back at him in the sky. Even though it was May it still held little heat, as if it were reflecting the current state of Adrian's heart.

But then it struck him, looking up there in the sky. Something so ridiculous that even Scarlett would be forced to listen to him after witnessing it.

It would be full in four days.

The moon.

CHAPTER TWENTY-FIVE

Scarlett

Scarlett felt akin to a zombie two weeks after Adrian had betrayed her. She had no tears left to cry. She had no feelings left at all. She was hollow. She was nothing.

That was when her father sent for her to visit the Duke house, and Scarlett's heart dared to stir back to life. If she could be welcomed back into the family – despite her shame – then Scarlett would be sure never to feel sorrowful again. And she would listen to her father, and Frances, and Sam, and everyone else who only ever had her best interests at heart. Even Andreas, who may simply have wanted Scarlett to stay away from Adrian Wolfe for being, well, Adrian Wolfe.

She put on the red dress. The one she had fled to her grandmother's house in. The one she'd been wearing when she ran into Adrian's arms. It was symbolic; if Scarlett was allowed back into the family then she would burn it to ashes and be glad of it. And if not...

Let's not think of 'if not'.

She wrapped herself up in her grandmother's cloak and kept her long hair loose and wavy around her face, to help hide her slightly hollowed cheeks that were proof she still wasn't eating properly, even two weeks later. Sam hadn't even been around for the last few days, with a gentle smile and a plea for her to look after herself. For he had fallen ill, her grandmother told her, which made Scarlett feel even worse for the distant way she had been treating Sam lately.

When he returns, Scarlett decided, *I will think of him better. I will treat him better, like he has always treated me.*

Scarlett's grandmother had been preoccupied recently – almost as much as Scarlett herself had been preoccupied with infuriating thoughts of Adrian. Perhaps she was deliberately leaving Scarlett alone, since she was determined that Scarlett should be strong and get over the folly of falling for a con-man all on her own.

Scarlett knew her grandmother was right. And it was what she planned to do – what she was *trying* to do. She just never knew it would be so hard.

She hadn't wanted to fall in love with anyone.

She had, anyway.

It was with a stomach sick with nerves that Scarlett stepped out of the carriage her father had sent for her and allowed a servant to see her through the ornate front doors and into the main body of the house. These weren't the doors she had run out from, two years ago – she had used the side door by the study – but it felt symbolic nonetheless to finally be welcomed back through the threshold of a house she had been shunned from for so long.

Scarlett was desperate that this would not be the last time she was allowed in.

The air in the house was far more serious than she had expected. Even the staff seemed in a far more stately mood than usual. And she was shown up to her parents' bedroom, rather than the parlour or her father's study. A horrible sense of dread began to creep over Scarlett; part of her wished to flee and run back out of the house.

But she stayed, and she was let into the room.

And there, helplessly pale and feverish in the large bed, laid Frances, Rudy and Elias, who were curled against their mother's arms. Her father sat in a chair by the bed, watching on helplessly with overly bright eyes.

"Papa –" Scarlett barely let out before he began to cry at the sight of her, rushing over and embracing his only daughter with shaking arms that did not seem to want to let her go.

"My love," he wept against her hair. "You came, you came. Rudy, Elias – look who's here!"

He pulled away from Scarlett so that she could tiptoe over to the bed. All three of its inhabitants seemed delirious, but upon noticing her presence both boys seemed to light up.

"Sister," Rudy said, his voice rattling, his breathing laboured.

"...missed you," Elias moaned, clearly in pain.

Scarlett sobbed. She couldn't stop it; the cries choked

and clawed at her throat until she allowed them out. She reached out a hand to each of her brothers. When they tried and failed to grab hold of her fingers she only cried harder.

And then another voice spoke.

"Scarlett," Frances called out weakly, her voice barely above a whisper. Her eyes rolled beneath their lids for a moment before she finally managed to open them. It seemed to take her a while to focus on Scarlett, but when she did she dragged a hand over one of hers. Scarlett eagerly took hold of it, intertwining their fingers so that Frances' hand couldn't slip away.

Scarlett could only watch her and cry. She had no words. All three of them were beyond mere sickness.

They were dying.

They were dying, and everyone in the house knew it.

"Frances, what can I do?" Scarlett eventually managed to ask, clinging to the question as much as she was clinging to the woman's hand. *Give me something to do. Anything. Tell me how to make things better.*

The woman smiled sadly, though it took effort to do so. "I have regretted it," she said slowly. "All this time, though I wouldn't admit it, I have regretted it."

"Regretted what?"

"Sending you away. Having you discover the truth. Hearing you call me Frances instead of mother. I regret it all."

"Don't say that," Scarlett immediately protested. "You were right to do it. I was in the way, I was –"

"You were not. You never were. I just couldn't see it. But, now..."

Frances coughed violently against her shoulder. When

191

she finally stopped the fabric of her smock was spotted with blood.

"Look after your father when we're gone, Scarlett. You were always a good girl. I should have loved you better."

"You loved me just the way I needed, Mama," Scarlett whispered, wide-eyed and genuine even though the words were technically a lie. Hadn't she always longed for an ounce of warmth from her mother – for her to act with Scarlett the way she acted with Rudy and Elias? It seemed like such a hollow, worthless longing, now.

For her mother was dying and her tiny, helpless brothers were, too.

Eventually Scarlett tore herself away from the bed and pulled her father out of the room with her, down the stairs to his study.

Scarlett stared at him, whose face was even gaunter than her own. "Why didn't you tell me sooner?"

"We thought they'd get better," he said, his expression pained and regretful. "It didn't seem like much at first. A typical fever. But it only got worse, and nothing Otto or anyone else could do would stop it. Otto thought it was poison, but he cannot find any in their system. He doesn't know why I'm unaffected."

"Poison?" Scarlett couldn't dare believe someone would poison her family. The Dukes were well respected and liked within Rowan – they had no enemies, and certainly none who would target a man's wife and children over the head of the family, instead.

"If it's poison, it's one that Otto and the healers do not know of."

"What about Nana? She has –"

"Your grandmother would be no more help than the

healers that we already brought to see them, my love," he interrupted, though not unkindly.

Scarlett thought of Adrian Wolfe, a man who might well know what was poisoning her family.

No, she decided bitterly, *the man I* thought *was Adrian might know. The real Adrian is a liar and a con-man. I wouldn't be able to trust a word he said.*

And even if she wanted to ask for his help, Adrian was long gone.

Scarlett bit back another sob. "Let me at least go back and get Nana. She might know something. She might –"

"Scarlett, please!" Her father stared at her pleadingly as his hands clenched into the side of his desk. "Don't make this harder on everyone than it already is. Otto doesn't think they have much longer than a day or two left. Let's not squander them looking for a cure that does not exist."

But Scarlett couldn't accept this. She wasn't ready to resign to the knowledge that her mother and brothers were doomed to die. Perhaps it was because she had only just become aware of their circumstances now, whereas her father had been dealing with it for days and days.

No matter the reason for it, Scarlett wasn't going to sit and watch her family fade away. Giving her father one, final hug, she ran off from the study and through the side door.

"Scarlett, come back!" her father shouted out after her. But Scarlett couldn't turn back, for if she did she'd never leave. It was a feeling she understood well.

She had to keep going. She had to work out how to fix it.

And she'd start by asking her grandmother.

CHAPTER TWENTY-SIX

Adrian

Adrian hadn't had an opportunity to find Scarlett on the day before the full moon – his first day transforming. He had just two chances left.

He felt inordinately foolish, hiding behind the trees closest to Heidi Duke's home in the hopes of spying Scarlett return when he still had full use of his human body. Today, however, it seemed as if his luck may finally have turned. Her nefarious witch of a grandmother seemed to have retired to bed early; if Scarlett would only return in the next hour or so then Adrian would have the best opportunity he'd had all week to explain himself...and to warn Scarlett of the poisons that were going to kill her family.

Adrian stayed stock still when his over-sensitive ears picked up the sounds of somebody travelling along the road through the woods. Though he was desperate to run out immediately, the years he'd spent stalking prey as a wolf taught him to stay exactly where he was until Scarlett appeared. He couldn't risk waking up her grandmother, after all.

It was only when he spied Scarlett's blood-red cloak – the weather had taken yet another cold turn – that Adrian dared to move a muscle. He stalked out to the edge of the trees where they met the road, not daring to make himself visible from the windows of Heidi's little house by stepping clear of the camouflage the branches afforded him.

If he was caught he was dead.

"Scarlett," was all Adrian said, so quiet that nobody but the woman mere feet away from him on the road could hear.

Scarlett whipped her head around to find the source of the voice, eyes narrowing in fury as they spotted Adrian. They were rimmed in red; clearly she had been crying.

"Go away, Mr Wolfe," she replied, though she had the sense to keep her voice quiet.

"Scarlett, please. You must listen to me."

"Oh, I *must*? I don't get a choice in the matter? So typical of you."

Adrian shook his head in frustration. After years of not truly caring about anyone but himself he was finding it next to impossible to frame his words in a context that did not include him.

He sighed. "Your brothers. Your step-mother. How are they?"

Scarlett seemed taken aback by the question. She sniffed slightly and rubbed at her eyes, further confirming that she'd just been crying. "Why do you care about them?"

"Does it seem like they've been poisoned but the doctor can't find anything wrong with them?"

"I – what? What do you mean by that, Mr Wolfe?"

"Scarlett, please. Get off the road." He gestured through the trees behind them, eyes darting over to her grandmother's house and back again. "We need to speak in private."

But Scarlett didn't like this idea. She took a step away from Adrian, towards the house. "Every word you've ever spoken to me has been a lie. Why should I trust you now?"

He felt like screaming, though Adrian knew he deserved Scarlett's mistrust. But he was running out of time; glancing up he saw that the sun had already fallen well below the tops of the trees. "Two minutes," he said. "Give me two minutes. Surely what I said about your family's sickness warrants two minutes?"

Scarlett seemed torn. She looked at her grandmother's house with a complicated expression, then at Adrian, then back again. But finally she relented and slowly followed Adrian through the trees. He took her to the small clearing where the silver birch tree that was Sam stood, simultaneously innocuous and sinister to his eye.

When he stopped walking Scarlett rounded on him, cloak whipping around her ankles as she did so. "Okay, Mr Wolfe. Explain yourself."

He had no time to waste.

He had to dive right in.

196

"Your grandmother is responsible for what's happening to your family. She's poisoning your step-mother and your brothers. I imagine you'd have a better idea as to why she's doing this than I would."

Scarlett's face was blank as she replied, "I don't believe you."

"I saw the dolls!" Adrian exclaimed, wringing his hands as he struggled to keep his voice down. He took half a step towards Scarlett, then, upon seeing her reaction, took a step back. "The straw dolls. Three of them. And I saw the poisons she was soaking them in. She's killing them slowly, so nobody thinks to consider it murder."

"What are you talking about? Dolls? Potions? What do you think my grandmother is - a witch?" Scarlett almost laughed the last question out. But upon seeing Adrian's dark, serious expression she reconsidered. "This has got to be a lie. I know my grandmother has some dangerous extracts and plants in her collection, but doesn't every healer? There's no reason to suspect her -"

"Scarlett, would I be saying *any* of this if I didn't have absolute proof of her wrong-doing? What reason would I otherwise have to pit you against your grandmother?"

"Oh, how about that ridiculous grudge you've had against her ever since she caught you trying to con her?" Scarlett bit out. She crossed her arms against her chest and turned away from Adrian. "The one that caused you to use me to get back at her. I'd say that would be reason enough to try and turn me against her. Just one last laugh for the clever Adrian Wolfe."

"Have you not even once considered why I hold that grudge, you impossibly ignorant little girl?!"

Adrian hadn't meant the words that came out of his

mouth. He really hadn't. But at that exact moment the sun finally set and an unbearable pain began to crackle down his spine, ringing through every nerve and begging for him to scream.

Scarlett turned around to face him immediately, her expression full of fury and contempt. "How *dare* you. How dare you say that to me, you –"

But her words caught in her throat as she watched Adrian struggle to stand. He staggered on the spot, eyes roving wildly for something to grab onto. Then he looked down at his clothes, remembering that he needed to remove them before he transformed lest he destroy them altogether.

He collapsed to the forest floor amongst a pile of dead leaves, fingers fumbling with the clasp of his cloak before struggling with the buttons of his waistcoat.

"Mr Wolfe, what are you doing? What's happening –"

"My boots!" he cried through gritted teeth. "My boots. Take them off. *Take them off!*"

The tone of his voice brooked no argument, and though Scarlett was still furious and disgusted by his insult she dropped to her knees and swiftly unlaced the man's boots, pulling them off as Adrian shirked out of his shirt.

"You want to know how I know Heidi Duke is a witch?" he muttered, sweat on the back of his neck turning icy cold in the air as his teeth clattered against one another. He forced his eyes on Scarlett, who looked terrified. "You want to know why I hold *a grudge?* All I wanted was for her to reverse what she'd done to me! Watch what your grandmother does to people who don't want to sell her soul-destroying curses and see whose side you're on, Miss Scarlett."

Adrian just barely pulled out of his leggings before his

198

bones began to break. He covered his mouth with both hands to hold in a scream. Every second of pain was made all the more agonising knowing that the woman he'd impossibly come to love was watching him, naked and vulnerable and monstrous.

Scarlett didn't move; she was transfixed. Her mouth gaped open as if she meant to speak but no words came out. And yet Adrian could see her cheeks glistening with new tears as her eyes grew wider and wider.

He had never wanted Scarlett Duke to see him like this.

After what felt like an eternity the pain stopped. Adrian shuddered as he slowly picked himself up onto his new legs, the dead, dark leaves falling from his fur as he did so. He didn't dare move closer to Scarlett. All he did was stare.

"Knock, knock, Mr Wolf..." Scarlett breathed. The words were oddly appropriate, being the first ones she'd spoken to Adrian in this form. Gingerly she crept forward on her knees, reaching out a hand until her fingers brushed against Adrian's wet, black nose. "You were... you've been watching the whole time."

Scarlett said nothing for a while. Her chest heaved in panic, though, as if she were struggling not to pass out. Adrian pushed his muzzle against her hand, reminding her that she wasn't alone. And then she whipped her head around, looking for something.

Or someone.

"Adrian, where's Sam?" she asked, voice dripping with dread. "He's not – he isn't sick, is he? He saw what my grandmother was doing, didn't he?"

Adrian couldn't answer with words, of course. He whined softly, licked Scarlett's hand, then turned and walked over to the silver birch tree. He sat beneath it, waiting for Scarlett to understand what he meant.

She stumbled over to the tree numbly, staring at the ghostly white branches in disbelief as she traced her hands over the grain of the trunk. "No..." she whispered. "She didn't...Adrian, tell me she didn't do this!"

He merely whined again. Scarlett collapsed beside him, back against the birch tree as she tried desperately to stifle a sob.

"Nana is trying to kill them. She's going to murder Rudy and Elias and my mother for...me. She's doing this for *me.*"

Scarlett looked down at herself, disgusted. She clawed at the fastening of her cloak and ripped it open, tossing the bleeding fabric onto the floor. She was breathing too heavily; her expression wild. If Adrian had been a man instead of a wolf he'd have wrapped his arms around her.

Instead, he crawled into Scarlett's lap and nuzzled his head against her shoulder, licking the edge of her jawline and whining until she finally looked at him again.

"I'm so sorry, Adrian," she said, very, very quietly. Her fingers found their way into his fur, holding him tightly as she buried her head into his ruff. "I'm sorry. I'm sorry. Please help me. Please –"

Adrian tilted his head and gently nibbled her ear, which was fairly difficult given that he was a wolf. But it was enough to shock Scarlett out of her crying, who pulled away in surprise as she reached up and touched her ear.

"That was a lot more painful than you were intending, I think," she said, almost laughing despite herself. "Or I would hope. I guess with you it could go either way. Are you telling me I need to calm down?"

Adrian didn't say anything, because he was a wolf. At

200

this point even *he* was getting tired of thinking such sardonic things. *I guess I can see why one might find me insufferably full of myself,* he concluded, altogether rather bemused despite the dire situation both he and Scarlett were in.

Scarlett smiled sadly as she rubbed a hand against Adrian's muzzle. "It's fairly obvious what you're thinking, even as a wolf. 'I obviously can't speak like this, little miss,' or, 'What do you expect me to do in response to your question? I'm a wolf!', right?"

Adrian pulled his lips back in what he could only hope was the lupine equivalent of a smile. To his relief, Scarlett laughed. She ruffled his ears.

"I think I might like you better like this, Adrian," she joked, "though given the circumstances you're not much use in this form, are you?"

Adrian snarled slightly at the insult, since he couldn't respond with his usual sarcastic charm. Scarlett seemed to get the point, though, and swatted his nose in response.

"Mind your manners, Mr Wolfe."

Oh, wonderful, Adrian thought. *She's having far too much fun with this. I'll never live it down.*

For a while Scarlett said nothing more, content to embrace the wolf that was Adrian while she cast occasional, furtive glances at the birch tree that was Sam.

Eventually she asked, "Can we get him out of there?"

Adrian nodded his head as best he could. Relief washed over Scarlett's face.

"Alright. Alright. That's good. And...how long are you stuck like this?"

He pointed his nose up at the moon in the sky, fat and luminous and not at all threatening to the eye.

Scarlett laughed bitterly. "But of course. Controlled by the moon. What a cruel sense of humour Nana has, to turn you into a wolf and Sam into a birch tree." The words came out in the form of a choked sob, which Adrian could do nothing about. He simply rubbed his face against Scarlett as his tail swept to and fro across her legs.

After a while Scarlett calmed down. She no longer smelled of fear, allowing Adrian to once more pick up on the usual scents he associated with her: vanilla, saffron and sandalwood. But now she also smelled of wolf. He didn't know how to portray this to Scarlett – to warn her to wash his scent off her before her grandmother found out.

"Tomorrow, when you're human again, we'll stop her," Scarlett said as she gently pushed Adrian off her and got to her feet. He nuzzled against her leg, feeling to his very core that he did not want Scarlett going anywhere near her grandmother's house.

He knew she had to.

Letting out one final whine, Adrian looked up at Scarlett's sad yet determined face. He nudged her hand with his nose, allowing Scarlett to scratch it before turning to flee through the woods. He knew he'd have to return for his clothes before the sun rose but, for now, all he wanted to do was run, and run, and run.

For all he knew tomorrow would be the last day of his life, or he and Scarlett would stop her grandmother and his curse would be lifted. For better or worse this was likely Adrian's final evening as a wolf.

He was going to make it count.

CHAPTER TWENTY-SEVEN

Scarlett

She didn't know how she found the nerve to walk through the front door of her grandmother's house. The kitchen – once so comforting and full of joy – filled Scarlett with disgust. She looked at the table, with its stains and its marks and its indentations.

That's where she sat and orchestrated the death of my family. Which is supposed to be her *family.*

Scarlett didn't know why her grandmother had done it. She wanted to know. She wanted to know the precise reason that a mother would want her daughter-in-law and precious grandchildren murdered. But the fact Scarlett was unharmed filled her with a sick, horrible certainty that it had to do with herself.

That only made her feel worse.

Her grandmother had already retired for the evening, despite the fact it was reasonably early. Scarlett was both greatly relieved and incensed by this – relieved because it meant Scarlett didn't have to confront the old woman immediately; incensed because she didn't understand how anybody could sleep knowing that they were slowly, tortuously killing people. *Children.*

Scarlett had to force back a sob as she made her way through to her bedroom as quietly as possible. She was starving but her stomach was writhing like a thousand snakes. She'd never be able to keep any food down. In the morning she would eat. In the morning she'd get her strength back and confront her grandmother.

She was grateful she did not have to do it alone.

Adrian, Scarlett thought ruefully as she undressed. Part of her was still furious and confused with him, of course. He had admitted to using Scarlett as a means to get back at her grandmother. But – now that she knew *what* her grandmother had done to him – Scarlett quickly found her anger dissipating. Adrian had simply wanted his life back.

And he mentioned not wanting to give Nana a 'soul-destroying curse'. Scarlett thought hard about everything else Adrian had said and done. How the first thing he had wanted Scarlett to do as soon as he saw her that day was to run. Clearly he had worked out her grandmother's horrific scheme then and there, which meant that...

"Saving me was more important than lifting his curse," Scarlett breathed out, her tiny, barely-uttered words swallowed by her pillow as she buried her face against it. And there had been no denying the way Adrian had looked at her – the fear, the desperation, the longing. Ultimately, in the end, Adrian had put Scarlett first.

Even if he took a typically twisted, Adrian Wolfe route to that decision. Scarlett wondered how he truly felt about her. What would the two of them be after they confronted her grandmother and, Lord help them, save her family? Could they repair what they had? Did Adrian even want that? Did Scarlett?

Tossing restlessly in bed she thought about Adrian, the wolf. He had been watching her for weeks. *Not just me,* Scarlett realised. *He was watching the house. He'd been keeping a close eye on what my grandmother was up to even as he crept up to my window and –*

Scarlett's face grew red and hot when she remembered discovering the wolf watching her dressed in nothing but her bed sheets. She had willingly let them fall. And if the wolf had been there from the moment Scarlett had taken off her robe...

"That pervert," she muttered despite herself, somewhat outraged. It was no wonder Adrian had been so convinced that Scarlett would fall for him, though, if he had interactions with Scarlett as a wolf to base her thoughts and behaviour on. She had been completely different with the wolf than she had been with people – open and bold and honest. Adrian would have gleaned far more from those interactions than he ever did watching her in the marketplace of Rowan.

Scarlett glanced at her window. She wished Adrian was behind it, pawing at the glass and demanding her attention. Staring at her with those amber eyes that she had always deemed inhuman. Unbidden she thought back to when Adrian had unceremoniously kicked her out of his room in Mac's tavern. He had explained it away as a fit; a seizure.

Now Scarlett knew better.

Her heart hurt merely thinking about it. Adrian had been in so much pain, and all because of the whims of Heidi Duke.

Does he have to go through that every night? Scarlett wondered with concern. *He ran off when the sun set after Andreas interrupted us, too.* But Adrian had crept into her room and spent the night once, too. Sighing, Scarlett resolved to ask Adrian about the rules of his curse once he regained the ability to speak.

And then we'll deal with Nana. We'll deal with the woman who turns men into wolves and trees, and poisons little children because they have somehow slighted her.

Scarlett didn't know how she fell asleep. All she knew was that she did and, when the darkness of unconsciousness fell over her, she dreamt. For the first time since her sixteenth birthday Scarlett dreamt of wolves and amber eyes and a woman who left a baby and ran away.

If not for that woman Scarlett's brothers and mother would be safe. For the woman who gave birth to Scarlett was not her mother and never had been.

She was merely a nightmare, haunting Scarlett with a life she could never have and never, she now realised, wanted.

*

"Red, dear, are you *ever* getting out of bed? It's almost midday!"

Scarlett forced herself awake with heavy, laboured blinks. She sat up in bed, rubbing at her eyes and wondering for a moment why her whole body felt raw and on edge.

And then everything hit her at once.

She dressed and stumbled through to the kitchen, smoothing flyaway hairs back as she sat down at the table. Forcing a smile on her face she grinned apologetically at her grandmother.

"Sorry, Nana. Clearly I needed to sleep."

Her grandmother came over and inspected Scarlett's face, turning her chin one way and then the other as she frowned. "Maybe you need some more. Why are your eyes red, Scarlett?"

Scarlett began to cry in earnest. She didn't even have to force it – merely thinking about her family, dying together at the hands of her grandmother was enough to warrant fresh tears.

The old woman hugged her fiercely; Scarlett struggled not to flinch. "Red, my love, whatever is wrong?"

"I-it's my mother, and Rudy and Elias. They're sick. They're dying. Did Papa say nothing to you about this?"

"This is the first I've heard of it," she replied as she pulled away. There was something odd about her expression when she added on, "But don't call that woman your mother, dear. I know it's easy to get sentimental hearing such news but you should still remember who and what she is."

Scarlett bristled. She had wanted to wait for Adrian to appear – indeed, she had to wonder where he was – but if her grandmother was going to say such things then Scarlett wasn't going to take the comments lying down.

"She *is* my mother," Scarlett bit back. "The woman who abandoned me on a doorstep is less than nothing to me. Frances raised me whichever way she could. I love her just as much as I love my father and my brothers."

Her grandmother was surprised by the retort. It took a little too long for her to fix her expression. "And what of your grandmother, Red?" she asked quietly. "Do you love Frances as much as your grandmother, who has always cared for you more than her? Who has always loved you more, and wanted what was best for you?"

"Nana –"

"They will die, Red. It's tragic, yes, but necessary. They were in your way. *Our* way."

Scarlett didn't dare believe her ears. Though she believed Adrian, it was a different thing entirely to hear her grandmother admitting to her crimes in such a cool, collected voice.

She feigned ignorance. "What do you mean, Nana? How are they in my way?"

Her grandmother's eyes flashed dangerously. "You really think I was going to let that woman get her way after kicking you out? Had she allowed you to stay in the main house as your father's heir then I wouldn't have touched her – or her little brats. Even after I was unceremoniously expelled from the house for supporting Richard's decision to keep you, I still would have left her alone." She paused, moving over to the open front door and closing it before pulling a curtain over the window. "You know, I never wanted Richard to marry Frances. It was your grandfather that insisted upon it. Forcing your father into a loveless marriage, just like I was. Of course, your grandfather didn't last long after that."

The horror of her words – the revelation that Scarlett never met her grandfather because his wife saw fit to get rid of him; the confirmation that Frances and Rudy and Elias' dire situation was because of Scarlett, and that her grandmother didn't seem to care about the evil

208

consequences of her actions – caused Scarlett to stand up and back away towards the door.

But her grandmother merely smiled. "Where do you think you're going, Red? After your little rendezvous with Adrian Wolfe last night I don't think I can trust you to set foot outside these walls."

Scarlett gaped at her in disbelief. "How did you –"

"I really did treasure that cloak, Scarlett. Perhaps don't leave it out for the wolves next time."

Her grandmother pointed into a dark corner of the kitchen. For there lay the muddied, shredded ruins of the once beautiful red cloak Scarlett had, until yesterday, been fiercely enamoured with. Now it made her feel sick to look at it.

"You won't get away with this," Scarlett muttered, though there was neither strength nor conviction to her words.

Her grandmother merely laughed as she put on a dark cloak of her own. She picked up a basket which hung by the door, filled with three straw dolls dyed a sickly, discomfiting greenish purple colour.

She pointed at Scarlett. "This woman shall not set foot outside this house. Until I return or should die let this spell hold true." Then she placed her hands upon the door and spoke to the house itself. "And do not let her out."

Scarlett shook with rage when she realised her grandmother had cast magic upon her. "You – you would put me under your control like this?"

"Just until your *mother* and her twins have sadly passed away. Now, I have a son to console and bring back under my wing. Wait and see, Scarlett; this will be good for you. With this you will have your previous reputation,

209

fortune and opportunities back. We both will. Know that I love you, dearly."

With a swish of her cape her grandmother was gone, leaving Scarlett standing in the kitchen alone. She hadn't even been given a chance to confront her properly – about Adrian, about Sam, about anything.

Furiously she let out a scream. A long, outrageously loud and soul-rending scream. Scarlett had never made so much noise in all her life.

But it didn't matter.

Her grandmother was gone and she was locked away.

Scarlett had lost before she'd even had a chance to fight.

CHAPTER TWENTY-EIGHT

Adrian

When Adrian heard Scarlett's high pitched, blood-curdling scream he feared the worst.

Heidi cannot have harmed her, he thought with increasing panic. *She can't.*

It had taken Adrian much too long to fully recover from transforming back into a human. The process had been blindingly excruciating, and seemed to take even longer because of the urgency with which he needed his true form back. It was as if Heidi Duke's curse *knew* what was at stake and was working against Adrian, hindering him at every possible turn.

A few more transformations like that and I'll either die

or not come back from my wolf form, he thought with chilling certainty. *If I don't die confronting the witch, anyway.*

Adrian spared barely a moment upon hearing Scarlett screaming, flinging on a shirt, leggings and boots before stocking up every secret pocket of his cloak and darting through the woods in the direction of Heidi's house. He wondered if the old woman would still be there...and what had happened to her grand-daughter.

"Let Scarlett be okay," Adrian muttered through his teeth as he rushed past tree after tree after tree, not daring to think she would truly be harmed. When finally the house became visible Adrian quickly checked on Sam Birch the tree, relieved to see that Heidi had left him that way instead of eliminating him as a precaution.

Once Adrian could be sure Scarlett was okay he'd set about saving Sam. They needed all the help they could get.

When he reached the front door Adrian was unsurprised to find that it wouldn't open. Steeling his nerves he kicked it with everything he had, which only left his body jarred with the force of the action. The door didn't budge.

He wasted no time in trying the kitchen window, instead, but the glass seemed suspiciously unbreakable. Adrian rushed around to the back of the house to try Scarlett's window instead.

When he spied her wrenching out the drawers of her dressing table through the window he almost laughed with relief. Other than looking sleep-deprived and frenetic, Scarlett seemed fine.

Well, as fine as I could expect, given the situation, Adrian thought as he banged his fist against the glass to get

212

Scarlett's attention.

Her face lit up when she saw him; it filled Adrian with an unbearable amount of love for the young woman in front of him.

"What happened to the house?" he shouted through the window, and then, "Where is your grandmother?"

Scarlett's face reverted to looking panicked. She rushed over to join Adrian at the window, holding up a hand against the glass as he instinctively did the same. To be so close and yet not touching was torment.

"She's gone. She trapped me. She put a spell on me!"

Adrian frowned. "Did she cast one on the house, too?"

"Yes! Adrian, what do I – what do we do?"

He smiled softly despite himself. He glanced behind Scarlett, noticing Jakob's silver snowdrop lying on the floor where Scarlett had unceremoniously thrown it aside in her haste to find something of use in her dressing table.

Scarlett followed his gaze with suspicion. She retreated from the window and picked up the beautiful, innocuous flower, returning with it clasped between both of her hands.

"Why were you looking at this, Adrian?"

His smile turned into a fiercely protective grin. "Because I enchanted it. The spell your grandmother cast on you will not work."

"You – when did you do that?"

"The night I crept into your room and eavesdropped on your conversation with Sam."

Scarlett seemed taken aback. "But that was before... you still meant to leave me. To use me. And you didn't

213

know what my grandmother was up to."

Adrian laughed bitterly. "I didn't need to know what she was planning to know I wouldn't want you to ever fall prey to her magic, after what she did to me. And Scarlett, though it won't mean much, I truly am sorry for -"

"You don't have to be sorry," she interrupted, before shaking her head and adding, "No. Take that back. You do. Very sorry. So sorry you'll want to spend the rest of your life making it up to me."

He gave her a lop-sided grin at the foolish, wonderful remark. "Do you mean that?"

"If you can help me save my family then I'm open to discussing it."

Adrian couldn't help but laugh. He never thought he and Scarlett would be able to repair their barely-begun relationship. Now, knowing that they could, he was determined more than ever to best Heidi Duke as quickly and as efficiently as possible.

To that end he forced himself back to the very real problem at hand. He stared at Scarlett seriously. "What *exactly* did your grandmother say to enchant the house? Do you remember?"

Scarlett frowned as she remembered. "She said, 'And do not let her out'."

"That was all?"

"I guess she thought the spell she'd put on *me* was more than sufficient."

"Good thing I'm an under-handed con-man, then," Adrian replied with a snort.

"We need to talk about that con-man thing after all of this is over."

"I imagine we do. But for now...it's exactly what we

214

need."

Scarlett seemed taken aback. "What do you mean?"

"Head through to the kitchen and wait by the door."

"Adrian –"

"Just do it."

And so Scarlett dutifully did as she was told. Adrian jogged back around to the front door, too, and when he saw Scarlett through the window he knocked upon the door.

"Adrian, what are you doing?"

"I have come for dinner, or have you forgotten, Miss Scarlett? Won't you please let me in?"

"I – yes?"

"Don't say it as a question. Will you let me in?"

"Yes; please come in, Mr Wolfe."

"Okay, try opening the door."

To Scarlett – and, if he was being truthful, Adrian's – surprise, the door swung open. Adrian stepped over the threshold into the kitchen where a stunned Scarlett stood. He wasted no time in closing the gap between them and embracing her, his lips finding hers and bruising them with kisses as if his life depended on it.

He supposed it did.

Scarlett wound her fingers through his hair, desperately keeping Adrian as close as possible even though they both knew the moment couldn't last for ever.

Eventually it was Adrian who pulled away. "Where did your grandmother put the spell on the house? Do you know where the straw dolls are?" he asked, more breathless than he had been after running all the way through the woods to the house.

It took Scarlett a moment or two to respond. Her eyes darted to the door, so Adrian closed it. "She took the dolls with her. As for the door, she placed her hands on it and said the spell," she explained. She narrowed her eyes. "How did you know you could open the door by asking if you could come in?"

Adrian scratched his chin. Then he riffled through some of his potions as he replied, "Just so long as you're not trying to get out, there's no reason for the door not to open. Now, to get you out, on the other hand..."

He let out a noise of satisfaction when he came across the vial he was looking for – it was pitch black and seemed to reflect no light whatsoever. When Adrian opened the bottle to pour some of the stuff on his fingers it seeped out like an ugly, poisonous sludge.

"What *is* that?" Scarlett asked curiously when Adrian smeared it into the grain of the wood.

"It blocks blocking spells and curses," Adrian explained. "I actually drink a little of it every day. It's disgusting."

"Why don't you just use that stuff you used on my snowdrop? So nothing will affect you?"

He gave her a side-long glance. "I have a bad curse placed upon me already. It wouldn't work. It would be like an oxymoron; I'm already cursed so the spell believes itself to have failed. Magic is a tricky business. You should be able to leave now."

Scarlett gazed at Adrian with something he hadn't seen from her before – reverence. "You know so much," she murmured as Adrian opened the door and Scarlett, with some trepidation, walked outside.

Nothing stopped her.

216

She was free.

He smiled in satisfaction. "I *did* tell you I learned much from my parents. And after what happened with your grandmother I made it my business to know as much about magic as I possibly could."

"I figured you had probably lied about your past to get me to feel sorry for you," Scarlett admitted.

"A reasonable thought. But everything I told you about me was the truth."

"Apart from the fact you turn into a wolf."

He chuckled. "I guess you're right. I don't really know how I was supposed to slip that into casual conversation, though. Do you?"

"Not really, no." And then, when Adrian headed to the garden and picked up a large, wicked-looking axe, she asked, "What are you doing with that, Adrian?"

He grinned; eyes shining with some kind of mad amusement.

"I have some firewood to make."

CHAPTER TWENTY-NINE

Scarlett

"You don't mean – you can't chop Sam down, Adrian!" Scarlett cried out in horror.

Adrian merely laughed. "How else do you propose we get him out of the tree?"

"I thought he *was* the tree?"

He shrugged, hefting the axe over his shoulder as the two of them walked through the woods towards the telltale silvery branches of Sam-the-birch-tree. "It's a bit of both. Either way, this is how we free him."

"Don't you have a potion or spell or something that can get him out?"

A sly, wicked smirk twisted up the edge of his lips. "Maybe."

"So use it!"

"Why should I waste one of my expensive spells on Birch?"

"*Adrian!*"

He laughed when Scarlett whacked his arm. "I'm kidding, of course. I have no such spell or potion on me. I'm not too familiar with transfiguration magic, given how taboo it is. It's difficult – near impossible, even – to find any useful information on the subject. And trust me...I would know."

Scarlett was silent as she considered this. But she didn't like the idea of cutting down the birch tree; not one bit. "What if it doesn't work?" she asked nervously when Adrian took a few swings of the axe through the air, testing his aim.

"If it doesn't work then he'll be turned back into a human when the spell-caster dies. You can see our predicament; we could really use Sam's help *before* that happens."

"I – I hadn't thought about the fact that Nana – that she would have to..."

Adrian put down the axe in order stroke the side of Scarlett's face with a hand. He looked at her sadly. "There's no way this can end with her still alive. I'm so sorry, Scarlett."

She gazed at her feet. But then, when she finally looked back up at Adrian, her eyes were set and determined. She held a hand out.

"Give me the axe."

"Scarlett?"

219

"It's my fault Sam ever got so involved in this. I'll cut him down...and face whatever consequences that result from doing so."

Adrian stared at Scarlett with pride. She wondered why. With a grim smile he picked up the axe and handed it over to her; she staggered under the weight of it for a moment before grounding her feet and finding her balance.

"Where should I chop?" Scarlett asked, uncertain now that the axe was actually in her hands.

"As close to the bottom as possible, I'd wager."

"You'd *wager*?"

"Just swing the axe at the tree, Scarlett. I doubt you even need to chop the whole thing down."

Scarlett remained dubious but, with no other advice to follow, she took aim at the base of the birch tree, inhaled deeply, and swung.

The steel-headed axe bit deep into the tree. With a struggle Scarlett removed it, then hacked at the tree a second time. A third. A fourth.

"Have you ever considered a career as a woodcutter?" Adrian asked, somewhat impressed. For Scarlett's cuts were in almost exactly the same place; Adrian knew that, had he been the one swinging the axe, the cuts would have been haphazard.

She rolled her eyes. "Sam taught me how to do it properly."

"How fitting that you're chopping *him* down, then."

"When do you think it'll be enough?"

Adrian walked over and inspected the tree. It seemed fairly close to falling under its own weight.

"Give me the axe, Scarlett. I'll finish it off."

Since she was breathing heavily and her forehead was shining with sweat, Scarlett dutifully complied.

Adrian didn't even look to see where he was swinging before he threw all his weight behind one strike and hit the tree. It swayed dangerously for a few seconds and then, when Adrian gave it a kick, fell over.

There was an overwhelmingly bright pulse of silver light; Scarlett closed her eyes and held a hand up against it. When finally she could see again the tree was gone, replaced with a very startled-looking Sam spread haphazardly on the forest floor.

He leapt to his feet with a cry, eyes darting wildly from Adrian to Scarlett and back to Adrian again. "I was a tree. I was a *tree.* I –"

"You were a tree," Adrian echoed back somewhat unkindly. "We get it."

"How much do you remember, Sam?" Scarlett asked, running a comforting hand up and down Sam's arm as he struggled to wrap his head around what happened to him.

He shook his head. "I – everything? Sort of? I heard you talking to me a few times, Mr Wolfe. And I was aware of Scarlett's grandmother coming to pick up her cloak this morning – Scarlett, your grandmother!"

"She knows," Adrian said. "She knows everything. Speaking of which, perhaps this is a conversation best had on the road. Care to help us take the old witch down and save Scarlett's family, Sam?"

Sam glared at him as if the answer was obvious. "I've only ever wanted to help her. Unlike you."

"If you could both cooperate that would be *wonderful,*" Scarlett cut in, struggling to reign in her irritation at their petty rivalry even in the face of mortal danger.

Adrian smiled easily as they rushed off. "But of course. I'm game if Birch is. After all, I could have left him as a tree."

"Why do you like this man, Miss Scarlett?!" Sam couldn't help but exclaim as he picked up the axe that lay forgotten on the ground before they rushed through the woods. All around the wolves were howling, even though it was the afternoon, but they knew Adrian's scent. They would not bother him after so long, even as a human. But they unnerved Sam and, to a much higher degree, Scarlett.

Adrian sidled up against Scarlett and brushed his lips against her ear, saying, "Don't worry. They're just talking to each other. They won't touch us. You're safe. Don't listen to the wolves."

Sam got his answer in that moment, in the quiet way Adrian reassured Scarlett and she immediately trusted him. He saw the way her face flushed having Adrian so close, and the change in her expression when she locked eyes with him, and he realised why Scarlett had been hit so hard when Adrian seemingly betrayed her.

She loved him, and she knew it. Sam never had a chance.

The townspeople of Rowan looked at the three of them curiously as they bolted along the streets, Adrian barely dressed and looking like he had spent the night in the forest (which he had), Sam ruddy-faced and carrying an axe over his shoulder, and Scarlett, who looked half a vengeful, beautiful phantom in her red dress and dark, unruly hair.

When finally they reached the Duke estate the grounds were eerily quiet. Scarlett glanced uncertainly at

222

the men on either side of her.

"Do we...just go in through the front door?" Sam asked, a look of blank confusion on his face.

Adrian considered the ornate gates. "Let me walk through first. Just in case."

He stepped forward before Scarlett could stop him. When nothing happened, both Sam and Scarlett followed him with some relief. When they reached the front door, though, they were surprised when it swung open to reveal Scarlett's father.

"Papa!" she cried out when she saw him. "Papa, where's my grandmother? She –"

"Who are these fellows, my love?" he interrupted. There was something not quite right about his expression. It was glassy and unnerving and set Scarlett immediately on edge.

"That's not important, Papa," she pressed on. "We need to get into the house and –"

"Oh, that won't be necessary. I think you should stay out here for the time being. I wouldn't want you to have to see your brothers. They're so sick."

Scarlett stared at her father, dumbfounded. She turned to Adrian, whose expression was pained.

"He's been enchanted. He's –"

But Adrian's next words were caught in his throat when he spasmed and collapsed to the floor. He cried out in pain and, when his spine began to snap and bend, Scarlett realised with horror what was happening.

"But the sun hasn't set! Why is this –"

"It was a mistake for you to try to come here, Mister Wolfe."

223

Scarlett's eyes darted back to the doorway, where her grandmother now stood beside her father. She was smiling an ugly smile that twisted her old, weathered features into something monstrous.

She stared at them all in disbelief. "You really think I wouldn't have set up counter-measures against the one man who could stop me? Especially since, it seems, he was able to undo my spells on the two of you," she added on, inclining her head towards Sam and Scarlett.

"But never mind," she continued on airily, as if Adrian wasn't howling in pain on the gravelled path as Sam stared on in horror and Scarlett bent down to try and fruitlessly help. "Red, dear, why don't you and Samuel come on in where I can keep watch over you? And as for our dear friend Mister Wolfe..."

Adrian had finally finished transforming. He stood there, trembling on four legs whilst he whined and shook his great, furred head. Scarlett thought that he still looked very much like he was in agony.

It was nothing compared to the look in his eyes at what happened next.

Heidi Duke snapped her fingers, and the grounds went up in flames.

For half a second Scarlett saw Adrian's pupils contract in his beautiful, amber eyes, full of sheer terror and animalistic panic that he couldn't push away.

He fled.

CHAPTER THIRTY

Adrian

He hadn't wanted to run. He'd wanted to stay and rip out Heidi Duke's damnable throat, freeing him from his curse once and for all. He'd wanted to save Scarlett's family.

Now he could do none of those things.

I didn't even tell Scarlett what to do with the straw dolls, Adrian realised mournfully as he continued to flee full-pelt out of the Rowan estate. *Just take a hint from the fire, Scarlett. Burn them, burn them, burn them.*

Adrian didn't stop running until he reached a stream that ran along the back of Scarlett's family estate. He'd had the sense not to run in the direction of the rest of

Rowan, where in all likelihood Adrian would be shot on sight. He was a wolf, after all, and that's what people were trained to do if they saw a creature such as him prowling along the streets.

I hate myself, he thought as he finally stopped, panting and deliriously terrified even now, away from the flames. He lapped at the cold, clean water of the stream, revelling in how it slowly brought him back to his senses. *I hate being a wolf. I hate being a slave to my instincts.*

If he were human he would have laughed bitterly at the irony of that statement. For hadn't he *always* been a slave to his instincts, from the moment both of his parents were stripped away from him? Adrian had looked out for nobody but himself, only doing what served his best interests or amused him. He hadn't done anything that went against his instincts – that helped someone else.

Until I truly got to know Scarlett. Until I fell in love with her. With a panging sense of regret Adrian realised that he hadn't yet told Scarlett his true feelings. *And now I may never get another chance.*

He looked back at the Rowan property, the grounds still very much alight with brutal, dancing flames. Adrian couldn't go near them. He *couldn't.*

He had to.

If Heidi Duke and her ensorcelled son were keeping a close eye on Scarlett and Sam then that meant they couldn't look for the poisoned straw dolls Scarlett said her grandmother had taken with her.

Not to mentioned the torn remains of Adrian's cloak – and the spells and potions that were hidden in the pockets – likely still lay where he had transformed. Even if the cloak burned to nothing everything stored within it would be safe, since Adrian protected anything of value in his

226

possessions against fire and water. He could only hope that Heidi hadn't taken the cloak inside with her.

It means I have to go through the fire, Adrian thought despairingly. But Scarlett was relying on him doing so. Her happiness depended on it.

Which meant Adrian's did, too. It was an odd sensation; one which he had not felt stir his heart for a long, long time.

And so Adrian rolled himself in the stream, drenching his outer coat in freezing water until it began to soak through to his thick, fluffy inner coat. Whining despite his resolve, and with his tail firmly between his legs, Adrian darted back towards the hellscape of the flaming Duke grounds before his animal instincts could force him against it.

The flames were licking up the sides of trees and bushes of all shapes and sizes; the grass turned to straw and then ash as fire razed it back to the very soil it sprouted from. Only the gravelled paths throughout the grounds remained unburned, but the air was hot and poisonous with choking, suffocating smoke. Adrian resisted breathing in as much as possible as he flinched from the heat, scrabbling across the gravel back towards the front of the house.

He spied his cloak where he had abandoned it – the fire had not yet reached it. And so Adrian bolted over and grabbed it between his teeth, pulling it along the path until he reached what looked like a side door into the Duke residence. Without hands to unstopper bottles and a human voice to utter spells everything inside was useless to him...but it wouldn't be to Sam or Scarlett. All he had to do was find the *right* magic for them to use.

With a grin that was literally *wolfish* Adrian thought of

the axe Sam had prudently brought along. He located the potion he'd used to get through the spell Heidi had put on her front door and held it gently in his mouth. If he could pour the putrid, black liquid over the edge of the blade then Sam would be able to use the axe to cut the witch down.

It was the only potion with a chance in hell of working. It was their best shot.

Adrian had to get inside the house first.

Peeking in through the glass panel in the door he saw that nobody was in the corridor. Standing up on his hind legs Adrian pushed down on the handsomely carved door handle until it finally gave way, then nosed the door open inch by inch until he just barely managed to squeeze through.

To think I'd ever have to waste five minutes trying to open a door, he bemoaned. Adrian never thought he'd explicitly miss having opposable thumbs, but with every passing moment spent as a wolf when he *needed* to be a man he decided never to take for granted the body he had been born with ever again.

If I survive, that is.

The first room he passed on his left was what appeared to be a study. The door was ajar, and the room was empty, so Adrian crept in to investigate. And there, sitting innocuously in a wicker basket, were the three straw dolls he had seen Heidi make, seeped in poison. Even with his limited colour perception Adrian could tell that the dolls were close to saturation, which meant Scarlett's family had perhaps hours left to live, if not minutes.

They might even been dead already.

But Adrian could not think like that. Carefully juggling the vial of blocking potion and the handle of the wicker basket in his mouth, he retreated from the study with the full intention of going back outside and flinging the wretched dolls into the fiery wreckage of the Duke grounds.

"What is a wolf doing in my study?"

Adrian flinched at the voice; it was Richard Duke, eyes glassy and expression lifeless like a human-sized doll. Had his mouth not been full he would have snarled at the man and snapped his teeth until he got past, but the things held by Adrian's jaws were too precious to let go of.

He tried to barge his way through the door but the man, unnervingly quickly, grabbed a poker from the nearby, empty fireplace and speared it straight through Adrian's right flank.

Thoughts of keeping hold of the straw dolls and the black potion were all but lost as Adrian yowled in pain. He struggled back onto his feet, though his right leg wouldn't take his weight, as Richard pulled out the poker with the intention of striking again.

"*Adrian!*"

Scarlett bolted towards him and pushed him free of her father, who struck the wall instead. She was followed by her grandmother who looked furiously confused.

"Why won't any of my magic work on you, Red?" She glared at Adrian. "What have you done to her, wolf?"

Adrian could do nothing but growl half-heartedly. Scarlett stroked his bleeding, matted fur even as he whimpered, her eyes full of horror at the blood pouring out of his wound. But he nudged her hand with his nose, urging Scarlett to pay attention to the dolls. She could deal with him later.

It took her a second to understand what Adrian was meaning as he glanced from the dolls to the door, where the fire could be seen roaring away through the glass. But then she nodded, grabbed the dolls and made for the door, slamming it open just as her grandmother screamed out.

"Stop her, Richard!" Heidi called out, making her way down the corridor to pull out the poker from the wall as her son chased after his only daughter. She glared at Adrian. "It's time I finish you off, Adrian Wolfe."

But then there was a *whoosh* of air behind her and Heidi only just ducked out of the way of Sam, swinging his axe so powerfully it smashed the wooden panelling of the wall when the blade connected with it.

"I should have burned you to the ground when you were a tree," Heidi glowered, carefully avoiding the man as she took a few steps back towards Adrian. "But it's no matter; Frances and the boys are breathing their final breaths. Even if my dear Scarlett burns the dolls it will be too late."

The grin on Heidi's face was more inhuman than any Adrian – even as a wolf – had ever smiled. When Sam swung his axe at the old woman once more he was shocked and appalled when it deflected off her, as if Heidi was made of steel instead of flesh.

She laughed maliciously. "You can't kill me so easily, Samuel. Now you, on the other hand..." She flung the poker at Sam with surprising strength and accuracy, slicing straight through the side of the arm he held the axe with. Sam let out a roar of pain as he dropped the weapon, clutching at the wound and staring at Adrian as if he must surely know what to do next.

But Adrian didn't. They were both injured, and Heidi was protected. Outside he could hear Scarlett shouting and protesting against her father. Every second spent fighting instead of helping Frances, Rudy and Elias only sent them further to their graves.

But then Adrian spotted the cracked vial of black potion slowly dripping into the carpet, and he acted without thinking. He lunged for it, breaking the glass open with sharp teeth until the inside of his mouth was coated with the disgusting liquid. Resisting the urge to heave and spit it out he skittered across the floor and crunched his jaws around Heidi's leg and, when she screamed, let her go and licked the axe, covering it in the same black potion that was also seeping into the puncture wounds on the witch's leg.

He shared the briefest of glances with Sam, who wasted no time in picking up the axe and struggling with it left-handed.

Just one hit, straight and true, Adrian begged, cowering into the corner when Heidi locked eyes with him and began to utter the beginning of a curse that he did not like the sound of at all.

But Sam's swing missed, and Heidi limped forward as if she didn't consider him a threat at all. She continued weaving her spell, and Adrian's heart suddenly felt like it was being crushed. He couldn't breathe. He couldn't see.

This is how I die, he thought deliriously. *In vain. Only fitting for a vain man.*

"Good-bye, Mr Wolfe," Heidi said with cruel satisfaction. "May you never –"

But her next words were cut off.

As was her head.

With one fell swoop Sam's axe found its mark and, with it, destroyed the vice-like grip the witch had on Adrian's heart.

231

As well as the hold she had on his soul.

"You're not so useless after all, Birch," Adrian muttered as he transformed back into a human faster than he'd ever transformed before, though he could barely stay conscious let alone speak. Sam didn't look at him, instead staring blankly at the headless, bloody corpse of the woman who'd once been his employer.

Heidi Duke was gone.

Adrian had nearly died for it, but he was free and he was, miraculously, still alive.

He only hoped the same could be said for Scarlett's family.

CHAPTER THIRTY-ONE

Scarlett

The realisation that her grandmother must have died was immediate. Her father let go of her arms, which he'd twisted painfully behind her back in his accursed attempt to stop her from burning the straw dolls that were killing their family.

Scarlett had no time to spare to see if her father was alright, or if he knew what was going on. She immediately picked up the basket of dolls where they had fallen on the gravelled path and flung them into the fire surrounding them, watching them smoulder a sickening green until the flames, finally, engulfed them.

And it was just in time; the unnatural fire receded into nothing a mere minute later, the power that had lit it in the first place now completely spent. Scarlett stared out at the destruction it had caused with numb, shell-shocked eyes – everything was all black and ash and ugly curls of smoke still hanging in the air. She spared a thought for the town of Rowan, thankful that the flames had not left the confines of the Duke estate.

"Scarlett? Scarlett!" her father called out, reaching for her desperately as understanding and intelligence finally returned to his face. He was panicked; horrified. "What have I done? What has *she* done?"

"We have no time, Papa!" Scarlett exclaimed as she grabbed his hand and dragged him back inside.

She retched at the horror lain out before her eyes once she set foot through the door. For there stood Sam, clutching at a deep gash on his arm even as his fingers, slippery with blood, dropped his axe to the floor. Adrian lay against the wall with his eyes closed, once more human and completely naked but for the thick layer of blood covering much of his skin. His leg was still bleeding badly; his teeth covered in black, oozing liquid that he spat out onto the carpet without opening his eyes.

And then there was Scarlett's grandmother, headless. Lifeless. Dead.

"S-Sam," Scarlett stuttered. "Adrian –"

"My cloak," Adrian coughed and spluttered, just barely managing to gesture back behind Scarlett. "And my...clothes, if they're not burned to a crisp."

Blindly Scarlett complied, locating Adrian's cloak by the door. His clothes, however, were in ruins. When she returned she glanced at her father, who was struggling to comprehend the scene in front of him.

"Can you get him...something to wear?" she asked. "Anything."

Adrian waved her over as her father nodded, then rushed into the servant's quarters before returning with a plain, cotton shirt and a pair of leggings. Weakly Adrian took the cloak, and the clothes, and struggled into the shirt before searching through his cloak. When he located a jar the colour of pale jade he opened it with trembling hands, ran his finger inside the jar to collect a small amount of similarly coloured salve and spread it across the wound in his leg.

He sighed in plain relief before flinging the jar at Sam, who caught it clumsily in his left hand. "That'll stop the bleeding and encourage the healing process, witch-killer," he mumbled. Adrian pulled on the leggings Scarlett's father gave him with some effort, wincing and biting down on his lower lip in pain when the material grazed his wound.

Scarlett moved forward immediately to kneel by his side when Adrian tried to stand up. "Stay where you are, Adrian! You can't move, you've lost too much –"

"Your wife," Adrian cut in, staring at her father. "Your sons. Where are they?"

The man glanced upstairs. "In the master bedroom."

"Show me." And then, directed at Sam, "Go get cold, clean water and hot tea. Tell the kitchen staff to prepare clear broth and bread."

Sam didn't baulk at the commands. He merely nodded and rushed off to dutifully comply.

When Adrian tried and failed to stand on his own Scarlett took his arm and slung it over her shoulder. She took Adrian's cloak and crumpled it beneath her other arm. "Do you really think you can save them?" she whispered, not daring to hope.

"If they aren't dead already," he said, too exhausted to

235

blunt his words. But it was the closest suggestion to a cure that both Scarlett and her father had heard so far, so the two of them exchanged a barely hopeful glance as he took Adrian's other arm and helped his daughter haul the man up the stairs.

"You look awful, by the way," Scarlett said when they reached the upstairs corridor. "Your clothes are soaked with blood already. You look like you bathed in the stuff."

"I must really love you, then, Miss Scarlett, to have ended up this way."

Scarlett said nothing. To hear Adrian confess *now*, of all moments, was shocking and inappropriate and so glaringly Adrian Wolfe than she couldn't help but choke back a laugh.

"I love you too, you arrogant, narcissistic, no-good con-man."

Her father raised an eyebrow as they reached the door to the main bedroom. "That's the worst endorsement I could possibly hear as a father."

"I could have said a whole lot worse."

Adrian snorted. "Charming."

He was gently placed down on a chair by the bed; Frances, Rudy and Elias weren't moving. For a moment Scarlett felt like her lungs had been filled with water. She couldn't breathe. Her vision went blurry. And then –

"Still alive," Adrian murmured, having checked their pulses. "Still alive and better than I could have hoped. Scarlett, my cloak?"

She passed it over with numb fingers, then watched in astonishment as Adrian carefully riffled through the pockets and folds of the fabric until he located everything he needed. Scarlett would never have been able to identify

236

even a single thing in Adrian's possession, yet there he sat nimbly mixing one vial of blue liquid into another as clear as diamonds before pouring in what looked to her eyes like sand and shaking the bottle vigorously.

When he was done the resulting solution was a brilliant turquoise, and as viscous as the black potion Adrian had used earlier on that day.

"Scarlett, help me out here," Adrian said, too focused on his work to look up at her. When she sat by his side he smeared some of the salve he'd created on her fingers. "Up their noses and on the roof of their mouth. Can you do that?"

Scarlett nodded before rushing to comply, just as Sam entered the room.

Adrian waved him over. "Excellent timing. Mix this into the water," he ordered, handing him over a sachet of powder.

"What's in there?" Scarlett's father asked, too curious to keep quiet any longer. "What's in the salve?"

"This and that," Adrian replied, sounding as sketchy and irreverent as ever. "They never really had any poison in their system, but it'll take a few hours for their bodies to fully register that. Their bodies are very weak; they're lacking the nutrients to recover properly." He glanced at Scarlett's father, who didn't like the sound of anything Adrian said at all.

He smiled slightly. "The salve will speed up the process of getting rid of the phantom poison's effects. The powder in the water is to help recover their strength, as well as to keep any pain at bay. When they're awake you must keep them all well hydrated and fed every two hours or so."

"So they're....my family is going to be –"

"They'll be fine. In a few days. Keep them all in bed for a week just to be sure, though."

Scarlett had never seen her father look at anyone the way he looked at Adrian. It was more than sheer gratitude – the man had saved his entire family. He needn't have, and he nearly died doing it, but he did it anyway.

When she was finished applying the salve and saw her brothers immediately begin to stir and their breathing ease up Scarlett let out a cry. She darted out a hand to hold her mother's when the woman's eyes slowly, laboriously began to open.

"Scarlett?" she coughed. Sam rushed over with a cup of water, clumsily holding it to her mother's mouth as she dutifully drank. When Sam moved away she smiled at her husband, who sat on the bed and stroked back her hair. "Richard, why are you all covered in blood? And who are these two young men?"

Adrian laughed, seemingly amused by the prospect of being referred to as young.

Scarlett resisted the urge to hit him across the head. "Mama, this is Adrian Wolfe, and this is Sam Birch." She reached out a hand to bring him back over. "They saved your life. They saved all of us."

Her mother beamed, and it lit up her gaunt, exhausted face. "Then it seems I owe you both a great debt of gratitude. Though perhaps we might wait a few days before talking through what happened."

"Absolutely!" Scarlett's father exclaimed. He looked at his daughter, then Adrian. "Scarlett, my love, perhaps you should see to Mr Wolfe's injuries downstairs. And – Sam Birch, was it?"

Sam nodded.

"Might I trouble you to keep helping me, just until I

238

can have a servant bring Otto Sommer to the house?"

He nodded once more. "Anything I can do to help. It's all I've ever wanted."

Scarlett was overcome with affection for the man. She took his hands in hers, reached up and kissed him, very gently. "Thank you, Sam. I don't know what I could ever do to repay your kindness."

He blushed furiously, running a hand through his blonde hair gone ruddy with dried blood. "Don't let Mr Wolfe get away with any more of his tricks and I'll call it even."

"Hah!" Adrian bit out. "As if she could ever do that."

Scarlett ushered him out of the room before Sam, glaring, could fire back a retort.

"You could stand to act a little more mature, all things considered," she complained as she helped Adrian down to a room where the staff stored medical supplies. She ignored the lifeless body of her grandmother. She had to. "That was my entire family in a room, you know."

"As if you could really expect me to be anyone other than me," he said, easing himself into a chair as Scarlett found a rag and began cleaning his face.

She smiled despite herself. "I suppose not."

"You already told your father I was an arrogant, narcissistic con-man, anyway."

"You missed out no-good."

"An important omission, I realise."

"Do you really love me?"

Scarlett stared at Adrian, her blue eyes suddenly full of uncertainty and doubt. Adrian may have simply said he loved her because of the adrenaline running in his system, revelling in the sheer feeling of being alive.

But his amber eyes held none of the doubts Scarlett's did. They were clear and intent.

"Scarlett," he began, running a hand through her hair to urge her closer, until their noses were almost touching. "I have lied to you. Betrayed you. Teased you. Mocked you. But my love for you is the one thing that's remained true throughout everything, no matter how despicable my actions were. I love you. I love you. And if you really could find it in you to accept a wretched, barely human waste of a man as a companion –"

"Shut up, Adrian."

"You won't even let me finish my confession?"

Scarlett rolled her eyes. "You already said the important part. I won't let you wallow in self-serving deprecation. Because what kind of woman would I be if I let the man I love do that in front of my very eyes?"

Adrian's face lit up. He smiled a smile full of sharp teeth and genuine, overwhelming joy.

"Won't you kiss me, Miss Scarlett?"

Her lips brushed his – a promise of many more kisses to come.

"As if you had to ask, Mr Wolfe."

EPILOGUE

Adrian

When Scarlett demanded Adrian take her away from Rowan and teach her everything he knew – about magic, about healing, about the world – Adrian had been shocked but only too happy to oblige.

He got Scarlett Duke all to himself.

It was a dream come true.

Almost a year had passed since Adrian, Sam and Scarlett had taken down her grandmother and saved the rest of her family. Once Scarlett was sure her mother and brothers would recover, the two of them had set off to explore other lands together, Adrian working as a merchant whilst Scarlett studied and studied and then studied some more. They had not been back to Rowan.

Now they were.

He watched fondly as Scarlett's screaming, delighted, identical brothers ran into her arms, bowling her over until she fell to the dusty ground. Behind them stood Richard and Frances Duke, smiling and laughing as Scarlett struggled back to her feet.

Samuel Birch was there, too. When Richard Duke had asked the man what he wanted in return for saving the family he had asked, unexpectedly, to learn. As the miller's son he'd had little opportunity to educate himself past basic letters and numbers. He wanted more for himself than the life he'd been born to inherit.

Adrian couldn't help but respect the man, though when they caught each other's eyes they both glared.

"Uncle Adrian!" Rudy – he thought it was Rudy – called out. Adrian didn't know when the boys had begun referring to him as such, since he and Scarlett had been gone all year, but he had a sneaking suspicion it had something to do with the exotic gifts he sent back for the two of them on a regular basis.

He grinned at them. "You're both so tall now. It won't be long until you outgrow your sister."

They both beamed proudly at the idea; Scarlett chuckled as she mussed up their hair.

"You have to keep eating your vegetables if you want to be taller than me."

"How was the journey home?" Richard asked, kissing his daughter on the cheek before shaking Adrian's hand.

"Horrible," Scarlett complained, making a face. "The sea was awful. So stormy – I honestly thought we were going to die more than once."

"Don't be so dramatic, Red," Adrian said. "It wasn't that bad. You just don't like travelling by boat."

"Touché."

Adrian glanced at Frances, before searching through his belongings and taking out a wooden box. He handed it over to her; inside was an ornate glass bottle filled with a liquid the colour of Adrian's eyes.

"I have it on good authority that your grandfather used to gift you this. Scarlett told me her father could no longer procure it, so I...took the liberty of sourcing it. There are a few more bottles in my luggage."

Frances opened the bottle, closing her eyes and sighing in contentment when she breathed in the scent. It filled Adrian's nose, too, which would forever be over-sensitive. Vanilla. Saffron. Sandalwood. Scents he was hopelessly in love with.

Frances enveloped Adrian in an embrace so tight he almost winced.

"Thank you, Adrian," she exclaimed happily. When she pulled away she looked at her husband. "And you had your doubts he'd treat our daughter well. The man's a charmer through and through, Richard."

"Precisely the problem," both Richard and Sam grumbled.

Adrian could only laugh as Scarlett glowered.

"It's not for any of you to decide if Adrian is good for me or not," she complained.

"Oh, certainly not," her father chuckled. "I doubt anyone would dare cross you now, daughter."

She frowned. "What do you mean?"

"He means you look powerful," Adrian explained for him. "Intimidating. It's a good look on you."

243

"Sister isn't scary!" Elias – or perhaps Rudy – bit out. "She's exactly the same!"

"You'll understand why she's different when you're older, boys," Frances said mildly. Adrian had to wonder if she would ever tell her sons what had really happened to them. Part of him wanted them to know – to know what their sister had done for them.

But a bigger part of him wanted them to remain forever ignorant. Scarlett would never want them to know, after all.

"You seem to have learned much on your travels, going by your letters," Sam said to Scarlett.

She smiled broadly, glancing at Adrian. "There's so much to know, Sam. And Adrian is a wonderful teacher."

He brushed his hand against Scarlett's at the remark, informing her that he took her words to mean something far filthier than her original intention. The tips of Scarlett's ears grew red, and Adrian was very suddenly reminded of the fact they had not rested, in a real bed, for days.

And so Adrian turned to Scarlett's parents with an apologetic smile. "The two of us are admittedly very tired from our journey. I hope you won't take offence if we rest for a while."

Frances nodded in understanding. "You're welcome to stay in the house, of course, but I took the liberty of having your grandmother's house prepared for you, Scarlett."

There was barely an edge to her voice as she mentioned Heidi Duke. For the sake of her sons – and her husband, and Scarlett – Frances was careful about how she talked about the old woman.

Adrian glanced at Scarlett out of the corner of his eye, wondering what she would do.

She smiled sadly. "Thank you, Frances. We'll head to Nana's house, if that's okay."

"It's yours whenever you're ready to come home permanently, my love," Richard said. "Though if you'd rather a new house was built better befitting your name then of course –"

"No," she interrupted. "I'll take her house. I love it. I always have."

And so Adrian and Scarlett headed for the woods with a final wave at her family and Sam, who once more glared thunderously at Adrian.

"You think he'll ever like me?" he asked as they wandered beneath the boughs of the trees, content not to walk too quickly.

"Do you think *you'll* ever like him?"

"I never disliked him. I merely enjoyed irritating the life out of him."

"You're a terrible person."

"I'm aware."

In stark contrast to the year before, the late April weather was pleasantly warm. The air positively teemed with life; songbirds, frogs and foxes could be heard calling to each other.

But no wolves.

"When's the next full moon, Adrian?" Scarlett asked nonchalantly.

"Twelve days," he replied immediately before grimacing when she laughed.

"Do you think you'll ever get that habit out of your system? Of knowing exactly when it is?"

"*You* spend almost seven years as a wolf every full

245

moon then tell me if you're likely to forget when the next one is."

Scarlett squeezed his hand in response, dragging him along the path through the forest more and more insistently with every passing minute.

"What's the rush, little miss?"

She stared at him pointedly. "I can't be the only one longing for a bed."

"I'm longing for something *to do* in a bed...or, rather, someone."

Scarlett didn't even blush at the comment. Rather, she glanced behind Adrian before raising an eyebrow, lips full of mischief as they curled into a smile.

"Must it be a bed?" she asked coyly. Scarlett began to unlace the front of her dress tantalisingly slowly, safely tucking away the silver snowdrop she now habitually kept on her person when the sleeves of the white blouse she was wearing beneath her dress slipped from her shoulders.

Adrian could hardly contain his excitement at Scarlett's sudden boldness. Without another word he picked her up, Scarlett wrapping her legs around his waist as their mouths found each other and Adrian walked them off the road and in amongst the trees.

When he reached a clearing where the ground was covered in thick, spongy moss, Adrian fell upon it with Scarlett in tow. Her fervent hands wasted no time in unclasping his braces and unbuttoning his trousers, even as his hands slid up her thighs beneath her dress and urged her closer.

It didn't take long before Adrian was inside her, Scarlett sitting in his lap and gasping as the pair of them rocked together, breathless and desperate for each other.

"What would your parents think, seeing you so bold and debauched?" Adrian murmured against her ear. "And in a forest, no less. Unthinkable."

"It's a good thing they will never know, otherwise they'd kill the man responsible for making me this way."

He laughed as he planted kisses down her neck. "I don't think anyone was responsible for making you this way except you, Scarlett."

Scarlett's hands found Adrian's face and turned his lips back to her own, kissing him as if it were the first and final time they might ever do so. They didn't speak again for a long, long time.

Finally, when the sun was well below the line of the trees they pulled apart from each other. They lay on the forest floor, hands and knees and hems of clothes stained green whilst their chests heaved and their faces slowly lost their flush.

Scarlett turned her head and stared at Adrian until he stared right back. Her luminous eyes glittered in the low light of the forest. Scarlett had always loved Adrian's eyes; she would never know how deeply he loved hers.

"Promise me something, Mister Wolfe," she finally murmured.

He smirked at the name. "Anything, little miss."

"Never marry me."

"Only if you never marry me, either," Adrian laughed, pulling Scarlett against his chest and burying his face in her hair. It smelled of everything important to him.

It smelled of home.

And, most of all, it smelled of Scarlett Duke.

EXTRA CHAPTER

Scarlett

"I'm so thirsty I could drink an entire flagon of water!"

"How about wine, instead?"

Scarlett laughed good-naturedly. "I suppose we've been travelling for a while now. It wouldn't hurt to stop here for the night and enjoy ourselves."

All around them were the signs of a midsummer festival in full swing. Lanterns were strung from poles and ropes and shop fronts, casting the small town in a warm, amber glow. The dusk air was filled with spicy, sweet and savoury smells that caused Scarlett's mouth to water and her nose to twitch, desperate to follow them to their source. The cobbled streets were laden with merchants selling everything from food to fireworks to mysterious items whose purpose Scarlett could not identify.

One stall was selling nightingales enclosed in ornate, golden cages, which several children were admiring with wide and covetous eyes. The birds sang out from the prisons, adding their wonderful voices to the cacophony of sound bombarding Scarlett's ears. She felt an aching sadness for them, and longed to set them free.

"I should have brought all my stuff with me," Adrian mused as he wound his way through the throng. Scarlett could see him sizing up groups of women who looked likely to fall for his charms - those who would eagerly spend all their money on his largely useless spells.

"Good thing we're not here on business, then," she said, before sliding her hand behind Adrian's neck and pulling his mouth down to hers. *Those women can keep their eyes to themselves,* Scarlett thought, when Adrian wrapped his arms around her waist and held her close. He enthusiastically reciprocated her kiss; even after two years their desire for each other hadn't once wavered.

When they parted Adrian was smirking. He glanced at the closest group of young women, who were noticeably disappointed. "Jealous, Scarlett?"

"Oh, never, but I don't much relish the idea of spending all evening watching every young and pretty thing falling at your feet."

"I could say much the same thing about you!" Adrian complained, "Though you seem to attract just about *every* man, not just the young and pretty ones."

Scarlett rolled her eyes, looped an arm through his and pulled the two of them down the street towards a well lit stall. It was true that she'd caught the attention of several men, but one look at Adrian was all they needed to know that they didn't stand a chance. For who could truly match a man such as Adrian Wolfe?

His head would grow three times as large as it is now if he knew I thought of him like that, Scarlett mused as she handed over several coins to the vendor in exchange for two large cups of spicy, dark-coloured wine. She relished the warmth of the liquid as it passed her lips and glided down her throat.

"This is truly excellent," she said, happily taking a larger gulp of the stuff just as she saw Adrian do the same. The merchant was pleased with their comments; he indicated towards several ornate, sealed bottles.

"If you like it, perhaps you would consider buying a few bottles to take along with you on your travels?"

Adrian grinned at the man as he handed him more money. "Or I might just buy a bottle to drink from tonight, and regret the migraine it gives me in the morning."

"I'm sure your lovely companion wouldn't want to deal with that," he replied, though he handed Adrian a bottle of wine nonetheless.

Scarlett could only laugh. "Trust me, I'll most likely have a headache alongside him. Have a good evening, sir."

The two of them visited a food stall next and bought smoked, salted potato dumplings and beef stew, before finding a vacant wooden table in the midst of a market square. The wood was gnarled and uneven, looking as if somebody had simply felled a tree, lain it on its side and declared their job of making a table complete. It made Scarlett think of Sam.

"I wonder how your woodcutter is doing," Adrian murmured. He finished his cup of wine in the space of a few seconds, then uncorked the bottle he'd bought and began swigging straight from it.

Scarlett stared at him. "I was just thinking of Sam, too. It's been a year since we've seen him."

"I'm sure he's working hard at ingratiating himself to your family, hoping your father realises that Sam is, in fact, the far superior match for his precious daughter than the wolf who stole her away."

"You don't mean that," she replied, swatting his arm in the process. The wine was already getting to Scarlett's head; along with the delicious food they were eating she was feeling altogether warm, hazy and satisfied.

Adrian raised an eyebrow. "Don't I?"

"Whether you genuinely do or not doesn't matter, anyway. It's hardly as if I'd rush back home crying that I'd made a terrible mistake in falling for a wolf."

"A wolf, you say?"

Adrian stilled at the voice. He turned just as Scarlett did the same. A dark-skinned woman who looked to be a few years older than Adrian was standing there, dressed resplendently in yellows and oranges and reds, like a flame. She had a cart with her full of bottles, scrolls and other miscellaneous items, some of which looked familiar to Scarlett.

"Are you a real witch, or a false one?" Adrian asked as he eyed the cart. Scarlett could tell by the twitch in his brow that he'd spied several items that he wished to have himself.

The woman smiled. "By the way you're looking at my potions I believe you already know. Though I'd prefer to be known a a witchdoctor, if it's all the same to you. I didn't spend years studying the art of healing to be reduced to a *witch*." She regarded Adrian curiously. "So are you a wolf, sir, or aren't you?"

251

"I was, in a fashion, once upon a time. I'm not anymore."

The woman rummaged through her wares until she found a small, narrow vial filled with metallic-coloured liquid. "Once a wolf, always a wolf, I think. Would you like to see what I mean?"

Scarlett stared at her, trying hard to understand what the witchdoctor meant. "What does that potion do?" she asked, before talking a nervous gulp of wine.

"It reveals if a curse still lingers in one's blood," Adrian answered for her. He never took his eyes off the potion. The liquid danced in the light of the lanterns, sometimes gold, sometimes silver, but always beautiful. "Or a spell," he continued, "or any other kind of magic."

The witchdoctor was delighted by his answer. "You are a magician, sir."

"I am. What can I do to get my hands on some of that potion? I have been searching for a vial for a long time."

Scarlett straightened up in surprise. She hadn't known Adrian was looking for such a thing.

Does he want it for mere academic interest? she wondered. *I know he could identify its component ingredients if he had a sample to work with. Or does he want it for something else?*

The witchdoctor grinned at Adrian. She threw the vial at him and he caught it, quick as lightning. "You may have it, if you satisfy my curiosity by drinking some of it now."

"He can't do that!" Scarlett protested, getting to her feet, but Adrian pulled her back down.

"It's alright," he insisted. "The potion is only temporary. It merely serves to confirm whether there's anything hiding in one's blood, and nothing more."

"A phantom of a curse, as it were," the witchdoctor said, eyes gleaming. "If you truly were a wolf before, I would like to see if you're still capable of returning to the form tonight. Transformation magic is rare indeed; it would be a privilege to see it."

Scarlett did not like this one bit. The three of them had drawn a very curious audience, too; all around them were dozens of festival-goers, watching with fascinated eyes as Adrian unstoppered the vial and held it up to the light.

"Adrian," Scarlett began, "You are drunk. Surely this a terrible -"

"You underestimate how wonderful such a potion is, Red," he interrupted, a wolfish smile upon his face that Scarlett had not seen in months. "And you do not know how much I long to know if your grandmother's curse still lingers within me. And we have a crowd! We cannot disappoint such an eager audience, can we?"

The crowd cheered at Adrian's remark. Scarlett almost laughed at his showmanship - this was Adrian Wolfe, the merchant, at work. It was only then that she became aware that perhaps the witchdoctor had been hoping this would happen, for people were now rummaging through her cart with enthusiasm. If Adrian turned into a wolf using one of her potions then everyone would know her wares were genuine.

What a great marketing ruse, Scarlett thought, sighing as she drank more wine.

"Be careful, then," she said, resigned to Adrian's decision regardless of the consequences it might bring.

Adrian nodded, amber eyes flashing in the twilight. He downed half of the potion, then stoppered the vial before handing it over to Scarlett for safekeeping. He looked down at his waistcoat and began unbuttoning it.

"What are you –"

"I'm rather fond of this waistcoat," Adrian said, smirking. "And my boots, too. I'd rather they weren't destroyed...if I really do transform."

The next few minutes were fraught with tension, though a half-undressed Adrian kept gulping down wine as if there was nothing wrong whatsoever. The crowd grew restless, as did Scarlett.

Just as she concluded that nothing was going to happen, Adrian lurched forwards and fell to the cobbled floor, clutching at his chest with nails that were rapidly turning into claws. Scarlett wanted to look away; it was frightening to see the man she loved twist and morph into something else entirely, but she owed it to him to look. It was *her* grandmother who'd inflicted such a curse upon him, after all.

The crowd were rapt and afraid in equal measure.

As they should be, Scarlett thought. *They do not know if Adrian will be a friendly wolf, or a feral one.*

The witchdoctor, however, moved closer to Adrian. She bent down, taking note of every popping joint and broken bone and reformed limb as his body became less and less that of a man, and more and more that of a wolf.

Eventually, after several long minutes of shuddering and twitching, Adrian-the-wolf got to his feet. He was panting heavily, tongue lolling out of his mouth, casting his strange eyes across the crowd before fixing them on Scarlett.

They are not so strange when he is a wolf, she reasoned. *They fit him exactly as they should.*

When Adrian's tail began to wag and he gambolled over to Scarlett, the crowd burst into enthusiastic applause. The wolf was clearly no threat, though Adrian was large and strong, and his teeth long and terrible. But how could they feel threatened by a wolf who rubbed his head against Scarlett's hand, and nosed at her waist until she bent down to hug his neck?

"My, my," the witchdoctor said, "a tame wolf. You are certainly a strange one, magician."

"He was close to losing himself when we broke the curse before," Scarlett said, a small frown of worry creasing her brow. She glanced at the woman. "He won't do the same now, will he?"

She shook her head. "As I said before, this is a phantom curse. Your love is in no danger...apart from the child about to grab his tail."

Scarlett laughed when she noticed the small boy reaching out for Adrian, who allowed him to touch him. He had always been great with children. He rolled onto his back, allowing the boy to scratch his stomach like a dog. The crowd couldn't seem to believe their eyes.

"He truly is a wolf," one man said.

"Look at the size of him!" said another.

A woman sighed. "But look how lovely he is!"

Even as a wolf they fall for him! Scarlett thought in disbelief. She traced a finger along Adrian's muzzle, ruffling his ears when he licked her hand and got back to his feet. When he stood up on his hind legs to reach the wine on the table Scarlett swiftly lifted the bottle away.

"None for you, Adrian," she teased, drinking from the bottle herself. "You had plenty before you transformed."

He whimpered, drawing several laughs from the crowd. Out of the corner of her eye Scarlett noticed the witchdoctor happily serving a hoard of customers; the woman would go to bed a very wealthy merchant.

255

"Shall we walk the streets, Adrian?" Scarlett suggested. The crowd murmured their agreement, and eagerly followed when Adrian padded forwards to lead the way.

The rest of the night was a blur of wine and lights and laughter. Scarlett had never seen Adrian enjoying himself as a wolf so much, though she supposed there had been nothing *fun* about his curse before. But now he was racing against confused yet happy street dogs, and play-fighting with big, burly men who relished the challenge of wrestling a wolf.

"This is certainly not a midsummer we're likely to forget," Scarlett told Adrian when they, finally, collapsed onto a bed in a nearby tavern, whose owner made an exception to allow Adrian to sleep there. It was hardly as if the man had ever had cause to give a wolf entry to his abode before, after all.

Adrian nibbled her ear as he curled up beside her. His large, fluffy tail covered Scarlett's legs, tickling her skin as he gently wagged it. She stroked his head.

"I could get used to this, you know," she said. "Wolf you is surprisingly good company. Though I still seemed to have to fend off interested young women."

Adrian merely stared at her. She giggled.

"I guess I *am* jealous. Good night, Adrian."

A lick across her face was his reply.

*

When Scarlett awoke Adrian was no longer a wolf, though he remained curled by her side where he had lain as one. He was watching her with eyes set alight by the sunrise, a grin plastered to his face.

"What's got you in such a good mood?" she asked,

256

rubbing at the promise of a headache within her temple. She really had drunk too much wine. "Now you know the wolf curse is still there, in your blood. We never really broke it."

To her surprise, Adrian laughed. "No, but now I also know there may be a way to control it. To flip it on and off, at will. The curse is there, dormant, merely waiting for me to do something with it."

"And what do you mean to do with it?"

"Who knows? I guess I'll have to find out."

"And how, exactly, will you do that?"

Adrian kissed her softly, his lips barely brushing against hers. She could feel him smiling.

"What do you think about searching for magic, Red?" he murmured. "Looking for cursed fools, and strange disappearances, and any number of wonderful things across the globe?"

Scarlett couldn't help but return Adrian's smile. He was never so handsome as he was when discussing magic.

"I'd say that sounds far more interesting that returning home, Mister Wolfe."

SNOWSTORM KING

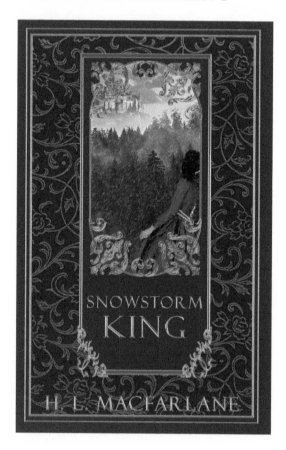

PROLOGUE

Rumour had it there was a magician staying in Alder for winter. He was from far to the south, where snow never fell. Everyone wondered why someone so used to warm seas and balmy winds would ever wish to stay up in the mountains in the middle of December, when Alder was largely cut off from the rest of the world.

This winter was particularly bad – the worst the mountain town had seen in generations, if the elderly were to be believed. Supplies were running low, and the winds kept destroying doors and windows and roofs. Food was scarce, and people were starving. The king was at a loss for what to do; he couldn't help his subjects even as the days of endless night drew themselves like a blanket across the town. It seemed like nobody would survive long enough to see the sun again.

And yet the mysterious man from the south had somehow made it up to Alder, despite the treacherous, ice-covered paths and the ever-present risk of an avalanche swallowing travellers whole at any given moment. He sought refuge with a tailor and his family, who had been clothing the town in their warmest fabrics at their own expense.

They'd have no business left if everyone died, after all.

The tailor had a daughter – a talented young woman named Lily who was destined to take over her father's shop. He'd had more than a few betrothal requests since she came of age, but he was determined to only accept a perfect offer for his precious daughter.

Lily had other ideas. She was bored of Alder and its people who all looked the same: blonde hair that flashed gold in sunlight and silver in moonlight; skin as pale as the snow that blustered around them; eyes so blue they put the summer sky to shame. She craved something different.

For this reason alone her father never should have allowed the magician to stay under his roof. Lily was fascinated by his olive skin, tightly curled, dusky brown hair, and hazel eyes. They were like nothing she'd ever seen before. She spent the long hours of winter showing the man how to sew, and embroider, and work with difficult fabrics. In turn he sneaked into her bed at night, whispering tales of other lands, of different people, and of magic.

When the magician was called to the king's castle the people of Alder were suspicious and desperate in equal measure. They feared magic – most all common folk did – but if the mysterious man could bring an end to the deadly winter slowly leeching the life from them then so be it. They could deal with *one* instance of magic in return for their lives.

Lily didn't see the magician again after he visited the king. Some say he was murdered. Some say he merely went on his way, leaving Alder the same way he must have entered it – using a spell. She was heartbroken. But the rest of the town rejoiced, for the storms that plagued the mountainside finally abated. That year spring arrived early, and would continue to arrive early for the following twenty years of the king's prosperous reign.

But Lily's encounter with the magician was not so fortunate. By the time summer arrived she could no longer hide her swollen belly from the people of Alder. Everyone wondered who she had fallen into bed with, for Lily said nothing about him, even to her parents.

When the babe was born that autumn it became obvious. The little girl had soft, tawny hair, reminiscent of the owls that hunted in the forest. Her eyes were as dark as pine needles, and her skin appeared kissed by the sun even though she'd never been beneath its rays.

Lily's parents didn't know what to do. They had no other children – Lily was their only, beloved daughter. They could not reject her, nor the baby she clutched to her chest protectively. They were a family.

So though the townspeople shunned the child, and Lily's marriage proposals ran dry, the tailor and his family continued to live a respectable life in Alder. For people always needed new clothes, and their clothes were the best. They had even sewn clothes for the king's two young sons, though the youngest was rumoured to be so tempestuous that he set the clothes alight after receiving them.

262

Lily's parents passed away before her child turned ten, leaving her to run the family shop alone. She never married, and was never foolish enough to fall into bed with another man who whispered sweet nothings into her ear again. She stopped dreaming of lands where the sun was warm, the days ever-lasting and the people were kind instead of cruel.

No. Those dreams were inherited by her daughter, Elina.

CHAPTER ONE

Elina

It didn't matter how inevitable the snow was every winter; Elina was always surprised when the first flakes fell. She hated the snow. She hated it down to her very core, and this year more than most.

For this winter was the worst anybody had experienced in twenty years. Elina might have thought this an exaggeration, had she not just turned twenty herself. She had lived through each and every one of those winters and could attest to the fact that this one, by far and away, was the worst.

Some said it was because the king had died, leaving his

youngest son to take over the throne. Everyone had wanted the elder son, Gabriel, to inherit, but Gabriel was at war protecting their country from foreign invaders. So that left his younger brother sitting on the throne until he returned – something nobody wanted.

Kilian Hale had developed a bad reputation as he'd grown and it had only gotten worse when he reached adulthood. That was what everyone said, at least. It wasn't as if Elina had ever met her new king...not that she wanted to, anyway. But she was no stranger to rumours, and the rumours surrounding the younger Hale brother were even more prevalent than the ones surrounding Elina.

A playboy. A drunk. A terrible temper. Prone to disappearing for days on end on some hedonistic, self-serving quest. In truth Elina envied this – the prince could go wherever he wanted and do whatever he wanted no matter what people said about him.

But now that prince was regent and he could no longer leave the mountainside on a whim. Not that he could have with the winter weather having hit Alder so viciously, of course. The snowstorms that plagued the area had already half-buried the town, and the paths leading down the mountain were death traps. The road leading to the castle itself was only just barely kept clear because of the forest that enveloped the twisting path, but the boughs of the dark, foreboding trees were growing heavy. Eventually they would be able to hold onto the snow no longer, and the road to the castle would be cut off, too.

"Are you sure you don't want me to come with you, Elina?" her mother, Lily, coughed. They'd closed their shop early for the day, as the town was holding a meeting about the bad weather. Supplies were beginning to run low so, as a collective, they needed to decide how Alder was going to get through the winter.

"Of course not, mama," Elina soothed, brushing her mother's hair out of her face and readjusting her blanket. Lily had been sick for a few weeks now, though apparently it was nothing she couldn't handle. Elina wasn't convinced. Though her mother was still one year shy of forty, and retained her elegant good looks that had been the talk of the town once upon a time, she had grown decidedly frail. The mild winters of years gone by ensured that she had never *truly* gotten sick, but this year was different.

"You can't go to the town hall all by yourself, Elina," her mother protested. "You know what they're like. They'll –"

"It's nothing I cannot handle," she smiled. "And besides, it's on their own heads if they ignore me. They need us to keep making blankets and jackets and leggings and gloves, and for that we need materials. They can't possibly snub me at the meeting."

Lily looked unconvinced. The town had only gotten worse in their treatment of her daughter since her own parents died. It didn't seem to matter how obedient or talented Elina was – her tawny hair, forest-coloured eyes and eternally sun-kissed skin marked her for what she was. The daughter of an outsider. A strange man. A magician.

Though some people didn't really believe the foreigner from twenty years ago had been blessed with magic, Lily knew the truth. For how could she not? But she had never spoken much about the man to Elina, in part because it pained her to talk of him and in part to save her from knowing just how shameful her mother had been.

But Elina wasn't deaf. She wasn't blind. She wasn't stupid. She heard what the townspeople of Alder said, and she saw how they looked at her. She knew she was different, and for that she was hated. But she loved her

266

mother fiercely, so not once did she ever consider blaming her for the way she was treated.

Elina kissed her mother on the forehead then wrapped herself up in her favourite blue cloak, made of fine, soft material that matched her dress. She pulled up the hood. "I won't be long, mama," she said as she opened the door, letting a blast of bitterly cold air through that had her wincing immediately. "I love you."

"You too, Elina."

The town hall wasn't far from the Brodeur tailor shop. If the ground hadn't been covered in a layer of thick, grey ice Elina would have reached her destination in under five minutes. But it *was* covered in ice, and Elina was always wary of walking on it in case she tripped and broke her neck, so by the time she reached the town hall the meeting had already started.

When she crept into the hall and tried to hide in the shadows at the back of the room a hundred eyes followed her.

Oh, wonderful, she thought. *I haven't even said anything and already I'm in the wrong.*

But to her relief nobody commented on her lateness. Apart from the occasional glare here and there Elina was ignored as the town head, Frederick, continued with his speech, for which Elina was grateful.

"It's not simply a case of rationing what we already have," Frederick said. "This winter seems set to last far longer than any winter we've had in twenty years. At this rate we won't make it past the end of January."

"This is all because the king died!" someone called out. "He had that magic from the foreigner, but it must have gone to the grave with him. We're all doomed!"

Several pairs of eyes darted towards Elina. She ignored

them. She knew this story by heart: her father had been a magician who, after impregnating her mother and bestowing the gift of magic to the king, disappeared forever. She never understood how the king could be so revered for this supposed deal whilst Elina's mother was scorned for bearing the magician's child. The double standard would have made her laugh, if it hadn't made her life so bitterly lonely.

"Let's not base our current situation on rumours and suspicion," Frederick said, ever the diplomat. "We need a solid plan to get us through –"

"Isn't there that travelling couple staying in Gill's tavern?" someone else interrupted. "You know the two. The woman's a healer, but the man – if ever I were to wager a man were a magician I'd place my bets on him. Perhaps we can convince him to broker a deal with the new king and –"

"Enough with the magicians!" the town head roared, finally reaching the end of his patience. "We cannot hope for magic to save us! We need to ask the prince regent to provide for us, like he should."

"Ha!" Daven the woodcutter spat out. "Have fun with that, Fred! I'd like to see our new *king* provide for anyone but himself."

Fred winced. "Prince regent," he corrected. "And we have to at least ask. It is his duty to hear us out."

"And will you go to barter with him?"

He shook his head. "I fear he will not listen to me. His Royal Highness is young, and impulsive. I believe it better to send a more *attractive* messenger."

Everyone knew what he was getting at – he planned to send a woman. A young, pretty woman who might tempt Kilian Hale into helping them on a whim. A whim was all they needed, after all. And rumour had it that he was just as handsome as his father had been in his glory days. The problem was, of course, his horrible attitude. When it came right down to it the woman of Alder loved Gabriel, his older brother, and not Kilian, who was as likely to imprison a woman as he was to bed her.

And so it was that nobody in the hall seemed very enthusiastic about volunteering to be a messenger, something which Elina wholeheartedly agreed with.

Clearly the town can't solve anything until someone has spoken to the prince regent, she thought as she silently made her way to the door. *I'm not needed here. I'll just slip out and –*

"Send the magician's girl!"

Elina froze. She dared not turn, for she knew all eyes were on her.

"Yes, send Miss Brodeur!" Daven agreed enthusiastically. "She's certainly pretty enough, and her link to the magician can't hurt."

Of all the times for someone in Alder to admit that Elina was attractive to look at, she would not have picked this moment. She'd been used to everyone ignoring her – for men to barely spare her a glance because of her bastard status and foreign appearance. It was something which she had loathed before. It had made her feel unwanted and ugly.

To be told she was pretty enough to be used as bait for Kilian Hale was *not* what Elina had wanted to hear. But the general murmur of agreement filling her ears told her the town had already made up their mind. Reluctantly she turned, keeping her expression as blank as possible as she took in the faces of the people in the hall. Most of them were looking at her with their usual distaste, though there was a sick layer of satisfaction behind their eyes at the idea of sending their least favourite townsperson to do their dirty work that hadn't been there before.

Frederick raised an eyebrow at her. "Miss Brodeur, would you be willing to do this?"

Elina wanted so badly to say no. But what would that achieve? She and her mother would only further be ignored. They needed to maintain a steady stream of business if they were to afford the medicine required to stop her mother's sickness from growing worse.

And Elina was sick herself. Sick of being lonely and ignored. If she could somehow convince the prince regent to help the town then surely she would not be so hated. She might become liked. Respected, even. She'd settle for merely being acknowledged.

So she nodded. "I can leave now, if it pleases you," she said demurely, though inside she was fired up and ready to shout at them all to see what she was doing for people who did not care for her.

See how selfless I'm being! Elina wanted to scream. *See what I'm going to do for the ungrateful lot of you!*

She said neither of these things.

With a sigh of relief at how easy and painless choosing a messenger had turned out to be, Frederick smiled at her. Elina couldn't help but flinch – nobody ever smiled at her, least of all the town head. She ran off without another word, knowing that if she spoke she'd say something she'd regret.

I can't disappoint them, she thought as she made her way towards the forest. *If I disappoint them I'll be in an even worse position than I was before. To improve my status I have to succeed.*

Elina stopped by a patch of ice and inspected her face.

Her hair was braided and wrapped around her head, which was how she usually wore it. A few curly tendrils had broken loose; she used her fingers to shape them properly. In the permanent grey of winter her hair seemed dull and dark compared to the rest of the people of Alder, but Elina could do nothing about this.

She stared at her reflection for another few seconds, the green of her irises as bottomless as the pine trees she was about to pass under. She would never look like she belonged in Alder.

She'd have to earn her place there instead.

CHAPTER TWO

Kilian

It took Kilian precisely two minutes of consciousness to come to the conclusion that he didn't want to get out of bed. His head was killing him, he was freezing, and his shoulder ached from having slept on it badly. He glanced at the mostly-empty bottle of vodka lying on the floor and winced.

That was definitely full when I started drinking yesterday.

With a groan he threw himself back against his pillows. But just when Kilian decided that, as king, he could simply choose to remain in bed no matter what anybody said, he heard a knock on the door. He ignored it, of course, but it didn't go away.

"Who is it?!" he roared, immediately regretting having shouted when his head rang painfully in response.

"Your Royal Highness, the messenger from Alder is seeking an audience again," came the timid voice of a servant Kilian didn't care to recognise the voice of.

"Send her away," he replied, waving a dismissive hand at the door even though the servant couldn't see it.

"Ah, you see, Your Royal Highness," the man said hesitantly, "as regent you really are obligated to listen to the spokespeople of your country, and this is the fifth time you've turned her away –"

"I am aware of my obligations," Kilian bit back. He rubbed his head. "Fine then. Don't turn her away, but don't let her in, either. Let me see what she will do whilst blatantly being ignored."

He could tell the servant didn't like Kilian's response one bit, but he didn't care. Shivering as he forced himself out of bed, he threw on a long overcoat that lay abandoned on the floor, staring dolefully at the blackened, empty fireplace opposite his bed in the process. He was about to call out for his personal servant to see to getting a new fire started, but then Kilian remembered that he'd fired him.

He'd fired most of the castle staff, truth be told. He couldn't stand them. All hired by his father or his elder brother. All of them judging every disappointing move Kilian made as if they expected nothing more from him than self-indulgent depravity.

Well, if that's what they expected then that's what they'd get. Kilian had kept on barely enough staff to keep torches lit and food cooking in the kitchen. He enjoyed the solitude. If he could get away with it he'd have fired every last soul in the castle – including himself.

Kilian never wanted to be king, even in a temporary capacity, and he wanted it even less now that it had been forced upon him.

Staggering over to the tall window in his room, which overlooked the grounds to the front of the castle and allowed him to gaze across the forest to the town of Alder, Kilian felt his mood worsen. The weather was truly awful – the last time it had been this bad he'd been just three years old. That time, the winter had been despicable simply through bad luck. The current bout of bad weather had nothing to do with luck, bad or otherwise, just like the twenty years of *good* winters that preceded it.

Kilian didn't want to think about that.

Clutching his overcoat tighter around himself against the cold, he gazed down to the heavy iron front doors of the castle. A woman stood there, huddled into her cloak and looking thoroughly miserable. This was, indeed, the fifth time in as many days that the messenger from Alder had coming seeking an audience with him. He had to admire her tenacity.

I suppose the town must be getting desperate, he thought, looking up at the endless white sky and its blinding, heavy snow. *The weather has been awful ever since my father died, and it's my fault. Not that I care. If they die that's one less thing for me to pretend to worry about.*

All Kilian had to do was keep the throne warm for his brother's return. Gabriel had been at war since summer, fighting in the borders for some reason or other that Kilian had never deemed important enough to remember. Any day now he'd come back – triumphant or otherwise –

and Kilian would be free of his responsibilities. He could leave the castle. Leave the country. He could go wherever he wanted.

In the meantime he was stuck inside a miserable, never-ending snowstorm. How could anyone expect him to *actually* do his job well when he'd never wanted it? His father should never have forced the position onto his youngest son if he'd wanted the kingdom taken care of.

But his father was dead and his brother gone. Now all Kilian could do was try to wrangle out some form of amusement to fill his days until he was free of the damn castle.

And I guess she'll have to do, he thought, a sly smile on his face as he gazed once more down at the woman in her blue cloak, almost invisible through the blizzard.

Kilian threw off his overcoat just long enough to dress in a white shirt and pair of trousers before sliding the coat back on top; his teeth were already chattering by the time he huddled against the fabric once more. His head was still killing him, so Kilian picked up the mostly-empty bottle of vodka from the floor and swallowed what was left. Fighting the immediate urge to vomit, he laced on a pair of boots, dragged a hand through his long, unkempt hair and slammed his door open.

Nobody was in the corridor, as expected. He wondered if he'd have to stop by the kitchen in order to get something for the pain in his head, though Kilian did not possess the patience to do so. When he reached the throne room he collapsed onto the overly-decorated chair, swinging his legs over one of the armrests as he dipped his head back over the other.

"Bring her in!" he called out to nobody in particular; he wasn't sure if anybody was even within earshot. "And get me some wine. In fact, bring me wine before you bring the girl." Kilian had priorities, after all, even if nobody else agreed with them. His first and foremost priority was always to be as drunk as he could physically get away with being, and he was at least a bottle of wine too sober for his own tastes.

A scrabbling by the door to the throne room told Kilian that his orders had been heard. Impatiently he waited for someone to bring his alcohol. When they did it was accompanied by bread, meats and cheeses. He waved that away.

"Did I say I needed food?" he demanded. But, upon feeling his stomach pinch in response, he waved the servant back. "Never mind. Keep it here. Now go away and fetch the girl."

Kilian scratched his chin as he guzzled down his first goblet of wine. A fine layer of stubble was growing; he needed to shave. He hadn't had cause to do so for days, though.

When was the last time I had a woman? he wondered. It had been at least two weeks. Resolving to have one sent to his rooms later that day, he shifted slightly on the throne when the sound of soft, light footsteps made their way towards him.

When the woman pulled down her snow-covered hood Kilian froze.

"Your R-Royal Highness," she said, shivering heavily as she struggled to bow. "M-my name is Elina Brodeur, and I c-come on behalf of Alder to seek your help."

But he wasn't listening. Kilian had never seen a woman like Elina Brodeur from his own country before. She stood out, dark and strange against the snow, reminding him of a man who had once come to the castle twenty years ago.

He straightened up on the throne and cleared his throat.

"You're the magician's girl."

CHAPTER THREE

Elina

The inside of Kilian Hale's castle was barely warmer than it had been outside. Elina's teeth were chattering so loudly in her skull that she barely heard the man's question. Well, it wasn't a question; more a statement of fact.

The prince regent looked at her with an expression of mild interest. "Well, aren't you?" he demanded.

Elina nodded. "He impregnated my mother, yes, but I would not say he was my father, and neither I his girl."

To her surprise Kilian snorted in amusement. "No, I

guess not," he said. He settled back against the throne, pouring more wine down his throat before continuing. "So, Miss...?"

"Brodeur. Elina Brodeur. Daughter of Lily Brodeur –"

"Yes, yes, I don't care. You came here seeking my help. What help exactly is it that you need?"

Something told Elina that Kilian knew exactly what the people of Alder needed. Going by his attitude, and the rate at which he was consuming wine, she concluded that he had merely approved an audience with her to provide himself with some kind of entertainment. The castle was empty, after all.

Disconcertingly so.

"Where is everyone?" Elina asked, glancing around the cavernous, dusty throne room. When she had imagined the inside of the castle this was not what she'd had in mind at all.

Kilian frowned. "Did I grant you an audience for you to criticise where I live?"

"I – no, I just –"

"Then tell me why you are here."

Elina struggled not to bristle against the man's standoffish attitude. He was royalty; he was *allowed* to be standoffish. She took in a somewhat shuddering breath, for she was still freezing. "This winter has hit Alder very hard. Too hard. We are running low on provisions – food, cloth, medicine, stone –"

"So you want me to provide the town with more?"

Elina kept her gaze steady. "Yes."

"Denied."

"...excuse me?"

"You heard me," Kilian said, glancing at Elina out of the corner of his eye with a smirk on his face that was begging for her to react. "No. I will not help your stupid town. You can all die. Now if that was all..."

"You can't be serious!"

"Oh, but I am."

"But so many people really *will* die if you cannot help – this isn't a joke!" Elina took a few steps forward, slipping on the snow that had fallen from her cloak and melted on the floor.

Kilian merely chuckled. "All the better for the kingdom if there are fewer people for me to rule. And besides," he pointed to one of the long, narrow windows, which were white with snow, "this kind of winter is made for culling the herd. You shouldn't expect everyone in Alder to survive this. So why even try to save them?"

Elina was torn between speaking her mind and keeping polite. This cruel man was her king, even if only until his far more capable brother returned. If she couldn't reason with him then the entire town would suffer.

She bowed her head. "Please, Your Royal Highness, I beg you to reconsider. I understand your sentiment, but –"

"You do, do you? And why would you understand such a deadly sentiment?"

"Because the people of Alder don't exactly like me, and I don't exactly like them, either."

Kilian seemed to consider this. "You would wish them dead for such a reason?"

"No," Elina murmured, shaking her head, "but I have

280

thought it nonetheless. Thinking such a thing and allowing such a thing to happen are different, though."

"Not when you're king, they're not," he joked.

Elina looked up; Kilian was watching her carefully with eyes as pale as glass. They were not the brilliant blue of the people of Alder; instead, they were as icy grey as the snow outside the window. Elina found them unsettling.

She supposed Kilian really was handsome, though his long, pale blonde hair was tangled and knotted down his back. His sharp jawline was covered in stubble, and it looked as though he had hardly bothered to dress for meeting Elina. He wasn't wearing enough to combat the cold which, upon further notice, had resulted in the man shivering almost as much as Elina was in her snow-sodden clothes.

He frowned at her. "What are you looking at?"

"You aren't wearing enough. You'll catch a cold."

"Says the woman currently half frozen to death."

"I wouldn't be if I had been granted an audience earlier, *Your Royal Highness.*"

Elina didn't know why she was baiting Kilian, but if the man truly wasn't going to help Alder then she didn't see why she had to remain polite.

He could lock me up in a cell and let me freeze to death, I suppose, but if that will be Alder's fate anyway then what does it matter?

Kilian brought his glass up to his cruel mouth and drank deeply. He swept his eyes up and down Elina, which she forced herself not to shy away from.

"You say your town does not like you. Why is that?"

Surprised by the question, Elina carefully considered her answer before replying. "It isn't so much that they

281

dislike me - that would involve them actually knowing me first. They simply do not wish to acknowledge my existence."

"Because of the magician?"

She nodded. "They don't like how different I look. And I was born out of wedlock, and my mother had many suitors at the time. She shamed my grandparents by doing so, though they loved her too much to let her - or me - go. Fortunately my mother is a talented seamstress, so she took over my grandfather's tailor shop, so the town's scorn for me means little and less."

"And yet, clearly, that's a lie."

Elina said nothing. Of course it was a lie.

"You would not be here if you didn't care for them," Kilian continued, almost to himself. "So tell me, Elina Brodeur, how *much* do you care for this town that hates you? What would you do for them?"

"I...what are you asking of me, Your Royal Highness?"

His lips twisted into a smile; Elina did not like the look of it at all.

"Become my personal servant. Wait on me, tend to my fires and my room and serve me food and wine. Do my bidding, no matter how humiliating that may be. Do all this and I shall provide Alder with the provisions it needs."

"Surely you must have far more qualified servants for such a role?" Elina asked, dumbfounded by the request.

Kilian shrugged. "No. I fired them all."

"You - why?"

"You may have told me about your pathetic, sob story excuse for a life, tailor girl, but that does not mean I have to tell you mine."

282

Elina said nothing. Kilian clearly wanted her to lose her temper. Or maybe he didn't; maybe he simply always spoke like this. Either way, Elina hated him for it. Frederick had wanted a young woman to beg Kilian for help on the hope that he'd take a liking to her and help her on a whim.

Well, this is clearly a whim, *but not the kind the town was thinking of.* Elina supposed this way was better. She hadn't wanted Kilian to take a *liking* to her in the way they'd been hoping. She didn't want to end up in his bed, giving up her virginity for the sake of a town who responded to her mother losing hers with disgust.

"...is there a limit to what you would have me do, as your servant?" she asked quietly, keeping her eyes downcast.

Kilian finished his wine and threw the glass to the floor, where it smashed. He picked up a thick slice of bread and tore off the crust, gnawing on it as he considered Elina's question.

"Maybe. Maybe not. I guess that's something you'll find out after accepting it."

"You act as if I *will* accept."

"Do you really have a choice? Something tells me you don't."

Elina hated being told this. Because of course she didn't really have a choice; if the town died then so would her mother. At least, for her, Elina had to endure the whims of Kilian Hale.

"I will not live in the castle," she said, looking up at Kilian as she spoke. He didn't seem to like this at all.

"You will. What if I require your assistance at night?"

"My mother is poorly; I will not leave her."

"Then have her live here too."

"We have the shop. It's our livelihood. I will not move her, or me. This is the only way I'll accept your proposal."

This is the only way I can tolerate your proposal.

Finally, after what seemed like minutes but was actually seconds, Kilian swallowed the bread he was chewing and nodded.

"Fine; live in the town that hates you. But you have to arrive at the castle before sunrise and stay until after my evening meal."

"Which is...?"

He grinned. "As late as I can make it."

Elina felt her temple twitch in irritation. "How long must I act as your servant?"

"As long as I want." And then, at the look of indignation on Elina's face, clarified, "Until winter ends. You will serve me for as long as your town needs assistance."

"And you will provide assistance immediately?"

"Yes."

Something told Elina her idea of immediately and Kilian's idea of immediately were entirely different things. But she didn't want to push her drunk, cruel king too far, in case he changed his mind.

With a yawn, Kilian stretched his arms above his head until his spine cracked in several places. He looked at Elina from heavy-lidded eyes hazy with alcohol.

"First order of business, Elina: run me a bath."

Elina had never wanted to do anything less in all her life.

CHAPTER FOUR

Kilian

"Where are the baths situated?"

"Oh, I have one in my room. Follow me."

Kilian lazily unfolded himself from his throne, sweeping past Elina as he exited through the door, not stopping to check if she was following him.

"Clean up in there," he ordered the same man who had served him food and wine. "Some utter heathen smashed my wine glass on the floor."

When Elina rushed to match Kilian's strides he did not slow down to accommodate her. It was far more amusing to watch the frozen, soaking woman struggle to keep up with him.

"I'm assuming you know how to light fires and prepare bathwater," he said.

"Of course I do."

He opened the door to his chambers and gestured towards the large, ornate bathtub. "Then get to it."

Elina stared at it in confusion. Her gaze lowered to the floor beneath it, which was scratched and damaged as if someone had literally dragged the heavy, ceramic tub into the room.

She glanced at Kilian. "Something tells me this wasn't supposed to be in here."

"It's easier to roll out of the bath and straight into bed if it's here," he explained simply, leaving Elina's side to wander about his room in search of a forgotten bottle of wine or vodka. Finding none, he collapsed on top of his bed. "If you don't get a fire going soon you're liable to genuinely freeze to death, so I suggest you be quick about it."

Elina straightened up at the comment. She unclasped her cloak and hung it from the door without waiting for permission to do so; in its absence Kilian could properly see her figure in the well-fitted, dark blue dress she wore.

Not bad at all, he thought appreciatively. *Not as tall as the rest of the women in Alder. Curvier, too.*

Kilian contented himself with watching Elina scurry around his room, cleaning the hearth before throwing fresh logs into the fireplace.

"There's more wood in the room over there," Kilian drawled, half-heartedly pointing to an adjoining storage room. "There's a water reserve and bowls for filling the tub in there, too."

Elina remained impassive as she said, "Why would the prince regent have a storage room for such things attached to his private chambers?"

"Because said prince regent is always cold, and likes to have firewood close at hand."

"So why don't you have a fire going constantly, if you're always cold?"

"Because I fired the staff, or have you forgotten?"

Elina paused. "You don't know how to light your own fire?"

"Why should I have to know how to do that?"

"Well if you're going to fire your staff it would be useful to know."

Kilian smiled. "Hence why *you're* here."

Sighing, and wearing an expression that very much suggested she thought Kilian was useless, Elina got to work starting a fire. Before long she had lit a spark, then the twists of paper she'd carefully placed between the logs caught fire, then eventually the wood itself. Within minutes a proper fire was merrily burning, though it was yet to give off any proper heat.

Wordlessly Elina moved through to the storage room to fill up a large bowl with water. When she gasped and returned with dripping wet, steaming hands, Kilian smirked.

"Have you never felt hot water before?" he asked sardonically.

"You have a thermal pool beneath the castle."

"Indeed I do. There are hot springs to the back of the castle, in fact."

287

Elina stared at her hands as if she couldn't believe it. "Why not use the hot springs to bathe, then?"

He couldn't be bothered answering such a complicated question. Instead, Kilian pointed to the window. "Have you forgotten about the blizzard? Why would I wish to bathe in *that?*"

She wrinkled her nose. "I guess not. At least this will make filling your bath much easier."

"Lucky for you."

Elina said nothing, though she removed the top layer of her dress and rolled up the sleeves of her undershirt before continuing to fill a large bowl with water, emptying it into the bathtub before refilling it once more and repeating the action over and over again until the tub was full.

The fire was well and truly hot by then; Kilian sighed in relief when he was finally able to feel his toes. In the flickering light he could see that Elina's hair was not quite as dark as her magician father, whose appearance was burned onto his brain even though he tried to forget about the man. It was almost burnished – a deep, intense copper colour that Kilian had never seen before. He thought it matched Elina's golden skin perfectly. Though she was still sodden, and her braid was a mess around her head, Kilian concluded that she really was quite lovely to look at.

I've picked a good servant, he thought, eagerly stripping off his boots and clothes in order to throw himself into the scalding bath. He wasn't expecting Elina to cry out in surprise and turn away in horror.

"Your – Your Royal Highness! You might have given me some warning!"

Kilian laughed as he eased himself into the water, which turned into a low moan of satisfaction as the heat seeped into his muscles. He leaned his head back to look at Elina. "What's wrong, Elina?" he asked casually. "Have you never seen a naked man before? Or is it simply that you've never seen a naked *prince* before?"

"I – you clearly know the answer to your question, Your Royal Highness," she stammered, keeping her back firmly to Kilian. "You don't even have anything to put in the bathwater! It's completely clear."

He shrugged. "Why would I bother putting anything in the water? All I need it for is taking away the cold."

Elina risked a glance over her shoulder; Kilian was satisfied to see her face was flushed. "You cannot clean yourself properly with water only, Your Royal –"

"You can stop it with the *Your Royal Highness* thing, Elina. Come over here."

She shook her head.

"Come here. That's an order."

Desperately looking like she wanted to protest, Elina crept towards the bathtub until she stood behind Kilian's head. He arched his neck further to stare at her as she looked down at him. This close up, he could see that Elina did not quite share the same eye colour as her father – not as far as Kilian could remember. Her eyes were greener, and the colour seemed purer, though in the firelight it still contained a few flecks of gold which he clearly remembered the magician's eyes having, too.

Elina darted her eyes away uncertainly. "What is it?"

"Comb my hair."

She looked as if she might object but, upon weighing up whether there would be much point, she drooped her shoulders and nodded. "Where's your comb?"

"By the mirror."

And so Elina retrieved the comb and, with obvious reluctance, slid Kilian's hair out from beneath his head to hang over the edge of the tub.

"There's a chair over there that you can sit on," he said, indicating over to his left. So Elina retrieved that, too, and sat down by Kilian's head. She seemed to hesitate before touching his hair, but when she did he said, "And be gentle, of course. No hurting me just because you can."

A flash of irritation crossed her face as if she was insulted that Kilian might suggest she would do such a thing. He remained on edge until Elina ran the comb through his hair a few times, stopping when she came upon knots and tangles to carefully unravel them with deft fingers. When it became apparent that she was going to do her job properly, he relaxed.

"You're very good at this," he murmured after a few minutes.

"I've worked out worse tangles in the wool and thread we use in the shop," Elina replied, voice quiet.

And then there was only the crackle of the fire to break the silence, though Kilian did not feel the need to add to the noise. Usually the whip of the wind outside was all he could hear but, for the first time in months, the wind was calm. Kilian was warm, relaxed, and actually enjoying himself – he couldn't remember the last time all three of those things had occurred at the same time. He wondered if he would have also enjoyed himself if he wasn't drunk, though he didn't care enough to find out.

When Elina finally stopped combing his hair he opened his eyes, which Kilian had not been aware were closed in the first place. He almost said thank you.

Almost.

"Where do you keep your clothes?" Elina asked as

she put the chair and comb back where she had found them.

He gestured to a room adjacent to the dressing table. "In there."

Elina disappeared inside. For a few minutes all Kilian heard were the sounds of her rummaging through his things; he wondered what she was doing. When she returned carrying a fine, woollen shirt and long, soft leggings before laying them on the bed he frowned.

"What are those for?"

"Wear them to bed. They'll keep you warm."

He stared at the clothes incredulously. "They're so thin. I don't believe you."

She put her hands on her hips. "You have nothing to lose by listening to me."

"I guess not," he replied, sinking beneath the water until it only just reached his hairline. When he resurfaced Elina looked away quickly. He grinned slyly. "How can you be so embarrassed by a naked body? How old are you?"

"...twenty."

"Ah, of course. That makes sense, what with the magician and all. So you're a twenty-year-old woman – two years past marrying age – and you're still this innocent?"

She bristled. "I shouldn't have to explain myself to the likes of you."

"The likes of me?" Kilian parroted back in interest. "Tell me, Elina, what do you mean by that?"

"I – you know what I mean, clearly. Otherwise you wouldn't keep looking at me the way you do, like I'm an object."

Huh. She's sharper than I thought.

"I guess that's true. In which case I apologise."

"That doesn't sound sincere at all."

He quirked an eyebrow. "So you won't accept even a semblance of an apology from me, despite the fact I'm the ruler of this land?"

Elina winced as she slid back into the outer layer of her dress and retrieved her cloak, which was stiff and dark with water. "You're the one who doesn't want me to call you *Your Royal Highness.* Something tells me the last thing you want is for me to treat you like a king or regent or anything remotely similar."

And then she opened the door and left without another word, though Kilian had not given her leave to go. Indeed, it was barely mid-afternoon. Yet he allowed it, for it was the boldest move anyone had made against him in a long, long time.

Hours later, when Kilian retired to bed, he decided to humour Elina's whims and dress in the clothes she had picked out. They felt thin and insubstantial; he prepared himself for a long, sleepless, freezing night beneath the covers.

Instead he fell asleep within minutes, as warm as if he were still in the bath, Elina combing his hair.

CHAPTER FIVE

Elina

"The prince finally granted you an audience?!"

"That's certainly one way to put it," Elina grimaced as she shed off every layer of her sodden clothing and slid into the bath her mother had prepared. She thought of Kilian's on-demand hot water supply with envy.

Lily Brodeur stared at her daughter, eyes bright with interest. "What do you mean by that? How did it go?"

"I...mama, how could that man be our king?"

Her mother laughed lightly. "So he really is still that bad-tempered. I always hoped he'd grow out of it. At least he won't be ruling for long."

"You talk as if you know him."

"I made clothes for Kilian and Gabriel once, back before I knew I was pregnant with you," she smiled. "Well, I helped my father make them. I went with him to the castle to deliver them. Gabriel was every inch the young prince - so elegant and composed - and he was only eight! But little Kilian was not quite four, and I had never met a child so tempestuous. He threw the clothes I made him in the fire!"

Elina gawked at her mother. "That can't possibly be a true story."

"Oh, but it is, I assure you. I wonder if he remembers?"

"He didn't seem to recognise my surname," Elina said, "though he was drunk, so that might explain it."

Lily looked at her in concern. "So what happened? You tried so hard to speak with him - I somehow doubt *my* daughter would leave without succeeding at what she sought out to do."

The comment warmed Elina's heart for a moment, though it was instantly doused as she explained her deal with the cruel, obnoxious sham of a ruler that was Kilian Hale. She watched as shock, disbelief and concern darkened her mother's pale face, grimly certain that she would try to talk her daughter out of her deal with the proverbial devil.

"Elina, you can't possibly -"

"It's only until winter passes," Elina spoke over her mother quickly. "Alder needs the supplies, mama. And *we* need Alder. We'll die along with everyone else if we don't get the help we need to get through the next few months."

Lily looked away from her daughter, discomfited. "I don't like it, Elina. If Kilian truly is as unreasonable as he seems then he might well simply be taking advantage of you with no intention of helping us at all."

"I have to at least try, mama. If, after two weeks, he still hasn't sent any provisions, I'll tell him the deal is off."

"He doesn't sound like the kind of man who would let you do that."

Elina sighed as she got out of the bathtub and towelled herself dry. "What would you have me do?"

"We could leave."

Lily's voice was very quiet as she stared at the fire currently roaring in the hearth. Elina shrugged on a shirt and some trousers and sat by her mother, inspecting her face. Her pallor was sickly and almost green, and her hands shook slightly. She was growing weaker by the day. A knot tightened in Elina's stomach at the unimaginable thought that her mother would not last the winter.

"Maybe when winter passes and your health returns," Elina said, forcing a smile onto her face. She unravelled the braid from around her head – her hair was still wet from the snow – and combed it through until she'd worked through the tangles in her wavy hair.

She was starkly reminded of combing Kilian's hair mere hours ago, though she didn't want to think about him. Once Elina had unpicked the knots, Kilian's hair had been lustrous, soft and shiny. It was paler than the blonde hair of the people of Alder, just as his eyes were paler, too. It was almost as if he were made of ice himself.

That would explain his callous attitude, Elina thought as she rebraided her hair, letting it hang down her back like a rope as she laced on a pair of dry boots and a dark green cloak that had belonged to her grandfather.

"Where are you going, Elina?" her mother sputtered in surprise. She coughed several times into her hands, taking a few ragged breaths before continuing. "You only just got back. And your hair is still wet."

She glanced out of the window. "I want to stop by the apothecary whilst the weather is still calm. I won't be long, don't worry."

As she had done with Kilian, Elina left without another word. Outside the snow was still falling, but it was soft and gentle and almost pleasant. It had been like that since Elina had combed Kilian's hair in the bath, flying through the air almost silently outside his window.

Don't think about him in that bath. Elina's face grew warm despite the cold, and she shook her head to clear it of her thoughts. She struggled along the ice-encrusted road until, with some relief, she reached the apothecary.

It was closed.

"Of course," she said aloud, watching her breath form a tiny cloud in front of her face. She couldn't go home without buying more medicine for her mother – their stocks were too low, and the way her mother was now Elina highly doubted she would get much sleep.

Maybe Erik or his wife are in the tavern, she thought, heading towards the establishment despite the fact she hated the place. Elina had never been welcome there; even when she had visited with her mother and grandparents as a child she had been shunned. It was the worst place to be ignored, surrounded by people having a good time. Enjoying themselves. Living in a world in which they pretended Elina did not exist.

And yet she pushed through the door of Gill's tavern despite all of that, because her mother's health was more important than her pride. Everybody looked at her as she walked across the bar, looking for Erik, the apothecary. Nobody asked her about how she was faring trying to broker a deal with Kilian.

She could tell by their faces they all hoped she would fail, even though their livelihoods depended on her succeeding.

They can go to hell, Elina thought as she concluded that neither Erik nor his wife were in the tavern. But then she caught sight of something unusual: black hair. Long, lustrous, wavy black hair. When the head of the woman whose hair it belonged to turned Elina saw one of the most beautiful people she had ever set eyes upon.

When she smiled at her, Elina looked down at the floor. "You stand out almost as much as me and Adrian," the woman said. Her voice was low and musical; lilting. "Won't you sit with us?"

"I – can I?"

She laughed softly. "Of course! You seem just about as welcome as us in here. Won't you tell us your name?" She indicated to the man standing behind her, who was looking for an available table. He flashed Elina a grin that she could only describe as *wolfish.* He had the strangest eyes she had ever seen – amber, like a sunset.

"Elina. I'm Elina Brodeur," Elina found herself saying, still enraptured by the two incredibly attractive people in front of her.

"I'm Scarlett Duke," the woman said, "and this idiot is Adrian Wolfe. Adrian, can't you find a table?"

The man named Adrian shook his handsome head. "There are none to be found. I guess we're eating up in our room. Miss Brodeur, who were you looking for when you entered the tavern?"

She was surprised by the man's observation; had the

strangers been watching her since she entered the place?

"Um...the apothecary," she said. "My mother is sick."

A flash of concern crossed Scarlett's face. "What ails her?"

"It's her lungs, for the most part. But she's always been frail. The cold has affected her badly this winter."

Scarlett glanced at Adrian. "How much stock do we have left?"

"Enough," he said. "Miss Brodeur, if you don't mind accompanying us up to our room I think we can help you."

Elina followed them numbly without really thinking. She wasn't used to people talking to her outside of the shop, and even then all conversation was kept short and professional. The only other stranger who'd talked to her this much was Kilian Hale, and he didn't count, because Elina wished he didn't exist.

When they reached the room Scarlett rummaged through a large trunk of vials, bottles and boxes that Elina would never have been able to make heads nor tails of.

"Let's see..." Scarlett murmured. "We have some eucalyptus oil from Asia – that'll help with your mother's breathing – and, let's see...peppermint, thyme and ginger for coughing and fever, and...oh! Powdered willow bark, for pain relief." She dumped several items in Elina's arms without warning. "Brew the herbs as a tea and sweeten it with honey. Don't let her take more than one finger joint's worth of willow bark in a given five hour period. You can put some eucalyptus oil in your mother's bathwater or add it to some boiling water and have her breathe in the steam. You can also pour a few drops on her pillow, to ease her sleep."

Elina stared at her in disbelief. "How do you know all

298

of this?"

Scarlett grinned; she tilted her head in Adrian's direction, who was drinking a tankard of ale he'd brought up from downstairs. "He taught me most everything I know, believe it or not."

Considering Elina had heard rumours that Adrian Wolfe was a magician at the town hall meeting, she did not doubt it. He really *did* look like a magician...whatever that meant. It was probably his eyes, or the white streak in his dark hair.

He scoffed at Scarlett's answer. "Believe it or not, indeed. I am very well educated."

"No need to show off, Adrian."

Elina's eyes darted between the two of them. "H-how much do I owe you for all of this?" she asked, lifting up her armful of remedies.

"Oh, just take it for free," Scarlett said. "Only... promise that you'll keep us company whilst we're in Alder. We could do with talking to someone local who'll be honest with us."

"...about what?"

"That depends," Adrian said. "How honest will you be?"

"Certainly more honest than the people downstairs would be."

He laughed amiably. "Oh, I like you. So tell me, Miss Brodeur; why can I smell magic upon you?"

She froze. Magic? On *her?*

"Adrian, don't scare her," Scarlett chided. She touched Elina's arm gently. "Pay him no mind. Adrian is a little more...sensitive to some things than most folk are."

"Are you here because of magic?" Elina asked.

"Possibly," Scarlett replied, her answer decidedly ambiguous. "We don't know yet. But now we're stuck here either way. So might you keep us company some nights and help us work out what's going on?"

Elina knew she should say no. She had too much going on with her mother's sickness and her stupid deal with Kilian Hale. But how could she resist the allure of *magic?* Elina was deathly curious.

Then she spotted a bag of bath salts inside Scarlett's trunk. Thinking of Kilian's bath, and how she never wanted to see him naked again if she could avoid it, she smiled slightly.

"Give me those bath salts and I'll gladly help you however I can."

CHAPTER SIX

Kilian

Elina Brodeur was acting unnecessarily servile. Kilian wanted her to snap and talk back to him, like she had done when she'd first left the castle. But she hadn't; instead, she demurely obeyed all of Kilian's orders without so much as a word of complaint. It infuriated him to no end.

And so Kilian got drunk, as he always did. He got so royally drunk he'd put the local alcoholics of Alder to shame. Not that he could know this for a fact, given he couldn't leave the castle, but the sentiment was there.

"Elina, get over here," he drawled. Kilian was spread

301

lazily over his bed, the sheets crumpled and creased beneath him as he rolled around with a bottle of vodka. He was well and truly wasted; so wasted, in fact, that he wasn't even aware that it was barely noon.

"Your Royal Highness, you have guests waiting for you in the throne room!" Elina exclaimed in horror when she dutifully rushed into Kilian's chambers.

"I told you not to call me that," he slurred.

"And yet I shall, because I have to," she replied, green eyes set with determination as she watched over the sprawling figure of the man who ruled her country, drunk out of his mind.

"But I am regent, and I told you not to. Dare you defy me?"

"Even so..."

Kilian knew she was being careful, and why; the fate of her entire town rested on her shoulders. He found it highly amusing that, in turn, what happened to Alder rested in *his* palms and that, if he failed to do anything to help them, it would be Elina who suffered for it. Elina, who hated the town that ignored her. Elina, who was trying to help them anyway.

He was determined to find out exactly *why* she was doing this.

It can't only be because of her mother, he opined. *She said her mother was sick, but so what? People get sick all the time. And it's not like I didn't offer to let them both stay in the castle. If her mother's health was all that mattered then Elina would have taken me up on that.*

"You really have to be in the throne room," Elina murmured, looking away when Kilian slid his hands beneath the waistband of his leggings to pull out the hem of his shirt. "Your guests have been waiting for a while,

302

and I highly doubt they'll be as patient as I was when I sought an audience with you."

Kilian barked out a laugh. "Probably not. And yet I won't see them, but I saw you."

"Your Royal Highness –"

"Stop calling me that."

"But you *are* a prince, and regent, whether you want to be or not!"

Kilian sat up and grabbed Elina's sleeve, dragging her towards him. "And what would you say if I told you I *don't* want to be in this position?" he asked, eyes glittering dangerously. Fear flitted across her face for but half a second as she gulped, and then it was gone.

"I'd say that you not wanting to be king is hardly a revelation. That much is obvious."

"You dare say that to my face but refuse to do away with my title? You make no sense, Elina."

She pulled her sleeve out of Kilian's grasp. "Maybe not, but I do not have to explain myself to you, either way."

"Yes you do. I'm your king."

"...then act like one."

Elina uttered those words so quietly that Kilian, in his drunken haze, barely heard them. For some reason they stung, though he knew they were true. Outside the wind rattled the stone of the castle, threatening to break through the window. He considered for one wild moment to allow the weather to get even worse, simply to strand Elina here, with him.

Let me watch her worry over her stupid town and her stupid mother who thought herself talented enough to make me clothes, whilst I lie here getting so drunk she

303

does not know what to do with me.

For of course Kilian knew who Elina's mother was. Or, at least, he had finally remembered after sobering up the day after they'd made their deal. Though he'd been very young Kilian remembered the encounter acutely. That winter had been bitterly cold, after all; his mother wanted him and his brother Gabriel wrapped in the warmest fabrics. Kilian had not wanted clothes spun by simple-minded commoners, though in truth the clothes were finely made. He'd thrown them in the fire, much to the horror of his parents.

If he were sober Kilian might have exhibited an ounce of shame remembering such an act. It hadn't simply been unbecoming of him, even at three – it had been unfair. The clothes had been lovely. Going by Elina's dresses and cloaks, her mother had only grown more talented in her skill with a needle. Lily Brodeur and her father had merely sought to clothe him in fabrics warm enough to keep out the winter chill, as had Elina when she looked out the right clothes for Kilian to sleep in.

But even so, Kilian didn't care. They were only clothes, and the Brodeurs were mere commoners. They could do whatever they wanted – travel wherever they wanted – and yet they clung to the side of the stupid mountainside even as it threatened to kill them. It was beyond stupid.

And so he ignored Elina's comment to act more like a king because, at least for him, he had never been given a choice. Kilian had to be king even if he was terrible at it, so terrible he would be. Elina could literally choose to leave at any point.

But she didn't.

"See to my guests for me," he muttered, pulling a

cover over his head as he took a swig from his bottle of vodka like a hungry newborn babe with milk.

"I cannot do that!" Elina protested. "I will not!"

"You would disobey a direct order from me?"

There was a pause. "If this is how you mean to treat me then yes. This was a mistake. You can keep your stupid deal; I won't be back again."

Kilian fell out of bed before he could stop himself.

"No!" he exclaimed, much louder than he had expected to speak. Elina's face went blank though he could tell she was, in truth, surprised. "No," Kilian repeated, calmer this time. He sat back down on his bed. "You're right; how could you possibly know how to deal with foreign diplomats? Go home. But come back tomorrow. I'll deal with them myself."

It was a back-handed apology if it could be called an apology at all. But it seemed to work for Elina, though Kilian doubted the same tactic would have the same effect a second time.

"Fine," she said, not looking him in the eye. "I shall take my leave, then."

She didn't say goodbye. She didn't even look at him. When Elina exited Kilian's bedroom he was tempted once more to trap her in the castle; to cause the snow to pile up so high and the wind to bite so harshly that she couldn't possibly take a single foot outside.

He resisted.

Instead, Kilian forced himself out of bed and into slightly more regal clothes, smoothed back his hair and left for the throne room.

I hate diplomats, he thought, sincerely wishing he was back in his room drinking himself unconscious.

CHAPTER SEVEN

Elina

Elina hated Kilian's castle. It was cold and dark and empty and...lonely.

Very, very lonely.

She had thought her life in Alder was isolated; it was nothing compared to what the king's life must be like living in such cavernous halls all alone.

"He did that to himself," Elina muttered as she ran Kilian a bath. She'd been working for the man for close to a week now. He was yet to send any supplies or provisions to Alder, so the town was still dutifully ignoring Elina. For all they knew she had completely failed at her task and was simply hiding every day to avoid their scorn and judgement.

She hated it. Kilian had her work every menial task he could think of – which largely involved making fires, fetching him more alcohol and, on occasion, preparing and bringing him food. Most of the time he simply wanted to keep her near to insult people or complain to her about nothing in particular. Elina largely suspected that all he wanted was to hear the sound of his own voice – that it ultimately didn't matter who he was speaking to.

It still shocked her somewhat that Kilian had actually spoken to the diplomats who had sought an audience with him a few days prior. One of the remaining servants had informed Elina of this fact the following day, though what she was supposed to do with this information she had no clue. She knew the diplomats were from the country waging war against them – the people Kilian's older brother, Gabriel, was fighting.

What can I do about that? she wondered as she added the final bowl of water to the bath. *What did that servant hope to achieve from me knowing that Kilian* actually *did his job? Were they suggesting that it was now my job to ensure he always did his?*

That was something Elina didn't want to be in charge of at all, especially considering how much else she was currently responsible for. Still, with the remedies Scarlett and Adrian had given her at least she didn't have to worry so much about her mother's health; she finally seemed able to sleep and the feverish chills that had plagued her for weeks had abated. For that Elina was eternally grateful, and was determined to sit down with the mysterious pair to tell them everything they needed to know about Alder and its people.

You smell of magic.

Elina couldn't get Adrian Wolfe's words out of her head. She was dying to know what they meant – and how Adrian had sensed magic from her in the first place. She could only conclude that he really *was* a magician. It was exciting, given that Elina had never met a magician before despite her 'father' being one.

But the thought was driven out of her head for her when Kilian entered his chambers, drunk as usual. Elina suppressed a heavy eye roll when the man tumbled onto the bed with an exhausted sigh, as if his day had been long and hard instead of short and full of nothing.

It was then that Elina remembered the bath salts she had so foolishly asked Scarlett for, so she retrieved them from the bag she'd brought with her and dumped a load of them unceremoniously into the bathtub. They clouded the water immediately, foaming around the edges of the tub whilst emitting a pleasantly foreign, spicy scent; Elina relished the smell as she breathed it in.

Kilian coughed. "What have you put in my bath, woman?" he demanded as he stumbled over to investigate, eyes bleary, red and slightly unfocused.

"Bath salts," she explained. "They're good for your skin."

"They make the water look filthy," he replied, surveying the steaming bath with distaste.

"Why would I make my life that much harder by trying to coax you into a dirty bath? I'd only have to run you a new one afterwards if that were the case."

Kilian didn't seem to like Elina's infallible logic, but his near-constant desire to be warmer than he currently was overrode that dislike. With another grimace at the bath he pulled his shirt up and over his head before

309

removing his boots and leggings, not bothering to turn from Elina as he undressed. She knew he did this because it embarrassed her, which only made her hatred for Kilian grow.

He did not respect her, not even in her capacity as a servant. She doubted he respected anyone at all.

But she *could* do something about Kilian's nakedness, at least whilst he was in the bath – namely covering him up with cloudy, steaming, exotically spiced water. And he didn't seem to have worked out her ulterior motives yet, which Elina was relieved about. She was fairly certain that if Kilian were aware of her intentions he would parade about naked in front of her just to make a point, no matter how cold he might be.

When he slid beneath the murky water's surface she bit back a noise of relief. It set Elina on edge to have the prince regent of her country stand in front of her in all his naked vulnerability, no matter how useless a ruler he was. She didn't want the implied responsibility of protecting him, after all. If someone were to come into Kilian's chambers looking to harm him, would he expect Elina to stand between him and his foe? She hoped not...for she certainly wouldn't do it.

"Comb my hair again, Elina," Kilian sighed, clearly already very content in his bath. So she retrieved his comb and the chair she'd sat on before and moved over to the bath and, without thinking, dunked the man's head beneath the water. She realised too late that she absolutely shouldn't have.

When Kilian broke the water's surface he was sputtering in indignation. "What on earth was that for?!"

Elina knew if she showed any weakness then he would take advantage of it. "You need to wash your hair," she

310

explained simply. "And now it'll smell nice when it dries."

"Who cares if it smells nice?" Kilian muttered, though he settled into the bath once more and arched his neck back for Elina to comb his now soaking hair nonetheless.

As compensation for dunking his head underwater – which, now that she'd gotten away it, Elina could admit to having enjoyed immensely – she was particularly gentle with combing Kilian's hair. She worked through it with her fingers as much as the teeth of the ivory comb, rubbing her fingertips against his scalp to ensure no undissolved bath salts remained.

When Kilian emitted a low groan from the back of his throat, she paused. He flashed her a drunken, warning glare.

"Don't stop that," he ordered. "I like it. Keep going."

Elina put down the comb and gingerly placed her fingertips back on Kilian's scalp. She didn't *want* to massage his head. She didn't want to do anything that would make him happy, even though making him happy would undoubtedly help Alder. But that didn't stop her hating the man...and she knew she was good at head massages. Her grandmother taught her, whom people used to pay to have massage their heads and shoulders.

She knew she had to swallow her pride. Being contrary for the sake of it would get her nowhere except out in the cold with no food to survive the winter. So Elina got to work, slowly and softly moving her fingertips in small circles whilst gradually increasing their pressure against Kilian's scalp. He closed his eyes, leaning his head back just a little more as if urging Elina's fingers to come closer.

Outside the window all was still, which unsettled Elina. Not being able to hear the wind rattle the window frame or hailstones pounding the glass made her think that the

311

eye of a storm must surely have hit, and that things were only going to get worse on her miserable walk back home.

Without thinking her fingers moved to Kilian's ears, sliding along their edge and down to his earlobes, which she rubbed between her fingertips before moving further down Kilian's neck and –

She stopped. Hands frozen in place on either side of Kilian's head, Elina wondered what had possessed her to travel further along his body than his ears. When Kilian opened his eyes and looked up at her they were hazy – no doubt from the alcohol, but Elina thought it might mean something else.

"I didn't tell you to stop, Elina," he murmured. Elina watched his lips as he spoke, which were wet from the bath. Her face grew red, though the heat from the fire did a good job of explaining that away. "Keep doing whatever you were doing."

With a small frown of uncertainty she crept her hands back up his head; Kilian responded by reaching up and covering her hands with his own, much larger ones. He pulled them down to his neck without saying a word.

Kilian didn't close his eyes this time. He kept them locked on Elina's face as she reluctantly worked out an inordinate amount of tension from his neck, moving onto his shoulders when he finally took his hands away from hers. But when she saw where his hands were going, even though the murky water obscured her from actually seeing anything, she recoiled away.

"I'm not – I'm not touching you for you to – to touch yourself!" she bit out, mortified.

Kilian's eyes flashed. "And why not? I'm the king. I can order you to do what I like."

Elina considered her next words very carefully. She

took a deep breath. "Please do not ask me to do such a thing. I don't want to be part of your...bedroom activities."

He chuckled at the remark, though there was a hardness to his expression that indicated he did not much like this turn of events. "Very well," he said, still smiling, "you may go for the evening, since I clearly have some *bedroom activities* to attend to."

Elina could do nothing but stare at him, until Kilian's genial expression broke and he indicated towards the door with his head.

"Get out. You need not come to the castle tomorrow."

When Elina stepped outside the wind had picked back up again with a renewed ferocity; her face was pelted with hailstones which very quickly robbed her of the heat in her cheeks.

She had walked out of one kind of storm and into a new one. She didn't know which one was worse.

CHAPTER EIGHT

Kilian

"Get out, get out," Kilian repeated, over and over again to his empty bedroom for nobody to hear but himself. He didn't understand: why had he reacted so physically to a *head massage?* Elina certainly hadn't intended it to be erotic in nature. He should know – he'd hired many a girl to perform exactly that kind of massage...only, they didn't stop at his shoulders.

It occurred to Kilian that he hadn't arranged for a woman to be brought to him since the day he'd decided Elina should be his servant. Clearly the tailor girl had unnecessarily distracted him. But he now had an insatiable thirst that needed quenched, so he barked out for a servant until one arrived.

They stared at him nervously; he didn't often let anyone into his chambers when he was bathing. "Bring a woman to the castle," he said. "Any young, pretty one will do." For a moment he thought about requesting she have brown hair, green eyes and sun-kissed skin, only to remember that likely the only girl in his entire country that fit that description was Elina.

The servant's eyes darted to the window. "Your Royal Highness, in such weather it might be –"

"Are you suggesting you cannot fulfil my orders?"

"Absolutely not! I – I shall see to it right away, sire."

The servant quickly retreated, leaving Kilian to his bath and his taut, frustrated body. Even *he* had to admit that he was getting too hot in the scalding water, though perhaps it was the scent of the bath salts that was getting to him and making him feel drowsy. Kilian wasn't sure what the steam smelled of exactly, other than the fact it was clearly exotic.

I wonder if Elina knows what the scent is, he thought as he hauled himself out of the bath, choosing to sit in front of the roaring fire to dry off instead of using a towel. An open bottle of wine that quite possibly had spoiled sat by the hearth; Kilian grabbed it and began eagerly swallowing the red liquid inside.

By the time a woman finally arrived at his door he had moved onto another bottle of wine, though Kilian had already been drunk before starting the first one. Now he was truly wasted.

The woman was young and pretty enough – all buttery hair, blue eyes and lithe limbs – but for some reason Kilian couldn't stand the sight of her, especially when she smiled. "Your Royal Highness," she began, "it pleases me to serve you –"

"Get out," he said, echoing the words he'd said to Elina. He turned away from the woman to stare at the fire, thinking of the way Elina's hair almost seemed to become alight when she was near it. It was annoyingly captivating.

"Your Royal Highness?" the woman asked uncertainly.

"I didn't stutter. Get out. I can't stand the sight of you."

She left without another word, leaving Kilian to sit, naked, in front of the fire, wondering what on earth he was doing to himself. His frustration would only grow if he left it unchecked. The tumultuous weather outside would get worse, too, though considering it remained terrible due to his constant bad mood Kilian did not care much for this point.

After a few moments he called back the servant he'd barked orders at before. "Arrange for grain, alcohol, cloth and firewood to be sent to Alder from the stores," he demanded.

"Now...?"

"In the morning, obviously!" Kilian exclaimed, beyond irritated with the servant's lack of common sense. "There's no point in having what's left of the castle's staff breaking their necks on the ice because it's pitch black outside, is there?"

"No...I'll see it done."

I should have just fucked the prostitute, Kilian thought grimly once the nervous servant once more left his room. But he knew that he wouldn't have been able to, even if the woman had spread herself out on his bed, wanton and lovely.

Kilian couldn't believe he had actually found a limit to his hedonistic, self-serving ways.

As with all limits imposed on him, he hated it.

CHAPTER NINE

Elina

"Elina, you don't have to work in the shop on your day off! You must be so tired."

Elina rubbed at her eyes before giving her mother an, admittedly sleepy, smile. "I'm fine, mama. The fact you've had to work in here all by yourself whilst I've been at the castle means *you* must be tired. And you're still sick!"

Her mother laughed lightly as she carefully folded a thick, lustrous wool blanket and wrapped it in paper. "I've been much better since you started giving me those medicines from Miss Duke and Mister Wolfe."

"I still can't believe how effective everything they gave me was, to be honest."

"I suppose that's what happens when you can explore the world and pick up remedies from exotic countries. It makes sense that they'd have access to far more potent medicines."

Elina watched her mother shrewdly as Lily sat down. She'd been mentioning moving away from Alder and travelling more and more frequently with every passing day. Before, when she'd talked to Elina about seeing the world, it had been framed as an old dream – something she knew she'd never truly get to experience. But now...

I think she might really want to leave. And if she does, and she truly is well enough to travel, then...that might just be the best thing to ever happen to us.

For of course Elina wished to leave Alder. The only thing keeping her there was her mother and the family business. If Lily Brodeur herself was finally serious about packing up and leaving then Elina would gladly follow. Briefly she thought of her father and if he was still alive. Was it so improbable to believe that they might find the magician that had changed Lily's and, in turn, Elina's life?

Outside the shop door the ever-present sounds of blasting winds and freezing snow were engulfed by another sound entirely. Elina and her mother cocked their heads to one side in almost identical fashion, listening intently.

She glanced at her mother. "What's going on out there? It sounds like half the town are shouting." When the door to the shop was thrown open the two of them winced away from the bitter cold. "Close the door!" Elina exclaimed before she even worked out who had entered in the first place.

"Ah, my apologies Miss Brodeur!" Daven – the

319

woodcutter – said as he struggled to close the door against the wind. Something about his tone took Elina aback. It was...genuinely conciliatory.

Lily smiled widely at Daven as he brushed snow off his clothes and walked towards the counter. "Daven Arner. I haven't seen you in here since your mother passed. How is the family doing?"

He flashed a glance at Elina before replying, "Struggling through the winter just like everyone else, ma'am. But now it seems that's all changed for the better."

"Oh?"

Daven looked at Elina once more, this time with an incredulous grin splitting his handsome face. He had never looked at her that way, not even when they were children.

"The king has sent through supplies for the town. And – what's more – it's double what we needed, and his servant said we'll be getting more in a few weeks! Elina – Miss Brodeur – how on earth did you do it?"

Elina stared at him gawkily. "What do you mean how did I do it?"

"Oh come now, Elina!" he exclaimed, having now completely changed to addressing her informally. "Everyone knew it was a fool's errand to ask Kilian Hale for anything. But you managed to get him to send *more* than we asked for? Did you...was there magic involved?"

She rolled her eyes before she could stop herself; from her chair her mother giggled. "Mr Arner, have you ever really thought me capable of magic? If you or anybody in the town thought that then people would fear and respect me rather than ignore me."

Daven had the sense to look uncomfortable and apologetic. What surprised Elina was that the expression

320

actually looked genuine. He ran a hand through his snow-soaked hair and looked away.

"Yes, well...I guess that's true. And it's - it's not fair that the people who ignored you were the ones who pushed you to help them."

Elina cocked an eyebrow and crossed her arms. "I seem to recall said person who pushed me into helping the town was *you*. 'Pretty enough' indeed."

Her mother burst out laughing when Daven's face turned beet red. She stood up from her chair. "Elina, if you need me I'll be in the back room starting on that jacket for Frederick."

"Mama -" Elina began, sincerely wishing not to be left alone with Daven, but her mother was already gone. She glared at Daven. "You can stop with the false gratitude now that my mother isn't around."

Daven looked ashamed. "I'm not - it isn't false gratitude. Elina, everyone is barely coping with the harsh weather. It's only because of *you* that we might pull through. I know there will always be people in Alder who won't respect or appreciate what you've done by virtue of you being, well, you, but I'm not one of them."

Shifting behind the counter and rearranging papers and ink in lieu of responding to the man, Elina was surprised when he placed his hands on top of said counter and leaned in closer to her.

"Mr Arner, what are you -"

"You didn't...you didn't go to bed with him, did you?" Daven murmured so quickly that it was clear he'd been mulling over the question for a long time.

Elina resisted the urge to slap him. "That was what everyone wanted me to do, was it not? That's what Frederick was *insinuating* at the town meeting. Does it

321

matter how I got the prince regent to send supplies to Alder?"

Daven looked torn. "No, I - I suppose not, but... Elina, I'm sorry. I should never have suggested you. I didn't even *want* you to do it. Not if you -"

"I didn't go to bed with Kilian Hale," Elina said flatly, brushing past Daven on her way to dust some shelves that definitely didn't need dusting. But he grabbed onto her wrist, preventing her from moving away.

"Mr -"

"You really didn't? He didn't touch you?"

Elina didn't know whether to be outraged or mortified; she settled for somewhere in the middle. "No," she said emphatically. "I don't know nor care what you think of me, nor anyone else in the town for that matter. But I care what I think about myself. And when it comes down to it, why should I bed the king for the benefit of a town that does not want me?"

"I want you."

"You - what?"

"I want you," Daven repeated, eyes bright and keen. "I always have, but I wasn't allowed. But my mother is dead, leaving me the head of my family. Nobody can tell me what I can or cannot want, now."

"The entire town would judge you."

"For what? Falling for the magician's girl who saved Alder? I think, once this winter passes, nobody will ever dare snub you, Elina."

Despite herself Elina lit up at the thought, even though she'd been relishing getting as far from the town as possible mere minutes ago. With a flick of her wrist she freed herself from Daven's grasp. "So, what you're saying is that you're only interested in me now that there's no risk to your reputation?"

"I –" Daven paused, shaking his blonde head as he laughed softly. "I guess it looks that way. But it's not really...it's not like that." He looked back up at her. "Let me take you for a drink some time. Or dinner. Let the two of us get to know one another and you can decide for yourself if my interest is superficial."

Elina clucked her tongue. "Considering how different I look from everyone in Alder I would never assume that you were even superficially interested in me."

"Elina, are you serious?" Daven stared at her as if he couldn't believe what he was hearing. "You're beautiful. And everyone knows it. It's part of the reason they hate you so."

She hadn't considered this angle before. "Why would anyone consider me beautiful when I don't conform to their standards of beauty?"

"Because pretty is pretty no matter whose *standards* you use."

Elina blushed despite herself. Aside from kind words from her grandparents and her mother she'd never received a compliment before – unless she counted the way Kilian looked at her hungrily and tried to touch himself when –

Do not think of Kilian Hale! she scolded herself. The last thing Kilian had intended to do was pay her a compliment when he acted the way he did. He merely viewed Elina as a plaything. Even sending the town supplies was all part of one big game he was playing with her to abate his boredom. But even so...

"I do not have much time these days for socialising, Mr Arner," Elina finally said, very carefully.

Daven's eyes grew wide. "That wasn't a no, was it? And call me Daven."

She smiled very slightly. "Not a no...Daven. But I work up at the castle most days, then help my mother out when I come back to Alder."

"You work in the castle?"

"As personal, tortured servant to the king," she said wryly. "That's how I got him to send supplies to Alder."

A flash of something Elina would, fifteen minutes ago, have never identified as jealousy crossed Daven's pale face. "You...don't need to do that for our sakes."

"Yes I do. Otherwise we'd die. I can put up with some abject humiliation for a winter – I've been doing it all my life, after all."

Daven didn't seem to know how to react to that. But then he grinned. "I go through the woods every morning looking for trees that may have been felled in the wind. Perhaps we might walk to the castle together some mornings and keep each other company?"

To Elina's surprise she actually liked the idea. Having someone to talk to that wasn't Kilian sounded like a dream. "I think I could agree to that."

"Wonderful," Daven said, still grinning. "I could pick you up from here tomorrow, then? What time must you leave?"

She grimaced. "Well before sunrise."

"Good thing I'm an early riser. I'll see you in the morning, Elina."

And with that he was gone, leaving Elina wondering what on earth had happened to her. In the space of fifteen minutes she'd been apologised to for having been ignored, thanked for everything she was doing for Alder, and confessed to for having been a man's object of desire for quite some time. She'd even agreed to something that could almost be considered courting.

All because of the whims of Kilian Hale. Elina still couldn't quite believe he'd stuck to his end of their deal.

"I have to thank him," she muttered darkly, knowing in her very soul that it was the last thing she wanted to do. But she barely had any time to mull over such an unappealing task when the door to the Brodeur shop opened once more, letting in, of all people, Adrian Wolfe.

He flashed a brilliant smile at her. "Elina Brodeur. I believe there should be a package for me."

Elina stared at him for a second too long before fumbling around the back of the counter until she located the blanket her mother had been wrapping in paper. She hadn't realised it was for Adrian but there, written on the paper, was his name. She passed it over to him demurely.

"Thank you," he said. "The tavern's rooms are awfully cold. I had it on good authority that your mother's shop was the best place for warm fabric."

She smiled at that, feeling her cheeks flush with pride. "It is, Mister Wolfe. That blanket is made of the softest, warmest wool you could find north of the equator."

Adrian considered her with interest. "Your mother told me and Scarlett about your father, when we came in to order the blanket. So he was a foreign magician?"

Elina shrugged. "That's what my mother says, and the whole town too. I'm assuming it's why you could *smell* magic on me in the tavern."

To her surprise Adrian shook his head. "No, that doesn't explain it. The magic on you is...stronger. Constant. As if you're in contact with it all the time."

Unbidden she thought of Kilian and his empty, foreboding castle. Working up there was the only change to her life that might explain Adrian's observation, after all. But she had no proof and, even if the prince regent *was* responsible for whatever magic was clinging to her, what could Elina even do about it?

She sighed. "I guess it's a mystery, Mister Wolfe."

"Adrian," he smiled. "Just call me Adrian."

"What is it with men and demanding to be called by their first names?" she said, thinking of Daven and, of course, Kilian, whom she was yet to address in any way he actually desired.

"Because names have significance, Elina, and it's only natural when you like someone that you want them to address you in a more familiar fashion. Otherwise you may as well be strangers." Adrian gave her a wolfish grin as he made for the door. "Don't forget to stop by the tavern soon to talk with me and Scarlett – she's extremely bored."

And then Adrian wrenched open the door and was swallowed by the snow, dark cloak swirling round his ankles making him look very much the image of a mysterious magician, just like Elina used to imagine her father must have looked.

CHAPTER TEN

Kilian

"Who is that man walking out of the forest with Elina?" Kilian asked the servant who was lighting the fire in his room. Though that was usually Elina's job and, indeed, the morning sky was still dark, Kilian had barely slept. He'd called the servant out of their bed to warm up his chambers and bring him wine, despite the ungodly hour. He knew why he hadn't slept, though he didn't want to confront the issue.

Kilian was supposed to have heard back from his brother by now. Gabriel and his army had to be well on course for returning from the country's borders, especially after Kilian had spoken to those diplomats. In a mere few days Gabriel was supposed to - finally - take over the throne from his younger brother.

And yet Kilian had heard nothing, and it only caused his mood to grow fouler. Watching Elina huddle next to some unknown man from Alder against the snow as she made her way to the castle didn't help.

The servant timidly approached the window to glance downward. She frowned slightly and then, with a nod of understanding, explained, "That's the woodcutter, Daven. He keeps the forest in check for the castle and builds houses in Alder."

"I thought nobody in Alder spoke to Elina..."

"Sire...?"

He waved the woman away. "You may go. What's your name?"

The servant seemed mightily surprised by this. She gulped slightly. "M-Marielle, Your Royal Highness."

"Go back to bed, Marielle. Take the morning off."

Knowing not to question this rare kindness, Marielle scurried off before Kilian could change his mind. In truth he didn't know why he'd granted her the time off. There had been something about the way she looked when she'd been hauled out of bed - like she wanted to complain about the indignity of it all but knew she couldn't - that reminded Kilian of the woman currently smiling at the woodcutter outside.

I'm growing soft, he thought, shivering inside his overcoat as he moved to his favourite spot by the fireplace and opened a bottle of wine. He didn't actually know what he'd say to Elina once she reached his chambers, considering how she'd left two days prior. But Kilian would be damned if he was going to let her know her rejection had any effect on him whatsoever.

"Your Royal Highness," Elina said after she knocked upon the door and entered. She was still smiling like she had done outside, with the woodcutter. Kilian hated how much it made her face glow.

"I'm assuming Alder received everything I sent over," he murmured, not bothering to correct Elina for, once more, referring to him by his title. "Going by your expression, I mean."

To his surprise she bowed slightly. "Thank you. It's more appreciated than you could possibly know, I'd wager."

"You'd wager?"

"Yes, because you don't care."

Kilian snorted into his wine despite himself. He waved her over. "Sit down and drink with me."

"The sun hasn't even risen, Your Royal Highness."

"And considering the weather you wouldn't be able to tell if it had, anyway," he countered, gesturing towards the swirling snow dancing behind the window. "So drink with me."

Elina grimaced but, knowing she couldn't refuse, took off her cloak and placed it close to the fire to dry off. She was wearing the blue dress she'd worn when she'd originally come to beg for supplies for her stupid town – the one Kilian had first imagined removing before he'd known anything about her.

He only wanted to remove it more now that he did.

"You wear a lot of blue for someone with green eyes," he said as Elina sat as far away from Kilian on the floor as she could whilst still remaining within the fire's circle of warmth. The distance didn't go unnoticed.

329

She stared at him with those very eyes, expression unamused as she took the bottle of wine Kilian passed her. "I wasn't aware I was supposed to dress to match my eyes."

"That's what most women do here."

"Yes, and their eyes are blue and the clothes are blue. What a wonderful coincidence."

"Your mother runs a tailor shop. Can you not simply make your own –"

"Are you telling me you want me to wear green, Kilian?" Elina interrupted testily.

"You just said my name."

It took a few moments for Elina to realise what she'd done and then, when she did, she gulped down slightly more wine than she could handle. Spluttering and coughing, she barely managed to ask, "Do you like me, *Your Royal Highness,* or am I mere distraction?"

He shrugged, laughing as he snatched the wine back from Elina. "Both, I suppose. Does it matter?"

"It clearly doesn't matter for you, so I guess it shouldn't for me."

Elina almost seemed to sigh as she stared into the fire, the flames reflecting off her almost-black irises like a mirror. The wine had stained her lips a deep red; before Kilian could find it in him to stop himself from doing so he was staring at them.

"I'd like to see you in green, to answer your question," he said, still not tearing his eyes away from the gentle curves of Elina's lips as she softly blew a strand of hair away from her face. "Or bronze, to match your hair, and gold, to match your skin. Anything but blues and whites and greys."

330

When Elina finally looked at Kilian again he tore his eyes away from her. "This is coming from the man who barely manages to pull on a shirt and trousers every day, and a threadbare coat that should have been replaced years ago." She pulled at a loose thread from his sleeve to prove her point; he merely laughed at the painfully true observation. When Kilian handed over the wine once more their fingers brushed against each other.

Neither of them did anything about it.

After an hour or two Elina murmured, "It's very warm sitting so close to the fire." Kilian wasn't sure how time had passed so quickly and so easily, though the only suggestion that it had passed at all was a lightening of the white sky. There was a slight sheen on Elina's forehead – evidence that she was indeed too warm – that made her skin seem more golden and lovely that it had been before.

"So take off your clothes," Kilian joked, not expecting Elina to follow his suggestion in a thousand years. It was to his surprise, therefore, that she slowly unlaced her boots and pulled them off before sliding out of the woollen hose she wore beneath her dress. Elina's fingers then made quick work of the top portion of her dress, leaving her in a white undershirt tucked into her long, blue skirt.

"You're right," she sighed happily as she took another swig of wine, which was colouring her cheeks quicker than the fire was. "Taking off some clothes *does* feel better."

Kilian made no effort not to stare, almost wishing for the room to be cold so he could see Elina's nipples through the thin fabric of her shirt. It wouldn't take much for him to slide the sleeves down, either. All he'd have to do is reach out and –

"Your Royal Highness."

Kilian's eyes darted towards the door, the serious tone

331

with which the interruption had been made immediately distracting him from the tantalising sight of a half-undressed Elina.

He frowned. "What is it?"

"Word from your brother."

He got to his feet immediately, not bothering to fix his hair nor put on boots before crossing his room for the door. When he saw Elina begin to stand up he waved her down. "Stay here," he ordered. "Run me a bath or something." She clearly knew better than to protest, so she demurely sat back down.

It was only once the servant had brought Kilian to his father's old strategy room that he spoke again. "What says my brother?" he demanded of the messenger who was shivering by the large, oak table etched with a map of the country and its borders. If Kilian wasn't so desperate to hear what the man had to say he might have ordered the servant to light a fire in the empty hearth.

He didn't.

"Y-Your Royal Highness," the messenger said, bowing slightly. "I come bearing unfortunate news. Your brother and his army have been delayed on the southern border, and it will take weeks for them to return."

Kilian wished he still had a wine bottle in hand simply so he could smash it. Instead he spoke very quietly, though every word was teeming with fury. "He's delayed? Why? How?"

The messenger shook his head miserably. "He would not say."

"He wouldn't *say*? He wouldn't explain his actions to his brother – his acting king? Is that what you would have me believe?"

"All he wished to relay to you was that he needed more time!"

Kilian smashed a fist against the table. "I don't *have* time to give him!"

"Sire, there is little we can do about it from here," the servant interrupted. Kilian vaguely recalled that the man had escaped being kicked out of the castle because he was one of the only servants who actually told him the truth about the things he overheard whilst working. "It would be better to send someone down to the border – to listen out for why the army is delayed."

It was a sound plan. If Gabriel didn't want Kilian to know what he was doing, then he'd have to go around him to get an answer. So Kilian nodded, the muscles in his neck and jaw so tight that he thought they might snap.

"You go for me, then. Bring someone with you. Not him," he said, gesturing towards the messenger with a flick of his head. "You have four days."

"F-four days...?"

"Ride quickly. Take my horse. *Now.*" He looked at the messenger. "And you...go back to where you came from before you went to war."

Both men left immediately without another word. Kilian paced back and forth by the table, hand to his head as he forced his brain to think. But he couldn't think. He could barely see. All he could feel was anger and –

Helplessness.

I don't want to be here, he thought as he left the strategy room. *I want to leave.*

CHAPTER ELEVEN

Elina

Kilian was acting strangely when he finally returned to his chambers. Elina couldn't place quite what was wrong – he seemed on edge, which was strange because Kilian was never on edge. That was largely to do with the fact he was always drunk, of course, but here he was, on edge *and* drunk.

Perhaps I'd know what was bothering him if I wasn't drunk myself, Elina thought as she finished pouring water into the bathtub, as per Kilian's request before he'd left with his servant. She'd been drunk a handful of times in her life, though only with her mother and usually whilst playing card games or after completing particularly difficult embroidery. It felt different to be drinking with a man – especially a man she didn't like who was also her sovereign.

Elina at the very least identified that whatever was wrong with Kilian obviously had to do with his brother. *Maybe not to do with his brother and more to do with the throne,* she corrected, thinking about how little he wanted to be king. Elina had to wonder if he cared at all for his sibling, given his attitude towards everyone else.

Kilian didn't speak a word to her as he stalked back to the fireplace and sat down, a bottle of vodka in hand from which he'd already drunk a sizable quantity. Elina resisted the urge to comment on it. She badly wanted to know what news he had received about his brother and their country's army but, at the same time, Elina thought she'd rather remain ignorant. She didn't want to become any more involved in Kilian's life than she had to be.

"Your bath is ready," Elina said as she tucked away an errant lock of hair than had grown loose from her braided crown.

Kilian did not look at her. He merely stared into the fire with dispassionate eyes. It was a world away from the look on his face when he'd stared at Elina undressing.

Only partially, she thought, blushing for nobody to see. *I'm still mostly dressed.* But mostly dressed was still more undressed than she'd ever been in front of a man before, and having the skin of her arms and chest exposed was making Elina feel self-conscious. And yet she didn't cover up; the alcohol in her system and the heat from the fire urged her against it.

"Your Royal Highness?" she eventually said when Kilian still made no motion to move. When she'd accidentally uttered his name before, Elina realised she hadn't liked doing so at all. It made her feel too vulnerable. Kilian's official title was much safer.

If men want me to use their first names to encourage closeness then I'd prefer to avoid them to encourage distance, she thought, even as part of her longed for Kilian to look at her like he had done earlier. Perhaps it was because of Daven's now very obvious interest in her, sparking a desire in her to be watched and wanted, as stupid as she knew that to be.

"You –"

"I heard you the first time."

Elina was struck by how flat Kilian's voice was. Uncertainly she took a few steps towards him, her bare feet soft and silent on the large, luxurious rug that sat in front of the fire. The air was full of steam from the bath, spicy and heady and fragrant. She inhaled it deeply before speaking again.

"What news did you receive from your brother, if you don't mind me asking?"

It took Kilian a while to respond. He swigged from his vodka bottle several times; Elina saw that his hand was shaking. Looking even closer she saw the muscles of his neck were bunched and tight – far worse than they had been when she'd massaged them two days ago.

"Gabriel and the army are delayed in the south," Kilian finally said. "For weeks at least. He didn't deign to tell me why."

"That's – these things happen. It's war. I'm sure there's –"

"If there's a reasonable explanation then Gabriel would have seen fit to tell me. He simply doesn't want to return."

Elina frowned. "Why would that be the case? When he comes back he'll –"

"Be king. I know. That's why."

"He doesn't wish to be king?" she asked, torn between curiosity and a burning desire to simply leave the conversation before finding out any more.

"I don't know," Kilian said simply, swirling the contents of the bottle in his hands round and round even as he looked as if he sincerely wished to smash it.

Elina tried to feign a smile. "If you don't know then perhaps you should find out."

"Do you not think I know that already? Or do you believe me to be stupid?"

"I – no. I suppose I don't."

He glared at her. "You *suppose*?"

In her drunk boldness Elina decided to speak her mind. "It's hardly as if you've given me much evidence either way. Other than your obvious cruelty and general disrespect for your country I hardly know anything about you."

Kilian's eyes flashed as he stood up and rounded on Elina. She held her ground, though she desperately wanted to take a step back.

"I don't understand you, Elina. You say you hate Alder, and with good reason. You could leave at any moment – literally any given moment – and improve your circumstances elsewhere, and yet you don't."

Elina frowned. "What's your point?"

"I would *kill* to be in your position – to have that opportunity to simply up and leave with a puff of smoke like that magician father of yours."

"Then leave."

"I can't!"

"Then you're no different than me, who won't leave Alder!" she exclaimed. "You say you don't care about anyone but clearly, deep down, you must do. There's some sense of responsibility in you that knows you have to look after –"

Kilian grabbed her arms with such ferocity that Elina took a step back; he followed. "You weren't listening to me," he growled. "I. Can't. Leave."

For the first time since Elina met Kilian she had to admit she was frightened of him. His fingers on her arms were like steel, bruising her skin even as she stood there. Pale, tangled hair was wild around his face; his even paler eyes aflame whilst he breathed heavily and his overcoat slipped from his shoulders.

Kilian looked mad – downright insane – and it was in that very moment Elina realised he quite possibly always had been.

"What do you mean you can't?" she whispered, too afraid to raise her voice.

"It means exactly that," Kilian said, unblinking. "It means that my father, on his deathbed, knew that Gabriel had to go to war and that someone needed to sit on the throne whilst he was gone. It means that my father also knew his second son would never do it, because said second son would rather spend his days in a foreign whorehouse drinking wine until he died. It means that my father subsequently knew he had to tie that son to the throne."

Elina didn't say anything. She merely stood there, trapped by Kilian's vice-like grip, until he spoke again. He laughed bitterly. "Your father really did gift mine with

338

magic all those years ago, when the winter was so bad it would put this one to shame. To him the spell that was cast was a blessing; I always thought it a curse."

"'You can control the weather of your country,' your father said, "with your heart and soul you will control the weather. You will become your country and your country will be you.' I was only three and yet I remember it word for word. It was terrifying, you see. Gabriel would agree with me, if you were to ask him in private."

Kilian finally let go of Elina to pick up his forgotten bottle of vodka and took a long draught of it, then thrust it out towards her. "Drink," he demanded.

"I -"

"That was an order."

So Elina drank, wincing at the burn in her throat as she swallowed the liquid. She took a careful step or two away from Kilian for fear that he would grab her again, but he didn't. He ran his hands through his long, tangled hair until his face was clear of it. In the firelight he looked gaunt and hollow; his cheekbones too well-defined and his jawline too sharp. Elina wondered when he'd last eaten properly.

"There were conditions to your father's magic, as there always are with these things," he said quietly. He glanced at Elina as he brought a hand up in front of his face, counting down each condition on his fingers as he spoke them. "One: the king - my father - could not leave the castle. The spell was tied quite literally to who sat on the throne. Two: the weather was linked to the king's mood. If he was happy and gentle then the winds and sun and snow would reflect this. If he was...less so, the weather would be harsh and stormy." Kilian paused, taking a breath before continuing. "And three: the spell *must* be passed on to the blood relative who succeeds the throne."

Elina's brain was numb. She couldn't possibly take in all of this information, not least when she was drunk and terrified. "...why did your father agree to the spell?" she found herself asking, though she didn't know where she found the strength to speak.

Kilian rolled his eyes. "The man was a fool. He loved his country, and everyone in it. He happily agreed to such stupid terms. And my mother...she was already ill, so she couldn't leave the castle anyway. He thought giving up his freedom was a small price to pay to be a good king. And he was, of course." Kilian looked out of the window, where the wind was howling so loudly it was if it wanted to scream at him. "My father was a good king – even I can admit that. He was calm, trustworthy and quick to love. You know how short and mild our winters have been. That was his doing."

Even though it felt rather like approaching a starving bear or wolf or mountain cat, Elina took a few tentative steps towards Kilian. He didn't look at her. "So he... passed the spell to you?"

"Against my will," he muttered, staring at the floor. "In the dead of night, when I should have been asleep but was, in reality, too drunk to even be unconscious, he loomed over my bed and cursed me to stay."

"Your father...he died in September?"

Kilian nodded. "He cursed me in summer, though, before Gabriel left. Clearly he knew I planned to run off. But because he still sat on the throne until his death, I didn't inherit his *powers* until autumn."

"That would explain this god-awful winter," Elina muttered despite herself.

She regretted it immediately. Kilian whipped around

and grabbed her once more, pushing her backwards until her legs slammed against the bathtub.

"Is this a joke to you?!" he screamed right to her face. "Am *I* a joke to you?"

"No, I –"

"Because that's what it seems like. No, that's what it *is* like – with everyone. You think I don't know what people say about Kilian Hale, the king they never wanted? The king they hope disappears? The king they expect to fail, so god only hopes that his saintly brother Gabriel returns from the war soon, right?"

"I didn't say anything like that!" Elina protested, though of course she was guilty of having such thoughts on numerous occasions. But that had been *before* she knew why Kilian didn't simply do everyone a favour and leave. Of course things were different now she knew.

And yet the person standing in front of her was nevertheless frightful and intimidating. Elina tried to lean away as much as she could; Kilian responded by picking her up and throwing her into the steaming bath.

"See, even you shy away from me and you're my *servant!*" he seethed, hands curled around the edge of the tub as Elina spluttered and choked on murky, salty water.

When she finally regained her breath enough to meet Kilian's gaze there were tears in her eyes. "I am not your servant," she said. "I never have been."

"Of course you are! Why else would you be here?!"

"Because you blackmailed me!" Elina cried out. When she tried to get out of the bath Kilian reached out and stopped her from doing so with a heavy hand on her chest. She continued to struggle nonetheless, water soaking through every inch of fabric clinging to her skin. "You wouldn't have helped Alder if I hadn't –"

"You really think I'd have let the town die?! Do you honestly believe I could have looked out of my window and watch people literally starve to death when there's enough in the castle stores to help them through seven winters, Elina?"

"Then why did you force me to –"

"Because I was lonely!" Kilian didn't seem to be aware of what he was saying. His fingers curled around Elina's shirt; he bent down until his head was just above hers, eyes wild and and angry and so bitterly sad that Elina realised she'd been a fool not to see how Kilian had felt before.

"You – why didn't you simply ask me to keep you company, then?" Elina asked quietly.

Kilian choked on a laugh that sounded more like a sob. "And would you have said yes?"

"...no."

"Then you see my problem."

"Ask me again."

Kilian blinked. He narrowed his eyes. "What do you mean?"

"Ask me again to keep you company."

There was a pause. Kilian looked at her, and Elina looked at him, and their eyes gave absolutely nothing away to the other.

"You..." Kilian murmured, voice barely audible over the storm outside that was his very own doing. "Will you keep me company?"

Elina tilted her head up, snaking a hand behind Kilian's neck before she could stop herself. She pulled his lips to hers.

"Yes."

342

CHAPTER TWELVE

Kilian

How had the events of the day culminated in such a moment – Elina's dark, wine-stained lips willingly pressed to his? Kilian's mind went blank. For one, blind moment, there was nothing. His body wouldn't move. Wouldn't react. And then –

Kilian reciprocated Elina's kiss with a ferocity and passion he hadn't felt in a long, long time. He collapsed into the bath with her, not caring for the water he displaced to the floor, drenching the rugs and wooden boards in one fell splash.

He couldn't get close enough, nor could he get his

hands through Elina's hair – her braided crown was secured far too tightly to her scalp. So Kilian made do with straddling her lap, bending low to deepen their kiss until he leaned back with enough force to pull Elina on top of him in a wave of steaming bathwater.

Kilian closed his eyes to protect from the sting of the salt in the water; when he opened them a somewhat dazed and heavy-lidded Elina was pressed against him, hands still entwined in his hair as she finally pulled her lips away from his.

"What was that for?" Kilian asked, hating himself for even asking the question when the mood had suddenly – finally – become good enough for him to find himself in such a suggestive situation with Elina.

Elina didn't look away as she replied, "Because you were right. I thought you a joke. Everyone else still does. Now, knowing the truth and...actually *looking* at you properly, I..." She paused, as if deciding whether she should utter her next sentence. "You're pathetic, Kilian Hale, but for the first time in my life I now know that it's not *all* your fault."

Kilian stared at her, too stunned to speak. When he burst out laughing he surprised even himself, considering how dark and angry he'd been mere moments before. He slid a hand down Elina's back, fingering the waistband of her skirt until he found the buttons that would loosen it. Elina's eyes darted downward when he proceeded to remove the material, her face red from heat and alcohol and embarrassment.

"So you kissed me because I'm pathetic?" he murmured, finally pulling the length of Elina's skirt from her body and tossing the drenched material unceremoniously to the floor. Her white undershirt barely covered her body to her thighs; soaked through as it was it

344

hardly hid anything at all. "How pathetic do I need to be for those hands of yours to wander downward, Elina?"

He was gratified when the flush of her cheeks crawled across her ears and down her neck. "I - I never said I *kissed* you because you were pathetic. Only that you're pathetic in general."

"Oh? Then why, specifically, did you kiss me?" Kilian asked, placing his hands over Elina's to guide them down from his hair, across his chest and to his navel.

"I - because..." she hesitated. Her hands wrung the edge of Kilian's shirt nervously beneath the water's surface; he was aching for her to move them further down. "Truthfully, I'm not sure," Elina finally answered. "I don't even think I like you."

Kilian chuckled, urging Elina's lips back to his own for another kiss. He slid his tongue into her mouth, running it across the edge of her teeth before biting gently down onto her lower lip.

"It doesn't seem to matter whether you like me or not, going by the situation we're currently in."

"Kilian."

He paused abruptly at the sound of his name which he, aside from her having mistakenly uttered it earlier, hadn't heard spoken by another person since before his father died.

"What is it?"

Elina looked a little uncertain. Kilian's hands found her thighs, repositioning the woman on top of him until she was properly sitting on the aching pit of frustration that had left him hard after most every encounter with her over the past week. She cried out in surprise.

"What did you – ah – stop trying to pleasure yourself

345

when I'm speaking to you," she complained when Kilian rocked her against him; a low groan whistled between his teeth at the sensation.

"Do a better job of speaking, then," he replied, hands roaming up beneath Elina's shirt even as he fumbled to hold a coherent train of thought.

"You said you liked me earlier. But is that simply because you're lonely? Is it because there's no one else? Is – this – because there's no one else?"

To that, Kilian could only laugh. "Elina, I'm sure you remember what happened two nights ago. Considering you were sober and I was wasted, I imagine you remember it much better than I do, in fact."

She frowned. "What are you getting at?"

Kilian sighed when he moved Elina against him once more, hands on her waist inexorably climbing upwards even as Elina watched him do so nervously.

"I called for a prostitute to be brought to my chambers as soon as you left," he explained, so off-handedly that it took a moment for Elina to realise what he'd said. When she did she tried to recoil, but Kilian only pulled her closer against him. His lips found her collarbone, trailing kisses across her wet skin. Beneath his mouth Elina was trembling; Kilian only wanted her more as a result.

"When the woman arrived I couldn't stand to look at her," he continued, his words barely a mumble against Elina's chest. "All I could think of was you. I sent her away – I, Kilian Hale, sent a prostitute away. Unheard of. So to answer your question, Elina Brodeur..."

He glanced upwards at Elina, her eyes glittering and dark as she stared back at him. "I don't just like you because I'm lonely. Granted that's how I got to know you, but that's not why I like you. And it's certainly not why

346

I'm physically attracted to you – I've wanted to bed you from the moment I saw you. But you already knew that."

"You saw me as an object," she replied, turning her head away until Kilian used a hand to make her look at him once more. "Viewing me like that is different from being attracted to me for *me*."

"I guess that's true. Which leads me to ask: though you profess not to like me, are you nonetheless attracted to *me* for me? Or are you, in your own words, viewing me as an object right now?"

Kilian glanced very pointedly downward; the meaning was not lost on Elina.

"I don't – I've never viewed you as anything less than a person."

"Merely a pathetic one."

"I – yes. And a cruel one. And a lazy one."

"And yet here we are."

Kilian kissed her before Elina could construct a response, and this time her hands moved on their own. They ran beneath his shirt, fingers gliding over soaking, slippery skin without quite touching Kilian where he was dying for her to.

When his own hands finally crept over Elina's breasts he paused, and pulled his lips away slightly from hers. "Nobody has ever touched you like this before, have they?"

She shook her head. "Nobody."

"Have you ever imagined someone touching you like this?"

"I – no. There's no man in Alder I could imagine ever *wanting* to touch me."

347

Kilian found this deeply sad and frustrating. How could an entire town be so narrow-minded simply because a baby was born a bastard to a foreigner? He wondered how the people of Alder would react to the dark-skinned people Kilian had met on his travels across other continents. Not well, he imagined.

"They are all fools," he said with surety, for of course they were. Except the woodcutter, who was a threat for Kilian to consider when he was not half-naked in a bath with the woman he so desired.

Elina laughed softly. "I know they are."

"When you go to bed tonight, will you think of me touching you?"

"When I...go to bed?"

Kilian nodded and, though he hated himself and his body was screaming at him not to do it, gently moved Elina away from his lap. "You are drunk. As much as I want this to continue, if I'm to prove I actually respect you then...we can continue this sober."

Elina's eyes widened in disbelief. "You're *always* drunk, Kilian. I doubt you're even sober in your sleep."

"I can't argue with that," he chuckled, hands reaching out for Elina even as he tried to resist doing so. "But from tomorrow I will be. Though god knows if either of us will like who I am sober."

She quirked an eyebrow. "I don't even like you as you are now, remember?"

"It's very quiet outside."

Elina seemed taken aback by the sudden change in topic. She cocked her head to the side to listen, a motion so irresistible that Kilian reached for her beneath the water's surface despite himself.

"You're right," she said. "It's quiet outside. I assumed..."

"You assumed what?"

Elina blushed. "I assumed the weather would get rather wild if you were – you know –"

"If I was half-naked in a bathtub with a beautiful woman?"

She nodded whilst Kilian laughed. "It was certainly bad enough after you left the other night. And I'll admit to having seriously considered stranding you here by getting in as tempestuous a mood as possible."

"*Kilian!*"

"I do love it when you say my name. At least I didn't though. That ought to count for something."

The look on Elina's face suggested she didn't entirely agree with this.

Kilian relaxed his head against the bath, content to watch Elina sitting mostly naked on top of his legs. "I definitely want to fuck you right now," he said, so casually that Elina almost choked in shock. "But I'm...okay with knowing I won't. That I can wait until a better time. When my head doesn't feel...cloudy. I don't know. It feels nice, though a certain part of me doesn't agree with that."

Elina's hands grazed against that *certain part* as if to affirm what Kilian was saying. He was gratified to see her gulp somewhat. And then he sighed, shaking water from his hair as he finally pulled himself out of the bath.

"I really need to sober up fast," he mused, mostly to himself, shedding his sodden clothes and wrapping himself in a large robe before finding one for Elina.

"I think this is the most modesty you've ever demonstrated to me, *Your Royal Highness,*" she said

349

coyly, placing the robe over her shoulders before hurriedly sliding out of her shirt. Kilian deliberately turned away, not entirely trusting his self-control to see Elina truly naked.

"Very funny. You're welcome to stay in the castle, of course, since your clothes are soaking -"

"Are there any servant's clothes I can borrow?" Elina asked instead as she wrung out her skirt. Kilian couldn't help but feel disappointed. He'd half-hoped she would want to stay in bed with *him*.

"I - don't see why not."

She smiled. "Thank you. My mother will be worried if I don't come home."

Kilian glanced out of the window. "It's still early, you know. Barely past lunchtime."

"Then I can tell her you were so magnanimous as to allow me a half-day because the weather turned fair. It might go a long way in making me like you."

He caught Elina's wrist and pulled her in against him. "That's not fair," he said, lips grazing her jaw as he spoke. "You could hold something like that over me for the rest of my life."

"Would that really be so bad? To have an annoying, human, moral compass?"

"That sounds terrible. That's the worst idea I've ever heard."

When Elina brushed her lips against Kilian's he knew it was time to say good-bye. "I'll find some servant's clothes myself," she said, "and then I'll be on my way. Have fun sobering up, Kilian."

"I'm still inclined to set a storm upon you the moment you set foot outside!" he called out after her once she'd strode across the room and opened the door.

"I don't doubt that. But if you want me back tomorrow then you won't."

And so Kilian had no choice but to let her leave. Grimacing at the feeling of walking on a rug drenched in cold water, he located his half-empty bottle of vodka and smashed it into the fireplace.

Part of him regretted it immediately.

CHAPTER THIRTEEN

Elina

"Elina, wait up!"

Elina glanced over her shoulder to see Daven racing to catch up with her. She stopped and smiled, though inside she wanted to run off to be alone. She had so much to think about, after all.

Too much, possibly. And she was still drunk.

Daven eyed her curiously when he finally reached her side. "Elina, why is your hair so wet? And are you in different clothes than you were wearing this morning?" he asked when her cloak shifted enough for him to see beneath it.

"The regent – ah – had a bit of a tantrum in the bath," Elina explained, for the first time in her life feeling a twinge of guilt about bad-mouthing Kilian Hale. Though what she was saying wasn't a lie, so to speak. It simply wasn't the whole truth, either.

"He shouldn't be having you bathe him," Daven bristled. "Surely he must have other servants who can do that. This isn't fair on you."

Elina shrugged as they continued through the murky forest, which was eerie in its stillness. She hadn't realised just how accustomed to the stormy weather she'd gotten.

How much I've become used to Kilian's foul moods, more like, she thought, smiling slightly at the thought. Though what had happened to Kilian was horrific – tragic, even – knowing that *she* affected his mood to the point of influencing the weather was...satisfying. Or exciting. Or terrible. Elina thought her feelings on the matter were probably somewhere in the middle.

"Elina, are you okay?" Daven asked, abruptly bringing her back into the present.

She laughed softly. "I'm fine. More than fine, really. I'm glad to have a half-day. I can help my mother out for a while."

"Ah, might I be able to interest you in coming for a drink in Gill's tavern? I don't want to push you, just...you said you didn't have much time because of working at the castle, so..."

Maybe it was because of the alcohol still in her system, or Elina's desire to show off to the people of Alder that she'd managed to do exactly what they thought she couldn't, but she nodded her head. "I'd be happy to, Daven."

It rather seemed that Daven himself was the happy one upon hearing her response. He walked her straight to the front door of her mother's tailor shop and even then seemed reluctant to part. But eventually he did, with promises to see her in the tavern after dinner, and Elina entered the shop much to Lily's surprise.

"Elina!" she cried out. "I was not expecting you back so soon. Are you – have you been drinking? What happened to you?"

Elina could only laugh. Or course her mother could tell that she was drunk. "It's a...story for another time," she said, "when I know a little more about it myself. I'm going to change and fix my hair then I'll come back and help you out."

Her mother *tsked.* "You absolutely will not. Go to sleep and sober up. Heaven knows you could do with the sleep, anyway."

"Dutifully noted. And..." Elina glanced at the front door. "I may be going to the tavern tonight for a drink, if that's okay."

"Are you meeting Daven?"

Elina blushed. "How did you know?"

"Oh come now," her mother laughed. "I've always known the boy had his eye on you. Nice to see he finally plucked up the courage to talk to you."

"I – how did you know *that?* I never saw him looking at me!"

The look on Lily's face was entirely sympathetic as she surveyed her daughter. "Of course you didn't. He only looked when you couldn't see. *I* saw, though."

"Why didn't you say anything?"

"Would it have changed your circumstances in Alder

if you knew? We both know it wouldn't. I didn't want to hurt you more than I already have by telling you about people who wanted to get to know you but couldn't."

"I..." Elina reached her mother's side and held her hand. "You have never hurt me, mama."

"I have; you've merely lived with it every day of your life so you cannot see it. Things would be different for you if you were –"

"Don't you dare say 'if I was like everyone else'. I don't need that, mama. I like who I am, and if the rest of the town are only acknowledging me now that I've helped them when nobody else could then that's on them, not you or me."

It was only in saying it that Elina realised it was true. She'd always wanted to be part of the town before – to look like them and laugh with them. But now she knew better. There was a world outside of Alder, even if she'd never seen it, and the opinions of one town meant little and less in the grand scheme of things.

Especially when the 'grand scheme of things' involves curses and weather magic and trapping a king in a castle.

Because that was the truth of it; Elina's problems were tiny compared to Kilian's. They didn't even matter. No wonder he'd been so disinterested in her 'sob story', as he'd put it, when they'd first met. Because Elina *could* leave at any point, really; it was fear holding her back.

Kilian couldn't so much as step a foot outside of his castle.

"Elina? Do you feel ill? Did you drink too much?"

She blinked, then shook her head as she smiled. "No, mama. I just have...a lot to think about. I'll go and sleep."

"I am so proud of you. Keep working hard and then,

when winter is over, let's leave Alder for good."

Elina had never given her mother a proper answer when she'd talked about leaving before. This time, she did.

"Absolutely. Spring can't come quickly enough."

*

When Elina arrived in Gill's tavern she was decidedly sober and full of nerves. She'd considered letting her hair hang loose but, as expected, she was too much of a coward to do it, even though she had decided hours before that she didn't care about fitting into Alder anymore. So her hair remained braided around her head, and she wore an inoffensive, dove-grey dress that nevertheless stood out for how finely made it was. Elina had made it herself, in truth, though the town did not know how talented she was. They only bought products her mother made, after all.

"Elina, over here!" Daven called out when he spied her. Nervously she made her way through the throng of thirsty tavern-goers, painfully aware of everyone's eyes on her. When she sat down Daven immediately handed her a tankard of ale, though she'd never drank the stuff before.

"A toast to Prince Kilian for providing us with the alcohol we're drinking, and to Miss Brodeur for wrangling it out of him!" he announced. To Elina's surprise people *actually* cheered for this, even though it meant cheering for her.

And then she was bombarded by conversation after conversation – answering more questions and speaking to more people than she ever had in her life. To her right Daven sat proudly, which didn't seem to be disingenuous at all. He *was* proud of her.

She wondered how proud of her he'd be if he knew what she'd been up to that morning.

Don't think about Kilian, Elina thought. Now was not the time. When she was back in her bed, alone, she could think about him. But even that caused her to blush. *He was the one who told me to think about him in bed, though he definitely didn't mean for me to mull over his problems.*

But how could she not? Now that Elina's own, highly insignificant, problem seemed to have been solved, she wanted to help him. She wanted to free Kilian from his prison.

A lustrous wave of dark hair by the stairs alerted Elina to the fact that Scarlett had come down to the tavern floor. Adrian wasn't with her. When Elina caught her eye the woman smiled, but shook her head as an indication for Elina not to join her. It sent a shiver up Elina's spine; what was going on?

Should I tell Scarlett and Adrian about Kilian's curse?

Of course Elina wanted to – how else could she help him, after all? But it wasn't her secret to share. She didn't have the right to talk to other people about it. And yet even so...

"Elina, did your mother make your dress?" a young woman around Elina's age asked, bringing her back out of her head. "It's gorgeous!"

"It's soft as sin, too," Daven added on, stroking a finger up the sleeve as if touching Elina was the most natural thing in the world. Again, she thought of Kilian, and how it felt like electricity was running through her whenever he touched her. She had wanted to run away from getting shocked just as badly as she yearned for the feeling. Daven's touch wasn't like that. It felt familiar and safe, though in truth they'd only been speaking to each other for two days.

"I made it, actually," Elina said bashfully, to the sound of a dozen envious cries.

"You must make me one in blue!"

"I want one with flowers embroidered in the bodice for spring!"

"Can you make an overcoat this soft?"

The comment gave Elina an unexpected flash of inspiration. Though she couldn't hope to help Kilian with breaking his curse on her own, she *could* do something about him always being cold.

And she could start with the ragged, threadbare excuse for an overcoat he practically lived in.

CHAPTER FOURTEEN

Kilian

Kilian had never been so cold. Which was saying something, because he was almost always cold. But without alcohol in his system to fool his brain into thinking he was warm he couldn't stop shaking. His body was wracked with painful jerks and shivers that set his teeth on edge.

His head was killing him, too; he'd never had so painful and so constant a migraine before. He had no appetite and, when he *did* eat, it wasn't long before he simply threw the food back up. A fever had broken across his brow which, even when setting him on fire, altogether felt like he'd been plunged into a biting lake of ice water.

But Kilian was no idiot. He knew he deserved each and every inch of pain his body was currently experiencing. It was a just punishment for keeping himself inebriated for the past nine of his twenty-five pitiful years. His system literally did not know how to cope without any alcohol. Dully he thought about calling the doctor in to help him only to remember that he'd fired the man for so unfairly allowing his father to die.

I am a horrible person, he thought, brain rattling in his skull as he shivered beneath several blankets on his bed. *It's no wonder nothing's happened with Elina since she got drunk with me.*

This wasn't strictly the reason, of course. For the past few days Kilian had been so ill and barely-conscious that he'd pushed Elina to help the other servants in the castle instead of looking after him. But still. He'd hoped she'd insist on waiting on him every moment of every day anyway, rather than take him up on his offer to leave him alone.

For Kilian was miserable alone. And he'd always been alone, so he was always miserable. It was only in meeting Elina that he could even acknowledge this, however, since to admit to being lonely was pitiable.

Yet despite calling me pathetic Elina is still here.

Kilian was ashamed by his drunken admission of loneliness to her, especially since she'd had no trouble expressing the same feelings to him from the very beginning with regards to the people of Alder. He'd never felt so dishonest.

"Shut up, brain..." he mumbled, groaning as he twisted in bed. It didn't do well to think about the person he'd become after all these years. And it wasn't as if Kilian had

360

drastically changed in personality when he'd started drinking; he had always been an unpleasant person. Elina's mother, Lily, would be able to attest to that, from when she watched in horror as three-year-old Kilian burned the clothes she'd so carefully made for him.

He was a snob. He was bad-tempered. He had a superiority complex a mile high. He was impulsive and cowardly and cruel-tongued and –

"I want Elina."

The words were barely a puff of breath upon the air in his room. Though the fire was burning brightly, Kilian's chambers felt like ice. Or, rather, Kilian himself felt like he was made of ice, in a furnace that could never melt him.

He was so cold.

Kilian could only really tell what time of day it was by when he spied Elina arriving at the castle in the morning, since when he wasn't lying in bed he was collapsed by his window, watching the wind relieve the forest of snow only for more to replace it.

She was almost always accompanied by the woodcutter, Daven, though occasionally another person or two decided to join their morning walk even though the weather was horrific and the hour ungodly. The fact that it was always *men* talking to Elina only served to make Kilian's mood worse – was she so oblivious as to not understand what they were interested in? It was clear as day from where Kilian sat, watching, even through the snow.

But Elina seemed to be enjoying the company. He couldn't help but wonder if, now she had been accepted by her town, she was no longer interested in Kilian, no matter how reluctant that interest had been in the first place. He had to remind himself that he'd forced Elina to get drunk the day she kissed him and they ended up in the bath together. Even Kilian could see how her actions could be explained as being the result of coercion rather than being voluntary.

It only made him feel worse.

Even though it was definitely colder outside than in his room he longed to be down there, amongst the swirling snow. He'd always hated the castle grounds before – for no reason whatsoever other than Kilian hated everything – but now they were tantalising. He couldn't set foot in the gardens, or the courtyard, or the forest. He couldn't use the hot springs, the only part of the castle and its grounds he would ever profess to enjoying.

He couldn't show Elina around all the places he used to hide from his parents and brother, or the spot in the forest where he'd disappear to with a stolen bottle of wine even as young as thirteen. Kilian had never wanted to tell anyone about his childhood before. And, now that he did, Elina didn't seem to be interested enough to listen to him talk about it. Kilian didn't like how that made him feel at all.

Rolling around in bed to try and untangle himself from a blanket currently wound around his leg, Kilian yelped in surprise when he accidentally overshot the movement and ended up on the floor. When he bashed his head upon the wooden floorboards his vision went white, then black.

*

When he came to, Kilian was still lying on the floor exactly where he'd fallen, feeling even worse than he had felt before. His head felt like it was going to split open, but when he retched nothing came out. There was nothing left for him *to* throw up.

The room was almost dark; the fire had burned low and the sun – wherever it had been behind the clouds – had clearly long since set.

I can't believe I knocked myself out for hours by falling out of bed, Kilian thought, laughing bitterly. But the only audible sound that left his mouth was a garbled cry; fumbling in the darkness he reached for a metal pitcher of water that sat on a table by his bedside. When he poured the stinging, freezing liquid down his throat more of it escaped his mouth than was swallowed, leaving trails of ice water running down his neck.

He wished the water were vodka. Or wine. Or ale, which he hated. He couldn't stand the pain of merely existing anymore. And so Kilian staggered to his feet, clutching his well-worn overcoat around himself as he tried desperately to find any kind of alcohol whatsoever in his room. When no bottles became immediately apparent, he began pushing chairs over and knocking down tables, smashing ornaments and vases to the floor in his quest to find something that would numb his existence.

There was nothing.

All he had to do was call for a servant and Kilian would be handed over anything he so desired. But if he did that then he knew he'd truly failed, and he'd never be able to stop drinking until his sorry excuse for a life was well and truly spent.

Kilian sagged against the window. For there was his answer – he *couldn't* drink, even if he found some irresistible volume of alcohol hidden away in a corner of his room that he was yet to upturn. He had to endure the unendurable until he was no longer in pain.

"How long will that be?" Kilian sighed, voice weak and insubstantial as he shivered violently. He didn't even have the capacity to shout for a servant, much less Elina, and he was the one who'd told them all to leave him alone. Kilian's solitude was his own damn fault, and he knew it.

In a moment of madness he undid the latch on his window, hauling open the man-sized panes of glass until he could stand on the window ledge and feel the full force of the wind buffet his entire body. It should have been strong enough to drag Kilian off the ledge and down, down, down to his death.

But he could not leave the castle, so the wind did nothing to him.

He was ashamed when tears began to well up in his eyes. Kilian wasn't even sure he *wanted* to die. He was certainly too much of a coward to run a blade through his heart or slit his throat or swallow poison or even let himself freeze to death. But falling through the window into a storm of his own making...

There was something poetic and circular about it, like it was the way Kilian was supposed to die. Except that he couldn't. Maybe that was why he liked it; it was something he could never have.

"Oh my god – Kilian!"

Elina slammed into his back and wrapped her arms around his waist, dragging him away from the window ledge as far as she could. Kilian didn't even resist.

"What were you – why were you doing that?" she asked, voice hysterical as she continued to cling to him. Elina was warm and Kilian freezing; he relished the embrace.

"I wasn't doing anything," he said weakly, which was technically the truth.

"Don't lie to me! You think I can't work out what you were –"

364

"I can't leave the castle, Elina. If I was going to kill myself it wouldn't be by jumping out of the window."

"That...that sounds like you tried, to see if it was possible."

Kilian didn't respond, confirming Elina's suspicions. He didn't want to turn around and face her when he still had tears in his eyes. But he was shivering so badly, and he hardly felt able to support his own weight.

"Kilian, why did you – why would you tell me to work with the other servants when you're like this?" Elina asked quietly. With utmost care she took a step backwards and, when Kilian followed, another, and another, until they reached his bed. Then she let go of him, shaking out and rearranging the pile of blankets upon it before gently pushing Kilian on top of them.

"Get in there. Now. I'm going to get the fire going again and bring you food, and you're *going to eat it.*" In the darkness she couldn't see his tears or, if she could, Elina didn't acknowledge them.

He stared at her, helpless. "I can't keep anything down. I can't feel anything except the cold, even in my stomach. It hurts, Elina."

Her expression crumpled. "Then why would you tell me not to look after you? I could have helped you!"

"I..." Kilian looked away. "I wanted you to insist on looking after me yourself. I wanted it to be your choice."

"Are you an *idiot*?!" she yelled, stepping forward as if to slap him but tripping on a box Kilian had thrown to the floor instead. She cursed aloud. "What did you do to your room? Why are you like this? Why are you –"

"I don't know what to do with myself. I want to die."

"No you don't." Elina's eyes were shining in the

365

darkness, overly bright and, Kilian realised, just as teary as his own were. "You don't want to die. You're going through withdrawal. You're starving. You're freezing. But you've been struggling through it for days now – if you wanted to die you'd have done it already."

Kilian said nothing. He didn't know *what* to say. He was so tired of everything, but he knew he couldn't sleep.

Elina sighed. "Get in bed. I'll sort everything out. Just...try and get warm."

And so Kilian complied, crawling beneath the covers whilst watching Elina struggle to close the window, start up a new fire until it was roaring, then ask a servant to bring through some food. She didn't try to clean up properly, merely pushing away things on the floor into the corners so that she wouldn't trip.

When the servant brought through a bowl of soup and some bread they didn't question the mess of the king's chambers, nor the state of the man himself. They merely handed Elina the food and ran off.

She perched herself on the bed, glancing at Kilian from beneath her lashes. "Sit up, Kilian. You can't eat lying down."

"I already told you, I can't keep any food –"

"Sit. Up."

He wasn't used to being ordered around. For a moment he considered chastising Elina for having the audacity to do so. Instead, he complied. "Are you going to feed me?" he asked, some of his usual sarcastic way of speaking finally returning.

When Elina nodded seriously and immediately shoved a spoonful of soup into his mouth Kilian was too surprised to retort. "I'm not going to stop until you're done with the whole thing," she said, bringing another spoonful of soup

366

up for Kilian to drink as soon as he'd swallowed the first one.

Twenty minutes passed in this fashion, during which time the fire began to properly heat up the room. But Kilian was still so cold, and the pain in his head was yet to abate. When he winced in response to it, Elina brought out a small vial of powder from a pocket of her dress, pouring it into a cup of water before handing it to Kilian.

He stared at the cup dubiously. "What are you giving me?"

"Powdered willow bark. You should have been taking it for the pain already."

"I don't need something like that to –"

"I'm not going to listen to a man who drinks his pain away tell me he doesn't want to take medicine that will do the same thing."

This version of Elina was ruthless. But Kilian realised it was what he needed, so he swallowed down the water in one go.

Finally she smiled. "Good. Keep sitting until that hits you, then lie down and go to sleep."

"You're not – don't go, Elina."

Kilian hated how desperate he sounded.

Elina moved the now-empty tray of food onto the only table that Kilian hadn't upturned. "I won't," she said quietly. "The weather is too bad for me to leave, anyway. You *did* say you wanted to trap me here, before; I should have expected this."

"I didn't –"

"I know you can't help it," she cut in. "You're in pain. It's okay. I'll help you through it, so just focus on not being sick."

367

He laughed weakly. "Easy for you to say. You're not the one who feels like this."

"True; I merely have to be able to stomach looking after you like this."

"Please stop making cruel jokes; it hurts to laugh."

Elina's lips quirked at the comment. "Noted. Close your eyes, Kilian. Just try and relax."

It was easier said than done. Even when the willow bark took the pain away from his head and settled his stomach, finally allowing him to keep down food for the first time in days, he was still cold. Too cold. The shivering wouldn't stop. Kilian sank below the covers, wondering how he would ever sleep.

"Elina," he said some time later, keeping his eyes closed so he wouldn't see her reaction when she invariably rejected him.

"...yes?"

"Lie in bed with me. Keep me warm."

She was supposed to say no. Any sane person would have said no.

"Okay."

CHAPTER FIFTEEN

Elina

"Okay?"

"That's what I said."

In truth Elina was terrified. She had no idea why she'd agreed to such a proposal, not least when Kilian was in such a state. But perhaps it was *because* of that that she agreed to lying in bed with him. He looked wretched. Defenceless.

Alone.

Not for the first time she felt fury rising in her throat that Kilian had thought it prudent to tell her to leave him

369

alone for days. But she was angrier at herself, for listening to him. Elina had been so excited by the prospect of creating a new overcoat for her stupid, immature king that she'd only too eagerly taken the reprieve from being by his side in order to work and work and work on the garment, hidden away in the servant's quarters until dark.

I won't have a king to gift the damn thing to at this rate, Elina thought as Kilian poked his pale head above the covers, still shocked that she'd agreed to lie in bed with him. But she could see him shivering – could *hear* his teeth chattering – and so she knew there was no way the man would warm up enough on his own. It also meant...

Elina's face flushed as she looked down at her clothes. She wouldn't be much use to Kilian as a body warmer if she kept them all on. With a sigh she began to unlace her dress, slipping it off as Kilian watched with wide, disbelieving eyes.

"Take that ragged overcoat off," she ordered without looking at him.

"You're being serious right now, aren't you?"

"Do you want to be warm or not?"

Kilian didn't respond, his silence being all the compliance Elina needed. He squirmed and struggled beneath the covers, whilst Elina wondered if she needed to remove her undershirt, too.

Surely not, she thought, but when she caught a glimpse of Kilian's expression – hungry despite the sickness that still lingered there – a brazen part of her lifted the shirt up and over her head before she could think better of it.

"Let down your hair, Elina."

It hadn't been the words she was expecting, in truth, now that she was standing naked in front of Kilian, the firelight casting her golden skin in a sunset glow. She fingered the braid wrapped around her head, somehow feeling far more nervous about letting down her hair than she was about being stark naked. But Kilian had practically seen her naked already – he hadn't seen her hair down. Apart from her mother nobody had.

Slowly, carefully, she unravelled the braid, working her fingers through her hair to loosen the curls until a cascade of wavy, tawny hair came tumbling down her back and over her shoulders. She glanced at Kilian from beneath her lashes, feeling somewhat uncertain, but that feeling was forgotten when she saw the way he was looking at her.

"You – you are so beautiful."

And though Daven had said the same thing, and though other people in Alder were beginning to make similar comments now, too, there was a world of difference in hearing them say Elina was beautiful and hearing *Kilian* say it.

It shouldn't affect me so much, she thought, though her cheeks were burning. *I already knew he liked the look of me. Him saying I'm beautiful isn't that important.*

Wordlessly Elina slid beneath the covers, heart hammering in her chest so loudly Kilian would definitely have heard it if the storm outside wasn't almost deafening. But when Kilian wrapped an arm around her waist and pulled her close she immediately recoiled.

"You're freezing!" she bit out. She'd never felt a human being so cold before. "And you're naked! I only told you to take your overcoat off."

Kilian snorted; Elina turned to face him, arms clutched protectively to her chest, though it was hardly as if either of them could see much in the dim light of the room, beneath the covers.

"Why should you be the only one naked?" he said.

371

"Hardly seems fair to me. And of course I'm freezing – I thought that was the point of you joining me. To warm me up."

"It...it is. But how could you possibly be so cold and still alive? Are you made of ice?"

His eyes were the colour of flint in the darkness, and at her comment they grew as hard as the stone, too. "Maybe I am. It would explain how heartless I am."

"You really are a pathetic excuse for a human being, Kilian."

He sighed, and some of the hardness in his eyes went away. "I know. What would you have me do? I *feel* pathetic. I feel wretched. I feel freezing."

With trepidation Elina reached a hand out and just barely touched Kilian's chest. She traced her fingers along his collarbone, brushing pale, tangled hair out of the way in the process. She took a deep breath, then wrapped her arms around the man's neck and pushed her body as close to his as she could possibly get it.

Kilian was so cold it physically hurt her to do so; Elina persisted anyway. She had to wonder if the curse had something to do with his abysmal core body temperature, and if that meant Kilian would be likely to run a constant fever once summer hit.

She nuzzled her head against his neck and mumbled, "Get warm and go to sleep," withholding a flinch when Kilian slid an arm around her waist and pressed his legs around one of hers.

"I'm fairly certain going to sleep isn't on my mind anymore..."

Elina glanced up; Kilian's expression was filthy. She noted with relief that his teeth were no longer chattering.

372

"This coming from the man who, thirty minutes ago, told me he couldn't keep any food down? I'd personally rather not do anything that involved you moving in the slightest, Kilian."

He bent his head down, brushing his lips against Elina's. "I needn't be the one doing the moving."

She dug her nails into his back. "Go to sleep!"

"Feel free to dig into me harder next time," Kilian smirked, but then he rested his chin on top of Elina's head and sighed contentedly. "I'll go to sleep. Thank you for this, Elina."

She didn't say anything; she wasn't used to hearing genuine gratitude fall from Kilian's tongue. Instead, she listened to the raging storm outside until it almost seemed to calm, but by the time she thought to look and see if it truly had she'd already fallen asleep.

*

When Elina woke she was facing away from Kilian, though he still held her close with an arm around her waist. It was very dark in the room – the fire had burned itself down to a smoulder. Outside the window it was almost silent. Almost. For it seemed as if, beneath the quiet, Elina could hear...something. Like the fall of snow on top of more snow, though she should never have been able to hear that, or the soft whistling of the wind winding through the forest, though she couldn't hear that either.

Elina was confused; why were her ears playing tricks on her? She wondered if it was simply because everything was so quiet where before there had been noise. It was discomforting. It set her on edge; caused her heart to pound.

It was then she realised Kilian was no longer freezing,

373

nor was he hot from alcohol and steaming bathwater. He was merely...warm. Warm against Elina's back, warm against her legs, warm against...

Oh.

Kilian shifted behind her, just enough that she could feel a very telling hardness pressing against her thigh. It sent a heat flaring up her that had entirely nothing to do with being nestled beneath blankets against the cold. Elina desperately wanted to turn – to see if Kilian was awake or aware of his own body – but she didn't want to risk rousing him if he was fast asleep.

She moved slightly, trying to find a more comfortable way to sleep against Kilian that didn't send her mind racing. When his hand ended up moving from her waist to brush past her breasts Elina sucked in a breath.

How can he be doing this fast asleep? How can he be driving me insane without even trying?

But then Kilian's hand twitched, and he just barely squeezed one of her breasts before proceeding to stroke her skin. His other arm snaked around her, pressing Elina's hips against him until she cried out.

"You're awake, aren't you?" she bit out, heart beating so painfully she thought it might jump out of her chest. Elina blew some of her hair away from her face, staring at her hands and wondering what to do with them – what *Kilian* wanted her to do with them.

"Evidently," was all he said, and it sounded so reassuringly like sarcastic, cruel, drunk Kilian Hale that Elina almost turned around and slapped him. But she didn't, and Kilian took that as permission to proceed with his exploration. His hands went roaming, sliding, pinching and squeezing every available part of Elina's body until she was writhing beneath them.

"St-stop it, Kilian," she stammered. "You're not well. You need to –"

"Don't tell me I need to sleep. I know what I need." A pause, and then, "Turn around, Elina."

She shook her head, so nervous she didn't trust her voice. Kilian clucked his tongue, affronted, before bending his head slightly in order to kiss Elina's shoulder where it met her neck. When he began sucking on it she raised a hand to stop him, but Kilian grabbed it and sucked her fingers, instead.

When he rocked his hips against Elina's she let out a moan despite herself.

"Do you really not want to do this?" Kilian whispered against her ear, voice all water over gravel and shiver-inducing.

"I...I don't know what to do," Elina admitted, voice barely audible even though everything was quiet. "What am I supposed to do?"

"All you have to do is turn around."

She turned.

Kilian's mouth found hers immediately, a hand in her hair tilting her head to meet his. Deftly he shifted Elina until she was no longer beside him but beneath him. She was shocked by the weight of him, for though Kilian hadn't eaten in days and had been ravaged by fever he was, ultimately, still a man who towered over her when she stood beside him.

When Elina pulled away from the kiss to catch her breath, Kilian watched her intently. His almost colourless eyes held the dying embers of the fire inside them. Along with his wild, tangled hair and sharp cheekbones he really did look like a man cursed.

Or possessed, Elina thought, as Kilian gently ran the back of his hand across her jawline with barely-contained desire. She could *feel* it on the air – the tightly-wound tension that he was dying to break. Longing to break. And she wanted it too. But she was frightened; how could she not be?

"I'll show you what to do," Kilian said, voice a low growl. "I won't hurt you. Just...stay here, beneath me, and help me chase the storm away."

"Well when you put it like that," Elina said, the edges of her lips quirking upwards despite herself, "then how could I possibly refuse my king?"

"Shut up," Kilian laughed, for just a second, and then Elina kissed him, and there were no more words spoken between them.

CHAPTER SIXTEEN

Kilian

When Kilian woke he discovered several things. One: his head no longer felt like it was being split open with a white-hot axe. Two: he actually felt hungry, and instinctively knew that he'd be able to stomach whatever he next ate. Three: he wasn't cold. And, most importantly, four: he wasn't alone.

Elina lay in his arms, sleeping softly with her head against his chest. Her long, bronze hair was almost as wild and unruly as Kilian's was, which wasn't surprising considering what they had spent much of the night doing.

He glanced out the window and almost cried in shock.

The sky was clear. Not a single cloud broke up the pale, glorious blue of it. By the angle of the sun – the *sun*, which Kilian could see for the first time in months – he estimated that it had to be just past noon. He wished the sunlight slanting into the room would reach his bed, so it could reflect off Elina's hair and skin and allow Kilian to see her for the first time as what she truly was: a woman far too warm and exotic for Alder, and Kilian's castle, and Kilian himself.

And yet Elina *was* with him, in one capacity or another. All he wanted to do was while away the rest of the day watching her sleep, but as Kilian thought that she seemed to rouse, turning away from Kilian to land on her back. She yawned, stretching her arms above her head as she slowly opened her eyes, taking a few moments to blinks focus into them before locating Kilian by her side.

She smiled sleepily. "Morning, Your Royal –"

"I'm rather certain I told you to stop calling me that. Numerous times, in fact."

"Sorry; that doesn't ring a bell."

Kilian smoothed back Elina's hair, clearing it from her beautiful face. "Did you sleep well?"

"I suppose I did, though I could do with more."

"So go back to sleep."

Elina seemed to consider this for a moment but, upon realising how bright the room was, immediately sat up despite her nakedness. She stared out the window, wide-eyed; Kilian stared at her, instead.

"It isn't snowing."

"I know."

"Or stormy."

"I know."

378

"The sun is out."

"...I know."

She glanced at Kilian. "Did you hit your head or forget to be miserable or something?"

He pushed her back against the pillows in indignation and ran a hand through his matted hair that was in desperate need of a wash. "Are you telling me you want to get stuck in the castle once more? Because I'm sure I could make that happen."

Elina laughed softly. She touched Kilian's knee. "You're still warm. That's good."

"You're talking like you expected to wake up and find me dead. I'm not as fragile as all that."

"Could have had me fooled. How are you feeling in general? Any pain? Fever?"

Kilian cocked his head to the side when Elina reached up to press a dainty hand to his brow. "I feel...normal, I guess. I don't really know what normal is, though. But no pain. Or numbness. Just..."

"Normal," she smiled. "I know what you mean. Are you hungry? Want me to go and prepare –"

"Do you really think I'm expecting you to act as my servant after everything that's now happened between us?" Kilian asked, shaking his head incredulously. "I'll have a couple of servants prepare the dining room, and we can have a bath and take our time before having breakfast...or lunch, considering the time."

Elina quirked an eyebrow. "*We* can have a bath before having lunch together? A lot of presumptions there about my willingness to spend time with you."

"I thought *I* was the cruel one, Miss Brodeur," Kilian said, feigning hurt as he collapsed beside Elina, turning his

379

head until their noses were almost touching. "Lately you've said far crueller things than I."

"You must be rubbing off on me."

Kilian said nothing; the look he gave Elina spoke volumes. Her face flushed a furious scarlet, but when she tried to look away Kilian slid a hand through her hair and pulled her back towards him. He kissed her, softly at first and then harder, harder, harder. By the time he was done Elina was gasping for breath.

His eyes glittered with desire as he watched her chest heave. "How are *you* feeling this morning, Elina?"

"As if...I spent the night in a man's bed for the first time."

"How apt. Do you care to spend another?"

Elina's brow creased uncertainly. "I really need to go home tonight. An afternoon, though..."

Kilian grinned foolishly, which for the first time was a good thing.

"That sounds good to me."

CHAPTER SEVENTEEN

Elina

"Elina. Elina...? *Elina!*"

Elina turned, surprised to see Scarlett Duke running through the glittering snow covering the forest path towards her. With the weather having been so glorious over the past three days they weren't the only people walking beneath the trees, basking in the scent of the winter sun beating down on dark pine needles.

She smiled bashfully. "Sorry, I was lost in thought."

"About something good, by the look on your face," Scarlett replied, linking her arm with Elina's as easily as if they were sisters. "Walk with me; keep me company whilst I stretch my legs."

Elina was only too happy to oblige. It was good for her to have a distraction, otherwise she'd end up daydreaming about Kilian once more. Not that daydreaming about him was a *bad* thing. Rather, it was a very good thing. It simply wasn't appropriate brain fodder during the daytime... especially not around other people.

"Sorry for not being able to speak with you when you were in the tavern the other day," Scarlett said, leading Elina out of the forest in full view of the castle. In the wintry light she could see that the smooth-stoned walls were not quite as grey as she'd first thought; there was a warm cast to the stone she hadn't noticed before. The warmth acted as a nice contrast to the slate blue roof tiles and delicate spires, which, during the multitude of stormy days Alder had been subject to so far, could barely be seen through the snow.

"That's alright," Elina replied, letting go of Scarlett's arm in order to hop forwards onto a stone-covered rock and slide back down to the path. "I was rather preoccupied, after all."

"Yes, it seems like the town has quite suddenly warmed to you," Scarlett said, a knowing smile on her face. "Particularly the man who was sitting next to you."

Elina's face flushed despite herself. "Daven. Yes, he's..."

"Oh, I see how it is. Something tells me you're not quite as interested in him as he is in you, though."

"I...yes. I suppose that's true. I haven't really thought much about it, to be honest."

"Because you've been thinking about someone else?"

Scarlett's eyes darted to the castle and back to Elina,

who was mortified.

"I don't - it's nothing like -"

Scarlett merely laughed. "I don't mean to tease you. You're just...very obvious. You remind me of me a couple of winters ago."

"I somehow doubt that," Elina said as she glanced at the castle. She wondered if Kilian was looking out at his kingdom through a window, wishing he could enjoy the sunny day just like everyone else. It made her heart hurt.

Scarlett watched her every expression carefully. "I really was especially naive and transparent when I was eighteen. It's only because of Adrian's debatable influence that I've grown any kind of sense."

"Wait, you're only twenty?"

Scarlett nodded. "How old did you think I was?"

"I...don't know. Not the same age as I am. You're far more mature than me."

"Two years of travelling will do that to you. If you stay in one place for too long you cannot grow."

Elina rolled her eyes. "You sound like my mother."

"Then she's a wise woman."

"And yet she could have left Alder whenever she liked - even *with* me in tow - but she didn't. If you can't take your own advice then what use is it to someone else?"

Scarlett smiled wanly, brushing away a fine layer of snow from a boulder before perching on top of it. "Everybody has different circumstances. Have you ever asked your mother why she didn't leave once you had grown a little older?"

"No," Elina sighed, hating the admission. She really *did* sound naive and foolish compared to Scarlett. She dropped down to sit in the snow, not caring about her cloak and dress getting wet. "No, I never have. I always just assumed she'd give me an excuse, like not wanting to leave the shop or hoping things would get better for me with the children my age."

Scarlett chuckled. "Those sound like valid reasons, not excuses. Your priorities change when you have a child."

"You..." Elina stared at her doubtfully. "Do you have a child?"

"No, but I have two much younger brothers. And...a complicated family history. So I understand how your mother feels?"

Elina knew she shouldn't pry. She did anyway. "How complicated is complicated?"

"My father fell into bed with a local girl months before he was due to get married and she got pregnant, then left the child – me – on his doorstep. He raised me with my step-mother, though I didn't know she wasn't my birth mother until I was sixteen. Things got worse for a while after that. Much, much worse..." Scarlett stared up at the sky; her blue eyes were slightly too bright. "But then they got better. I'm very close with my step-mother now. In fact, I'd never even call her that. She *is* my mother, just as she always has been. You're crying, Elina."

It took Elina a few moments to process Scarlett's final sentence. When she did, she frantically rubbed her face with the heel of her hand until the tears were gone. "I'm sorry," she mumbled. "I can't believe I asked such an intrusive question. You didn't have to tell me all of that."

Scarlett merely smiled. "Your mother told me and Adrian about your father; I'm merely returning the favour, since you did not get a choice in whether we found out about your past or not."

Elina swallowed a lump in her throat that threatened more tears. A shiver ran down her spine as melted snow began to seep into her clothes. "Did you ever think about finding her? Your birth mother, I mean. Did your father tell you anything about her?"

"Yes and no. I wanted to know for so long – what did she look like, what was her family like, did my father know where she was – but when it came down to it I realised I didn't need to know. I started seriously asking myself what I would *do* if I found her. Ask her why she left me on my father's doorstep? That much was obvious; he was wealthy and she was not. He could raise me without any shame whereas a young mother with a child born out of wedlock would be scorned...but you know this very well already."

"Yes, rather well," Elina laughed bitterly. "Though I'm finding that it bothers me less and less with every passing day. The scorn, I mean. And being ignored. Being lonely."

"Is that because the townspeople are paying attention to you now?"

She shook her head. "No. That's...nice. It's gratifying, too, don't get me wrong. But it's hollow at the same time. They're only accepting me now that I've managed to do something *worthy* of their acceptance, even though I've been making their clothes for years and helping keep them warm."

"So what else changed?"

Elina glanced at the castle before she could stop herself and immediately regretted it.

"I *knew* you must have your eye on someone, but a king? You have very high standards!" Scarlett grinned. Elina was tempted to throw a snowball at her.

"He isn't even the king, not truly," she grimaced. "He's the prince regent."

"Doesn't make a difference from where I'm standing. Does he know how you feel? Have you told him? What does he think about -"

"I think you're overwhelming Elina," came a low, melodic voice. Adrian approached them from the forest, dark red cloak starkly contrasting against the perfect snow. When he reached Scarlett, perched on her boulder, he kissed her gently.

Scarlett pouted. "I wasn't really. I just got excited."

Elina laughed nervously. "It's fine. And it's... complicated, I guess." She looked at the castle once more, thinking of Kilian trapped inside. "Can I trust the two of you?"

Adrian's reply was immediate. "Absolutely not."

Scarlett swatted his arm. "Don't be cruel. Is your mother not faring far better than she was before, Elina?"

Slowly, she nodded.

"And have I not just told you about my own past?"

She nodded once more.

Scarlett smiled. "Then I'd say you can trust us."

Elina said nothing for a few moments, still staring at the castle. When eventually she spoke her voice was soft and quiet. "He can't get out. Kilian - the prince regent, I mean - is stuck in the castle."

Adrian and Scarlett grew serious immediately. The man's eyes glittered with interest; leaning against the boulder Scarlett was sitting on he gestured for Elina to continue.

She sighed, then committed to telling them the rest.

She wasn't sure at first if she could remember everything Kilian had said about his curse, given that she'd been drunk at the time, but as she spoke Elina realised she'd learned almost every word by heart. When she finished explaining Scarlett looked sad. Adrian's face was unreadable, his strange, amber eyes staring at the castle as if he might be able to see through the stone. Elina wondered if he actually could.

"That would explain the magic on you," he murmured, still looking at the castle. "Elina, did your royal friend happen to tell you anything about *how* the curse was said? For example, what his father was doing when he spoke the words, or whether they were spoken directly to his son or to an object?"

She shook her head. "Kilian told me he was in bed, and that his father must have thought he was asleep. All he heard were the words; I don't think even he knows more than that."

"Hmm."

Elina didn't know what else to say. She'd always thought that if she told Scarlett and Adrian about Kilian's curse that they'd be able to immediately help her. She hadn't thought about how complicated magic itself was at all.

She felt so foolish.

"Elina, can you get us some more information?" Scarlett asked.

Adrian nodded his assent. "Can you wander the castle and see if there's anything...unusual?"

She frowned. "Unusual how?"

"You'd know it if you saw or felt it, I think," Adrian said, which was infuriatingly vague. "Anything else you can get the king to remember would be helpful, too. And don't forget the servants. They might know something their sovereign doesn't."

Bleakly Elina thought about how Kilian had fired most of them. She wondered if she could find some of them in Alder, now that the townspeople were speaking to her.

So she nodded. "I'll see what I can find out."

"In the meantime..." Adrian glanced upward. "Perhaps try and keep the moody king in a pleasant frame of mind. I rather like the sun."

"Adrian!"

He smiled warmly for Scarlett. "You agree with me, though."

"Of course I do but you have no *tact*."

"But it's obvious Elina must have had a hand in the king's better mood. Elina, I don't suppose you're currently bedding –"

"*Adrian!*"

Elina could only watch the pair of them enviously. Their relationship was so easy. So...free. She had never witnessed a pair like them before.

They're certainly a far cry away from me and Kilian, who spend half our time at each other's throat and the other half of the time feeling miserable for ourselves.

The thought gave Elina pause. Was she really thinking of herself and Kilian as a *couple?* Could they really be described as that? She didn't think so. For if Kilian's curse was broken he'd run away as fast as was physically possible, regardless of whether Elina went with him or not. She wondered if he'd even want her to go with him.

And would I want to go, either?

But such thoughts were premature. Elina first had to

388

focus on a solution to Kilian's curse. Freeing him from his prison wasn't going to be easy, after all. It might even be impossible, and he would be stuck in the castle for the rest of his life.

She didn't want to think about that.

CHAPTER EIGHTEEN

Kilian

Kilian was lounging by the large, ornate windows in the dining hall. They offered an expansive view of the grounds to the back of the castle, including his beloved hot springs. He hadn't looked at them since he'd been forcibly handed the throne. He couldn't bear to.

But he was doing a lot of things he couldn't bear to do before, including being sober and treating what few servants he had at his disposal kindly, so Kilian figured he could handle looking down on the one part of his country that he actually liked.

And Elina was down below, exploring on uncertain

feet, which was the primary reason Kilian was looking out of the window in the first place. He'd never admit that to anyone, though. He didn't even want to admit it to himself.

I'm sickeningly soft with no alcohol in my blood, he thought with a grimace. *Even my outward appearance is soft.* Kilian scratched his chin; it was clean-shaven and smooth. His long hair, which used to run past his shoulders in matted knots, was meticulously washed and combed and braided, keeping it away from his face.

His clothes were unstained and fresh; his ragged overcoat was nowhere in sight. The embroidered waistcoat he wore over his white shirt made Kilian feel oddly constrained, though he supposed that was a given considering he'd been living in shirts three sizes too big for him with ineffectual trousers and little else.

Though he would never say he was happy about it, he looked far more like a prince that he'd ever done before. Kilian could tell the servants felt the same way, though they were still nervously testing the air with their 'reborn' regent. It was reasonable of them to expect that Kilian would simply grab a bottle of vodka and revert to who he was two weeks before, after all, so he couldn't blame their shifty expressions and furtive footsteps.

I need more staff, he thought, tearing his eyes away from the window in order to look around the dining room. Kilian had wanted to eat in here with Elina after she'd spent the night in his bed; it hadn't happened. The room had been too filthy, with most everything in it covered in dust. It had since been cleaned to its former glory, but it was only one room out of dozens in the castle. He couldn't expect three servants to ever hope of keeping the place in check.

Kilian laughed derisively as he returned to watching

Elina. His original intention of making the castle so filthy and neglected simply so Gabriel would have to deal with fixing it when he returned from war seemed so stupid now. Immature. Pointless.

Worst of all, it would have only proven to his brother just how useless he was. This wasn't something he'd ever cared about before – rather, he had thrived on disappointing him – but now things were different. Kilian had a clear head. He wasn't in pain. He could *think*. And though the cold was still there, seeping into Kilian's very soul and demanding he drink to forget about it, he could resist. If he fell prey to it then all he was doing was dying.

Kilian didn't want to die. He knew that now. All he wanted was to be free, and to do that he had to get his act together and work things out. For curses could be broken if he could only work out how.

And she may be the key. Kilian tracked Elina through the window with hawk-like eyes, observing her every movement. There didn't *seem* to be anything magical about her, but it wasn't as if magic was inherited like the colour of one's hair and eyes. But Elina was smart and could see right through Kilian. Most importantly, she hadn't abandoned him. She *wanted* to help him. And, though she might not yet be willing to admit it, Kilian knew that Elina liked him, even though he was an entirely unlikable person.

He had never wanted someone to like him before; having women be superficially attracted to him for a single night had always been enough. But Kilian wanted more for himself now. He wanted to *give* more to Elina.

"She's so beautiful," Kilian uttered, words fogging the window as he traced Elina with a finger against the freezing glass. The sun – which was more Elina's doing than Kilian ever wanted her to know – shone brightly in her hair, bringing out copper and gold and red tones usually hidden in the brown. Her skin was soaking up the sun like a sponge; it had already grown a shade or two darker in the week since the weather took a turn for the better. It made her look even more out of place against the snow.

Kilian longed to go somewhere together with her where snow didn't fall at all.

When I'm free, he thought longingly. *If that ever happens.*

It was dizzying to Kilian, how much he liked Elina. And he could never tell her. Or, rather, wouldn't. Despite everything that had happened so far – all of the ugly confessions, unruly behaviour and deadly storms – part of him was too prideful to admit how much the woman affected him.

I want to fix myself by myself. I don't want to fall apart the second she's gone. I need to be better than that.

For of course Elina could never be expected to leave with Kilian if that's what he ended up doing. Likewise, he couldn't demand that she stay either. Part of him itched to order her to do what he wanted simply because he could, but he buried that awful inclination away.

No. Elina deserved to decide what she wanted to do with her own life – to have free choice. How could Kilian deny her the one thing he was stripped of, after all?

A flash of movement outside brought Kilian out of his head. Elina was nowhere to be seen. For one agonisingly long second Kilian didn't know what to do or think, for at the end of the day if Elina had somehow been spirited away what *could* he do, stuck in the castle as he were?

But then Elina appeared – in the hot springs. She had fallen in, resurfacing from the water with a shocked and appalled expression on her face.

393

Kilian couldn't help it; he burst out laughing, the mirthful sound echoing around the dining hall and amplified ten times over. Elina couldn't hear him, of course, and she was unaware that she was being watched as she slipped and struggled out of the hot springs and onto the snow, shivering violently within seconds.

"Marielle!" he called out, knowing that the servant in question was probably nearby. Perhaps because she was the one he'd first shown kindness to, Marielle had in turn been the first of the castle's staff to warm to him. And now that Elina was far less Kilian's personal servant and more a willing companion, Marielle had stepped in to fill her shoes.

"Yes, sire?" she asked politely as she stepped foot into the dining hall.

"Prepare a bath in my room. I rather think somebody needs it."

Sneaking a glance through the window, Marielle's lips twitched when she spied Elina. She nodded her head at Kilian before retreating from the hall. Once Kilian could no longer see Elina through the window he, too, exited the hall, stalking purposefully down the main corridor. Knowing that Elina wouldn't be using the front doors but rather the servant's entrance, he took a few detours with quickening strides, hoping to reach the door before Elina entered the castle.

He made it just in time to catch her coming in, sodden, freezing and looking thoroughly ashamed of herself.

"Have a nice swim?" Kilian chided, his voice full of laughter he could barely suppress.

Elina's mouth widened into a shaky, wordless O at the sight of him. His lips quirked upwards at the expression, then with no further comment he bodily lifted Elina over his shoulder and carried her away.

She cried out in surprise. "K-Kilian, what are you –"

"You've given me plenty of baths; it's high time I gave you one."

Elina had nothing to say in response, though Kilian felt her heart rate accelerate against his back as her hands clenched and unclenched his shirt.

A coiling down below his stomach told him the bath was unlikely to be a solo one.

CHAPTER NINETEEN

Elina

"Kilian...?"

Elina spoke his name very softly, testing to see if the man was awake. But Kilian was fast asleep beside her, snoring quietly as he rolled onto his back. In the moonlight he was so pale Elina thought he looked more a statue than a living thing. Only the gentle rise and fall of his chest belied the fact that Kilian was a mortal, breathing man.

Kilian was looking much better now that he'd gotten over his alcohol withdrawal. His appetite had voraciously returned, too, and he'd started taking much better care of his appearance. Though he'd been handsome in his wild, unkempt state, now that Kilian was groomed and fed Elina came to the conclusion that he was undeniably beautiful.

With a tentative finger she prodded his cheek. Nothing. Kilian didn't even stir. And so Elina slowly crept out of bed, locating her undershirt on the floor before realising that she'd definitely wake the sleeping prince if she tried to lace on her dress.

She glanced at the door leading to Kilian's cavernous selection of clothes that he rarely touched. Slipping on her undershirt, Elina tiptoed over and perused through his trousers with only the light from the moon to guide her eyes. Eventually she came across a dark pair that seemed as if they were far too short for Kilian – likely a relic from his younger days. As quietly as possible she pulled them on, somewhat impressed that they fit reasonably well if she ignored how tight they were around her hips.

Elina knew where the creaky floorboards were in Kilian's chambers by now, so it wasn't difficult to largely avoid them in order to sneak out to the corridor. She teased tangles out of her hair with her fingers and braided her hair down her back as she walked, alternately peering then shying away as she passed through shadow, then moonlight, then shadow as a result of the tall, narrow windows that punctuated the walls.

Now that she had left Kilian's room Elina had to admit that she really didn't know what she was looking for, surrounded by swathes of empty, cold, magic-ridden castle walls.

It's hardly as if Adrian and Scarlett were helpful on that front. They were so vague! How am I supposed to know what I'm looking for when I see it? It's not as if I'm well-versed in magic myself.

Real magic – true, powerful curses and spells – was so rare these days. Elina knew from the books she'd read growing up that some countries didn't believe it existed at all. For a while in her youth she had entertained this idea, simply because she wanted to hate her so-called magician father rather than long to meet him.

Elina had no such naivety to fall back on now. She knew magic was real. The dangerous kind.

She had to work out what was going on.

Though Elina had spent almost a month in the Hale family castle she was still unfamiliar with much of it. Kilian had only recently wanted the place cleaned up after months of allowing it to go to ruin, so aside from his own chambers, the servants quarters, throne room and dining hall Elina didn't know what much else of the castle was actually used for.

She climbed down the grand staircase first; the dining hall was at the bottom, with a sprawling ballroom attached on its left. Vaguely recalling that Kilian once told her there was a library to the right of the hall, she tentatively pushed on what was hopefully a promising door.

Peering through the darkness, and treading on feet made silent from a layer of dust, Elina realised very quickly that the room wasn't a library so much as a parlour room which happened to contain a few bookshelves.

I suppose Kilian would consider that a library, she mused, using what little light was available to try and discern the titles of the heavy tomes closest to her. *He doesn't seem like much of a reader.*

Many of the books were handsomely-bound encyclopaedias and atlases. A few were record books, full of lists of farm stocks, taxes, town names and various other things Kilian definitely needed to know about but deliberately hadn't bothered learning.

But nothing stood out. If Adrian was sure Elina would *know* what she was looking for when she saw it then it definitely wasn't in the parlour. Exiting, she briefly tried the dining room, which she already knew likely held nothing of interest. She paused in front of several portraits of the royal family through the years, smothering a laugh when she came across one in which a scowling, huffing boy of around four seemed to try his best to ruin the portrait.

That must be Kilian, she thought, sparing a look at his older brother Gabriel, who looked every inch the perfect prince. *My mother thought so, too, but if he really was 'perfect' then why has he still sent no word back to Kilian about why he's delayed at the border?*

Shaking her head, Elina left the room and headed back up the grand staircase, and then up a further set of stairs that headed in a westward direction. The entire wing of the castle she entered was grandly decorated; it didn't take her long to realise that she must be in the *actual* king's chambers. It was only in realising this that Elina acknowledged that Kilian's chambers were, indeed, his own rooms. He'd probably lived in them from infancy.

He doesn't strike me as the kind of person who'd take over his parents' room, even if it was *the king's bedroom,* she mused. When she reached a highly polished, heavy set of wooden doors Elina felt her heart beat quicken. An overwhelming desire to run back downstairs to Kilian's bed without continuing her search hit her, but upon noticing that one of the doors was ajar her curiosity overtook that desire.

The door swung silently outward despite its weight. Inspecting the lushly carpeted floor Elina noticed that there were footsteps through the dust, leading to a desk the size of Elina's own bedroom back at her mother's house.

She walked towards it, careful to tread only in the footprints already embedded in the dust. On top of the dark, gnarled grain of the table sat a silver locket, shining in a narrow ray of moonlight that had wormed its way between the heavy, velvet curtains covering a full wall of the room.

Elina agonised over whether to touch it. But, just as when she couldn't help asking Scarlett about her complicated family history, Elina's reluctance quickly burned away in the face of something new and interesting. She picked up the locket, appreciating how the silver was etched with a complicated, beautiful pattern of vines and flowers on both sides.

When she pried it open a lock of silvery-blonde hair fell to the floor. Panicking, Elina only just managed to grab it before it brushed against the dust, securely replacing it back inside the locket and flinging the piece of jewellery onto the table before running out of the king's chambers without so much as another glance around.

I don't care what Adrian said, she thought as she fled down the stairs, *I have no idea what to look for. Even if I combed the castle a hundred times I'd come up blank.*

When she reached the bottom of the grand staircase Elina became aware that her hair had come undone from its braid. She shook it out and, in the process, saw the door to the ballroom out of the corner of her eye. She'd never been in before. It had only recently been cleared of dust, and Elina knew she'd be lying if she said she didn't want to look inside. So she walked over as quickly as she dared and opened the door, taking a moment to adjust to the relative blinding brightness of the room over the corridor.

Much of the southern wall of the ballroom was made of gilded-framed glass, providing a full view over the castle grounds and the mountain on which it was nestled into. The windows let in an overwhelming amount of moonlight, casting the enormous room in silvery, ethereal light. It was freezing, but that somehow added to the magical feel of the room. But the feeling was magical in the poetic sense; Elina sensed nothing awry about the place.

Taking a deep breath – though she wasn't sure why she was nervous – Elina entered the room, bare feet echoing on the polished floor. For a few moments she imagined herself dressed up to dance, instead of in an insubstantial white shirt and a royal prince's old trousers. She twirled and leapt across the length of the room, reassured by the quickness of her feet and her sense of balance. It had been too long since Elina hadn't been wrapped in restrictive winter clothes.

Spring can't come quickly enough, Elina thought. This time, however, the thought had nothing to do with leaving Alder alongside her mother. No, it had to do with spring feasts and summer dances and swimming in the mountain lakes and forcing Kilian along to experience all of these things with her – things she had previously experienced alone or not at all.

Elina knew she had to get back to bed. She'd been away too long and Kilian was sure to notice her absence soon. But the feeling of *space* around her – a space with nobody in it but her and the moon – was intoxicating. It was somehow the closest thing to freedom she had ever felt.

"Dancing by yourself seems awfully lonely."

Elina stopped so abruptly at the voice that she tripped over her feet. For there, by the doorway, stood Kilian, yawning good-naturedly and looking ridiculous in his ragged overcoat. It made her think of the one she was making him – the one that was mere days away from completion.

She almost grinned, but something about the way Kilian was looking at her now that he'd finished yawning stopped her. "I didn't mean to wake you," she said quietly, her voice reverberating off the walls turning it to a shout.

Kilian flicked his eyes downward. "Are those my trousers?"

"Possibly. Want them back?"

"No; they look good on you," he replied, shaking his head slightly. Kilian's hair caught the moonlight, turning it to silver. Elina had never once cared for the way the blonde hair of Alder looked beneath the sun and the moon before, but it was different with Kilian.

Everything was different with Kilian.

"Why are you in here, anyway?" he continued, walking towards Elina whilst flinching at the freezing temperature of the floor.

"I...couldn't sleep."

"You should have woken me up."

"You were too peaceful to wake up."

Kilian barked out a laugh as if the notion of him being peaceful was too incredulous to believe. When he reached Elina he bowed deeply, though it seemed more a mockery of a bow rather than a sincere one, especially considering his wretched clothes and slept-on hair.

Elina eyed him warily. "What are you doing, Kilian?"

"About to ask you to dance, of course," he replied, eyes glinting in the moonlight like ice as he held out a hand. "Though I must admit to being rather bad at it,

402

given that I tend to avoid any and all social events befitting my station."

Elina slid a tentative hand into his; a shiver ran up her spine when he snaked his other hand around her back, beneath her shirt. "I thought you *enjoyed* such events so you could get drunk and disappoint your family?"

Kilian laughed harder at that. Pulling Elina closer to him, he took a step back and then another when she followed. Clumsily he spun her beneath his arm. "The point being that I was drunk instead of dancing, or too busy falling into bed with a -"

"I get it," Elina cut in, rolling her eyes. A few steps later and Kilian seemed to have found some kind of rhythm to follow and, a few steps after that, Elina almost felt as if they were beginning to glide across the floor. She frowned. "I thought you said you were bad at this?"

"I am, comparatively. My brother's outstanding at it; my parents were even better. But I guess the lessons they forced me to attend as a child haven't been entirely obliterated by my alcohol consumption throughout the years."

"You are so spoiled."

"I know."

When Elina reached up and kissed him Kilian looked somewhat surprised. But then he ran a hand up through her hair, crushing her lips back against his with an intensity that stopped their dancing altogether.

"What were you really doing, wandering the castle in the middle of the night?" he asked, voice a low, unsteady growl that told Elina it would be a long time before either of them fell back asleep once they returned to Kilian's bed.

She smiled slightly. "Looking for magic."

"Did you find any?"

"No." Elina pulled Kilian towards the door by his hand, interlacing her fingers through his. "Only you."

CHAPTER TWENTY

Kilian

Kilian was spending more and more of his time sat by various windows in the castle, watching the world go by whilst he was locked up inside. Especially when Elina returned to her mother's house, though at his insistence those occurrences had grown less and less frequent. He knew he should feel bad for taking up all of her time.

He didn't.

Kilian simply didn't have it in him to feel guilty about tearing Elina away from her mother and the town that now loved her in order to satisfy his own desires to be with her. Drunk or not, that part of him would never change. He felt good when he was with Elina. Useful. Motivated. Wanted. And he knew Elina enjoyed spending time with him too, so at the end of the day Kilian reasoned his selfishness wasn't hurting anyone.

But then he thought of Elina's mother, Lily, who Kilian had to constantly remind himself had been ill. She'd been the primary reason Elina had accepted his original deal; considering how unfairly he'd treated Elina back then she clearly had to love her mother very much to put up with him in exchange for her health.

I suppose I can't expect everyone to have an unhealthy relationship with their parents, like me.

Not for the first time in recent weeks Kilian thought of his own mother. He'd never had a bad relationship with her, so to speak, but because she'd been so sickly after giving birth to Kilian and largely committed to bed rest for her health he had hated her. She'd always been too unwell to spend time with him. The looks his father gave him were even worse, too; they told Kilian all he needed to know, even as a child.

Kilian's father blamed him for his wife's deterioration. It was unbearable. It was almost a relief when his mother died shortly after his sixth birthday, though in truth Kilian had grieved in secret, when nobody was watching. Always in secret.

He supposed that habit had carried on throughout his life – to acknowledge feelings only when alone.

Because I was lonely.

That was what he'd screamed at Elina, the moment he finally started to let her in even though he hadn't wanted to. She could have retreated. Could have run away. Instead, she stayed, and now Kilian couldn't imagine coping through a single day within the castle without her.

"I need to do something for her mother," he decided aloud, thinking about perhaps insisting a little stronger that Elina bring her up to stay in the castle. That way she could spend more time with her mother without Kilian having to sacrifice his own time with her.

He laughed derisively at how poorly-functioning a human being he was. *Lily Brodeur has her shop. That was one of the reasons Elina never wanted to move her to the castle. Who am I to ask the woman to give up her family's business simply for my benefit?*

Kilian's heart lightened immediately when he spied Elina making her way across the snow towards the castle. She was struggling with a large box in her arms; curious, he spared a few seconds to check his appearance in a mirror - something he'd never have done for anyone before - then lounged back on his bed as if he hadn't been impatiently watching and waiting from the moment he opened his eyes that morning for Elina to arrive.

His heart was thumping painfully in his chest. It wasn't like Kilian to be nervous, but ever since his and Elina's midnight dance in the ballroom it constantly felt as if he had something lodged in his throat. It was uncomfortable and suffocating.

Part of him knew that what was 'stuck' in his throat were all the words he wanted to say to Elina but never could. And yet there was something else, too; an uncertainty about what Elina had actually been doing, wandering the castle in the dead of night when he was asleep.

She said she was looking for magic. But what? And why? Or...for whom?

If she had been wanting to help Kilian then Elina would have asked him to help in her search. He knew the

407

castle far better than she did, after all.

When Elina came through the door and smiled at Kilian strewn out on his bed all suspicions were forgotten. He didn't want to dwell on such things, especially when he was already obsessing over what his brother was up to. The servant Kilian sent down to the border was yet to return, even though he was two weeks late.

It would definitely have taken him longer than four days as a round trip, so I was being unreasonable with my time frame, but even still...

He shook the thought from his head. "What's in the box?" he asked Elina curiously when she placed it onto the bed beside him. "Secrets? Magic?"

Elina laughed softly. "No. Nothing like that. It's...a gift."

"For me?"

"No, for me. Of course for you, Kilian."

The look of tolerance on Elina's face at his stupid question filled him with unbearable affection for her. The lump in his throat returned; Kilian gulped it down. "Can I open it now?"

"Unless you want to lie there and stare at a box all day whilst I stand and watch you watching it."

He smirked. "Point taken."

But when Kilian sat up and reached out to take the lid off the box Elina grabbed his hand, her expression anxious and somewhat embarrassed.

"I'm – I'm still nowhere near as good as my mother is but I did try really hard with this and I hope you like it and –"

"Shut up, Elina."

Kilian took her hand away, altogether more interested in the gift now he knew Elina had made it herself. When he lifted the lid of the box she stood there, nervously biting her lip as if she were silently pleading for Kilian to like whatever was inside.

She needn't have worried, for when Kilian unfolded the long, high-collared, elaborately embroidered overcoat from the box he was instantly enamoured. The fabric was a dark, moody blue dashed through with silver thread that shone like gold in the light from the fire – like his hair. The interior fabric was soft and luxurious against his fingertips, promising to insulate him against the cold when he wore it. The buttons were engraved with a pattern of vines and flowers that seemed oddly familiar, though Kilian couldn't place it.

When Kilian didn't speak or react Elina only grew more worried. "Do you –"

"I love it. This is – why did you make this for me? *When* did you start making this? It must have taken weeks."

She blushed. "Just under three. I didn't do much else other than make it whenever I wasn't with you. I...decided to make it after we got drunk together. I couldn't stand watching you wear that ridiculous, moth-eaten overcoat of yours, and then the colour scheme and embroidery pattern came to me so quickly it almost felt like I had no choice but to make it."

Kilian was torn between trying on the garment and pulling Elina down onto the bed with him, to demonstrate his gratitude the only way he knew how – physically. But then he thought of the lump in his throat, and how his life would be so much better if it simply disappeared.

"Elina," he began, avoiding her eyes at first through

sheer nerves. "I don't know how to thank you. For everything."

"You don't have to thank me, Kilian. I didn't do any of his for your gratitude."

"The fact you did anything at all for *me* means you get it regardless," he quipped. Gently placing the overcoat on top of its box Kilian got to his feet, gesturing for Elina's hand. When she gave him it he enveloped it in both of his; her skin was hot against his own. "I had no idea just how much I would come to depend on you when you first started working for me. You've completely changed me."

Elina wrinkled her nose. "I don't really think I've changed you, Kilian. You just didn't know who you were. And you're still insufferable and lazy, even though you've definitely gotten far more tolerable since you sobered up -"

"You really know how to ruin a moment, don't you?" Kilian laughed, shaking his head incredulously. When he locked eyes with her he realised how stupid it had been to pretend his feelings for her were trivial.

There were anything but.

"Elina -"

"Sire?"

Kilian and Elina frowned at each other, then simultaneously looked at the door. For there was the servant Kilian had sent to find out why his brother was delayed, looking uncertain and confused by the scene he had walked in on.

Kilian let go of Elina's hand immediately and stalked over to the man. "What have you found out?" he demanded, now on edge and nervous for an entirely different reason than confessing to Elina. Outside the wind violently buffeted the window, as sure a sign as any

410

that Kilian had little to no control over his own feelings once they were forced to the surface.

"Your Royal Highness, he..."

"He's what?"

"He's..." The servant looked at the floor. "Missing, sire. Your brother is missing. He has been since that first messenger was sent."

Kilian roared in fury, the sound all but drowned out by the rapidly-forming storm outside. He turned from the servant, fervently pacing his room as the reality of what Gabriel being missing meant.

It means he isn't coming back. It means I'm stuck here. It means I must be king.

"Get out," he muttered to the servant. The man was only too happy to oblige, scurrying out of sight just as Elina reached his side and touched his arm.

"Kilian, there's a solution to all of this. You just have to stay calm and –"

"What do *you* know?!" he screamed, wrenching his arm away from Elina's hand as if she had burned him. She stared at him in shock.

"Kilian –"

"No, don't talk to me in that tone. You have *no idea* what's going on in my head right now."

"You have to find out if your brother is still alive!"

"Who cares about that? Dead or alive, he's gone, leaving me here to rot –"

"He's your brother!"

"*I don't care!*"

"Then you're an even worse liar than you think!" Elina screamed back at him. Kilian was momentarily taken

411

aback – he'd never heard Elina raise her voice like this before. "There's no way you don't care for him," she continued on passionately, "he's all the family you have left."

Kilian averted his eyes. "Just because family matters to you doesn't mean it has to matter to me. I'm the one whose *father* cursed him to stay a prisoner forever."

"At least you had a father! And he clearly cared for you, whether you believe that or not. Have you never wondered what his true reasons were for placing you on the –"

"You know *nothing,* Elina. Nothing at all."

She glared at him. "If you would just *tell* me then I would."

"I don't owe you that. I don't owe anyone anything."

"I wouldn't want you to tell me because you feel like you owe me!" she cried, attempting for a second time to touch Kilian's arm. He shrugged her off. "I want you to tell me because you...want to tell me. Because you –"

"Just get out, Elina."

She blinked in surprise. "What?"

"Get out. Now."

Elina glanced out the window at the howling, wretched blizzard obscuring the sky. It seemed like a distant dream that the sun had ever been visible. "Kilian, don't –"

"Now!" he ordered, voice like thunder to match the storm. "Don't come back."

For a moment it seemed like Elina would protest. There were tears streaming down her face; Kilian fought back the urge to wipe them away and apologise – to beg her to stay. But then she set her mouth in a grim line, pulled up the hood of her cloak and swiftly departed

Kilian's chambers without another word. It was only when the echoing of Elina's footsteps were silenced that Kilian collapsed onto his bed and buried his face in the heartbreakingly beautiful overcoat she'd slaved away to make him.

It's better this way, Kilian thought, hating himself, but hating Gabriel more. *I should never have gotten close to Elina in the first place. I should have stayed alone, just like I have been from the very beginning. I could never have expected her to stay with me if I'm locked in this castle forever.*

If he had never let Elina in then turning her away would not have hurt quite so much.

Kilian had never been in so much pain.

CHAPTER TWENTY-ONE

Elina

"And here was me thinking we'd already had the worst of the winter weather."

"This is the ugliest storm to hit Alder for years."

"Even worse than when the magician –"

"Definitely worse than when the magician stepped in."

Most everyone in Gill's tavern glanced at Elina, then, though it wasn't out of spite or annoyance. Because of her they had enough supplies to make it through the awful winter, even with this new barrage of snow and hail and thunder. She doubted she'd ever be spurned by the town

414

again. But she was still the daughter of the magician, so of course whenever he was brought up they thought of her.

"You'd think, after twenty-one years, they'd have something better to talk about," Lily sighed. Now that Elina had been accepted by the town, her mother had decided to venture out with her to enjoy the warmth and atmosphere of the tavern. Elina knew it was a thinly-veiled excuse to keep watch on her – she hadn't exactly returned from Kilian's castle in the best state of mind the previous day, after all.

Elina's only response to both her feelings and her mother's comment was to tip back the rest of the contents of her tankard of ale down her throat. She didn't know what else to do. She felt useless. Kilian had been beside himself with fury; Elina didn't think she'd ever seen a person so angry. But it wasn't simply that Kilian was *angry*. No, in the moments after learning that his brother was missing he'd had the expression of a doomed man, his life having been forcibly ended before it had ever really begun.

She sighed. Kilian's reaction wasn't even over-dramatic. In reality anyone would react the way he had if they were being forced to stay trapped inside the same building forever performing a role they never wanted. But what Elina didn't understand was Kilian's lack of concern about his brother's wellbeing.

It's impossible that he doesn't care for Gabriel, she thought, though in reality Elina could not be sure of this, given Kilian's personality. But the mere fact that, before they'd been interrupted, Kilian had clearly been planning to tell Elina something important – something about his feelings for her – suggested Kilian was not quite as heartless and callous as he pretended to be.

But Elina could do nothing to help him, not just

415

because he had sent her away but because Elina had no idea how to help him. Kilian had been right; what *could* Elina do?

Nothing, except stay by his side and support him. But he doesn't want that.

Sadly she thought of the way Kilian's face lit up when he saw the overcoat Elina had made him. She wished she could go back to that moment and stay in it, when curses and storms and thrones had been the last things on either of their minds.

"Elina? What's wrong?"

She shook her head, a small, humourless smile on her face. "Nothing, mama. I'm just...I don't know. Stuck."

Lily frowned at her daughter. "Stuck? How so? Has Daven –"

"It's nothing to do with Daven," Elina said quickly. In truth she hadn't thought about Daven since she first slept with Kilian. For her mother to bring him up now felt bizarre and out-of-place. It made Elina realise that she really had outgrown Alder and its people, even if they were welcoming to her now.

"So his brother really isn't missing?"

"You really think he could go *missing*? No, he ran off, I'm telling you."

Elina's ears pricked up at the conversation the group of men were having behind her. Noticing the change in her expression, Lily didn't try to continue their conversation. Instead she listened carefully alongside her daughter.

"How would you know that?" Fred, the town head, demanded. Clearly he didn't believe the other man.

"I was the one sent back to the castle to tell Prince

416

Kilian that his brother was going to be delayed for a few weeks. It was all a ruse to buy Gabriel some time."

"But why would he do such a thing? To run off when there's a war going –"

"The war's done," the man interrupted. "As soon as Prince Kilian spoke to the foreign diplomats everything was tied up and sorted."

Kilian doesn't know that, Elina thought. It felt like her heart was simultaneously frozen and beating far too quickly.

Frederick clucked his tongue. "What in the world is going on? How as a country are we supposed to deal with a king who keeps our armies down at the border just so he can use them as a ruse to *run off*? And for what purpose?"

"A woman. It's always a woman."

"Why not bring the woman back with him and take his place on the throne?"

"Do you really think anyone in their right mind wants to live in a country where the winters are like *this*?" the man asked. Elina didn't need to see him to know that he was gesturing out the window towards the storm. "She's not from around here; she's from much further south, apparently."

"But living in a castle, married to a king...who wouldn't want that?"

Elina stood up abruptly, surprising everyone in the near vicinity. Her mother grabbed her arm.

"Where are you going, Elina? If you want to head home –"

"The castle," she muttered. The men who were talking stared at her, confused and unsure about what was going on. "Kil – the prince regent needs to know what's going on."

The messenger who'd been sent to tell Kilian of his brother's delay grew pale. "You cannot tell him. It was his brother's orders to keep him in the dark."

Elina rounded on him. "Tell me, who sits on the throne? And who has run off? You should have told the truth from the beginning. You have no idea what you've done."

"What I've – what have I done?!"

But Elina stormed out of the tavern before the man had finished his sentence, though her mother was shouting for her to return. She was furious. She was heartbroken.

I scorned Kilian for not caring about his brother when clearly his brother does not care for him.

Tears began to well up in Elina's eyes, burning painfully when the bitter wind blew against them. It really was too cold and tumultuous and dangerous to be outside. But if the weather was the way it was then Kilian himself could only be worse. Elina needed to see him. Talk to him. He needed to know what his brother had done.

When she finally reached the castle Elina could not feel her hands nor feet nor face. She was beyond freezing; even so, she struggled to the servant's entrance to the castle and banged upon the surface. But the door was locked, and after a few minutes Elina had to conclude that nobody was going to let her in.

Staggering through the snow drifts she made her way to the monstrously large front doors of the castle, once more pounding her numb, ice-cold fists against the wood and iron.

"Kilian, let me in!" she screamed. The wind carried her voice away as if it were nothing more than a whisper.

She hit the door again. "Let me in! Let me in! Let me in! Kilian, I need to talk to you!"

But there was no response. Elina couldn't even see well enough through the snow to know if Kilian was watching her from a window. And so she continued to bang against the door and shout until her throat was raw and her voice was hoarse, even though it was futile.

Eventually she could keep it up no longer. The cold began to make Elina tired – dangerously tired – so she leaned against the door. A few minutes later she slid down to the snow, her legs having lost the strength to keep her upright.

"Kilian," she cried, her voice barely audible even to her. "I'm cold."

He didn't answer.

CHAPTER TWENTY-TWO

Kilian

Kilian had been staring at a bottle of vodka for hours now. Every time he picked up the bottle, opened the lid and placed it to his lips something stopped him, which only made him more furious.

I want to drink, he thought. *I want to forget everything.*

He knew it was impossible.

Now that he was in full control of his senses he didn't want to willingly take them away. Kilian needed to work out a way to free himself of the curse placed upon him by his father, and for that he needed his brain to be fully

420

functioning. But he couldn't work out *what* to do, or how. He didn't have access to a magician or even books on curses and spells to work from. Not for the first time, Kilian regretted how little he'd paid attention to the education his parents had so desperately tried to force upon him.

When the window rattled in its frame Kilian jumped; it sounded dangerously close to shattering. With a sigh he dragged himself over to make sure the latch was securely in place, wincing at the noise the wind and hailstones made against the glass. He could see nothing outside but darkness and swirling, never-ending snow. With a sadistic grin Kilian thought of the town of Alder, the people fearfully huddled in their houses and clinging to the hope that the storm would soon pass.

It won't, he thought. *I'll make sure of that.*

He knew it wasn't fair, to punish other people for something his brother had done to him, but even if Kilian wanted to he wouldn't have been able to stop the freezing blizzard. He was too unstable; too furious; too lost.

When a tentative knock on the door drew Kilian's attention away from the window, he pulled his old, ragged overcoat a little closer against his chest and called the person in. He couldn't bear to look at the one Elina made him after how he'd treated her, much less wear it.

Marielle took a few steps into Kilian's chambers. "Your Royal Highness, please pardon the intrusion."

"That depends on what the intrusion is for," he replied, rubbing his temple to try and force a nagging headache away. Kilian didn't want to have to deal with people right now if he could at all avoid it.

"Miss Brodeur was attempting to enter the castle through the servant's door. We didn't let her in."

"Good."

Marielle glanced at Kilian uncertainly before casting her gaze to the floor. "She moved to the main entrance. I don't think she's left yet."

That gave Kilian pause. *What's she thinking, travelling to the castle when the weather is so bad? She's a fool.*

"She'll get the message and return home soon enough," he said, hoping it to be true. "She's not stupid."

"It doesn't seem like she –"

"Thank you for letting me know, Marielle. You may go."

Kilian rushed back over to his window but, as before, he could see nothing but darkness and snow. Straining against the roar of the wind he tried to hear Elina shouting, but of course he couldn't. With any luck she'd already given up and gone home.

I can't see her, he thought. *I just can't. Not after what I said. And if I am to be trapped here forever then I don't want her feeling obligated to stay in Alder for my sake. She should just leave and forget about me.*

Such a thought hurt Kilian, ripping at his heart more than the cold ever could; he didn't *want* Elina to forget about him. But the chances of him being able to break his curse were so low. It wasn't something Elina should have to bear.

"Go home, Elina," he muttered into the darkness, before retreating to his bed and collapsing on top of it.

Kilian lay there for a while, staring up at his ceiling with sightless eyes in the hopes that eventually he would fall asleep.

He didn't.

After an hour or two he swung back up to his feet with

the intention of wandering down to the kitchen to grab some food, though he wasn't hungry. But he had nothing else to do, and nothing new to think about.

Loneliness felt so much worse after knowing what it felt like to *not* be lonely.

A nagging impulse pushed Kilian to stop by the front doors first. They were heavy, and there was nobody around to help him open them, so he was reluctant to even try. But even so...with a whistle of breath through his teeth Kilian struggled to open one of the doors just wide enough for him to peer outside. At first he saw nothing out of the ordinary. No people. No shouting.

Kilian felt a wave of relief wash over him, though it was mixed with a keening sense of regret that he hadn't simply let Elina into the castle in the first place. And then –

A snow-covered figure fell through the gap in the door, a glimpse of blue material and dark hair only just visible beneath the ice that was dislodged when the person hit the floor with a thud.

"*No,*" Kilian mouthed, horrified beyond words. With shaking hands he dragged Elina inside and slammed the door behind them, holding her close to his chest as he stood and ran for help.

"Marielle!" he screamed. "Somebody! Anybody! Help me!"

Kilian could hardly bear to look at Elina's face as he ran for his room. She was unconscious; he couldn't even tell if she was breathing. And she was *pale,* a word Kilian would never have used to describe Elina's complexion before. She was colder than any living thing had a right to be.

When he reached his bed he gently placed Elina down upon it and removed her stiff, frozen cape and placed his head to her chest, checking for a heartbeat. It was just barely there.

"Run a bath!" he ordered a shocked Marielle when she appeared at the door. "Not too hot," he added on, remembering what his mother used to tell him about people who had been out in the cold for too long.

Kilian unlaced Elina's dress, silently apologising for doing something so shameful when she wasn't conscious. But he had to; he had to remove every last piece of snow-covered, sodden clothing that she had on. When she was naked Kilian held her in his arms and lay beneath the covers, smoothing snow out of her hair as he anxiously watched her blue lips, wishing they'd hurry up and return to their usual, irresistible colour.

"You idiot," he muttered through chattering teeth, "you obstinate idiot." Elina was so cold she almost burned his skin. Belatedly he wondered if this was what she'd felt like when Kilian had asked her to keep *him* warm in bed two weeks ago.

No, this must be worse. I don't see how I was ever this cold.

"S-sire, the bath is ready."

"Tend to the fire," he ordered, "then head to the kitchens and have some food prepared. Soup. Tea. Anything easy on the stomach." A few minutes later Marielle vacated his room, then Kilian lifted Elina out of bed and gingerly placed her in the bath. Marielle had done her job properly; the bath was a gentle temperature. The now roaring fire seemed to be competing with the wind outside in an effort to make as much noise as possible.

Kilian desperately wanted the fire to win.

Finding a cloth, he soaked the material and gently

scrubbed Elina's face and washed her hair. "Come on, idiot," he begged her unconscious face, watching as her cheeks slowly began to regain some colour. "Wake up. You have to wake up."

It took a while before Elina's body finally seemed to return to an almost normal temperature, but she still didn't rouse when Kilian took her out of the bath, dried her off and dressed her in the large, luxurious robe she'd worn before, after the two of them had drunkenly taken a bath together. Then he sat her against his chest in front of the fire, feeling her heartbeat gradually speed up against his hand.

Marielle had been and gone with the food Kilian had requested before Elina finally, tortuously, began to wake. Her dark lashes fluttered, and a low moan escaped her lips.

"Elina!" Kilian cried out, turning her around to face him. "What were you thinking?! Have you lost your senses completely? What's *wrong* with you?"

"Kilian...?" Elina slurred, her brain struggling to work out where and when she was. But after a few blinks she finally seemed to properly wake up, and she tensed in Kilian's arms. Her eyes went wide. "Kilian – your brother –"

"You think I care about my brother right now?!" He crushed her against his chest, burying his face into her damp hair as he willed himself not to cry. "You almost died and you want to talk about my *brother*?"

But Elina feebly pushed him away with what little strength she had. "Kilian, you have to listen to me, please! You really think I sat in that storm just to tell you off again?"

Kilian was pained. He didn't want to talk about

425

anything else that wasn't to do with himself and Elina. The rest of the world could burn – or freeze – for all he cared. Just so long as Elina was okay. But if she had really, stupidly risked her life to talk to him about his brother...

"What about Gabriel?" he sighed, pulling over the bowl of soup Marielle had brought in and handing it to Elina. She drank straight from the bowl with a serene, grateful expression, before growing serious once more.

"He hasn't gone missing. He ran off."

"...what?"

"I heard in the tavern," Elina continued. "The messenger who first came to tell you Gabriel was missing was talking to the town head. The war's been over for weeks, but he was keeping you in the dark to use the fighting on the border as a ruse to run off with a woman. Kilian, I'm so sorry – I should have believed you in the first place. He –"

"Gabriel really isn't coming back?"

Somehow the news stunned him, even though it was what Kilian had been thinking for weeks anyway. But it was one thing to believe something without any evidence. It was another thing entirely to find out that, all along, he'd been right to doubt his brother.

Gabriel had abandoned him, and it stung like nothing else ever had.

Elina clutched his hand. "Kilian, I'm so –"

"It's fine. I'm just glad you're okay. *I'm* the one who's sorry for telling you to leave."

She said nothing in response to Kilian's apology, even though he never apologised to anyone. But she smiled, and that was all he had to see.

He ran a hand through his hair. "Guess I really am

stuck here," he said, trying to keep his voice as even and casual as possible. "Guess I'm going to have to make peace with that fact before I freeze everyone to death."

Kilian wasn't expecting Elina's eyes to light up. She stared at him in earnest. "Kilian," she began, "do you think you could remember exactly what your father said and *how* he said it when he placed the curse on you?"

He frowned. "Yes...why?"

"Because I might have a magician that can help."

CHAPTER TWENTY-THREE

Elina

It was an odd feeling, sitting in the strategy room of the Hale castle with Kilian, Scarlett Duke and Adrian Wolfe. Kilian was holding Elina's hand so tightly it almost hurt; he'd hardly let go of her since her brush with icy-cold death. It was reassuring, and gratifying, too, but it was also terrifying. It reminded Elina of just how close she'd stupidly come to killing herself...and what that would have meant. She'd have left her mother all alone. She'd have left *Kilian* alone, and he'd have never known what his brother had done.

Elina resolved to never act so rashly and stupidly ever

again.

"So how did the two of you end up in such a miserable place like Alder in the middle of winter?" Kilian asked Scarlett and Adrian.

Scarlett smiled. "We've been travelling around for the past couple of years following rumours of magic. Most of the leads we followed turned out to be false. Imagine our surprise when we met Elina and realised we had finally come across true magic!"

Kilian raised an eyebrow. "True magic from Elina?" He looked at her suspiciously. "I thought you didn't know any magic."

"Oh, she definitely doesn't," Adrian said, "but this castle is crawling with it. Her working here brought her in contact with it, so when we met her I could sense it."

"I find that hard to believe."

"And why is that?"

"I can't *feel* magic in here and I'm the one who's cursed."

Adrian laughed, his amber eyes bright with amusement. "That's because you don't know what it feels like. In time you would."

"I've been cursed for months, magician, is that not time enough?"

"Try years."

Kilian's eyes narrowed; even Elina looked at Adrian in surprise.

"You've been cursed for years?" she asked, curious.

"Yes," Adrian replied smoothly, as if the issue of being cursed didn't bother him whatsoever.

"What kind of –"

"A story for another time," Scarlett interjected. "I feel like the subject of your *own* curse, Your Royal Highness –"

"Call me Kilian."

"The subject of your own curse, Kilian, is far more pressing," Scarlett finished. "Was your father definitely not touching anything when he cursed you?"

Kilian shook his head. "I wasn't facing him, and I was blind drunk, so I don't know. But I don't think so. The words were identical to the ones Elina's father spoke the first time, and *he* wasn't holding anything."

Adrian nodded. "Do you have anything of your father's?"

"Like a ring or a jacket?"

"No. Hair or bone or skin. Something *from* him."

Kilian thought carefully for a few moments, eyes staring sightlessly at the ceiling as he pondered the question. Then he nodded. "I'll be right back."

They waited for Kilian's return, Elina feeling curiously impatient. She wanted badly to know about Adrian's curse, and why he needed something of Kilian's father, and what their next move was going to be, and –

Kilian returned holding a familiar silver locket. He was staring at it with an odd expression on his face. "This was my mother's," he said. "She kept a lock of my father's hair in it. Stupidly sentimental. I suppose I'm glad of it now."

Then it seemed like a switch flicked on. He looked at Elina, then back at the locket. "The buttons on the overcoat you made me – the pattern on them matches this."

Elina's face reddened. "I may have found it when I was sneaking about the castle," she admitted sheepishly.

"The pattern was so beautiful I couldn't help but replicate it. And it's not like I went rummaging through any drawers...it was just lying there on a table."

"I was looking at it myself earlier that day," Kilian mused, sitting down and handing the locket over to Adrian. "I don't know why."

"Maybe you're not so bad at sensing magic as you think," Adrian quipped, clicking open the locket and grasping the lock of hair between his fingers, a frown creasing his brow. It only deepened as time wore on.

"What is it?" Scarlett asked.

Adrian glanced at Kilian. "Give me some of your own hair."

Somewhat dubious, Kilian brought out a pocket knife and cut off a small quantity of hair from the bottom of his braid and handed it over to the other man.

After a few long moments of silence Adrian sighed. "Your father didn't curse you."

"I – what?"

"There's no magical link between the two of you. Your father had the spell cast on him, yes, but he isn't the one who transferred it to *you*."

"How do you know that?" Elina asked.

"It's...complicated," Adrian admitted. "It's not easy to explain. But there's a link missing. The identity of the curse placed on Kilian doesn't match his father." He stared at Kilian. "Did you ever talk to your father about the curse after it was put on you?"

He shook his head. "I didn't speak to him at all. But that wasn't anything new – I avoided being in the castle as much as possible. I only stayed after the curse was put on me because I knew my father was going to die soon, and if

I was anywhere else in the world when that happened then the curse would kill me for leaving the castle."

Nobody spoke for a while. Kilian, Scarlett and Elina all watched Adrian as he mulled over the unexpected problem at hand.

Eventually he asked, "Do you have anything of your brother's?"

No one needed this explained to them; the insinuation was obvious. Wordlessly Kilian left the room and returned a few minutes later with a brush laden with pale blonde strands of hair, handing it over to Adrian before sitting down.

It didn't take long before Adrian nodded. "It was Gabriel, no doubt about it."

Kilian banged a fist upon the table. "I don't understand! How did that happen – I thought that –"

"The only way to know what happened is to speak to your brother yourself."

"But he's run off!"

To everyone's surprise, Adrian shook his head. "He's about five miles away, and heading this way. Seems he hasn't run off as far as you think."

Kilian's mouth was wide in disbelief. "How do you know that?"

He waved the hairbrush. "There are perks to being a magician."

Elina squeezed Kilian's hand. "I guess you'll get your answers one way or another sooner rather than later."

But Kilian's face was blank; Elina couldn't tell what he was thinking at all.

"What am I supposed to do when he shows up, if he

432

doesn't tell me anything or simply leaves again?" he asked quietly. "If he has no intention of taking over then how can I force him to?"

Nobody answered.

Nobody knew.

CHAPTER TWENTY-FOUR

Kilian

"Are you sure you don't want me here with you?"

"No; I need to talk with him by myself."

Elina fussed with the buttons of Kilian's overcoat before he sat down on the throne. He was wearing the splendidly embroidered one Elina had made him, having finally thrown his old one in the fire. Paired with dark trousers, supple, leather boots, a clean-shaven face and his hair elegantly tied back, Kilian for once looked every inch a king.

All for a meeting with his brother, in which he'd have

to try his hardest to push said role onto him. Kilian had no idea what to do or say; the whole endeavour seemed impossible.

The weather had cleared up since Kilian had warmed Elina back to life. She'd spent every night in the castle since then with him, and most of the daytime, too. It kept him settled and in control, even though Kilian rather felt like he might explode at any given moment.

But he couldn't have Elina with him when he spoke to his brother. It was something he had to do on his own if he wanted to settle things once and for all. That didn't make it any easier to watch Elina squeeze his hand, smile reassuringly at him and turn to leave, though; Kilian grabbed her wrist and pulled her back to him, landing a kiss upon her forehead without really thinking of what he was doing.

Elina glanced up at him through her eyelashes, the blush that spread across her cheeks unbearably pretty. "What was that for?" she asked softly.

"For nothing at all. For everything. Thank you, Elina."

When she broke away from him she rolled her eyes. "You don't have to keep thanking me for every little thing, Kilian. It's not like I'm going to disappear if you act like your usual, ungrateful, cynical self."

Kilian laughed into his hand before regaining his composure. "I suppose there's no point in acting like someone else around you. I have to at least *try* and appear level-headed and diplomatic if I'm to talk to Gabriel properly, though."

"So you're trying it out on me first?"

"No," he said. "I simply wanted to thank you."

Elina looked torn between leaving the throne room and returning to Kilian's side once more. "I'll be in the parlour room with Scarlett and Adrian in case you need me."

Kilian nodded.

And then Elina was gone, leaving him alone on the throne, pretending to be king. Kilian felt like he was going to be violently sick; his stomach was churning and his heart palpitating so badly he wished for alcohol to calm his nerves. But he persisted, keeping his back straight and his face calm when, finally, a knock on the door signalled the arrival of his brother.

Gabriel Hale looked regal even in the simple travelling clothes he was wearing as he entered the throne room. It was something about the way he held himself and walked with a purpose; when the two of them had been out in public Gabriel had always been recognised for what he was, whereas Kilian could slink off to a whorehouse without being noticed at all.

The brothers shared the pale eyes and even paler hair of their father, but Gabriel's jaw was more squared-off that Kilian's, and his cheekbones wider. He had a handsome face that screamed trustworthy. And Gabriel was just as even-tempered as their father had been. He never had a cruel word to say about anyone, and he was diplomatic to a fault in arguments. Everything about him was perfectly suited for being king.

Except that he had run away.

"Gabriel," Kilian drawled. "You don't look all that missing to me."

His brother grinned. "Well aren't you a sight for sore eyes up there, Kilian. You actually got dressed properly to greet me!"

He rolled his eyes. "Hardly. Where have you been? I've heard...conflicting reports about what's been going on at the borders. Is it true the fighting is over?"

Gabriel nodded. "There were some skirmishes I had to deal with that delayed the whole process, but yes. Thank you for dealing with those diplomats a few weeks back."

Kilian kept his suspicions from showing on his face. If the conversation Elina overheard was to be believed, then the fighting had been over weeks ago, and Gabriel was lying.

"I was informed that you were missing," he said, choosing his words very carefully. "I was worried."

Gabriel burst out laughing; the sound irked Kilian. "You, worried about me? I don't think so Kilian. I thought you were a better liar than that. I know you were only concerned about me taking the throne off your hands."

"And is that not what you've returned to do? You *are* the king, after all. And god knows nobody wants me to do it – least of all me. You know how useless I am."

Something flashed across Gabriel's face that Kilian didn't like the look of at all. He stared at his brother sitting on the throne and shook his head. "Maybe you *are* useless, Kilian, but it's because you never try. Can't you put some effort into something for once?"

"Why should I? I'm merely prince regent. The throne is yours, and now you're back."

"No, Kilian. I'm not."

"...excuse me?"

Gabriel ran a hand through his glossy hair. "This is a courtesy visit, brother. I won't be back. I have no intention of taking the throne – of being tied to it. My heart belongs elsewhere."

437

Kilian stood up immediately, pounding down the steps from the throne to reach his brother. Gabriel was taller than him; Kilian hated that he was. "I was never meant to be king," he seethed. "I'm not the one who should be trapped here."

"And yet you are. Father must have seen something -"

"*I know it was you!*" Kilian screamed. "I know it was you who cursed me, Gabriel!"

Gabriel seemed taken aback by this for a few moments, but then he schooled his expression and an easy smile crossed his lips. "I guess there's no point in asking how you know that. Either way, *you're* the one stuck in the castle, little brother. Not me."

Kilian glared at him. "Why did you do this to me? *How* could you do this to me?"

"Because father wouldn't," Gabriel explained. "I begged him to do it. I didn't want to stay here, on the mountainside. I wasn't ready to be trapped in the castle; I still had so much I wanted to do."

"And you think I didn't?!"

Gabriel laughed incredulously. "Tell me, Kilian, what have you ever done with your life? Nothing. Some responsibility will do you good."

"I don't want this!"

"And neither do I." Gabriel rounded on him, eyes glittering dangerously. "When father passed the curse on to me I guess he expected me to return from the borders as soon as I was sent word he was on his deathbed. For all he knew I *had* to, otherwise the curse would kill me. Tell me, how did he react when I never returned? Did he realise what I'd done - that I'd passed his damned magic on to you?"

438

Kilian looked away. "I didn't speak to him. I wasn't even there when he died."

The laugh that was emitted from Gabriel's mouth was warped and cruel. "But of course you didn't. Classic, responsibility-shirking, closed-off Kilian at his finest. I suppose you get points for consistency, though had you only talked to father you'd have realised he never wanted you tied to the throne in the first place."

"You're...unbelievable," Kilian muttered. His hands were shaking; he curled them into fists. "Do you really think I'll let you leave the castle knowing all this?"

Gabriel shrugged. "And what can you do to keep me here? Nothing."

Kilian punched him in the face, but what he wasn't expecting was a sharp pain in his stomach in return. He looked down.

Gabriel had stabbed him.

"You...son of a bitch..." Kilian breathed.

"You won't die from something so minor, little brother," Gabriel said as he removed the knife and let it clatter to the floor. "I just need you incapacitated long enough for me to get far from here. Goodbye, Kilian."

Kilian didn't stay conscious long enough to watch his brother leave.

CHAPTER TWENTY-FIVE

Elina

When Elina found Kilian passed out on the floor of the throne room in a pool of blood she screamed. She'd never been one for raising her voice before, but in the past few days she'd found herself being louder than she ever had been. Shouting at Kilian. Wailing at the weather because of Kilian. Crying out *for* Kilian.

"Somebody help me!" she exclaimed, holding her hand to the wound in Kilian's stomach and putting as much pressure on it as she dared. On the floor by his side lay an ornate dagger, its intricately carved blade stained crimson. "Why wasn't anyone around to stop this?" she demanded when a couple of servants rushed into the room, followed by Scarlett and Adrian. "Why did nobody stop Gabriel?! Where is he?"

One of the servants looked back towards the doors. "He – we didn't know to stop him! We received no orders to detain him, and it's not as if Prince Kilian kept any personal guards in the castle – he got rid them all!"

Elina was too panicked to even be angry with Kilian for such a stupid move. Her eyes darted from Kilian's ashen face to the servants and back again. "Call a doctor. There must be one in the – oh, no. Don't say it."

They shook their heads sadly. "His Royal Highness let him go, too."

She almost pounded her fists on Kilian's chest. "You're an *idiot*!" she cried, not caring who heard her talk about the prince in such a way. But then Scarlett and Adrian knelt down beside her, and Scarlett calmly undid the buttons of Kilian's overcoat and removed it. Elina could hardly look at the dark fabric stained even darker with his blood.

"Elina, we'll handle this," Scarlett said. "Go ahead to Kilian's room and wait for us there."

"But –"

"Just do it," she interrupted firmly. Elina had never heard Scarlett speak in such a commanding tone before, but she wasn't in a position to protest. With one final, agonised look at Kilian's deathly pale face Elina got to her feet and stumbled to his chambers, flinging herself onto his bed when she reached it.

She wished there was a storm outside to mask the sounds of her crying, but outside it was eerily calm. Elina hated the silence. She hated what it insinuated.

"Don't you dare die, you coward," she muttered into a

pillow. "Don't you dare."

*

Two hours passed before Kilian slowly came to. Adrian had propped him up in bed against several pillows; as soon as he began groaning and muttering Elina immediately roused from where she had been dozing, curled up beside him. She poured a glass of water and brought it to Kilian's lips before he'd even opened his eyes.

"I - hold on," Kilian spluttered weakly. He waved the water away. "Give me a minute. Ah, that hurts..." He looked down at his now tightly-bandaged stomach, mildly impressed. "Who patched me up? There's no doctor nearby."

"Scarlett did," Adrian replied. The woman in question was asleep in front of the blazing fire; nobody made a move to wake her. "Care to tell us what exactly happened, Kilian? Though I imagine it's not too difficult to put the pieces together."

Kilian took the glass of water from Elina and drank the entire thing before answering. "What I wouldn't give for that to be vodka," he joked, though his voice was strained as if trying to be funny physically hurt him. He took hold of Elina's hand, which was shaking. "I'm okay, Elina. Even Gabriel said I wouldn't die from the wound. I do not think he intended to kill me - merely to prevent me from going after him."

"That's - that's just as bad!" Elina cried, winding her fingers through Kilian's in a desperate attempt to get closer to him. She wished Scarlett and Adrian weren't in the room, so she could hide under the covers with Kilian and pretend the rest of the world didn't exist.

But that would solve nothing, even though it was all she could do personally for Kilian. Elina had never felt so useless.

Kilian smiled humourlessly. "Probably. Either way, he admitted to being the one who cursed me. He never wanted the throne, it seems. Clearly I should have tried harder to get to know my brother when I had the chance, then I might have seen this coming early enough to do something about it."

"Did he – did Gabriel say *why* he didn't want the throne?" Elina asked uncertainly. "Did he mention the woman he's supposed to have fallen for?"

"I didn't even get to ask about her. All Gabriel said was that he didn't want to be trapped here when he still had so much he wanted to see and do. It's not exactly a sentiment I don't share."

"But being king was *his* responsibility, not yours!"

Kilian stayed silent.

After a few moments Adrian spoke up, though he sounded very much like he didn't want to. "You know what you have to do to get out of this, don't you?"

"Does it really have to be this way?"

"The only other way to remove the curse is for another blood relative to take it on. You have none, other than Gabriel, and he's made it clear that he has no intention of holding the throne."

Elina stared at Adrian, confused. She narrowed her eyes. "What do you mean, Adrian? Kilian, what is it you have to do?"

Kilian hesitated. "I have to kill him. I have to kill my brother."

"No!" she cried, horrified. "Why? Adrian, surely

there's something you can *do?* There must be another spell, or a counter-curse, or –"

"Elina, the magic your father performed was very, very complicated. I'm still struggling to work out exactly what he did, and how he did it. The surest way to remove a curse once and for all is to destroy the one who cast it... trust me, I know this all too well."

Adrian's eyes darted to Scarlett's sleeping figure as he spoke, and he was relieved to see she hadn't woken up. He smiled gently for Elina. "There is nothing else to be done about it. Kilian has to kill his brother."

"But, then..." Elina stared at her fingers entwined with Kilian's. "If you kill your brother to free you of the curse, who will then be king?"

Kilian laughed bitterly. "A problem for another day. I have to force Gabriel back to the castle first before we think about that." He stared out of the window, a frown shadowing his brow. "How long was I unconscious?"

"About two hours," Elina said. "Why?"

"Gabriel couldn't have gotten far in two hours with all the snow on the ground, even with the fair weather this afternoon. He should still be in range to feel the full brunt of a tempestuous little brother."

"Kilian?"

He grinned, eyes gleaming like the drunk madman Elina had first met. "Time to whip up one hell of a storm."

CHAPTER TWENTY-SIX

Kilian

Kilian had never so viciously enjoyed being in control of the weather. Though Elina wouldn't let him leave his bed to sit by the window, he could still hear the horrendous noise of the storm and imagine the carnage it was causing just fine.

It hadn't been difficult for him to produce the storm. Kilian was in pain, and he was furious with his brother, as well as feeling betrayed. Part of him still couldn't quite believe Gabriel had stabbed him, even if it wasn't meant to be lethal.

He came into the throne room knowing he'd have to

do something like that to keep me from stopping him, Kilian thought, barely keeping his temper in check at the memory of the cold, icy blade sliding into his stomach. *If I ever had any qualms about killing Gabriel before, I don't now.*

The plan was simple enough; if Gabriel was to have a hope of leaving the mountainside then he'd have to come and make his peace with Kilian. When he showed up, he'd be taken to Kilian's rooms to talk to him. Then, when he got close enough, Kilian would cut him with a knife coated in an evil-looking poison Adrian had given him. The blade would barely have to scratch the surface of Gabriel's skin; all the poison needed was one, tiny entryway to his bloodstream.

"Easy enough," Kilian muttered, stomach smarting when he tried to reposition himself in bed. Scarlett had done a superb job of tending to the stab wound – it wasn't even bleeding any more. But internally he was still suffering, and the plant extracts Kilian had been given to help with the pain were beginning to wear off.

Good, he thought. *Let the pain make the blizzard even worse.*

Four hours had passed since Kilian woke up. It was dark outside, and almost time for most people to retire to bed. Dully he thought that he'd rather like to join them in that regard; to fall back against the pillows with Elina in his arms, warm and safe and thinking of nothing but each other. But that was something to look forward to *after* the not-so-simple task of murdering his brother. Kilian grimaced at the thought.

And then...

He couldn't shake what Elina had asked upon finding out that Kilian would have to kill Gabriel. Who *would* be

446

king once Kilian was free of the throne? Although he wanted nothing more than to run away and never think about it ever again, Kilian knew that he couldn't. Not if he wanted Elina to stay by his side and respect him as a human being. He couldn't leave the country in upheaval. He couldn't allow Alder to struggle through the next winter with no provisions put in place to help against awful mountainside weather.

When he heard a knock on the door Kilian flinched. "Who is it?"

A pause. "You know who it is, brother."

Gritting his teeth against what was to come next, Kilian called out, "Come in, then."

Gabriel was completely soaked through and half-covered in ice. When Kilian indicated towards a chair deliberately placed by his bedside, Gabriel instead headed straight for the fire to warm up his hands.

"I won't apologise for what I did," he said, back turned to Kilian as he basked in the heat from the flames.

"I wouldn't expect you to. And yet you're here because you have to ask me to let you leave, which stabbing me was supposed to prevent. Clearly you're not as smart as you think you are."

Gabriel chuckled. "Or perhaps I underestimated how petty you are, Kilian."

"I wouldn't call my reaction to being *stabbed* petty."

"...I guess not. Let me leave, little brother."

"And why should I?"

Gabriel left the heat of the fireplace to sit down in the chair by Kilian's bed. He locked his eyes on his brother, running a hand through his sodden, frozen hair to push it away from his face.

447

"There's a woman, Kilian," he said very quietly. "I met her last year, at a ball. I never thought I'd see her again, but in summer she was travelling through our country. I spent some time with her, and fell completely in love with her. When the fighting broke out at the border I begged for her to go back to her home country, but she would not go. I wrote her so many letters before I was forced to travel down there myself."

Gabriel chuckled. "She's so stubborn. I knew I couldn't face never seeing her again, but I couldn't ask her to give up her freedom and live in this forsaken castle just for me, either. That's the main reason I passed the curse onto you, Kilian. If I hadn't I wouldn't have been able to be with the woman I love."

Kilian said nothing. His hand was wrapped around the handle of the poison-soaked knife. All he had to do was reach out and nick Gabriel's hand. But his brother's words were keeping him from moving, for of course he understood exactly how Gabriel was feeling.

"...did you not think I felt the same way, Gabriel?" Kilian asked, so softly his words were almost lost to the wind and the roar of the fire. "That I didn't want to be stuck here all alone?"

Gabriel eyed him awkwardly. "You – you've always been alone, Kilian. You never wanted to be with anyone, and that certainly didn't seem to change when you reached adulthood. You never loved anybody."

"That's not true, and you know it. Don't try to deflect responsibility by believing me incapable of love."

"Our parents are dead, Kilian. Who is there left for you?"

Kilian was overwhelmed by a wave of anger at such a remark. "You truly think I couldn't meet somebody new to care for?" he accused, eyes blazing. "Do you believe nobody would be able to put up with me long enough to care about me back? Is that it?"

"I..." Gabriel stared at his hands, then back at Kilian. "Truthfully, yes. You're my brother, and I love you as best as I can, but you and I both know that you're not a good person."

"Then why would you have me be king?!"

"Because my love for Selene is greater than my love for my country."

Kilian frowned. "Is that her name? Selene? The woman you love?"

His brother nodded.

"It sounds Greek."

"That's because she *is* Greek."

And then, to Gabriel's surprise, Kilian burst out laughing. "How did we end up so similar when we're so different?"

Gabriel stared at him, expression dubious. "What on earth do you mean?"

"I'm in love with the magician's girl," Kilian said, closing his eyes and reclining his head against the pillow in stupid, nonsensical mirth. "I'm completely, shamelessly in love with her, and she's desperate to leave Alder, and I cannot go with her."

"You aren't...you're serious, aren't you?"

He nodded. "Of course I am. She's been by my side throughout the entire winter. I started acting more like a king for her. I stopped *drinking* for her. I fixed the weather for her. Not that any of that matters, ultimately."

"Kilian –"

449

"Just go, brother. Go back to your Selene and live the life you always wanted to have."

Even as Kilian spoke the words he hated himself. He didn't want to be stuck in the castle forever. He wanted to kill his brother and be free of it all. He wanted to run away.

He simply couldn't do it.

For the first time in what felt like years, genuine affection spread across Gabriel's face. "Do you mean that?"

"No. Yes. Of course I do. I hate you, but I still can't force life imprisonment on you...even if you *did* stab me. So go. Don't let me see you again."

Gabriel smiled slightly. "I hope that last part isn't true. I would love for you to meet Selene one day. And I'd like to meet the magician's girl –"

"Don't push your luck," Kilian interrupted, waving his hand toward the door. "Just...go, Gabriel, before I change my mind and make it so cold outside you freeze to death where you stand."

When Gabriel ruffled his hair Kilian raised an arm to stop him. The knife was still in his hand; his brother stared at it sadly.

"You really did mean to kill me."

"I did before. You cannot blame me for it."

"...I guess I can't. I'll come back to see you in summer, Kilian. Try not to destroy the country before then."

"You don't get a say in the matter!" Kilian called out as his brother left the room. He sagged against the pillows, dropping the deadly knife to the floor. He'd lost all will to do anything.

I guess this is my life now, he thought, staring

450

sightlessly at the window as the wind and snow and hail finally began to let up. *Maintaining my temper and being diplomatic for the sake of other people. Great.*

As Kilian drifted off to sleep he almost hoped that, come morning, he wouldn't wake up.

CHAPTER TWENTY-SEVEN

Elina

"You've done such an excellent job of fixing his overcoat, Elina."

"You'd never have known Kilian bled half to death wearing it."

"Adrian!"

Elina laughed softly. The three of them were sitting by the fire in her mother's house, drinking wine whilst Elina finished up the repairs to Kilian's overcoat. When her mother came in with a tray of food both Adrian and Scarlett's eyes lit up.

"Thank you, Lily!" Scarlett exclaimed, which was echoed by Adrian. The two of them had grown close to Lily during their stay in Alder; Elina suspected they talked about her mother's affair with the magician as well as digging up old and embarrassing stories about Elina herself. She was glad for it; her mother relished the company.

"Don't mention it," Lily said, sitting down in her favourite chair by the fire before being handed a goblet of wine from Adrian. "You really have done a wonderful job repairing the coat, Elina," she remarked as she observed the fabric. "When you brought it back to the shop my heart almost broke in two. You worked so hard on it."

"Yes, well, it was just about the only thing I managed to do of use for Kilian," she muttered.

Elina hadn't wanted Kilian to kill his older brother. That didn't change how distraught she was that Kilian was now stuck forever in a castle he hated, doing a job he'd never wanted in a country he was desperate to escape from. He'd given up everything for his brother's happiness, even after what Gabriel had done to him. It wasn't something Elina could understand, since she had no siblings herself, so all she could do was respect Kilian's decision and support him.

He hadn't unceremoniously kicked Elina, nor Scarlett and Adrian, from his castle after Gabriel left. But Kilian also hadn't spoken much, choosing instead to sleep and keep to himself, so the three of them had returned to Alder three days after he'd let his brother go. Elina wanted nothing more than to stay by Kilian's side and tell him everything would be fine, but she knew it was a lie.

Nothing was fine. And, if Elina was being honest, she wasn't sure if she had it in her to stay in Alder the rest of her life for Kilian's sake. He certainly wouldn't allow her to in the first place – Kilian had made that much very clear from the moment he'd first heard Gabriel was missing. It demonstrated just how much he'd grown as a person, even if Kilian would deny such growth.

It only made Elina feel worse.

Adrian gently kicked her ankle, knocking her out of her reverie. "There's nothing you can do, Elina, short of chasing after Gabriel and killing him on Kilian's behalf."

Elina made a face. "Don't tempt me."

Scarlett sighed into her wine. "It's not fair. On anyone. Your country will suffer from having a king who does not wish to lead, and their dissent will in turn negatively affect Kilian. And that's not even touching upon the personal issues the curse brings up. I don't think Kilian will last all that long locked up."

"The only reason he's still alive is that he's been too much of a coward to kill himself," Elina admitted, a cold shiver crawling up her spine despite the heat from the fire. "Something tells me he's becoming less of a coward with every passing day...and that's not a good thing."

From her chair in the corner Lily watched her daughter with an expression full of sympathy. "Elina, he might yet prove to be stronger than you all think he is. Didn't he properly work with those diplomats before? The ones that *actually* ended the fighting?"

Elina nodded. "But I had to *force* him to speak to them."

Her mother smiled. "But even so, Kilian did do his job. And he chose not to kill his brother, even though that meant tying himself to the position of king. I think he's far more magnanimous than any of us have given him credit for."

"Mama, that's not the problem," Elina said, head

drooping sadly. "Kilian could pour his heart and soul into being a good king – and actually manage it – but that doesn't change the fact that he's trapped in the castle. He can't even go out into the castle grounds! And the weather entirely depends on him keeping level-headed. Kilian...he was already halfway to madness when I met him. Being cooped up for the rest of his life will only make things worse."

There was silence in the room for a long time after that, for Elina spoke the truth. They could all try their best to help with improving Kilian's circumstances within the boundaries that had been set, but that didn't change how restrictive those boundaries were in the first place.

Eventually Lily downed her wine and allowed Adrian to pour her another glass. "If only Alesandro were here."

Elina stared at her. "Who's Alesandro?"

"Why, your father, of course. Have I – have I never told you his name before?"

"No," Elina said, shaking her head. "And everyone in town called him 'the magician'. I had no idea."

"That's...I'm sorry I never told you, Elina."

Elina waved a dismissive hand. "It doesn't matter. He's not my *father* anyway."

"And yet his blood runs through you nonetheless."

A smash by the fireplace caught them both by surprise; Scarlett had dropped her goblet on the hearth, spilling burgundy wine and glass all over the floor. She was staring at Adrian with wide eyes, which he returned with a look of baffled understanding.

"Of course," he murmured, scratching his chin before beginning to pick up the shards of glass from the floor as if in a trance. "Scarlett, why didn't we think of that before?"

"We were too set on the curse itself. And this wouldn't even be a counter-spell. It's just a...coincidental curse."

Lily and Elina glanced at each other in confusion before setting their eyes on Adrian. "What are you two talking about? What would be a coincidental curse?"

Adrian grinned wolfishly. "Elina, do you think you could cope staying by the king's side for the rest of his life?"

CHAPTER TWENTY-EIGHT

Kilian

Kilian was staring out the window again. This time, however, he wasn't in his own chambers but in the ballroom. The large, expansive windows along the southern wall faced the back gardens of the castle, much like the dining room windows did. He watched sightlessly as the water in the hot springs bubbled and rose as steam, a keening sense of longing filling the pit of his stomach.

He'd largely recovered from the physical trauma of being stabbed, though the mental trauma of the act was something Kilian doubted he'd ever fully get over. He had been the *better person.* He had been the bigger man to his brother, who had always been the golden son.

And he'd been punished for it.

With a sigh he rolled off the windowsill, stalking across the ballroom floor towards the exit. He thought of his and Elina's midnight dance as his footsteps echoed off the walls. It felt like it had happened a thousand years ago when, in truth, it was barely three weeks ago.

So much can happen in so short a space of time, he thought, sighing once more as he made his way up the grand staircase. Kilian didn't really know where he was going – he didn't want to return to his chambers, which were beginning to feel suffocating. He wasn't hungry. He didn't feel like striking up a conversation with any of the servants, nor reading a book in the parlour room. In frustration he collapsed onto the second-from-bottom stair, leaning against the railing as he stared dispassionately at the main doors into, and out of, the castle.

Kilian thought of finding Elina by them, half-frozen to death. If she hadn't literally fallen through the gap in the open door onto the castle floor then Kilian would not have been able to drag her inside.

"How stupid," he muttered, a horrible shudder wracking his body at the thought of having not been able to save Elina because of her father's curse. His stomach twinged in pain; Kilian bent over double until it subsided.

He had no idea how long he sat on the stairs, silent and alone. There was no wind nor snow nor rain to interfere with the quiet, though the sky remained permanently overcast with thick, grey cloud. Kilian could just about control his temper enough to keep the storms at bay, but he was too miserable to let the sun through. He wondered if he'd ever see it again.

When a loud knock on the front door reverberated

around the hall, it took Kilian a moment to respond.

"Who is it?" he called out, leaving the staircase to stand by the heavy wood-and-iron door.

"Kilian?" a familiar but muffled voice exclaimed back. Elina. "What are you doing standing by the door?"

"I don't know."

"Are you going to let me in?"

Kilian considered this for a moment. He knew he had to end things with Elina before it became impossible for him to do so. She needed to be free of any and all lingering responsibility towards him in order to leave Alder and finally live her life. But if he never saw her then he never had to end things, so Kilian seriously considered telling her to leave.

"I can practically hear what you're thinking, *Your Royal Highness*," Elina said sarcastically.

"Technically it's Your Majesty, now," he quipped back. He drooped his head in resignation as he struggled to open the heavy door. "Fine; you can come in."

Elina was stark and beautiful against the snow, in a green dress the colour of pine needles that was astounding layered over the golden tones of her skin. In her arms was a familiar box.

"I come bearing gifts," she announced. "Well, the same gift as before. I repaired your coat."

"I thought you didn't have a green dress," Kilian said, frowning when Elina made no move to enter the castle. "Aren't you going to come in? It's cold by the door."

"I never said I didn't have a green dress – only that I didn't want to wear green," she replied, decidedly avoiding Kilian's question. She twirled on the spot, allowing the skirt of her dress to spin around her. "Do you like it? My mother made it for my eighteenth birthday. I can't believe I was too self-conscious about the way I looked to wear it. Seems pointless now."

Kilian crossed his arms. "It's lovely. Now come in. I can't feel my fingers."

She flashed a mischievous smile. "Why don't you come out here and let me warm them up?"

"Are you drunk, Elina? How could I leave the castle?"

"Just try it."

"No."

"Do it for me."

"Elina," Kilian complained, running a hand over his face in exasperation. "I'm not in the mood for whatever game it is you're playing."

But Elina's face had turned serious. "I'm not playing a game. Try and take a step outside, Kilian."

"Elina –"

"Please."

Kilian felt wretched. Whatever it was Elina was hoping for wasn't going to work. After all, what had changed? Absolutely nothing. But clearly it was important to her, so reluctantly he edged his feet to the door's threshold. He looked at Elina. "I'm not wearing shoes."

She shrugged. "Doesn't matter. Just try it."

Kilian's heart sped up despite himself, thinking that what he was about to do was incredibly stupid. As soon as he reached out to take a step some invisible force would prevent him from doing so, and that would be the end of it. He inched a foot forward.

Nothing happened.

Frowning, Kilian tentatively took a step out onto the

snow, and then another. There was no hook pulling him back inside, nor a wall stopping him moving forward. No, there was only freezing, biting snow beneath his feet, urging him to walk faster and faster until he reached Elina's side.

He stared at her in wonder. "What happened? What did you – what did you do, Elina?"

She beamed. "Adrian and Scarlett have cursed me."

"They've – what?!" Kilian sputtered. "Have you lost your mind?"

Elina merely laughed. "It's nothing bad. In fact, I'd say it's fairly wonderful."

"...what did they do to you?"

"It was my mother's idea, technically," Elina explained, opening the box in her arms and taking out the beautiful overcoat she'd made for Kilian before passing it over to him. He dutifully shrugged it on. "She said something about me having my father's blood. Magician's blood."

"I don't understand," Kilian complained. "I thought we already established you don't possess any magical ability?"

"No, but I still contain the blood of the one who created the spell cast upon the Hale family," she said. "So Adrian managed to weave some...balancing magic, if you will, against your curse. Or maybe 'neutralising' is a better word for it." Elina seemed to ponder this for a moment before shaking her head. "Either way, it negates your own curse. There's only one condition."

"I don't like the sound of that. Elina, I don't want you to have to give up anything for my –"

"Let me finish, Kilian," she laughed. "The condition is that I have to stay by your side. The spell is distance-

461

sensitive, so I can't be further than a few metres away from you in order to keep your curse at bay. Adrian thinks up to ten, maybe, but told me not to push it –"

Kilian cut her off with his mouth upon hers. He couldn't believe what he was hearing. The curse put on him would be lifted *and* Elina would stay with him? Moreover, Elina was the literal reason he could be free of everything in the first place?

"You'd really stay with me for me to be free?" he asked, voice trembling as tears filled his eyes. Kilian didn't care if he looked weak. Not in front of Elina.

She brought a hand up to cup his cheek; above them the sun just barely managed to break through the clouds, lighting the very edges of her hair on fire and adding gold to the green of her eyes. "Of course I'll stay by your side, Kilian. You love me, don't you?"

He choked on a laugh. "*I* love *you?* And what about the other way around?"

Elina wrinkled her nose. "That's up for debate. I guess you'll have to put up with me first and find out."

"This really isn't all a dream? This is really happening?"

"Yes, you idiot."

"Then for the love of god can we get back inside? Otherwise I'll have no feet left with which to wander the world with you."

Elina's lips curled into a sly smile.

"Yes, Your Majesty."

EPILOGUE

Elina

"That's – Your Majesty! Oh my – Gill, get the good wine out! Your Majesty, I –"

"I'd prefer vodka, if you have it," Kilian said mildly, his expression blatantly amused at the looks of shock on the faces of everyone in the tavern. When Elina spied her mother, Scarlett and Adrian sitting at the back of the tavern she linked an arm through Kilian's and wound him through the throng of stunned townspeople.

To her right she spied Daven, staring at her in amazement. She felt just a tinge of guilt that she had not yet properly rejected him. Hopefully walking into the tavern in arm with the literal king would let him down better than Elina ever could with words.

"So you have deigned to drink with the commoners, Your Majesty?" Adrian drawled, face flushed from alcohol. He was clearly rather drunk; Scarlett swatted his arm good-naturedly.

"Careful about what you say when you're drunk. You don't want a repeat of last time when that witchdoctor turned you back into a –"

Adrian laughed the rest of Scarlett's sentence away, just a tinge of embarrassment colouring the red of his cheeks. Elina was deathly curious.

"What were you turned into?" she asked, just as Gill herself brought over an ice-cold bottle of vodka to their table, along with a very good bottle of red wine.

"On the house, of course," she said, her face growing redder than Adrian's when Kilian beamed at her. With his perfect cheekbones, crystal-blue eyes, immaculately-braided hair and expensive clothes it was no wonder Gill was besotted with the sight of him. Out of the corner of her eye Elina spied most of the women of Alder looking at him longingly.

"I preferred you when you were scruffy," she muttered, so quietly only Kilian could hear.

He grinned. "Are you jealous, Elina? Because I'd rather say *I'm* jealous of the way all the men were looking at you when we entered here."

Elina rolled her eyes. "They were not."

She cried out in surprise when Kilian snaked a hand through her hair and pulled her in for a long, lingering kiss. When he let go his eyes were glittering in amusement. "Well, just in case, now they all know both of us are unavailable."

464

"You...behave yourself!" Elina pushed him away and grabbed a goblet of wine, face unbearably hot with the knowledge that most everyone was looking at her. But it was a good kind of embarrassment. She was pleased that Kilian had absolutely no qualms in demonstrating his affection for her in front of everyone.

"And for the record, magician," Kilian said as he settled down onto a chair, throwing a shot of vodka down his throat before continuing, "I very rarely drank with people of the same station as me. I was far more likely found passed out in whorehouses or seedy taverns hidden down back alleys or –"

"Kilian, everyone is listening to you!"

He glanced around the tavern and, sure enough, each and every person in the building was attentively listening to his every word. Kilian shrugged. "It's hardly as if my social proclivities were unknown. And besides, I won't be king for much longer anyway."

"Oh?"

It was Lily who had spoken, who until now hadn't met a grown-up Kilian. He smiled, standing up only to kneel in front of her and kiss her hand. Her eyes widened in shock.

"Miss Brodeur, I have a great deal to thank you for. For bringing Elina into the world when everyone else would have suggested otherwise. For raising her to be the kind of woman who wouldn't let me get away with throwing my life away. For instilling in her the desire to do more than simply live in Alder. But, most of all...I wish to apologise."

Lily looked down at him uncertainly, the blush that spread across her cheeks making her look far younger than she was. In that moment Elina saw the beautiful woman who had raised her – the one who had seduced, and been seduced by, a mysterious magician.

"What could you possibly have to apologise to me for, Your Majesty?" she asked politely.

Kilian's gaze was steady as he said, "Once upon a time a wonderful woman spun a spoiled, angry little boy a set of clothes that were far too good for him. The boy set them ablaze, for no reason other than the fact that he could. It was certainly not one of his finer moments."

Lily laughed. "Please get up, Your Majesty. All is forgiven. I'm happy enough to see you wearing clothes from my family at all, even if it took you twenty-one years to accept them."

He glanced down at his blue-and-gold overcoat before looking at Elina. "Your entire family are certainly very talented. So, tell me, Miss Brodeur, I heard that you're looking to travel with your daughter come spring. Would you be entirely averse to a third person joining the party? I've always wanted to visit Greece."

Lily frowned, as did several people in the tavern. "Your Majesty, I don't understand. How can you come travelling when you have a country to run?"

When Kilian caught Frederick's eye, the man stood up. Elina struggled to hold back a smile; Kilian had thought long and hard about what to do with regards to the crown.

"Over the coming months I'll be working with representatives from each of the major towns to form a democratic government," he announced, for the whole tavern to hear. "I think it's about time our country moves away from a monarchy; it's outdated and...problematic." He shared a glance with Elina, who laughed into her hand at the understatement.

466

"I think most everyone – particularly in Alder – can agree that I'm not fit to sit on the throne," Kilian continued. "I would be far more comfortable knowing that I have absolutely nothing to do with the maintenance of an entire country. This does mean, however..."

There was a general air of uncertainty at this final sentence. Elina almost hit Kilian for pausing for dramatic effect, especially when he knocked back another shot of vodka.

"This does mean that there's nothing protecting the country from a harsh winter. We'll have to work collectively to ensure that what happened twenty years ago does not repeat itself. We cannot be unprepared for such horrific weather again. There will be no magician protecting the land. No mild-mannered king controlling the skies for your benefit. No curses or spells or enchantments making us special."

The room was silent for a few moments, and then it erupted in an overwhelming wave of noise.

"I *knew* the curse was real!"

"The king really was controlling the weather? That's insane!"

"Does that mean Prince Kilian – King Kilian – was responsible for the awful weather over the past few months?"

"Hey, keep your mouth shut. He's right there..."

Kilian merely laughed at the comment before turning his attention back to Elina and the rest of the table. She stopped him from picking up another glass of vodka.

"Pace yourself, Mister Alcoholic."

"I can handle *three* measures of vodka, Elina."

She quirked an eyebrow. "On your own head be it.

467

But if you pass out in the forest on the way back through to the castle it won't be my fault."

"At least the two of you might actually make it that far," Scarlett complained, struggling beneath a now unconscious Adrian happily dozing on her shoulder. "We're supposed to be leaving in the morning! There's no way Adrian will be willing to go anywhere with the hangover he'll doubtlessly have come sunrise. If only he could still turn into a wolf, we could have left tonight."

Kilian and Elina stared at her in shock. Lily, however, looked unperturbed; clearly she was privy to Scarlett and Adrian's full history.

"Did you say *wolf?*" Elina exclaimed.

Scarlett nodded.

"As in...an actual wolf," Kilian added, "not some metaphorical wolf?"

She nodded again. "It's a very, very long story. Perhaps one for the next time we cross paths."

"And when would that be? How are we supposed to find you?"

"Oh, I have no doubt we'll find *you,*" Scarlett said, smiling mysteriously. "We have your hair after all, Kilian."

He scratched his head. "You can curse me using that, can't you?"

"Do you really want the truth?"

"...no."

"Then we can't curse you using it," she laughed.

Elina and Kilian glanced at each other, slow, sheepish smiles spreading across their faces. Even though they had managed to free Kilian from the throne, and negated his curse, and Elina had finally made peace with her father being the magician who set everything off in the first place, that didn't mean they were free from the touch of magic. It would likely follow them wherever they went.

But, for the first time in their lives, they could finally accept that.

EXTRA CHAPTER

Kilian

"Kilian, it's still too cold to use the hot springs and you know it."

"Hence why we need to get into the water as soon as possible."

Kilian didn't wait for Elina's retort; he threw her unceremoniously into the water, clothes and all. When she broke the surface, spluttering and gasping for air, she glared at him.

"I didn't bring a spare set of clothes. I'll freeze on my way back to the castle."

"You can wear my coat," Kilian replied simply, sliding out of his clothes quickly before stepping into the bubbling water himself. His mouth slid into a grin. "Or you could return naked. I'd rather like to see that."

Elina made a wave of water with her hand and sent it crashing towards him. "As if I'd do that. I'm worried that if the weather stays like this our journey down to Greece will be delayed."

Kilian shrugged. "That's what happens when one can no longer control the weather. Blizzards in March. Sleet for rain. Beautiful."

"Maybe I should keep my distance from you just to give the roads a chance to clear..." Elina muttered, turning away from Kilian as she spoke. He pulled her back to him, sitting her on his lap and biting her lip when Elina cried out in surprise.

"If you stayed far enough away to keep me trapped in the castle then the weather would get *worse,* I'd wager," Kilian said. He kissed her softly. "Are you so sick of me already, Elina?"

She rolled her eyes, then pushed away from Kilian in order to swim a few curious strokes across the pool. "You'd know it if I was, Your Majesty."

"I'm not –"

"You *are,* at least until those documents up in your office are completed and signed," Elina countered, causing Kilian to sigh.

He knew he had to finish looking them over. He knew he had to sign them. Kilian simply...couldn't be bothered. *This is precisely why I'm demolishing the throne, of course,* he thought as he relaxed against the side of the hot springs. For how could he face sitting in an office, worrying over paperwork, when instead he could content

471

himself with watching Elina swim through clouds of steam and swirling snow?

She still has her clothes on. That needs to change.

"Take off your dress," Kilian complained, waving a hand in Elina's general direction as he did so. "The water feels much better against naked skin, you know."

"Oh, so it's not simply because you want me to undress for your own benefit?"

"I never suggested I didn't think that, too."

Elina paused in the middle of the pool, reaching her toes down to touch the smooth stone surface beneath her before unlacing the front of her dress. Her eyes never left Kilian's as she did so, her expression torn between amusement and exasperation.

"Let down your hair," Kilian insisted, after Elina was blessedly freed from her clothing.

She shook her head. "Absolutely not. That will definitely cause me to freeze on the way back to – *Kilian!*"

Kilian lunged for her, sliding an arm around Elina's neck to drag her below the surface of the water. He wrapped his legs around her waist, keeping her firmly in place as he unfurled the braid she had pinned around her head with deft fingers. When he finally let Elina go she kicked him away, outraged.

"You can't just – what sort of manners do you have to push a woman down into a body of water, Kilian?" she demanded, the moment she broke through the water once more.

He didn't answer; he didn't have to. They both knew he had less than no manners until it benefited him to pretend he had some. Instead, Kilian watched with growing hunger as Elina's wavy, tawny hair spread out

472

around her golden shoulders in the water, rippling and undulating like it was made of magic.

"You look like a mermaid," he said, taking another few paces back in order to truly appreciate the sight of Elina in all her naked, ethereal splendour. Kilian didn't think he'd ever grow tired of the sight of her, especially against a backdrop of snow and steam and hot, bubbling water. They were the very foundation upon which he had gotten to know her. Upon which he'd fallen in love with her.

A small, pleased smile curled Elina's lips. She glanced downward at her hair winding its way all around her through the water. "Have you seen a mermaid before, to compare me to such a thing?"

"If I said I had, would you believe me?"

"No."

Kilian chuckled. He swam across to the other side of the pool, then back over to Elina's side. "You're right not to believe me. I don't even *know* if you look like a mermaid. They might be horrific, ugly creatures to look upon. They might be green. They might be -"

"I'm surprised, Kilian," Elina interrupted, raising an eyebrow. "It's unusual to hear you actually interested in something. To want to *know* something that serves you no benefit in knowing."

Kilian could only laugh. "I guess you're right. It would be unusual if I didn't become at least a little fascinated with all things strange and magical after everything I've been through, though. Don't you agree?"

"Are you honestly asking if 'the magician's girl' understands your interest in magic?"

"You never seemed that inclined to understand it."

473

"That was before," Elina muttered. She lowered her head into the water and exhaled a stream of bubbles. When she resurfaced she sighed. "I never wanted to be associated with my father, remember? But things are different now. And what with us leaving for Greece soon..."

Kilian placed a hand beneath Elina's chin, turning her head to look at him. Her winter-forest eyes looked decidedly uncertain.

"We do not have to seek out your father if it scares you," he said, not unkindly. "We can venture down with your mother and then head off on our own adventure once she's safely in Greece. Nobody will force you to -"

"But that's the thing," Elina cut in. "I *do* want to meet him. I want to get to know him. I want to know...why he never came to see my mother again."

Kilian frowned. "Did he know about her pregnancy?"

"Mama said she wasn't sure," she replied. "She never told him, but he was a magician. He had his ways, probably."

"We should have asked Adrian if it were possible for him to work out such a thing, then we wouldn't have to speculate."

"Yes, well it's not as if we thought to ask questions like that before he and Scarlett left," Elina said. She removed Kilian's hand from below her chin in order to arch her neck back to stare up at the wild, white, evening sky. "I wonder when we'll see them again."

Kilian joined her in looking upwards. "Scarlett certainly made it out like it wouldn't be long. Though the woman is rather mysterious so who knows what she actually meant."

"I guess we'll just have to wait and find out."

Elina smiled. "I guess we have to do a lot of that. Waiting and finding out, I mean. About Scarlett and Adrian. About my father. About whether the country will be fine without a king."

"And whether I murder Gabriel next time I see him for being an arrogant, all-knowing piece of –"

Elina's mouth on Kilian's swallowed the rest of his sentence. "We both know you'd never do anything of the sort," she said, her words whisper-soft against Kilian's lips. "Just imagine him arriving to visit you in summer, instead, only to find you gone and the monarchy entirely erased."

The thought elicited a rough, throaty laugh from Kilian. How he would love to see the look on his brother's face upon discovering that Kilian was no longer tied to the throne. That Kilian – and people who *cared* for Kilian – had discovered a way to get around the Hale curse that Gabriel had not.

"I've been wondering for a while now about something," Elina murmured, after a few moments of her doing nothing but planting affectionate yet absent-minded kisses on Kilian.

"What is it you've been wondering about?" He pulled her closer against him, revelling in the feeling of every inch of Elina's wet, hot skin on his. He was very close to wishing to talk no longer in favour of something far more physical.

She kissed the end of his nose. "Once there's no longer a king, will your curse still stand? Or will it be negated entirely? It's hardly as if you father asked mine about the hypotheticals of the curse before having it placed."

Kilian paused to consider this for a moment. He grinned. "I guess we'll have to –"

"Wait and find out," Elina finished for him, giggling softly.

"Speaking of," he said, sliding a hand down to Elina's thigh to hitch her leg around his waist, "I've been very patient since we got into the hot springs, but I'm done with *waiting*."

Elina blushed and looked away, though she was smiling. "And what would that be for?"

"You."

THE TOWER WITHOUT A DOOR

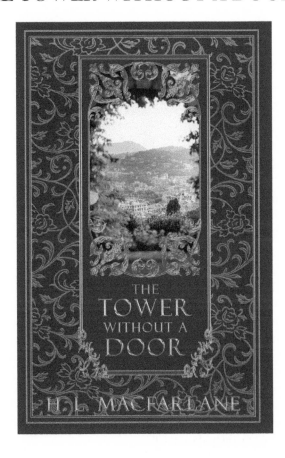

PROLOGUE

Nobody liked the king much, and the people of Willow least of all. Golden-haired and handsome Pierre Saule was a war hero, though, and well-respected and intimidating enough that neighbouring countries did not wish to cross him. For that he had managed to cling to the throne for ten years, despite his cruel disregard for the common people he was supposed to rule.

In contrast his beautiful wife, Mariette, and his brother, Francis, were beloved by all. Francis tempered his older brother's bad behaviour by acting as the head of his council and, with the help of a powerful wizard who had served in Pierre's army for years, ensured that the country did not fall into ruins. Mariette worked with a team of loyal doctors to bring better health care to those too impoverished to pay for it, and spent more time on the road touring the country than she did in the royal city of Willow or the palace itself.

479

When she gave birth to a baby girl two years after Pierre had taken the throne, the kingdom rejoiced. With Mariette and Francis there to teach the child she was sure to become a better ruler than her father, the common folk said.

Over the next eight years the Princess Genevieve grew into a bright, intelligent and well-mannered young girl, whom even her father came to adore. She had his golden hair, and his green eyes, and thought that he could do no wrong. Perhaps it was a narcissistic kind of love on the king's part, but it was as close to true love as Mariette had known the man to be capable of.

For though the pair kept up a united front to the kingdom, behind closed doors the king and queen often argued. Mariette should spend more time in the palace, Pierre would say, even as his wife prepared for another tour of the country alongside Francis that would keep her away for two months. She would respond in kind – that it should be the king himself who joined her on the tour, not his brother – but Pierre would not listen. He didn't want to mingle with the common folk. In order to punish his wife he would refuse to let her take Genevieve along on her tours, though he knew he was hurting his daughter in the process, too.

Every night before Mariette left the palace she would comb her daughter's golden hair, singing soft lullabies and telling Genevieve how much she loved her. Genevieve longed for such nights with her mother; when she and her uncle were gone all she had was her father, who stayed in a perpetual bad mood when they were both away.

And then, on the eve of Genevieve's eighth birthday, the fragmented, fragile peace that had been so hard-fought for within the palace was broken. For Mariette and Francis had long-since been more than what they seemed, hiding their passion for each other from the king at every turn. But it had been common knowledge in every little town and village the two of them had visited; the people simply loved them enough to keep their secret. But eventually rumours began to spread to the wrong ears, and the king finally learned the full extent of what had been going on for years behind his back.

For it was not only the king who had golden hair and green eyes.

Furious and humiliated, and unable to look at the little girl he had always thought his own, Pierre had his wizard spirit Genevieve away to live out the rest of her days in the man's enchanted tower, without so much as an explanation to the princess about what was going on. He imprisoned his wife in the palace – a punishment only fitting for a woman who thrived on exploring the country. When he discovered that the wizard had long since known of her infidelity Pierre imprisoned him in the palace, too, upon pain of death of his eighteen year old son should he try to escape.

The king had planned to behead Francis for his treachery. He wanted nothing more than to watch his brother die, after all. But his pride was stronger, and he did not want his country to know just how humiliated he was. So, instead, Pierre banished his brother, ordering him to never set foot inside the country he loved so much ever again.

The king pretended to his kingdom that everything was fine, and informed the people that both Mariette and Genevieve had fallen ill, explaining their absence from the public eye. When eventually his wife was forced to bear him a son, Pierre rejoiced. He did not need his 'daughter', now that he had Prince Louis. His line and rule would continue as intended.

It was perhaps some ironic twist of fate that his young son grew up genuinely sickly. Even the king's wizard could do nothing for him. Everyone knew the boy was unlikely to reach adolescence, so time and again the wizard urged for Pierre to bring back Genevieve.

Yet the king's pride was too great. Genevieve was not his daughter. He would not give his brother the satisfaction of having his child sit upon the throne. Many times he tried to produce another heir but Mariette was too frail from her imprisonment to have another child. Pierre did not want to marry again, or father a bastard, for doing so would involve having to admit to his country that there was a problem he could not solve on his own.

Eventually the king was forced to concede that bringing back Genevieve may be his only option. The girl did not know her father was, in fact, her uncle. Pierre could train her for the throne under the belief that she was still his. Genevieve had always adored him, after all. She was the only one who had.

And so he ordered his wizard to magic her back to the palace from his enchanted tower. Pierre would ensure his daughter trusted only him; not her mother. Everything would be fine. Nobody would ever know Genevieve had been locked away far from the palace for so long.

But something unexpected happened.

When the wizard cast the spell to bring the princess back, she didn't appear.

Genevieve was gone from the tower.

CHAPTER ONE

Genevieve

Today marked the end of Genevieve's twelfth solitary year, which coincided with her birthday. Twenty years since her birth, and more than half of those spent with nobody to touch or talk or listen to. She no longer wasted her time – though she had so much of it – wondering why she had been spirited away to the tower in which she now lived. For it was a pointless endeavour, as there were no answers to any of Genevieve's questions.

"What do you think we've been sent for breakfast today, Evie?" she asked aloud the moment she'd woken up and stretched her arms above her head. Genevieve was a troublesome mouthful of a name, especially if one was going to talk to herself. 'Evie' was much better.

Evie talked to herself a lot. What else was she supposed to do when there was nobody else to talk to?

When she was first sent to the tower and discovered food and supplies magically appeared there twice a day Evie had hoped she'd eventually meet the person responsible for doing so.

Twelve years later and there was still no sign of the elusive person.

When she was a child, back in her father's palace, there had been a wizard. They'd gone to war together back before her father took the throne. The man was the most powerful wizard Evie knew...not that she knew any other wizards, of course, but if he worked side-by-side with the king then Evie could only assume he was the strongest. She had never known his name, for she hadn't been allowed to speak to the wizard nor ask after him. But she heard people call him The Thorn Wizard, so that's what she'd called him, too.

Evie had wondered for a while, back when she was eight and nine and even ten years old, if Thorn was the one sending her food. She was sure he was the one who'd sent her to the tower in the first place, so it made sense to her child's brain that he was making sure she didn't starve.

"None of it makes sense," Evie murmured as she rummaged through the basket that had appeared whilst she was sleeping. "Not a single thing."

The food inside was the usual – bread and cheese and apples and a few slices of cured meats. A pitcher of water. Nothing out of the ordinary. No cake or pastries or anything special to mark her birthday. Most of her meals consisted of similar fare, and it was never enough. Either the person sending Evie food still believed her to be eight years old or they were cruel. She was *twenty,* and needed an adult's portion of food.

Because of this Evie was on the skinny side, and was

484

shorter than she remembered her mother being. But she hadn't seen the woman in twelve years; for all Evie knew she was actually of a height with her now.

It wasn't just food she was hungry for. No, what Evie craved was knowledge. Of what happened on the eve of her eighth birthday that resulted in her being sent to live in an enchanted tower with no door. Of how far she was from Willow, and the palace, and her family. Of whether any of her family were still alive at all. Of what lay outside the solitary window that was Evie's only proof that a world out with her tower in fact existed.

She padded over to the windowsill even now to look outside, bringing with her the basket of food to pick it apart with mindless, fidgeting fingers. Evie allowed her hair to hang out of the window, if only because it was the one part of her that could.

For Evie's hair was so long it now trailed on the floor behind her feet when she walked. She might have cut it, if there had been something sharp in the tower to cut it with. But all she had at her disposal was a bed, a bathroom, a table and tall, near-endless bookshelves. They didn't seem so endless now that Evie was twenty; she had read most every book on them, and some of the tomes more than once.

None of those things could be used to cut her hair. Evie had considered using a candle to burn it, once, but she scared herself out of doing it. One of her most treasured memories of her mother had been of her combing her golden hair, singing softly all the while, until Evie's locks were soft and shiny and lustrous.

I looked after it as best I could, mama, Evie thought, glancing down to where its ends hung several feet below the windowsill. Sometimes she would spend an hour or two braiding it into elaborate hairstyles that she found in books; usually Evie let it hang loose and free and bothersome.

She gnawed off a hunk of bread and slumped her shoulders as she chewed. It was a beautiful early summer's day. The sun shone brightly in the sky promising that, by midday, any sensible person would be seeking shade from its glaring rays. It lit up every strand of Evie's hair until it looked like it really *was* made of gold. It was one of her favourite things to see.

Below her – far, far below her – was a sloping, grassy meadow that met a forest on its right hand side. The trees along the closest edge were broad and low-boughed and lost their leaves in autumn. But she could see further into the forest from the height of her tower, where the trees were dark and evergreen. It looked dangerous and foreboding.

Evie longed to explore it.

Perhaps it was because this was her twentieth year. Perhaps it was because she wanted to get back to her family and find out why she'd been sent away. Perhaps it was because all of her clothes were too small and she was always hungry. Perhaps it was because she had run out of books to read.

Whatever the reason, today was the day Princess Genevieve was going to escape from the tower, or die trying.

She hoped she wouldn't die trying.

Evie had shredded any clothes she'd been sent over the past twelve years – save for one or two dresses to actually wear – in order to weave the fabric into ropes. She'd learned how to make them properly from one of the books in the tower. Individually they more than supported her weight.

But now they were all tied together in order to make a rope whose end dangled about five metres above the meadow, and she had to hope it would support her weight until she reached the final inches of it. Evie didn't relish the fact she'd have to brace for a fall to the grass. She'd probably break an arm or an ankle; she hoped she'd be able to use the rough stone surface of the tower to climb down the last few metres instead.

There was a lot of *hoping* going on in this plan.

But Evie was nothing if not an optimist, and if she stayed in the tower for much longer she'd likely die of boredom or loneliness, anyway.

"Or I might starve to death," she posed to the air, sighing dramatically as she finished her meagre breakfast. But Evie knew she was just as likely to slowly waste away until she was old, when time itself would finally – finally – give her an escape from her living hell.

An optimist, indeed.

With nothing left to lose, Evie tucked her hair behind her ears and grabbed her makeshift rope. A lurching in her stomach as she approached the window once more told her that she was definitely not as confident about her plan now that she actually had to follow it through.

"You have nothing to lose but yourself," Evie breathed, closing her eyes for a few moments whilst she tried in vain to settle the erratic beating of her heart. Then she tied the rope to one of her bedposts, checked its stability by tugging on it several times, dropped the rest of the rope through the window, and –

"Oh my oh my oh my, I can't do this," Evie cried, the moment she tried to position herself on the windowsill to abseil down the tower. She clung to the rope in terror, forcing her weight backwards until the only part of her body still in contact with the tower was her bare feet. She'd never been sent shoes once in twelve years. But, then again, who needed shoes when they were locked up inside a single room?

With all the strength of will she could muster, Evie dragged her feet downward an inch. Two. Three. Already her arms were protesting against supporting her weight on a rope that was beginning to chafe the skin of her hands.

And then she slipped. Evie fell two feet in absolute terror, screaming, before she managed to wrap her legs around the rope to hold herself in place. It felt like her muscles were made of water; any moment now they would give way and Evie would fall to the ground below and perish.

She sobbed, closing her eyes to the world as if that would somehow make everything go away. "I can't do it I can't do it I can't do it I'm going to die I'm going to – *ah*!"

For at the very moment that Evie felt her hands losing their grip once more, a much stronger pair of hands grabbed the rope from above her and yanked her back to the windowsill. She kept her eyes closed until the same pair of hands pulled her through the window and roughly threw her to the floor.

Evie's heart had been throbbing before; it was nothing compared to how painful it was now. She'd nearly died, and for what? Managing to climb down all of three feet from the tower window – two of which had only been achieved through falling?

It took Evie a few seconds before her brain finally kicked in and reminded her that someone had saved her life.

Someone. A person. A human being.

She flung her eyes open.

A man stood there, face covered in stubble with hair overgrown across his eyes. A ragged cloak hung from his shoulders, obscuring the rest of his tall frame. Though Evie couldn't see his face properly she had the overwhelming feeling that he was glaring at her.

She didn't speak. She didn't know what to say. All she could do was stare.

The man bent low to regard her. Evie, tangled in her hair and the rope and with muscles made of water, did not move away.

"Who," he began, disturbingly quietly, "are you?"

CHAPTER TWO

Julian

"I said – who are you?"

The young woman Julian had only just hauled through the tower window merely stared at him, unblinking.

Can't she speak? he wondered. *Or can she not understand me? Perhaps she has been instructed not to say anything.*

But then, after a few more moments of silence broken only by laboured breathing, the woman answered him. "Evie. Genevieve. Princess Genevieve."

Julian was too stunned to hear the 'Princess' part. He narrowed his eyes. "What were you doing trying to enter my tower?"

"I...what?"

"Why were you trying to get in here? What were you

looking for? Who sent you?"

Genevieve stared at him in disbelief. "I was trying to *leave* the tower! So it's yours? Why have I been locked up in here for twelve years? What did I do?"

Oh.

Julian hadn't expected such an answer. Why would a young woman be trapped in the Thorne family tower? It didn't seem reasonable. It sounded like a lie. But Julian had been travelling for almost thirteen years, in an effort to stay as far away from home as possible.

Genevieve could be telling the truth.

He swept the hair currently obscuring his view away from his eyes and regarded her critically. Genevieve certainly didn't look like a spy. Her powder blue dress was finely made, but it was too short in the skirt which ended just above her knees. It was bordering on downright outrageous.

Perhaps she is a thief and stole the dress, which is why it doesn't fit, Julian supposed.

Yet the dress was not the most outlandish thing about the scrawny young woman currently trying to inelegantly right herself from her position on the floor, for Genevieve's sun-coloured hair was longer than she was. When she finally stood Julian watched as it pooled by her feet like liquid gold. She regarded him with green eyes devoid of suspicion or fear, which given the situation she was in didn't make any sense.

Genevieve looked half-starved, though not in the gaunt, desperate way Julian had witnessed in the faces of many an impoverished village. No. There was...something else. The woman in front of him was hungry for something that wasn't just food.

She was, quite simply put, the most bizarre person

491

he'd ever seen.

"Why should I believe that you've been trapped in here for so long?" Julian demanded, standing back up to his full height as Genevieve brushed herself off.

"Well, why should I believe that this is your tower?" she countered. "Twelve years here and I have not seen you once. I haven't seen anyone at all."

Julian's spirits fell just a little. He'd almost hoped his father would have somehow appeared in his son's absence, though of course that was impossible. His father was dead.

He rubbed at the furrows near-permanently creased into his brow. "Just suppose I hypothetically believe you. Why have *you* specifically been locked in here?"

Genevieve looked at him as if he were stupid. Julian was taken aback, and a touch affronted. Nobody ever looked at him like that.

"I told you already," she said. "I'm Princess Genevieve."

"The princess and her brother have been sick for years. They are bound in the palace until they recover." Julian might have spent thirteen years avoiding Willow but that didn't mean he was ignorant of the goings-on in the royal city.

Genevieve dropped the long, make-shift rope she'd just begun untying from one of the old, rickety bed posts. It landed on the gnarled wooden floorboards with a dull thump. Her eyes seemed altogether too bright; Julian almost looked away from them, her expression was so intense.

"I have a brother? I have -"

"Louis," he elaborated for her benefit. Whether Genevieve really was the princess or not, Julian knew that the conversation would only move along if he gave her all the information she craved. "He's eight, I think. So why have you been locked up here all this time?"

She didn't seem to hear him. Instead Genevieve jumped back over to the window and sat on the sill. "A brother. A baby brother. And my mother? My father?"

"Excuse me?"

"Are they alive?" Genevieve asked without looking at him. The fact she was ignoring his questions in favour of barraging him with her own annoyed Julian to no end.

"Yes," he replied, fighting to keep his tone polite. "But Queen Mariette has also taken ill. Nobody knows with what, though. She hasn't been seen away from the palace grounds in years."

Genevieve absorbed this information in silence.

Julian supposed that she looked enough like King Pierre to be his daughter, what with her golden hair and green eyes, and she was of an age with the princess. But that wasn't proof enough of *being* the princess. Genevieve could have been lying about being trapped in the tower for so long. She might simply be insane.

He turned from her, inspecting the room his father had so often retired to in order to read and practice magic. Julian had never liked the tower much, preferring instead to stay at home in their handsome, well-made house on the outskirts of Willow with his mother. That was, until she died. After that Julian had spent just as much time in the tower as his father had until the man mysteriously disappeared.

Julian liked the tower even less now, years later. Though, looking closer, he had to admit that the solitary room inside it did indeed look lived in. Perhaps Genevieve was telling the truth.

"You're a wizard...right? Can you get me out of here?"

Julian was so lost in his head that he didn't hear her questions at first. But then he turned to the so-called princess, who was now watching him instead of the window with a hopeful expression on her face.

He nodded, thinking that the sooner he got Genevieve off his hands then the sooner he could sleep for three days straight and figure out what to do with the rest of his life, now that he was home once more.

"I'm a wizard, yes."

"Hence the poofing in out of nowhere," Genevieve said, excitement colouring her voice. Julian didn't like the ardent way she was looking at him at all, so he turned his face away from hers.

"I'll send you to Willow, but not to the palace. I don't want to get arrested. You can seek an audience with the king yourself."

Genevieve clucked her tongue unhappily. "I didn't mean - I don't want to be spirited off to Willow. I just want you to send me down there." She pointed to the meadow at the base of the tower. "I've been stuck here for so long. I'd prefer to travel to Willow on foot."

Julian laughed before he could stop himself. It was cruel, he knew, but he didn't care. "You? Walk to Willow? Have you seen what you're wearing, little girl, or the state of your hair? Do you have any supplies? Money? Do you know how long it would take to reach the city? Do you even know the way?"

"I...no," she admitted, with some hesitation. But then Genevieve shook her head, stood up from the windowsill and smiled brightly at Julian.

Oh, lord, no.

"You could take me!" she babbled excitedly. "I mean, this is *your* tower. Don't you want to know why I've been locked up in here all this time?"

"No."

"And you could update me on what's been going on in the country the past twelve years," Genevieve continued on, as if she hadn't heard Julian. "And then, when I reach the palace, my father will reward you handsomely for helping me find my way back home, and then –"

"I said *no*," Julian cut in, louder this time.

Genevieve frowned. "But why not? Do you not pity me for being locked up? Are you so callous a man that you would not help a person in need?"

"Absolutely."

Neither of them said anything, though Genevieve's cheeks puffed out as if she was holding back from yelling profanities. He wondered if she even knew any, given that she must have been a child when she was first locked up.

Julian glanced at the window. "Last chance for me to send you straight to Willow, *princess.*"

"I shall walk," she said, resolutely ignoring his jibe, "if you would be so kind as to point me in the right direction."

I should just send her to Willow regardless, Julian thought as he reluctantly joined Genevieve by the window. He pointed east, through the forest. "That way," he murmured. "Stick to the outskirts of the woods as best you can and you'll reach a small town by nightfall. From there you can find someone to give you better directions to Willow."

Genevieve didn't reply. She stared in the direction Julian was pointing, frowning slightly against the sun. A small spray of freckles crossed the bridge of her nose, he noticed. He began joining them together in his head, forming constellations, when Genevieve turned her attention from the forest to Julian himself.

"What's your name?"

"I don't have to tell you that."

"No, you don't, but it would be nice if you did."

God, she's annoying, Julian thought, though he reasoned there was no harm in giving her his first name.

"...Julian," he finally answered.

Genevieve inclined her head politely. "Thank you for saving my life, Julian, and thank you in advance for releasing me from your tower."

"Don't die on the road," Julian said, unsmiling, before raising his left hand and clicking his fingers. And just like that Genevieve was gone, only for her to reappear down in the meadow, several paces away from the tower.

She looked up at Julian in awe; her golden hair caught the breeze and blew behind her like a cloak. "That felt so strange!" she exclaimed. "Thank you!"

"Go away!" he yelled back, then turned from the window to investigate the rope Genevieve had presumably constructed to escape. It was surprisingly well made. If she'd been a little stronger – better fed, with muscles given a chance to develop properly – Genevieve likely would have made it to the meadow unharmed.

But Julian didn't want to think about her any more. All he wanted to do was sleep.

Several hours later he lay awake and uncomfortable on a bed that smelled completely different from when he had last used it thirteen years ago. It smelled of the 'princess', he knew. The entire room did. He couldn't escape it.

But Genevieve was no longer Julian's problem. It was up to somebody else to help her now. So why couldn't he stop thinking about her?

"She wasn't wearing any shoes," he muttered, reluctantly rolling out of bed to pack a bag before he could stop himself. "Who doesn't own shoes?"

CHAPTER THREE

Genevieve

"Yes, just let a young woman walk barefoot into the woods," Evie muttered, though in truth she was too excited to be all that angry with the wizard who'd - reluctantly - helped her.

For how could Evie allow negative feelings to befoul her mood when she was beneath the boughs of an old oak tree for the first time in her life? Even when she'd lived in the palace, or ventured into Willow, she'd never stood under such a gigantic tree.

But soon the soft, spongy grass beneath Evie's feet would turn to pine needles and sharp twigs and stinging weeds. They would make quick work of her soft, unblemished flesh, she knew.

If only she had shoes.

Julian told her to avoid wandering deeply into the woods, so Evie hoped the ground wouldn't get too uncomfortable to walk on. And then, when she reached the town he'd told her about, she could finally buy a pair of shoes that fit.

"With what money?" Evie asked aloud, stopping in her tracks as if floored by the question. But of course she needed money; it was hardly as if she could announce herself as the Princess Genevieve and expect the town to help her out. After all, she was fairly certain Julian did not believe she was the princess, and he had far more reason to believe her than an unknown town would.

He should have given me some money, at least, Evie grumbled, though in truth that wasn't fair. Julian had offered to magic her all the way to Willow - she had brought the problem of money and shoes and shelter upon herself. But she had to live with her decision to recklessly walk herself to the royal city, so with a sigh Evie continued on her journey.

*

"Ouch!" she exclaimed after several hours of walking. It was not the first time she'd made such a proclamation, and it wasn't simply because of her aching, bleeding feet. For Evie's hair kept getting caught on branches and roots and snagging painfully; eventually she was forced to carry her hair in her arms to avoid catching it on anything.

Now that it was past noon Evie had to admit her mood had decidedly taken a turn for the worse. Her stomach grumbled insistently, and she knew little and less about which plants in the forest were edible. Her hands were chafed raw from the number of times she'd had to catch the rough bark of a tree trunk to stop herself from falling when she stumbled.

499

And the sun. Despite the fact Evie was beneath the trees it still beat down on her through the canopy, pricking her skin with unbearable heat. There was a sheen of sweat all over her which Evie was desperate to wash away. And she was so thirsty, too. Once she acknowledged her thirst it was all she could think about, until her mind was so busy daydreaming about water that Evie tripped over an exposed tree root and fell flat on her face.

"This is ridiculous!" she decried, spitting out a mouthful of dried earth and leaves in the process. She crawled over to the tree whose root had upended her and collapsed with her back against it, then closed her eyes to the dappled sunlight. For a while all Evie did was run her fingers along the tree's roots as her chest heaved with exhaustion.

"I can't do this," she murmured, thinking of her failed attempt to escape from the tower. If Julian hadn't shown up when he had done then Evie would have died.

Her stomach lurched unpleasantly at the mere thought of the tetchy, unkempt wizard. Even when Julian had pushed some of his dark hair out of his eyes Evie had not gained all that much more insight into his appearance. It left her feeling unsatisfied, that he should have seen her lying on the floor like a crazed fool, whilst Evie saw so little of the first human she'd had contact with for twelve years.

Julian was not a nice man, Evie decided. He had called her 'little girl' and refused to give her even the most basic of supplies.

"And he wasn't curious about why I was in his tower at all!" Evie complained, crossing her arms over her chest to emphasise her mood. "If I'd discovered a princess locked in my own tower then I'd want to know why she was there."

In truth Evie just as badly wanted to ask Julian questions about his own life. She'd had nobody but herself to talk to for so long, after all. And he was a wizard, and clearly connected to what happened to her on her eighth birthday.

"Well you'll never see him again, so just forget about him," Evie said, before brushing off her now filthy knees and clambering to her feet. She winced as they took her weight, and wondered how she could possibly keep going. And then she heard it.

Water.

A stream! Evie thought, delighted, and all complaints about her aching, bruised and bloodied feet were forgotten in favour of chasing the beautiful sound of water over pebbles. It took her a while to find it, for within the forest the sounds of the water echoed and reverberated in some places and were absorbed by moss and close-knit trees in others. By the time Evie finally felt moisture beneath her feet the trees overhead had changed from broad-leaved to evergreen, and there was no more sunlight filtering down to the forest floor.

But Evie did not care. Just a few minutes later she stumbled across the stream itself, though it was narrow and insubstantial. Another few minutes of impatient walking later and the stream grew wider and deeper. She stepped into the shallows and sighed contentedly. The bracing water soothed her feet and tickled at her ankles. Bending low she scooped some of it up and brought it to her parched lips, eagerly lapping at the water until she had her fill.

After that Evie was still hungry, but at least her thirst was sated. She decided there was no harm in following the stream for a little while longer, since it was still mid-afternoon. She had plenty of daylight left to find the nearest town, and now that she'd rested for a few moments and drank her feet no longer seemed so sore.

It was therefore to her surprise when, after about an hour of following the silvery path of the stream, Evie found what appeared to be a road. It was reasonably well-maintained considering it carved its way through the middle of a forest, so she began to follow it. Above her the afternoon sun beat down on her back, though soon it would dip beneath the trees as evening crept upon the woods.

"Why didn't Julian tell me about the road?" Evie wondered, once more annoyed at the wizard. "It would have made my journey so much easier." She could only assume he'd told her to walk beneath the trees on the outskirts to make her journey longer and more irritable in response to Evie having refused his offer of going directly to Willow.

"So petty," she grumbled, before making her way along the road in the general direction of east. Evie fashioned conversations that she might have when she reached the town as she walked. She knew they were unrealistic, and probably unhelpful, but they helped to pass the time as the sun lowered in the sky.

"Why yes, kind sir, I do indeed look like I've been locked up for years, but that would be because I have. Thank you for noticing. Would it be at all possible to spend the night in your inn?"

"Unfortunately this is the only piece of clothing I possess, madam. Might I trouble you to spare me even the simplest of clothes?"

"As you can see I am not wearing shoes and have suffered for it. I would appreciate any help you can give me in procuring a pair."

But Evie was distracted from her ramblings when she heard the sound of several people laughing not too far ahead of her on the road. She was reaching a bend that promised to lead to the exit of the forest and the town ahead, which was likely obscuring the source of the voices from her.

What do I do? Evie worried. *Do I go ahead and try to catch up with them? Or do I stay back and wait for them to go?*

Her meeting with Julian had been disastrous, after all. Though Evie had spent her entire journey excited to talk to other people, now the very thought daunted her. She looked down at her arms, laden with her hair as if it were a babe.

I look weird and suspicious, I suppose. If they don't ignore me they will likely tease me. But it wasn't as if Evie could make herself look more presentable when she reached the town, so what did it matter if some strangers on the road saw her?

Then she realised the voices were getting louder and more boisterous. The group was heading her way and unless Evie hid beneath the trees she would meet them. She took a deep breath, figuring that it was better late than never that she saw people who weren't bad-tempered wizards like Julian. For all she knew the strangers would take pity on her and help her.

So Evie continued purposefully along just as the sun began to set the tips of the trees aglow. She reached the bend in the road at the same time the strangers did – a group of five men who looked to be about as old as Evie remembered her father being, though they looked far less elegant and refined than he had been.

Their cheeks were ruddy; two of them were holding

bottles of what Evie was fairly certain was wine, though perhaps it was something stronger. It wasn't as if she had any personal experience with alcohol given that she was locked away at eight years old.

One of the men cocked an eyebrow when they spied her. "And what have we here?" he said, slurring his words slightly.

So they won't ignore me, then, Evie thought. She held her arms as close to her chest as possible even though they were full of her long, tangled hair. She didn't know if she should speak or not. Would the men take offence if she didn't talk to them?

A second man took a step towards her and looked her up and down. "You're injured, my lovely. Would you like some help?"

Though the question was a nice one, the man's tone and expression were not. Evie flinched back; the group of strangers laughed.

"You scared her, Jack! No point in scaring her. She might run off."

"She won't be running anywhere in the state she's in," Jack replied, indicating towards Evie's feet. "What happened, little girl? Were you attacked and robbed?"

This time they waited for Evie to reply. Yet her voice was caught in her throat and wouldn't come out. She had never been scared of people before. But now...

When the man named Jack lurched forwards to grab her Evie yelped and stumbled away. The men only snickered harder.

"So she *does* have some life left in her," the first man said, a horrible gleam in his eyes as he circled around Evie. "That's good for us, then."

"P–please leave me alone," she stuttered, as all around her the group closed in and blocked off her escape. When someone grabbed her hair and yanked her to the ground she cried out in pain.

Evie struggled to get back to her feet even as Jack pushed her down once more. "Alf, keep hold of her hair!" he ordered the man who'd pulled Evie down in the first place. He grinned at her, showing Evie all of his dirty, yellowing teeth. "It shouldn't be difficult when she has so much. Have you never cut your hair, girlie?"

Evie merely wriggled beneath him. "Let me go! Let me go! Let me –"

"I'd like you better if you stayed silent."

"Ah, same here, but that doesn't mean I'd go to such lengths to shut her up."

Evie froze – as did the group of men. For it was not one of them who had spoken.

It was Julian.

Evie twisted her head until she caught sight of the scraggly wizard. His lips were contorted into a snarl, and his eyes – entirely free of hair for the first time – were glowing with anger.

No, not with anger. They were literally glowing, like burning, red–hot coals.

"Now, if you'd be so kind as to let my idiotic companion go," Julian said, "then I might not be inclined to burn all five of you to ashes."

CHAPTER FOUR

Julian

Julian was furious for several reasons.

First: that Genevieve had bothered him enough into actually packing a bag full of supplies to go out looking for her.

Two: that when he'd sent out a spell to find her location in the outskirts of the forest, he'd instead discovered that she was on the road, which was infamous for its thieves and brigands.

Three: that he had not warned her of said thieves and brigands.

And four: that the aforementioned brigands had found Genevieve and would have done any number of unspeakable things to her, had Julian not arrived just in time.

He was largely mad with himself, of course. Julian could have prevented all of this had he ignored Genevieve's ridiculous wish to walk to the royal palace and had magicked her there, instead.

But he didn't want to acknowledge his self-directed anger, when five wonderfully deserving targets for his fury stood in front of him.

The man closest to Genevieve had sneered at Julian when he'd first appeared, though he'd recoiled at the sight of Julian's eyes. He didn't *have* to make them glow. It was a pointless waste of magic, really. But it scared people who had little knowledge of spells and alchemy, and if the sight of burning eyes was enough to send the brigands on their way then Julian would actually *save* magic.

Burning five men to ashes took a lot of power, after all.

"I won't warn you again," Julian said, voice loud and commanding and imbued with the very real threat of fire magic. He took a step towards the group, avoiding making eye contact with Genevieve. He didn't think he could take any more of her terrified face than he'd first seen when he found her, struggling against the men holding her down.

Two of the group stumbled backwards, but did not leave. The other three stayed where they were, and drew out several filthy-looking knives.

"You think you can scare us with your parlour tricks, wizard?" one of them said as he brandished his weapon.

Julian waved his hand in front of him and the man's blade shattered into pieces. Then his shirt began to smoke and smoulder, which he promptly threw off as he yelped in pain.

"That will be your skin next time," Julian said as the man attempted to stamp out the fire that was beginning to engulf his shirt. "So tell me: is it really worth your lives to see how much of my magic consists of *parlour tricks?*"

And yet still two of the men did not back down. Julian glanced at Genevieve before he could stop himself; she was watching him with unabashed awe in her eyes. It made him uncomfortable, so he looked away before she could realise his gaze had been on her.

"I don't think you have it in you to burn us," one of the men said, "or else you'd have done it already."

Julian shrugged his shoulders. "I suppose that could be true. It could also mean that I don't want to waste precious magic on people such as you. But you've irked me enough to push me into action." He sighed. "Good bye, gentlemen."

The men barely had the opportunity to draw breath into their lungs to scream before Julian clicked his fingers. But he did not set them alight.

He stunned them.

One by one they dropped to the ground with heavy thumps. The man closest to Genevieve fell on top of her; Julian expected her to push him off. When she did not he grew concerned and closed the gap between them.

He had accidentally stunned her into unconsciousness, too.

"Oops," he murmured, though a smile curled his lips. There would be no idle chatter to bother him as he took her to the nearest town, which suited him just fine.

Julian unceremoniously pushed Genevieve's would-be rapist and potential murderer to the side and then, upon seeing the state of her legs and arms and feet, swept her into his arms. She barely weighed a thing compared to the heavy bag across his back, though her hair was irksome.

"Why have you never cut it, you fool?" Julian

wondered aloud as he picked the bulk of Genevieve's hair up and placed it all in her lap. He'd have to rectify the length of her hair himself, it seemed, once they reached an inn.

Julian could have transported the two of them straight there but something gave him pause. He didn't know what. But it was still light enough in the summer twilight to finish the route to the nearest town on foot, and Genevieve weighed barely more than a tall child, so even though it seemed like madness Julian chose to walk the rest of the way.

Now I sound like her, he thought, looking down at Genevieve passed out in his arms. *Walking. Why would a wizard walk anywhere?* Now that the young woman was still and quiet Julian could see that she really *was* a young woman, despite her weight and childish demeanour.

If she gained some weight she might even be pretty.

Julian quickly pushed the unwanted thought away. Genevieve was already more trouble than she was worth; he had saved her life not once but twice in the space of a single day. He dreaded to think what tomorrow would bring.

"Ugh, tomorrow," he muttered, hating himself even more for coming to the aid of the woman in his arms.

Then Julian heard the sound of footsteps and froze.

"Who goes there?" he demanded, putting on his commanding, magical voice once more. The air sizzled with the power of his words, warming Genevieve's skin and putting some colour back into her gaunt, exhausted cheeks.

When a man crept out of the forest Julian was fully prepared to stun him like the others. But then he held up his hands in surrender and smiled.

509

"Just a regular traveller," he said. "I was spooked by all the noise I heard, so I hid in the trees. Didn't want any trouble. Is the little miss okay?"

Julian didn't reply, instead squeezing Genevieve a little closer to his chest before he could stop himself. He looked the man up and down – in the twilight Julian could make out blonde hair going grey at the temples, light coloured eyes and skin wrinkled with middle age. He was wearing well-made but plain clothing, and carried two bags over his shoulders. There was a sword on his hip.

A merchant, perhaps, Julian thought. *Or an ageing sellsword. Either way he is none of my concern.*

When Julian moved to walk past him the man cried out, "You're not going to harm her, are you?"

"Of course not!" Julian spat out. "What do you take me for, old man?"

"A wizard, I suppose. A powerful one. That girl in your arms would stand not a chance against you."

"I will not harm her," Julian said, when he noticed his potential foe had his hand on the hilt of his sword. "I mean to take her back to her family."

An odd look crossed the man's face, and Julian felt himself frown. There was something...off. Something uncanny.

"Do I know you?" he asked.

The man shook his head. "I would think I'd remember such a foreboding wizard. Anyway, I shall take up no more of your time. Take care of the girl for me."

And then he was off before Julian could ask any further questions. He stayed stuck to the spot, too baffled to move, until he felt Genevieve beginning to shift in his arms.

510

He sighed. There was no way he could cope with another hour of walking with her conscious. And talking.

"Magic it is, then," Julian said, and with a snap of his fingers they were gone.

CHAPTER FIVE

Genevieve

Evie regained full consciousness with a start, though her brain had been trying to claw its way back for a while before that.

"Where am I?" she demanded, swinging into an upright position in an unfamiliar bed in an unfamiliar room. Two lanterns were lit, casting a warm glow across sparse furniture and off-white walls. Curtains were drawn over the window, so Evie could not tell what time it was.

And then her stomach growled painfully, bending her over double.

"Fix that," a gruff voice muttered, followed by a small loaf of bread hitting Evie on her temple. "There's soup on the table."

She spied Julian sitting on a chair in the darkest corner

of the room, glowering at her. To her left there really *was* a bowl of soup sitting on a small bedside table, so Evie picked it up with both hands and revelled in its warmth.

"Thank you," she tried to say, though it came out as more of a croak. Noticing a pitcher also sitting on the table along with a cup, Evie put down her bowl in order to pour herself some water. She drank the lot down so quickly that it took her a beat too long to realise the liquid wasn't, in fact, what she had assumed it was. Coughing and spluttering, Evie held a hand to her throat and tried to rub away the burning the liquid had caused.

In the corner Julian was cackling with laughter. "Serves you right for not looking at what you were drinking, little girl."

"I am *not* a little girl," Evie protested around another cough. "I'm twenty years old today. What is this vile stuff?"

Julian frowned slightly. "It's wine. Have you never had wine before?"

She shook her head. "I've been locked up for twelve years, remember? The last time I had *soup* was before that."

"What have you been living on, then?"

"Bread, mostly," Evie replied, picking up the loaf Julian had thrown at her. "Cheese. Apples. Sometimes dried meat. Water to drink. That's about it."

"No wonder you're so skinny," he said, casting his invisible gaze across Evie. Julian's eyes were once more covered by his dark, overlong hair. It annoyed her, but she didn't say anything. The wizard had saved her life twice today, after all. It would not harm her to show him some manners, though he seemed disinclined to extend the same respect to her.

513

Evie ate in silence for a while, during which time Julian got up and left the room. When he returned he was carrying a pitcher that *actually* contained water, left it by Evie's bedside, then took the half-full pitcher of wine over with him to the chair.

Julian took a long draught of the stuff. "Let me know when you begin to feel light-headed. I'll put you to sleep when you do; I don't imagine your tolerance for alcohol is particularly high."

"I don't want you to put me to sleep again!" Evie exclaimed.

"Ah, I didn't mean to, before. I got carried away."

The side-eye she gave Julian implied she definitely didn't believe him. The man finished off his cup of wine, poured another and then moved over to sit on the end of Evie's bed. She put down her finished bowl of soup on the table and inched away from him.

He grimaced. "I just wanted to check that you're okay."

"I'm fine, thank you."

Julian arched an eyebrow. "Are you sure? You were covered in cuts and bruises when I found you. Your feet at the very least can't be in the best of states."

Evie felt a twinge of pain lancing down her leg even as he spoke. The dull ache of her feet crept up her nerves in earnest, telling her that Julian was correct. She looked down at her hands. "I guess I'm not feeling great."

A pause. Julian gulped down more wine before saying, "I told you to stay to the outskirts of the woods. It was the *one thing* I told you to do. Why did you ignore me?"

"I thought you told me that just to inconvenience me!" she replied, bristling. "You weren't exactly very nice to

514

me, Julian."

He shook his head in disbelief. "Why in the world would I have done such a thing? I saved your life when you were hanging out of the tower, or don't you remember? Just because I wanted you gone didn't mean I wanted you to take one step outside and immediately walk into trouble."

Evie said nothing. She knew she had acted brashly, and immaturely. If she had been not so naïve about the world around her then perhaps she'd have been more inclined to take Julian's directions to the town more seriously.

"Did those men – did they do anything to you?"

"No," Evie replied quietly. She looked away from Julian. She didn't want to think about the strangers on the road; it was too frightening to dwell on what they would have done had Julian not come to her rescue. "They pulled on my hair and bruised me when I fell, but that's all."

She ran her fingers through her hair as she spoke, wincing when she met tugs and tangles along the way. It was a mess. It would take her many painful hours to clean and untangle it all.

"Right, that's it," Julian announced, before putting down his wine and closing the gap between them. "I'm cutting your hair."

"Don't you – don't you dare!" Evie cried, squirming out of the way when Julian attempted to grab hold of it. He slung an arm around her waist instead, hauling her back to his side.

"What's so important about bloody *hair* that you would let it become so cumbersome?!" he yelled.

"There was nothing to cut it with in the tower!"

515

"So let me cut it for you now!"

"No!"

"You brat, stop squirming and –"

"Stop yelling in my ear! Let me go!"

As soon as Julian realised he had pinned Evie to the bed he let her go and recoiled away. Evie's face was flushed. She was beginning to feel light-headed, which she put down to the wine. And her dress was in disarray, barely covering her at all. If she didn't have so childish a figure she'd probably have been embarrassed.

Julian ran a hand through his own hair and clenched his teeth in frustration. Now that Evie could see his face clearly she realised he was younger than she'd originally thought; he was perhaps only ten or so years older than her. By the way he spoke to her Evie would have assumed he was closer to fifty.

He glared at her. "What is honestly *so important* about your damn hair, little girl?"

"Stop calling me that," Evie replied, deliberately ignoring Julian's actual question. She didn't want to tell him about her memories of her mother brushing her hair and sending her off to sleep – those were hers and hers alone. In a world where Evie had so little, her memories were more precious to her than anything.

It seemed to Evie as if Julian knew she was deflecting. "Calling you what?" he asked, as if he didn't know exactly what he'd just called her.

Evie rolled her eyes. "Little girl. Brat. I told you; I'm not a child."

"So, what, should I call you *Princess*?" he asked scathingly.

"Just call me Evie."

"I thought your name was Genevieve?"

"It's too long. Call me Evie."

"*Fine...*Evie." Her stomach flipped upon hearing Julian call her by the nickname she'd given herself. She didn't like that at all. When he glanced at her Evie realised his eyes were blue. "If you won't let me cut your hair then at least allow me to do *something* about the state it's in," he insisted. "It will only get worse on our way to Willow."

Evie's spirits lifted, all previous unpleasant feelings forgotten immediately. She drew herself up onto her knees. "You're coming with me?! You're actually going to show me the way?"

"Don't make me regret this before we've even begun," Julian said, sliding a hand over his face in obvious exasperation. "Something tells me you would still refuse me magicking you to the city despite what happened in the forest, so I have no choice but to accompany you."

She nodded at the wizard's observation. "What would *you* want to do if you'd been locked up for twelve years, Julian? Would you not want to explore the world before returning home and maybe getting answers to your questions that...you might not like?"

Julian stared at her, baffled. "You're more astute than I thought."

Evie laughed bitterly, though she hated the sound. "How many times do I have to tell you that I'm not a child? I know that my return to the palace may not be what I hope it will be. But still I have to hope, otherwise what's the point?"

He sighed, then motioned for Evie to turn around. Obediently she did so, though she flinched when she felt Julian's hands pulling her hair away from her; it had tucked itself beneath her legs in their fight on the bed.

517

"I'm not going to cut it, I swear," he muttered. He brought his fingers to her scalp, massaging them into the roots of her hair with surprising gentleness. "I'm just going to work some magic."

Evie's heart lit up at the prospect. "You're giving me magic hair?"

"Don't be ridiculous. I'm simply working magic *upon* it. Now be silent, and be still."

Evie's skin tingled as Julian worked on his spell. She was faintly aware of the fact her hair was lit around its edges in a fiery way akin to Julian's previously glowing eyes. It sent a shiver down her spine, to think of him full of furious magic and ready to kill someone at a moment's notice.

"I told you not to move," he complained.

"I can't help it!" Evie protested. "Your magic tickles!"

Julian made a noise of disgust at the comment, but then he put his hands on Evie's shoulders and roughly pushed her off the bed towards a mirror hanging on the wall. Evie hadn't seen her reflection in anything larger than a cup of water for twelve years; she was nervous to see what she looked like.

But she didn't even notice her body, nor her face – not at first, anyway. She only had eyes for her hair.

Julian had cleaned and untangled every last golden strand of it, and had woven it into so intricate a braid that Evie couldn't tell how and where it started. The style brought her hair off the floor, the end of the braid only just skimming her ankles, which was far more practical for walking and running and just about anything else Evie could think of.

"Julian, this is –"

"Don't you dare thank me," he muttered, before heading for the door. "I did that for my own benefit, else I'll end up having to carry you to Willow just so you don't trip up over your damn hair. We leave immediately after sunrise."

And then he slammed the door and was gone, leaving Evie to stand in front of the mirror alone.

In contrast to her glorious, shining hair, the rest of her was underwhelming. Evie's skin was sickly pale, and there were shadows beneath her eyes. The bones of her elbows jutted out too much, and her cheekbones were too prominent. There were barely any signs that she had an adult woman's body, though Evie remembered her mother's figure had been invitingly curvy. She longed for the rest of her to match her hair – to look as beautiful as her mother and father.

"Guess I need to eat more," Evie decided, returning to the bedside table to retrieve the half-eaten loaf of bread from earlier. "I want to look my best when I return to the palace."

For there was nothing else Evie could control about the situation, and she knew it. She didn't like it one bit.

Perhaps it was because of the wine in her system, or the fact that she had a full stomach for the first time in years, but that night Evie fell asleep so quickly she might have been inclined to believe Julian had put a spell on her.

Maybe he really had.

CHAPTER SIX

Julian

"How long does it take to get to Willow on foot?"

"Ten days, as the crow flies."

"But we are not crows."

"I am aware, Evie."

"So how long will it take?"

"Longer if you keep asking me."

When Evie came to a halt on the gravelled road in a huff it was all Julian could do not to yell in frustration.

She crossed her arms over her chest, the elaborate braid Julian had woven into her hair swinging behind her like a pendulum. "Why can't you just tell me the answer instead of making fun of me?"

"*Fine.* It will take about four or five weeks, as I wish to stop by several towns on the way. Lord help me survive so long in your company. Are you satisfied now?"

"Very," Evie grinned, unfolding her arms and skipping on ahead of Julian in barely-concealed delight. He had a growing suspicion that Evie wanted the journey to Willow to take as long as feasibly possible, despite the fact she was eager to reunite with her family.

But she was aware that she may not get the welcoming she desires when she arrives, Julian mused. *For all we know it was her parents who sent her away in the first place.*

Julian had to force himself to keep walking instead of freezing to the spot. He was thinking as if he truly believed Evie was, indeed, the princess. But what evidence had she provided to support this? Other than having blonde hair and green eyes – traits not as rare as they once were a generation or two ago – there was nothing about Evie that suggested she was royalty.

She was polite and well-spoken, Julian supposed, but any girl of reasonable birth would sound like her. And she had not yet talked of her life before the age of eight – such as when she deliberately dodged Julian's question about her hair – which either suggested Evie was lying about being a princess or didn't want to talk to Julian about her childhood.

Which is bizarre because she won't shut up about everything else.

He watched Evie bound even further ahead of him like a collie dog. He'd bought her a brown cotton dress with a white undershirt from the innkeeper's wife, whose adolescent daughter had outgrown them. Despite the fact Evie was twenty – which Julian still struggled to believe – the clothes fit her much better than her previous dress

521

had, though she refused to throw that one away. He also procured her a pair of boy's trousers and a lace-up shirt as a change of clothes, as they were the only other garments he could find to buy.

Lastly, he'd made Evie a pair of shoes. Well, they'd been his and he'd enchanted them to perfectly fit her feet. Clothes Julian could cope with not being a precise fit on Evie; shoes he could not. If her shoes were too big or too small then she would complain about it and he would suffer a migraine for the duration of the journey to Willow.

Genevieve didn't look too bad now that she'd been cleaned up and clothed in something that fit her, though Julian wondered if she merely looked better because of her hair. He had to admit that he'd probably used more magic on it that was strictly warranted – he certainly hadn't needed to fix it in such an intricate hairstyle – but it looked so beautiful he scarcely cared. For as long as Julian could remember he'd been using magic for practical purposes only, to hone and enhance his offensive, defensive and enchantment skills. To use it for purely aesthetic reasons (though admittedly the underlying spell to keep Evie's hair out of the way was a useful one) was a rarity for him.

But now Evie's hair was a work of art. The innkeeper's wife had been in awe of it that very morning, and many of the early-rising townspeople had stared at her as they left. It left Julian feeling distinctly proud of his work, though he'd never say as much out loud.

Evie, however, had grown self-conscious. "They will think I'm not pretty enough for such hair," she'd admitted, very quietly. If Julian had been a nicer, more patient person he'd have comforted her. As it was, he disliked early mornings and had instead snapped at her to

522

finish eating breakfast as quickly as possible.

The girl had eaten like a piglet, though Julian could hardly blame her. If Evie had truly been stuck in the tower eating nothing but bread and cheese then of course she was ravenous. He made a mental note to stock up on extra food in every town; he had a feeling she'd devour it all.

"You know, you wanted to cut my hair even though your own desperately needs a trim," Evie said, breaking a blessed ten minutes of silence. Julian wondered if that was the longest stretch of peace and quiet he'd get over the next month.

"My hair doesn't trail on the floor though, does it?" he countered, darting out of the way when Evie reached up to try and touch it. "Even if I let it grow for twelve years it wouldn't be as long as yours."

"Is it not annoying to tie it up? I'll admit it's an improvement over letting it hang over your eyes, though."

Julian scratched the side of his temple. He wasn't used to having all of his hair tied back in a knot, but it made sense. He had to keep on high alert during the journey if he wasn't simply going to transport them using magic, so keeping his eyes clear was a necessity. But now everything seemed too bright, and he had to make eye contact with people, and he hated it.

"And are you not boiling to death inside that cloak?" Evie remarked, fingering the fraying edges of the material. "At least buy yourself one that isn't so damaged –"

"Are you quite done with criticising my appearance, *Princess*?" Julian asked through gritted teeth.

Evie said nothing. She merely stared at him expectantly until he gave in and answered her question.

He sighed. "I'm used to concealing myself from other

523

people," he finally explained. "As a wizard, it's not a good idea to let someone see if you have a particular solution or spell or weapon on you. And you don't want them to know if you have injuries. And you don't want other wizards and spell-wielders to use any old scars or defining features to their advantage. Better to keep it all hidden, even if it *is* uncomfortably hot beneath a cloak in summer."

The answer would have satisfied the average person. Evie was not average.

"What do you mean by other spell-wielders?"

"Magicians," Julian said, making a left off the rood to cut through a small strip of woodland to a stream. He needed to refill his water skin to combat the scorching heat of the midday sun. "Alchemists. Doctors."

"Doctors are spell-wielders? What's the difference between a magician and a wizard?"

He crouched low beside the narrow, gurgling stream and dunked his container into the water. It wasn't as cool as Julian would have wanted, given the heat of the day, but it would have to do. "What doctors can achieve these days is practically akin to magic, one might argue," he murmured. "Some of them know just as much – if not more – than an alchemist or experienced herbalist knows about the properties of poisons and mind-altering substances."

"And magicians?"

"Generally wizards are born with an affinity for magic whereas for magicians it's far more of a learned skill. They also mostly deal with curses and transformative magic instead of combative and defensive spells, for the most part, though admittedly the line between magicians and wizards is becoming blurred."

Evie paused to consider this. "You transformed my shoes and enchanted my hair. Does that not make you a magician?"

"And now you see my point," Julian said, standing upright once his water skin was filled and stretching his shoulder muscles until they cracked. "One day the two words will likely become entirely synonymous. But I'm far better versed in combative magic than the average magician. Or average wizard, truth be told."

"Was the magic you used on those men combative?"

He nodded. "Or defensive, as the case may be. Stunning them did no harm – it merely allowed us to escape."

I must surely have given her enough to think about for the time being, Julian thought as they picked their way back to the road through the trees. Evie jumped up and grabbed a couple of apples from a low-hanging bough; she threw one to him before happily biting into her own.

"I can't fathom how you're still hungry," Julian mused. "You ate enough for three people at breakfast and we're only an hour out from the next inn for lunch."

Evie shrugged. "You might have noticed I could do with gaining a little weight. And when will I ever have an opportunity to be a glutton like this again?"

"You *are* aware that I'm the one paying for your food, yes?"

"And when we reach the palace I shall have my father repay you for every meal. You *are* aware that he's the king, yes?"

"So you keep reminding me," Julian mused, before taking a tentative bite of the bright red fruit Evie had tossed him. It was deliciously sweet, though he personally preferred the sharper, green variety. He glanced at her out of the corner of his eye. "You haven't told me anything about your childhood, Evie."

"I know."

"Why not? It would lend some credit to your story."

To Julian's surprise, Evie chuckled. It wasn't her usual, childlike laugh; it was an altogether more adult sound. When she turned her head to smile at him with her woven, golden hair framing her face and the sun turning her irises to emeralds, Julian saw glimpses of a woman who really *could* be King Pierre's daughter.

"Because I have no reason to tell you," Evie said, "just as you have no reason to tell me about you. Or were you expecting me to spill every secret from my childhood when you so clearly do not wish to divulge anything about that tower of yours, or why you were absent from it for so long?"

Julian didn't reply.

Evie was right, and it infuriated him to no end to admit it.

CHAPTER SEVEN

Genevieve

Over a week had passed since Genevieve had nearly died trying to escape Julian's tower. In that time she had annoyed the man so much that he'd been driven to bark at her to shut up on no fewer than nine separate occasions, though Evie rarely heeded his demand for longer than half an hour.

And yet despite how often she spoke she still refrained from telling Julian anything substantial about her life before being trapped in the tower. Sometimes Evie wondered if that was irritating him more than her never shutting up; other times she was fairly certain it was the incessant talking driving him insane.

Either way, Evie was revelling in finally having company – even if Julian was quiet, angry, tired and bored most of the time.

"What do you think of – Evie, for the love of god, we just had lunch!"

Evie had picked up a pastry from a market stall, paid the vendor and already taken a large bite from the delicious baked good before Julian had noticed what she was doing. She grinned bashfully.

"Sorry," she said around mouthfuls of buttery pastry and sweet raspberry jam. "I was still hungry."

Julian raised his face to the sky and closed his eyes. Evie was familiar with the gesture; he did it when the two of them were around other people and he wanted to resist shouting. "I told you not to make me regret giving you money to buy things."

"But you shouldn't regret me eating, Julian!"

"It's a perfectly acceptable regret," he countered. "At this rate we'll run out of money barely halfway to Willow."

Evie stuck her tongue out. "I know you have most of your coins hidden somewhere in your cloak and bag. There's no way we'll run out of money before we reach the palace."

Just as Julian was about to retort the vendor who'd sold Evie the pastry burst out laughing. The pair of them turned to the woman, surprised and confused.

"Don't the two of you make such a funny couple!" she said. "And your hair is so beautiful, miss. Do you braid it yourself? Or does your lovely companion do it for you?"

Evie pulled Julian away before he could begin spouting angry protestations about being mistaken for a couple, all the while trying to smile at the woman with her pastry firmly between her teeth.

"Why did you do that?" he demanded, before ripping half of Evie's pastry from her mouth and unceremoniously

528

shoving it into his own. She glared at him for half a moment then continued consuming what he had left her. "All I was going to say to that woman was that she was mistaken; why would I ever be together with a skinny, brattish, annoying –"

"You're going to have to find another word for 'annoying', Julian," Evie said mildly. "It's getting awfully boring." This was not the first time the pair of them had been mistaken for a couple, after all; considering they were a man and a woman travelling together it was only natural for the towns and villages they passed through to assume as much.

Evie didn't mind being viewed as a woman in love, wandering the country with her partner. Even *if* the partner was a tetchy wizard who somehow never got enough sleep to satisfy him, though he insisted on getting up at daybreak. It certainly beat staying in a tower all by herself.

"I think 'annoying' works just fine," Julian replied, before directing Evie down the market street to a green-and-gold shop front. "I want to go in here. Can I trust you to stay out here and not cause any trouble? Or will I have to magic your mouth shut and tether you to the door?"

She swatted his arm. "I can behave. Why can't I just come in with you?"

"Because my business is my own."

"Typical."

"Says the woman who talks at length about nothing but stays silent on anything meaningful."

"...fine," Evie conceded, before crossing her arms and leaning against the shop front. "But don't keep me out here for long or I really *will* misbehave."

Julian's eyes glittered at the pseudo-threat, almost on

the cusp of glowing with magic. Both he and Genevieve knew fine well she would not do anything of the sort. She said such things to rile him up and, to Julian's dismay, it usually worked.

He needs to do something about his temper, Evie thought as Julian wordlessly left her side to enter the shop, a bell above the door chiming prettily when he did so. She shifted on the spot, trying to readjust her arms across her chest to make herself more comfortable.

The clothes Julian had bought her merely a week ago were beginning to grow tight. Evie liked the feeling of it, for it was proof that she was finally gaining weight, but in another few days they would likely become unwearable.

She glanced down at her chest. Every night, when she was left alone in her room in whichever inn Julian had picked for them to stay in, Evie would look at herself in the mirror and wonder if she was any closer to looking as grown up as her mother did. She supposed it *was* working – her hips and her breasts were certainly curvier than they had been a week ago, and Evie's face no longer looked gaunt and underfed. But it wasn't enough.

She wanted her body to match her beautiful, golden hair. The magic Julian had worked upon it was quickly becoming both a blessing and a curse to her.

"I was never so narcissistic back in the tower," she grumbled, "though it's hardly as if I knew what I looked like, either."

Out of the corner of her eye she noticed than several passers-by were glancing at her, some of them more than once. Her hair really *did* stand out, what with its length and colour and intricate, weaving hairstyle. Julian's magic repelled dirt and grease from it, and kept her hair from forming flyaways and tangles, so Evie hadn't unravelled the braid even once. It meant it looked perfect at all times.

Unlike the rest of me.

"No, Scarlett, I am *not* getting involved with that."

"But Adrian –"

"Absolutely not. There's just...far too much drama involved with something like that."

Evie tried not to make it obvious that she was watching the unusual couple bickering a few metres away. They were possibly the most beautiful people she'd ever seen. The man's jet-black hair was broken by a solitary white streak, and there was a single hanging emerald adorning one of his ears that matched his green waistcoat. He looked the epitome of a charming gentleman...except for his amber eyes, which had a predatory edge to them that reminded Evie of the wolves her mother used to tell her about before bed.

The woman also had black hair, though it was thick and wavy and tumbled over her shoulders. She wore a deep red dress so finely made that many of the female townspeople sighed with longing as they passed her. Her face was pale and fair, with the hint of a smile on her lips that suggested she knew a secret nobody else was privy to.

I think they might be even odder than me and Julian, Evie decided, just as the wizard himself exited the shop and returned to her side.

He frowned at the couple she was watching. "Who are they?" he asked, immediately suspicious. He held a small bag in his hands from the shop, though he slid it into the folds of his cloak before Evie could ask what he'd bought.

She shrugged. "I don't know. I think they might have been talking about us, though."

"How do you know?"

"Just a hunch. They're going in the opposite direction to us, anyway. It probably doesn't matter."

Julian didn't look satisfied with Evie's answer but he took it nonetheless. "Come on," he said, "we still have hours of travelling to go before we reach our stop for the night."

"Why don't you dress like the orange-eyed man back there?" Evie asked after a while. "You might actually look good."

Julian clucked his tongue. "Hardly one of my top concerns, Evie."

"Don't you want to find a wife?"

He didn't reply; his silence spoke volumes.

That would be a no, then.

"Do *you* want a husband?" Julian countered, much to Evie's surprise. "When you return to the palace and take up your place as princess, I mean. You'll probably have to."

"I hadn't really thought about it seriously," she admitted. "I guess marriage is still an abstract concept to me."

"Better to keep it that way," he mumbled, so quietly that Genevieve almost missed it. She chose not to reply; it was a subject she realised she'd rather not discuss.

That afternoon they travelled together in uncharacteristic, awkward silence for the first time.

Evie didn't know why it bothered her so much.

CHAPTER EIGHT

Julian

It was just before midnight and Julian couldn't sleep. Normally he collapsed into bed the moment he reached an inn – walking all day was exhausting, and Evie's incessant chatter even more so.

Except for today. He and Evie hadn't spoken since the marketplace in the previous town, which Julian didn't understand. Had she stopped talking to him because he'd asked her about whether she wanted to get married?

It can't be that, surely, he thought. *Evie said herself she hadn't even considered the idea all that much. That it had been a hypothetical situation, since she reasonably assumed she would never get to leave the tower.*

But then why had she stopped talking? Julian had felt so awkward in the silence yet he couldn't find the words to break it. And Evie had a faraway look plastered to her face, as if she wouldn't have heard anything Julian said even if he *had* spoken.

With a sigh he lurched out of bed, slid on his boots and headed towards the inn's tavern, thinking that perhaps some ale would ease him into unconsciousness. He hesitated for a moment when he passed Evie's room, running his fingers along the grain of the wooden door as he did so. He wondered if she was asleep, or whether he should ask if she wished to join him.

The thought almost made Julian laugh. *Here I am with a perfect opportunity to be alone and I'm considering deliberately asking Genevieve if she wants to annoy me? Ridiculous.*

And so Julian left her door and continued downstairs. There were a mere handful of men still sitting in the tavern, though the ones at the bar respectfully kept their distance from him when he walked up to it. Even without his cloak on, and wearing a simple white shirt and trousers, Julian exuded an aura that told people to stay away. That he was unusual. That he was powerful. He supposed that was his magic's doing.

It never keeps Evie away, Julian mused as he ordered a tankard of ale. *It's like she doesn't know or care about it, or cannot feel it.*

"Fancy seeing you here, wizard."

He turned; several stools away sat an oddly familiar figure. When he moved over to sit by Julian he recognised him as the man who'd hidden on the road when Evie was attacked.

Julian frowned. "I thought you were travelling in the opposite direction from me?" he asked. "How did you end up here?"

The man's shaggy, greying blonde hair shook as he

laughed. Julian realised that maybe it really *was* time to cut his hair, or at least tidy it up – the stranger looked half-mad.

"I'm not heading towards any particular destination," the man replied. "Haven't had one for a while now. I just go where I feel like going."

"I can relate to that," Julian said, thinking of the past thirteen years of his life. Looking back he felt like most of it had been a waste – he had no standout memories from his period travelling abroad. No notable people to drastically affect his course in life; no stories to tell of monsters felled and villages saved; no sweeping, epic romances that would likely make Evie blush. All Julian had done was improve upon his magic, which he could have done anywhere.

I may as well have been trapped in a tower all alone.

As if reading his mind, the man asked, "How's the girl? Did you get her home?"

Julian nearly told him that Evie was still with him on reflex, but remembered to be suspicious at the last second. "I did," he said, narrowing his eyes as he took a long draught of ale. "Glad to be rid of her."

"That's not very nice, wizard. I'm sure she was quite lovely."

"And how could you be so sure of that?"

He shrugged. "A hunch."

Julian realised he'd been right to be suspicious; the stranger clearly knew far more than he was letting on. Julian could not be sure for what purpose he was interested in Evie, so he downed his ale, nodded at the man and promptly left the tavern. He didn't want to say something that gave the stranger more information that he already had, after all.

I'll have to keep a closer eye on the road, Julian thought as he crept up the stairs and passed Evie's room. *I don't want to be followed or –*

A thump came from behind Evie's door. Julian froze in front of it, wondering what had caused the noise. Just as he concluded that it was probably no more harmful than the young woman falling out of bed in her sleep – Julian snickered at the thought – he heard Evie stifle a sob.

He slammed the door open to check on her before he could stop to think things through. Evie *was* on the floor, both blankets and her long, long hair twisted around her legs and waist like serpents. But there was nothing amusing about her having fallen from her bed.

Evie's face was ashen, eyes glazed over in horror as she sobbed and sobbed.

Julian didn't know what to do. He knew he couldn't stay standing there merely watching Evie, either, so he closed the door behind him and took several tentative steps towards the young woman on the floor, though Evie didn't seem to realise Julian was there.

"Evie?" he asked, voice a little uncertain. He bent down by her side and reached out a hand to check her temperature; Evie recoiled from it with such force that her head thumped against the wall.

"You fool!" Julian exclaimed before he could stop himself. This time he bodily picked Evie up despite her trying to wriggle away and placed her back in bed. He pinched her pale, tear-stained cheek. "Wake up already. Wake up. What happened?"

Evie blinked several times and looked down at her trapped limbs. Wordlessly Julian set to work untangling her; she trembled beneath his fingers. *I've never seen her so scared,* he thought. *Not even when she was hanging out*

536

of the tower was she this afraid.

"Evie, what happened?" Julian asked again, forcing his voice to be altogether far gentler than it had been the first time.

She shook her head miserably. "It was just a dream. A nightmare. I'm fine."

"Clearly not. Tell me what happened."

When Evie sat up against the headboard and drew her knees to her chest Julian chose to sit beside her. Usually being in such close proximity to Evie resulted in him wanting to scream at her or throw something in annoyance, but not now. Julian felt an overwhelming urge to protect the small, shivering woman in front of him, whose impossibly long hair was beginning to unravel around her face.

I need to put some magic back into her hair, Julian noted as he reached a hand out to tuck a lock of it behind Evie's ear. She watched him do so with wide, unguarded eyes.

"Why do you care so much about a nightmare, Julian?" she asked. Her voice was barely audible.

"If a woman who I know to be fearless enough to climb out of a tower window using a rope made of clothes can be reduced to *this* after a dream," Julian said, waving a hand in Evie's general direction, "then of course I care. What did you see that was so bad?"

Evie didn't look at his face. She sighed, then wrapped her arms around her knees. "I was back in the tower."

"That doesn't seem all that bad."

"It was surrounded by thorns," she continued, as if Julian had never interjected. "They were everywhere. Black and twisting and sharp. They grew in through the

537

window and trapped me where I lay. I couldn't escape them. They cut into my skin, and then they cut deeper. It was like being suffocated; I could only watch them close in on me as they slowly killed me. It was..."

Evie didn't finish her final sentence. It didn't matter which word she used to describe what happened – horrifying, frightening, terrible – it clearly would not do the experience any justice.

Julian felt an uncomfortable finger of ice creep down his spine. That Evie had dreamed of thorns unsettled him deeply. But he hadn't told her his surname, so there was no explaining away her dream as subliminal based on things she'd heard.

It can't be prophetic, Julian thought. Evie had displayed no signs of magical talent so far. *But can a mere 'bad dream' really be bad enough to send her into such a panic?*

"You think it's stupid," Evie mumbled into her knees. "You think *I'm* stupid."

"You and I both know I don't think that," he chastised. "Just because you're insufferable and oftentimes an idiot doesn't mean you're stupid."

Julian was pleasantly surprised when Evie laughed at the remark. He smiled slightly. "If you're feeling better then I'm going to head back through to my –"

"No, don't go!" Julian stared down at his sleeve; Evie had grabbed it before he'd even had the opportunity to stand up. Her fingers clenched through the material down to his skin, promising fingertip-shaped bruises in the morning if Evie didn't let go soon.

He raised an eyebrow. "Where do you propose I sleep, then? On the floor? Because I'm not doing that."

"Sleep in the bed with me," Evie said. There was

absolutely no trace of an ulterior motive on her face – but then again, there never was. "Please," she added on, when it became clear Julian was going to decline. "Please stay."

The two of them stared at each other for a long time, Julian frowning and thinking whilst Evie's green eyes were bright and pleading. Another lock of hair fell across her face; when Julian reached forward to place it behind her ear he knew he wouldn't leave.

"Fine," he sighed, exasperated. He hauled off his boots and lay down beside a victorious Evie. "You win. This is a one–time thing, though. I don't much revel in the idea of squeezing onto a narrow bed with a skinny brat for company."

Evie swatted his face; this close together she barely had to reach her hand out to do so. "I'm not so skinny now. And I'm not a brat."

"You really are. Look what you're having me do! All because of a nightmare. You're such a child."

When Evie smiled at him Julian could help but breathe an inward sigh of relief. Things were back to normal between the two of them after their awkward afternoon of silence, which Julian was glad for despite his preference for quiet.

"Good night, Julian," Evie said before snuggling into the crook of his arm.

"Don't you dare fall asleep there!" he complained, though Evie had already laced her hand through his to bring it over her shoulder. Julian could have kicked himself for giving into her ridiculous request, but when Evie's breathing slowed and she fell back into a far more restful slumber than before he forgot to be annoyed.

Just once, he thought. *I can indulge her just once.*

There was a growing problem, however. This close

together Julian realised something about Evie he'd have rather not had to deal with. For Evie was right: she wasn't a brat. She was a woman.

And Julian's body was reacting to that even as he screamed at it not to.

This was going to be a long, awful night.

CHAPTER NINE

Genevieve

It was just before dawn and Genevieve was wide awake. She had slept comfortably for a few hours after waking from her nightmare, but the feeling that she wasn't alone in her bed was quick to rouse her when the room began to lighten.

Julian, Evie thought, too cowardly to turn and see his sleeping face behind her. *I can't believe I asked him to share a bed with me. I can't believe he* accepted *my request to share a bed with me.*

It seemed like madness that she'd asked him to spend the night with her. But Evie hadn't really expected Julian to agree to keep her company – she was just an idiotic child reacting badly to a nightmare, after all.

Although he said I wasn't stupid. He was almost kind to me.

Evie didn't know what to do now that she was awake. The bed was narrow and Julian was tall. There was barely enough space for him on it – let alone Evie, too. It meant she was pressed up against him, her legs interlaced with his.

A furious blush began to creep up Evie's neck. *I only have an underdress on and it's currently bunched around my thighs!* But Evie didn't dare reach down to fix her clothes; she didn't wish to risk waking Julian up. His soft breathing tickled Evie's head, sending errant strands of hair wafting over her face.

The magic's come undone, she thought, picking up a lock of golden hair and inspecting it for signs of having been stuck in a braid for a week. But there was not a single crimp or crease or wave to it – Evie's hair was as straight as if she'd kept it unbound and free instead of tied up.

She huffed out a small breath of air. *Magic is so strange. Where does it come from? How did Julian learn to be a wizard? Was he just born this way?* He did *say wizards tended to be born with an affinity for magic.*

With every passing day Evie longed to learn more about him, despite the fact she was wary of telling Julian anything about herself. At this point she wasn't sure why she was keeping her childhood secret; Evie trusted the wizard, after all. For how could she not? Julian had saved her life twice, then chosen to help Evie travel to Willow on foot, and now he was even comforting her when she had bad dreams.

Don't dwell on the dream, she thought, though it was difficult not to. It had been so vivid – so alarming – that when Evie had awoken all she could see around her were thorns. They'd threatened to overcome her; to entrap her; to control her. They represented everything Evie had tried to escape from, the moment she'd decided to climb out of the window of Julian's tower.

She squeezed her thighs together in discomfort only to remember, too late, that one of Julian's legs was between them. Evie's previous blush grew bolder. She was thankful the wizard was far more clothed than she was, otherwise things would probably have been much worse.

This is still the most indecent I've ever seen him, though, Evie thought. She craned her neck around in order to try and peek at Julian without disturbing him. But he was fast asleep, so Evie risked slowly sliding her legs away from his to turn and face him.

In stark contrast to what he looked like when conscious, Julian's face was serene as he slept. Without a scowl on his face he looked younger, once more reminding Evie that he really couldn't be much more than a decade older than her. Although, given their current situation, she sincerely wished she *hadn't* thought about such a thing.

Stop it, Evie, she scolded even as she held the fingertips of her right hand millimetres from Julian's face. But she couldn't help it; she wanted to know if she could feel...something. Anything. A sign that Julian held the power to set things on fire – to just as easily stun a group of men as he could enchant a young lady's hair. She wanted to feel that buzz of magic that made her heart sing when his blue eyes began to glow like molten glass.

Then Evie tried to see past the magic she was longing to feel. Beneath it, Julian was a tired man desperately in need of a shave, a haircut and some new clothes. In that respect he was not so dissimilar to Evie herself.

He's really strong, Evie mused, casting her gaze along the line of Julian's shoulder and down his arm. He'd carried her onto the bed the night before as if she'd weighed nothing at all. *And that's not to mention how easily he pulled me back into the tower when I was falling!* But hidden beneath his cloak Evie had never seen whether Julian actually had the frame to support such strength, or whether he'd used magic to help out every time.

Now she knew. Despite the fact Julian always appeared to be old and tired and unkempt and resigned he was, in fact, a perfectly healthy man who was probably stronger than most even *without* magic.

And he is handsome, I suppose, Evie thought despite herself. *Though it's not as if he seems to care about his looks all that much. When you're a powerful wizard I guess it doesn't matter if women fawn over you for your blue eyes or not.*

It made Evie hate her own growing narcissism. Did she honestly care so much about becoming beautiful like her parents? Was that really all she had going for her? She was a *princess.* Beautiful or not she would have opportunities abound once she returned to Willow and the royal palace.

Her stomach lurched at the thought, so Evie turned from Julian and closed her eyes as if doing so would somehow eliminate all her doubts. But they lingered, ruining the warmth of the sun as it crept over the horizon and ventured through the window into the room.

Just what was waiting for Evie when she returned to her parents? Would they be glad to see her? Or would they be angry? Why was she sent to the tower in the first place? What could the eight-year-old Princess Genevieve have possibly done to warrant such a cold, cruel punishment?

And why was it *Julian's* tower?

"Shh," Julian mumbled against her ear, clearly still fast asleep. Evie hadn't said anything out loud; she had to wonder if Julian's power extended into being able to read her mind. She didn't like that idea one bit.

Perhaps he is dreaming of telling me to shut up, since he has to do it so often when awake, she thought, which was a far more appealing explanation. Evie almost giggled at the idea of her annoying the wizard even in his sleep, but then Julian slung an arm over her waist and pulled her in against him and all such amusing thoughts were lost.

Evie's eyes darted downward to Julian's hand, which rested on her stomach. For there was the thrum of magic she had longed to feel earlier, pinning her in place against him. It wasn't uncomfortable; rather, the peculiar sensation was almost pleasant. Like Julian was keeping her safe.

But he's doing it in his sleep, she thought. *Does he know he's doing it? Just how powerful is he?*

As if in protest to Evie's brain running through a million questions at once Julian squeezed her against him just a little tighter, and her mind cleared. For soon the wizard would wake up, and then he'd go back to being his usual, dour self. Evie would likely not get an opportunity to spend time with him like this again.

I guess I should make it count, she thought, before snuggling against Julian's side in much the same manner as she had done when he'd first agreed to share her bed. But things were somehow different than they had been hours before, in the dead of night. Evie felt altogether like she was growing up at a rate far faster than she had done when she was alone in the tower. Sleeping beside a grown man she was not married to was not something she was supposed to do...especially not when her thoughts towards said man were beginning to verge on impure.

But Evie was content to push such troubles off onto another day, along with everything else she had to worry about. The morning sun, and Julian's soft breathing, and the knowledge that she was free from the tower, was enough to satisfy her.

For now.

CHAPTER TEN

Julian

Ten days had passed since Evie's nightmare and, just like that, the pair of them were more than halfway through their journey to Willow. Julian should have felt relieved. Soon he'd be able to wash his hands of the young woman beginning to encroach on all his thoughts and he could go back to his unremarkable life of trying to improve his magic for a goal he could never reach. There was just one problem.

Julian was beginning to wish his journey with Evie *wouldn't* end.

It wasn't that she had suddenly become less annoying or less exhausting to look after. No, everything was pretty much the same as it had been from the very beginning. But the closer they got to Willow the more Julian felt like they were being followed, and the more he became aware that perhaps there was something from Evie's childhood that would tell him why.

Given how reluctant Evie was to tell him anything, despite all that they'd been through so far, Julian concluded that whatever it was wasn't going to be pleasant, and that the two of them really would be better off never going near the royal palace.

"How is your hair a mess *again*?" Julian complained when he spied Evie return from a market stall in the town they were passing through, arms laden with a heavy basket full of food. "I only enchanted it five days ago." Her golden hair was coming undone around her face; with her dishevelled dress and rosy cheeks Evie looked decidedly as if she'd taken a tumble through a meadow with a young lover.

Except that's just what she looks like all the time because she has absolutely no self-awareness, Julian thought, grabbing the basket of food from Evie's arms so that she could tuck her hair behind her ears.

She smiled bashfully. "I guess my hair is as greedy as I am. It must love your magic quite a lot."

He snorted in amusement at the comment. At least Evie was honest about her insatiable appetite. "Sounds about right. I think you need more clothes."

"I *know* I need more clothes." She looked away and blushed as she spoke, which at first confused Julian. But then he noticed the way some of the local boys were looking at her, eyeing the way her breasts were just a little too visible above the neckline of her dress, and how the curve of her hips brought the hem of her skirt above her knees.

The dress I found her in fits her better than this one now, Julian thought, before unceremoniously handing

548

Evie the basket of food to carry once more simply to cover her chest. It wasn't just that she looked indecent in such an ill-fitting dress – it was that the pair of them travelling together when Evie looked like that made *Julian* feel indecent, too. Had he really been so blind to Evie's situation that he was only realising the discomfort she must be feeling now, almost three weeks after they'd first set off on their journey?

Out of the corner of his eye a flash of movement caught Julian's attention. Just a hint of someone sliding between two market stalls, but it was enough for him to know that he and Evie were definitely being followed through the town.

He rummaged inside his cloak and fished out several gold coins before sliding them into the basket Evie was holding. He bent low towards her ear, then pointed down a side street. "Buy yourself something that fits better from there. I'd say buy *several* things that fit you but you seen intent on tripling in size by the time we reach Willow, so there's no point."

Evie smiled softly at the comment, though it didn't reach her eyes. She glanced at Julian a little uncertainly. "What's going on, Julian?"

"Just do as you're told. Please," he added on, when it seemed as if Evie was going to protest. Instead she merely stared at Julian long and hard; he resorted to finding constellations in her freckles just as he had done the first day he'd met her. The sun had brought them out over the last three weeks; they were much easier to see now. But Evie didn't budge even as Julian continued to stay silent.

Then he pulled a gold coin out from behind her ear, like a common street magician, and she burst out laughing. "Okay, okay, I'm going," Evie said, waving back at Julian before heading in the direction he'd pointed out.

He watched her walk away with a smile on his face, though when he spied the same boys as before leering at her it quickly turned into a scowl.

He sent out a thread of magic towards them – not enough for the boys to notice, but strong enough that Julian could keep track of wherever they went whilst he searched out whoever was following him. If they got too close to Evie he would know; the magic in her hair made certain of that. On more than one occasion Julian had wondered whether he should tell her that part of the enchantment he'd cast on her was a tracking spell, though ultimately he'd decided against it.

Nobody wanted to know they were being watched. Followed. Under constant supervision.

Least of all Julian himself.

It didn't take Julian long to work out where his and Evie's stalker was hiding. He crept along one side street, and then another, and finally down a dark, hidden alleyway blocked off by a large market stall selling trinkets and vases. When he spied a shadowy figure leaning against a rough stone wall Julian recognised him immediately.

"You," he spat out, sending fiery magic down to his fingertips in order to light the alleyway in front of him. For the stalker was no other than the greying, middle-aged man whom Julian had met on the road the day he'd saved Evie's life, then in the tavern a week later before her nightmare. "I should have known."

The man smiled humourlessly. "You *did* know, wizard. You simply hadn't done anything about me following you yet."

"Give me one good reason not to blast your head from your shoulders," Julian demanded, taking another step forwards and sending enough magic to his fingers that the air began to crackle and spark around them. He was satisfied to see the man flinch back from it all.

"You're strong," he said. "Very strong."

"Are you hoping to compliment me into letting you go?"

"Not at all. I'm merely glad that the person protecting Genevieve is more than up to the task."

Julian froze; his magic faltered. "How do you know her name?"

The man's eyes darted around as if looking for someone. "You *are* being followed, you know. Not just by me."

"I'm aware. How do you know Evie's name?" Julian repeated, his tone altogether more demanding this time.

To his surprise, the man's serious expression broke for a moment. When his eyes lit up Julian took a moment to realise they were green.

"Evie," he said. "Mariette would love to know she goes by that. My brother didn't like it, though, so she never went by Evie in the palace."

Julian's brain was working overtime to try and connect the dots, much like he did with Evie's freckles. *She's really the princess?* he thought despite himself. All this time Julian had only half-believed her. Evie could just as easily have been driven insane from being stuck in the tower for years, or from hitting her head, or –

"You are surprised to learn that the woman you're with is Princess Genevieve."

It wasn't a question.

Julian shook his head, dismayed by his own lack of knowledge. "Not surprised. Merely..."

"You thought she was lying about it?"

"How much do you know, stranger?" Julian asked, frowning. He returned a little magic to his fingers, for all the good it would do. "Have you been listening to our conversations?"

"Only in the beginning," the man admitted. "I had to be sure I could trust you to keep her safe, so I listened to everything."

Julian didn't like this at all. He hadn't known they were being followed in the beginning.

"You don't need to look so upset," the stranger laughed. "I've learned a thing or two about cloaking myself from a wizard's eyes."

"So I only became aware of you following us because you wished it to be so?"

He nodded. "I'd hoped you'd have more time to move Genevieve to a place far from here by now, but that hasn't been the case, so..."

"You don't want Evie to go home?"

The man laughed incredulously. "Do you not recognise me yet, Julian?"

He paused. "Should I?"

"Aside from my physical similarity to the king, and my knowledge of Genevieve's upbringing, the fact I was the one who convinced your father to work on the grand council after the war was over should have informed you of who I was."

"But that was..." Julian's voice trailed away as he thought back to his childhood. "I was a boy then. Only eight. I thought it was the king who came to see my father directly."

"Pierre hates to travel. He sent his brother in his

stead."

Oh.

"You're Francis Saule."

"In the flesh."

Julian's eyes narrowed. He returned his hand to his side, snuffing out the magic within it in the process. "You were exiled. For –"

"For a lie," Francis interrupted. He snorted. "Well, my dear brother lied to the country, that is. He made me out to be a war criminal. In truth what I did was far worse...to him, anyway."

"Speak plainly or not at all," Julian said. The thread he'd sent out after the local boys was beginning to tug, warning him that they were far too close to Evie.

Francis' eyes were hard. "I hurt his pride."

"That doesn't explain a damn thing and you know it."

"It should," he said. "You must know how proud our dear king is."

"I've spent the last thirteen years travelling, twelve of which have been spent avoiding dealing with my father's death." Julian had never been so honest – with a stranger, no less – about his father. But this man, the king's brother, had known Jacques Thorne. He might have been a stranger to Julian but he was not to his father.

Francis' smile was sad and genuine. "Perhaps it's for the best you haven't been around to witness the king's character. I'm sure he would ensnare you for your powers had you stayed close to Willow."

Julian ignored this. Nobody was going to trap him, least of all the king. He never intended to work for anybody he had not chosen to help himself. "What did you do that hurt your brother's pride so much that he

553

exiled you?" he asked.

"I fell in love with his wife."

Oh no.

"And she fell in love with me."

Please stop.

"I fathered a daughter the king always believed to be his."

He isn't stopping, Julian thought, dismayed. He wanted to cover his ears with his hands – to block out all the drama and betrayal he had accidentally walked right into, the moment he'd saved Genevieve's life.

"Genevieve was sent to your father's tower to live in isolation," Francis continued, as if he took no notice of Julian's distraught expression. "She was never told why. My brother...he loved her, in his own way. He couldn't stand to look at her after he found out her true parentage. The fact he's looking for her now must mean he's aware she's no longer in the tower. He –"

"Wait," Julian said, holding out a hand as he attempted to take in Francis' deluge of information. "Just wait. The king had Evie – the princess – sent to my father's tower. Why? Why, specifically, Thorne tower?"

Francis shook his head sadly. "Because he worked for my brother, and was the most powerful wizard he had at his disposal."

There was something about the man's explanation that didn't feel right. Julian wanted to press him for further answers but the thread of magic connecting him to the boys lurking after Evie pulled against him more insistently than ever. She was leaving the shop, and they were there, waiting for her. Julian had to get her first.

"Don't let her reach the palace," Francis said, reading

Julian's intention to leave the alleyway from his face. "Pierre *can't* get hold of her. Stay off the roads. Keep her safe."

"You lost the right to tell Evie what to do the moment you allowed the king to trap her in a tower," Julian uttered, so angry on her behalf that his eyes began to glow. He turned from the king's brother, stalking back through the throng of the marketplace until he found Evie standing nervously by the entryway to the tailor's shop.

She beamed when she saw Julian, evidently relieved to no longer be on her own. "Julian, what do you think of -"

"We're leaving," he muttered, grabbing Evie's arm and pulling her away from the predatory stares of the boys lingering nearby.

"Julian, what's wrong with -"

"Nothing. We just have to leave."

But everything was wrong with Julian. Evie really was the Princess Genevieve, and the king had really banished her to Thorne tower. Julian's *father* had been involved, somehow, and shortly thereafter he'd disappeared and died.

He was missing some vital pieces to the puzzle, and he had no idea how to find them. There was only one thing Julian knew for certain.

There was nobody either himself or Evie could trust except each other, and nowhere was safe.

Julian spared half a glance at the princess, knowing full well what her response would be to his next statement.

"I hope you like camping."

CHAPTER ELEVEN

Genevieve

"Camping?!"

"Yes, camping. As in, sleeping outdoors in a field, preferably a forest, with absolutely nobody around and -"

"Julian, I know what camping is. I just haven't experienced it before, given that I was *locked in a tower for twelve years* and -"

"And you're a princess," Julian finished for her. "Yes. I know."

Evie frowned for nobody to see. Something was wrong with Julian. *Well, something has been wrong for a while now, but this is different. Something happened to him when I was in the tailor's shop.*

She hurried along behind him, struggling to keep up with Julian's long legs even as his grip tightened on her arm. The town was well behind them now; Evie had to wonder what he was so concerned about. Back at the marketplace she'd thought Julian was worried about the young men who kept stealing glances at her. It had reassured Evie to know that he was looking out for her, but it became quickly apparent this extended to more than keeping away amorous youths.

"Julian, please, slow down!" Evie insisted when they reached a tall, ancient oak tree. It signalled the beginning of a forest so large that she couldn't see where it ended.

He turned, letting go of Evie's arm in the process. Though his eyes were on hers it seemed altogether like Julian was looking through her, instead. She didn't like it. It was only when he took the basket of food Evie had been precariously holding against her chest that he finally seemed to see her.

"Your dress is nice," Julian mumbled before looking away.

The comment should have made Evie happy – had he complimented on the dark green, leaf-embroidered fabric outside the tailor's shop then she'd have been ecstatic. As it were, Evie knew Julian was deflecting from telling her what was really going on. But the two of them had been doing that to each other from the very beginning, so she sighed and moved past Julian into the forest. He wordlessly followed.

"Was it expensive?" he asked after ten minutes. Evie almost laughed, then slid her hand into one of the pockets sewn into the dress and threw a number of coins at Julian without looking to see if he caught them. Going by the string of curses he bit out she could only assume each and every one of them fell to the forest floor.

"Not so expensive as to be worried," she said, slowing

her steps until Julian had finished picking up the coins. "The woman working in the shop loved my hair so much that she gave me a discount, I think. Is my hair meant to charm people, Julian? What did you weave into it?"

He glanced at her. "It shouldn't charm people, *per se.* But it's meant to disarm them, and make them trust you."

"Why would you put that in my *hair*?"

"So that nobody bothers us with suspicious questions," Julian answered simply. "The fact you got a well-fitting dress out of it is an unexpected benefit."

This time Evie *did* blush at the mention of her new clothes. It was an adult dress, made for a woman instead of a child. It cinched in at her waist and accentuated her curves without squeezing or hurting her, and the wide skirt actually fell below her knees. It was cut low across her shoulders, exposing Evie's collarbones and the hollow of her throat. It was still a far cry from the opulent dresses she remembered being popular in Willow back when she was a child, but it was a fine improvement upon what she'd been wearing before.

Evie spun on the spot before jumping onto a fallen tree trunk. She grinned at Julian. "It really is a nice dress. I forgot what proper clothes felt like."

Julian was silent. Even an hour or two ago he'd have likely passed comment about how it wouldn't surprise him if Evie had *never* known what being in proper clothes was like, simply to insult her. But now he had nothing to say.

Something is wrong, Evie thought, more sure than ever before. *If I ask him what's happened will he simply ignore me again?*

And so the two of them weaved through the forest in silence for a while, Evie leading the way even though she didn't know where she was going. Her hair continued to unravel as it had been doing since that morning until it was once more long enough to trip her up; by the time the braid became completely undone the sun had set over the trees, casting the pair of them in pre-emptive twilight.

"Julian, are we going in the – ouch!"

"Will you watch what you're doing, you idiot?!" Julian exclaimed, dropping the basket of food in order to catch Evie before she fell to the forest floor. Her hair was entangled around a low-hanging branch, preventing Evie from walking any further until she was set free.

She stared at him dolefully. "I wasn't the one who wanted to leave the road so urgently. Why haven't you magicked my hair back into a braid, anyway?"

Evie thought Julian wasn't going to reply as he delicately unwound her hair from the branch. It always unnerved her to see him use his hands for such small, everyday tasks when she knew how much power he could hold in them.

But there was no magic sizzling in them now. There was no magic around Julian at all.

"I can't enchant your hair right now," he admitted. "Not until we find another town where someone else's magic can cover the trail of me doing it."

Evie flinched when her hair snagged on a thorn-covered vine twisting along the branch. Julian pulled out a knife from somewhere within his voluminous cloak and cut the offending greenery to pieces before gently removing it from her hair.

"I didn't know magic left a trail," Evie said, voice quiet as if she were whispering a secret.

Julian nodded sagely, though he didn't look at her. "All magic does. An experienced tracker can find a specific wizard or magician if they know what to look for."

"And...someone is looking for you? Or...me?"

Eventually, with one final twist of his fingers, Julian set Evie's hair free. He indicated for her to sit down on one of the tree's massive, twisting roots, then knelt down behind her, pulled out a comb from his bag and got to work untangling her hair from the bottom-up.

"Julian, you really don't have to do that," Evie began, feeling her face grow hot even as the air slowly grew cooler around them. When night fell she imagined it would be cold this far inside the forest.

He chuckled humourlessly. "If I don't want you to become a permanent fixture of the forest I'll have to. Do you really want to entangle yourself on every branch, thorn and flower in this place?"

"No..."

"I could still cut it, you know."

Evie gasped at the thought, outraged. "You know I won't allow that!"

"Then tell me why."

The request was so softly made Evie thought she had imagined it at first. Julian had asked her about her hair before, of course, but she'd resolutely kept silent on the matter. Part of her still wanted to keep her answer to herself, though not for her original reason. Yes, Evie's memories of life in the palace were all the proof she had of who she was. For a girl with no material possessions who'd lived a solitary existence, they were more important than diamonds.

But Evie no longer lived in a lonely nightmare in the tower, and over the past three weeks she'd had more of a life travelling with Julian than she'd ever had before, even when she lived in the palace. Though she'd always treasure her childhood memories, they were no longer quite as precious as they once were.

"In the evening," Evie began; her voice took on an almost sing-song quality to it. She recognised the shift in tone as belonging to her mother, and she smiled. "In the evening before I went to bed, whenever my mother was home in the palace, she would come to my chambers with a comb as golden as my father's hair, and a brush so soft it would put a baby's hair to shame. Well, that's what mama said, anyway."

"Whenever she was home?" Julian interjected politely. Evie could hear him working through knots and tangles in the lower half of her hair; she shivered pleasantly to think of how it would feel when he reached her scalp.

She tilted her head backwards to look at him. "She wasn't home often. She was always travelling with my uncle."

There was something about the way Julian's eyes shone that made Evie think he was about to set the forest alight. But then she blinked and the glow disappeared, suggesting that all she'd seen was some last ray of sun flashing within his blue irises.

When Julian put his hands on either side of Evie's head to tilt it back to its original position she didn't protest. His fingers brushed against her neck. She resisted the urge to move closer to them – to feel them dig into her skin instead of merely whispering across it.

"So your mother would comb your hair, and you treasure the memory, and that's why you don't wish to cut it?" Julian asked, so matter-of-factly that Evie scowled, all previous unruly thoughts about the man vanished from her mind.

"Well when you put it like that it sounds stupid," she complained. "But I was eight, and I never got to see her

561

much, and she would be so gentle and sing songs to me and tell me how beautiful my hair was."

"When you put it like that it *still* sounds stupid," Julian remarked, sliding the comb through the roots of Evie's hair until it no longer snagged even once. He worked his fingers through it, separating her hair into three sections before beginning to braid it. "Though I understand, I guess."

Evie hesitated before asking a question that had been on her mind for days. She twisted her hands in her lap, wondering if Julian would avoid answering her as he had with everything else so far.

"What is it you wish to ask me?" he murmured, so close to Evie's ear that she let out a cry of surprise. He snickered. "If it's about my childhood I'll do my best to answer you, since you've told me about your hair."

Fighting against the throbbing of her heart, Evie asked, "Where are your parents? Were you close with them?"

"Both dead." A pause. "I was closer with my mother than I was my father, but then she died when I was fifteen. Her death brought me and my father closer together than we had been before."

"When did your father die?"

"About twelve years ago," Julian replied. His fingertips grew a little rougher against Evie's scalp as he answered her, but then they slackened once more when he reached her neck.

"How old were you?"

"Eighteen."

"Ahh."

Evie could feel Julian frowning even though she couldn't see him. "What is '*ahh*' supposed to mean?" he asked, making quick work of the rest of her hair as he braided it down her back.

"I've been wondering about your age for a while now, since you act like such an old man."

He clucked his tongue. "I'm ten years older than you, you brat."

"Not old enough to act like my father."

"When have I ever acted like your father?!"

Evie turned her head; Julian had finished braiding her hair and was beginning to coil it around his hand like a rope. She couldn't help but laugh, seeing him kneeling amongst pine needles and leaves and dirt with an affronted expression upon his face.

"You scold me all the time," she said, "and tell me what to do. And warn me not to misbehave, and -"

"That's because you'd die half a dozen times every day if I didn't," he complained, finishing winding up Evie's hair before flinging it over her shoulder and watching the braid fall into her lap. "I wouldn't say that's me acting like your father. I think you've just spent far too long away from people that you've forgotten what it's like to be looked after."

"Sometimes I think the same thing about you," Evie mumbled, looking away from Julian as she stood up. Her braid was still long enough to trail on the ground, but she could easily hold it up from the forest floor in her hand. "Thank you for fixing my hair."

"It's just as much for my benefit as it is for yours," he said, ignoring Evie's first comment. He stood up, brushing leaves from his cloak before making his way further into the forest. Evie picked up the long-forgotten basket of food from the ground, replacing a few apples that had rolled out of it.

He said that the first time he fixed my hair, Evie thought as she wordlessly followed Julian beneath the murky boughs of the trees. *Yet if he truly only wanted to keep it out of the way he would never have spent so much time and magic on it.*

The two wound their way deeper and deeper into the forest until Evie was stumbling over unseen roots rather than her hair. She was cold, and tired, and her feet hurt, and her eyes could scarcely make out anything in front of her. But just as she was about to complain Julian stopped in front of her.

"We'll camp here for the night," he said. "I can hear a stream close by. Can you go and fill up our water skins?"

Numbly Evie did as she was told. All she could think about was warming up by a fire and falling asleep. But when she returned from the stream it didn't seem as if Julian was preparing a fire at all.

"We can't risk the smoke," was all he said, answering the question on Evie's face without telling her anything about who he didn't want to see said smoke. She grimaced.

Tonight was going to be a long, cold night.

CHAPTER TWELVE

Julian

Evie was shivering in the tent and there was nothing Julian could do.

The tent was made of hide, and it kept the wind and water out, but that didn't stop it from being cold. Even with the two of them taking up most of the space within it the air still had a bite to it.

It's never summer in the middle of a forest at midnight, Julian thought, glancing at the huddled figure turned away from him on his right. Evie had taken the top layer of her dress off – insisting she didn't want to wrinkle it – but that left her in a white underdress that was too thin to provide much warmth. The blanket Julian had given her wasn't much thicker, either; given that he usually used magic to heat up he'd never thought much about carrying a heavier one.

"Are you sure you can't light a fire?" Evie asked after a while, the words coming out a little unevenly as her teeth chattered. Julian felt wretched about the fact he couldn't, since he was warm simply by virtue of having honed fire magic within himself for so long. He was unlikely to feel cold for the rest of his life.

"You know I can't," he replied, not unkindly. He watched as Evie shifted her long braid of hair over her shoulder, hugging it closely to her chest as if it might provide some warmth. Julian reached a hand out to comfort her, then thought better of it and pulled it back. "Were you ever this cold in the tower?"

In the darkness Evie nodded. "There were times in winter I thought I'd die. I was never sent enough firewood to sufficiently warm up the room, and I had to forgo heating my bathwater for much of the season. Not the most pleasant of memories."

"I hadn't thought about the fact you must have been sent supplies," Julian admitted. He inched over a little closer to Evie, deciding that if she was too cold to sleep then the least he could do was talk to her until she was exhausted enough to fall into unconsciousness. He could have knocked her out with barely a hint of magic, but if the people tracking them down knew what they were looking for then they'd work out Julian's location immediately.

"Twice a day for twelve years," Evie said. She looked over her shoulder at Julian, eyes shining in the darkness. "You'd have thought whoever banished me could have at least ensured I had enough to eat and didn't freeze in winter."

Especially since it was your father, or uncle as the case may be, Julian mused. But Francis had said the king loved Genevieve; was his love so easily broken that he would

566

doom his false daughter to spend more than half her life starving?

"Why is it so *cold*?!" Evie exclaimed a moment later in frustration. She huddled into herself as tightly as she could. "It's almost July. *July*. It should not be so cold."

"The depths of evergreen forests are their own little worlds," Julian said, staring up at the hide tent above them as if he could see straight through it. "In some countries there are entire races who rule the forests, and the lakes, and all the hidden places humans should never dwell upon for very long. Magical people who can look like exactly like you but are as dissimilar from humans as can be."

When he heard Evie shift over to face him Julian resisted smiling. He had hooked her with a tale enticing enough for her to forget the cold; he just had to keep it that way.

"Have you met them before?" she asked. "These people?"

Julian nodded. "Once or twice. Both encounters were pleasant affairs, truth be told. They were amused by my powers. I think, had I not been a wizard, I would not have made it out of their forest alive."

Evie sidled a little closer to Julian, her eyes rapt and alert. This time he *did* smile, for how could he not? She wanted to hear more about the world – to counter her ignorance with knowledge. It was a feeling Julian could more than relate to.

"You said they live in lakes, too. Are they fish?"

He chuckled, then raised his hands above him. There was just enough difference in the levels of dark shadows inside the tent that Julian could make vague, fuzzy silhouettes appear upon its faded surface. He twisted his hands into a horse's head, then a seal, and then a fox.

"They take on many shapes," he explained. "Water horses and sleek-skinned seals by the shore, or murky-faced merpeople deep below the surface. The one I met was a fox, though. I don't think he wished to be one."

"I would rather be a fox and have the freedom to roam about than be trapped as a human in a tower," Evie said, reaching her own hands out to attempt to recreate the fox Julian had made. Hers was smaller than his, and for a few moments they amused themselves by dancing the make-believe animals across the tent. Then Evie brought her hands back to her chest and shivered. "Are there really magical people like that, Julian, or did you just make them up to distract me?"

He raised an eyebrow at the ludicrous suggestion. "Do I strike you as the kind of person who could make such creatures up?"

"I'm not sure," Evie admitted. "I don't know much about you, truth be told."

"You know enough."

"Then that must mean there's not all that much to you."

"You wound me, Princess Genevieve."

An awkward pause followed Julian's words. Evie stared at him with wide eyes. "You haven't called me that with any sincerity even once before now. What changed?"

Julian looked away. "Nothing. Everything. I don't know. I guess I believe your story now, whereas I doubted it before."

"And why is that?"

He didn't want to tell her about what the king had done, or that her real father was his brother, or that it had been Julian's father who had spirited Evie away to her prison in Thorne tower. He didn't want to tell her about the fact Francis wished for Evie to stay as far away from Willow as possible, or that the king was looking for her.

He wanted Evie to stay just the way she was, unspoiled by the cruelty of her selfish family.

"Come here, Evie."

She hesitated. "What do you mean?"

"I mean come here," Julian repeated, indicating for her to lie closer to him. With one fluid motion he pulled his shirt away from his body, much to Evie's surprise. He grimaced at the look on her face. "I'm much warmer than you. It's the magic in me. Consider this my attempt at rectifying the fire problem."

Evie reached out a hesitant hand to touch Julian's chest but, upon feeling just how warm his skin was, forgot all her doubts and cuddled in as close as she possibly could. Julian resisted the urge to flinch away from her chilly, clammy touch.

"Why did you not tell me to do this earlier?" she demanded, voice muffled against Julian's shoulder as she eagerly wrapped her arms around him. "I'd have fallen asleep hours ago!"

"Yes, and I'd still be awake," Julian mused.

Evie looked up at him through her golden eyelashes. "What do you mean?"

"I mean that you're annoying. I thought you knew that by now."

"If I were the warm one and you were cold I'd have offered to do this from the very beginning."

Julian sighed good-naturedly. "I know. That doesn't change anything, though. Now settle down and go to sleep."

"I know you're only offering to do this to deflect from answering my questions, you know," Evie said after a while. Her body temperature had risen enough that Julian no longer wished to recoil from her, and found to his horror that he was enjoying the feeling of having her lying there against him.

"Go to sleep," he repeated, the words becoming muffled in Evie's hair. Her long braid snaked across the floor of the tent behind her; Julian wondered how she even coped with such a frustrating abundance of hair when sleeping.

If she had a husband he would insist she cut it, just so that it didn't interfere when they –

"Julian?"

He shook his head to remove any and all traces of such a dangerous train of thought. "What is it?" he asked, a little sharper than he intended.

Evie's breath tickled against Julian's skin, setting his nerves on edge. When she shifted position one of her thighs ended up far too close to his groin; he closed his eyes and willed unconsciousness to take over as quickly as humanly possible.

"Have you been with many women before?" Evie asked, a question no other adult could likely ask in such an innocent manner. "Whilst you were travelling, I mean. Or before that, when you were younger."

Julian sighed. "Why are you asking me that?"

"Because I was –"

"Locked in a tower. Forget I asked."

He didn't answer her question, hoping that Evie would eventually move on from it and fall asleep. Her fingers just barely pressed into his back, sending a shiver running up his spine. Julian tried to ignore it, but then Evie dug her nails in a little more insistently.

He grabbed onto her hair without thinking and pulled Evie's face up to look at him. "What are you doing?" he growled. "Go to sleep!"

But her eyes were determined. "Why won't you answer my question?"

"Just what is that you want from me, Evie?"

"Stories," she said. "Experience. Why can't I get to know what *living* feels like, after so long on my own?"

God damn it, Julian thought, irritated beyond belief at Evie's infallible logic. For hadn't he only just acknowledged and approved of her thirst to learn of the world around her?

He hung his head in resignation; overgrown locks of his hair brushed against Evie's face. "I've been with a few women. There. Happy now?"

"No."

"And why not?"

"You didn't explain *anything,*" she protested. "What were the women like? Was it fun? What did they think of you?"

"I suppose you could just touch me and find out!"

Julian had meant to be mocking; Evie *was* touching him already, after all. But when she glanced up at him the expression on her face suggested she'd taken him seriously.

"I can?" she whispered. Her voice hitched on the question in a way that drove Julian wild. Was she really *that* excited by the prospect? It was flattering, to say the least.

But dangerous. Too dangerous. Evie was a princess, and Julian was protecting her. It would be a huge violation of her trust, not to mention how inappropriate it was and –

"Fine," he muttered, immediately regretting the word the second he saw Evie grin in delight. "You have five minutes to bother me; after that you're going to sleep without another word. Got it?"

"Got it," she said, nodding seriously, though there was a mischievous glint in her eyes that suggested Evie might just push past the five minutes anyway.

But then her fingertips ran down his back, and Julian forgot to care. He hadn't been with a woman in a while, given that he'd largely kept to himself the past couple of years, and his nerves had been shot ever since he'd kept Evie company after her nightmare.

This is wrong, he thought. *This is a mistake.*

Evie slid her hands across Julian's waist until she reached his stomach before creeping up to his chest. Her eyes followed her fingertips, watching the way they pressed into his skin almost reverently.

"...having fun?" Julian muttered after a couple of minutes had passed. Evie nodded, though she bit her lip instead of saying anything. She wasn't looking at him, instead casting her eyes downward to the laces of his trousers.

Lord help me.

When Evie's hands roamed towards his waist Julian jerked away.

"Please don't," he said, pulling Evie's hands back up until they were cupped between his own, in front of his face. "I can assure you that you don't want to do that."

Evie merely frowned in annoyance. "How can you

572

possibly know what I want to do, Julian? And I still have two minutes. Why can't I –"

He planted a kiss against her hand, the action silencing her mid-sentence. She stared into his eyes, which he knew were likely too bright with the promise of barely-fettered magic. Evie slid the hand Julian had kissed away from his own, stroking the line of his jaw with about as much force as a feather. When she reached his hair Evie pushed it back, running her hand through it until it fell across his face, where it had lain before.

She was pressed right up against him; every curve of her body finding another inch of Julian's skin to touch. He couldn't take it; it was unbearable.

"Why can't I want this?" Evie asked, managing to get her question out in its entirety this time. "Am I really so annoying, Julian?"

He held his breath for a second. Two. Three.

"Yes," Julian said, and then his mouth was on hers. He rolled Evie onto her back, hands roving beneath her dress to cling to her hips, her waist, her breasts – anything he could find. Evie eagerly reciprocated, flinging her arms around Julian's neck even as her legs did the same around his waist.

He groaned when she bucked against his groin. She parted her lips to let in his tongue; Julian imagined doing something similar with an altogether harder body part. He pressed down upon her, burying Evie into the blanket, the floor of the tent, the soft ground of the forest below, until there was nowhere deeper he could push her.

He needed more. He needed –

"We need to stop," Julian gasped, wrenching himself away from Evie as if she were made of flames. He held a hand over his eyes. "Good lord, Evie, we can't do this. I

573

can't do this."

There was nothing but the sound of laboured breathing for a while. Eventually Evie asked, very quietly, "Is it because you don't like me, or because I'm Princess Genevieve?"

"The latter," he replied. "Of course it's the latter. I'd never have gone this far if I didn't like you."

"...thank you for your honesty," was all Evie said, and then she turned from him.

Julian didn't dare open his eyes again that night.

CHAPTER THIRTEEN

Genevieve

Neither Julian nor Evie brought up their first night sharing a tent together for the remaining part of their journey to Willow, though they spent another week and a half sleeping inside it every night. But whenever they camped deep into the chilly depths of a forest Julian wordlessly removed his shirt and allowed Evie to huddle close to him, for which she was grateful.

But her heart hurt, and Evie could neither understand it nor do anything about it. Julian had thrown away her burgeoning feelings before she had even accepted them for what they were. She knew that, at the very least, she should be happy that Julian had not rejected her out of dislike but, rather, out of a sense of duty and responsibility. Given the fact he'd been looking out for her ever since he'd saved her from those men on the road,

Evie could hardly be surprised by this turn of events.

That doesn't make his rejection sting any less, she thought sadly as she finally entered the city of Willow. Julian was walking a few paces ahead of her, keeping to himself. He was on high alert for – something. Or someone. Evie couldn't tell; it wasn't as if Julian had informed her about what was going on. But his antsy energy had her on edge, too, making it impossible for Evie to appreciate the beautiful, intricate architecture of the city in which she'd been born.

It was both alien and achingly familiar to her, as if Evie's mind itself had invented the place in a dream. Not that she'd dreamt of cities or palaces or even her royal heritage all that much over the past few days. No, all she'd dreamt about as she and Julian made their awkward way towards Willow was Julian himself.

Evie couldn't stop thinking about the way he'd looked at her before he gave in and kissed her, or the ferocity with which he'd pushed her below him. The weight of Julian on top of her – the feeling of having every inch of his skin against hers – had been driving her insane ever since. Evie had wanted more. *Needed* more.

But Julian had pulled away.

Damn him being responsible and righteous just when I craved for him not to be, she cursed, dolefully watching the man stalk through the throng of the crowd. All Evie had wanted over the past few days was to ignore Julian until he kissed her with desperate longing once more, but though she'd followed through on the former Julian had not done the same with the latter.

And now it's too late. We've reached Willow and soon I will probably never seen Julian again. I should not have ignored him simply because he hurt my pride.

But was it really her pride Julian had hurt? Evie hadn't spent enough time with other people to have any pride in herself as a woman. Then was it her pride as a princess that he'd broken? The fact that he'd rejected her for the one part of her that she could not change – a part of her she could have demanded he accept if she'd really wanted to?

Evie laughed bitterly. *I could never do that.*

Julian stopped to look back at her, concerned. "What's the matter?"

"Nothing," she said, waving him away. "Nothing at all. I'm just nervous." It wasn't untrue; Evie's stomach had been lurching and roiling all morning. She hadn't eaten anything at breakfast – much to Julian's surprise.

His face softened. "Everything will be fine, Evie. And if it's not...well, that's what I'm here for. And on the subject of what I'm here for..."

Evie frowned as Julian regarded her critically. She *had* to frown, otherwise she'd blush as red as a summer apple beneath his gaze. "What is it?"

"I think it's probably safe to work some magic on your hair once more," Julian said, darting his head back and forth as he looked for somewhere quieter to perform the enchantment. "And you could do with a more expensive dress."

Evie picked at the sleeve of the one she was wearing. "But I like this one. It's like a forest."

"I never said you had to get rid of it, only that you need a new one. You want to look your best to meet your parents, do you not? And your brother?"

She froze at the mention of her brother, Louis. Evie had chosen not to think about him ever since Julian had first brought him up. This was partially due to him telling

577

her that Louis was sickly and unlikely to survive childhood, but for the most part it was because Evie couldn't imagine having a sibling. He would be the age she was when she was sent to the tower, after all. It was unfathomable. Unknowable.

It scared Evie to no end.

"Evie?"

She shook her head. "Yes, okay. Let's make me look my best. Only..."

Now it was Evie's turn to cast a critical eye over Julian. The wizard was hidden beneath his stained and ragged cloak, and though most of his hair was tied back there remained a few errant strands covering his eyes. Julian's stubble had grown to the point of it almost being considered a beard; Evie longed to see it gone.

"No," Julian said, upon realising what Evie's expression meant. "No. I'm fine just the way I am."

Evie crossed her arms over her chest. "If *I* need to look more presentable when I'm already in a nice dress then you definitely need to look better, Julian."

He pointed at her. "You and I both know that it's your hair that's the problem. It's a travesty."

"Still not cutting it."

"Even if I agree to cut *mine*?"

Evie faltered. It was an appealing bribe. However...

"No. I don't want to cut my hair...even if it's only for another few days. And besides, you *have* to cut your hair."

Julian cocked an eyebrow. "Oh?"

"I'm the princess. You have to do what I say."

So much for never using that against him.

To her relief, Julian laughed. "If that is the only thing

578

you can think of to demand of me then fine, I will. But let me fix your hair first, *then* we can set about getting new clothes and fixing me."

"You don't need *fixed*," Evie muttered as Julian pulled her down a near-abandoned alleyway. Had he not been a wizard Evie would never have gone down such a street; even now there were hungry eyes on them, busy calculating how much money they were likely to be carrying. But then Julian's eyes began to glow, and his fingertips turned Evie's hair to liquid gold, and they scurried away in fear.

Evie sighed contentedly as Julian enchanted her hair. She'd missed the feeling of it – of hot, bubbling magic coursing through every strand as he weaved and braided the lot of it into so elaborate a hairstyle even the aristocrats of Willow would be envious.

When Julian was done and pulled his fingertips away from her scalp Evie felt a keening sense of regret. It was, most probably, the last time he would ever work his magic on her.

Well, in the literal sense, she amended, watching longingly as Julian rolled out a kink in his shoulders and shook his hair from his eyes. When he smiled at her his expression was so guarded against her it hurt Evie's heart.

"Shall we go shopping, then?" he asked. But Evie shook her head, and Julian's formal smile disappeared. "What's wrong?"

"I...think I want to buy a dress by myself. Can we find an inn first so that we can meet back there when we're both done?"

The meaning behind her words was plain for Julian to translate: *I can't pretend that everything is fine between us any longer.*

579

He regarded Evie for so long she almost repeated her request. But then, finally, Julian inclined his head, then pulled a small bag of coins from his cloak and proffered them to her. She took it wordlessly, being careful not to touch his hands. They were abuzz with magic, as if Julian could no longer contain it for some reason.

"Let's find a good inn for the night, then," he said, "though I doubt any inn will seem *good* once you return to the palace."

"Trust me," Evie replied, lips quirking into a smile despite her bad mood, "anything will feel like luxury after spending eleven days sleeping in a tent."

Julian snickered. "Fair point. Here's hoping neither of us need ever find ourselves in a tent again."

Evie didn't reply; she merely followed Julian out of the alleyway and down the main street as he searched for an inn. Going by the purposeful way he wound his way through the crowd he already had a place in mind. But it didn't matter how lovely the room was that Julian paid for Evie to sleep in that night – she knew she would be sleeping in it alone.

And though camping had been hell, and she had hated most every part of it, it was a hell Evie would gladly live through again and again if it meant she did not have to say good bye to Julian.

CHAPTER FOURTEEN

Julian

Julian watched his reflection in the mirror as if he did not recognise the person staring back at him. For the first time in months – years, even – he was clean-shaven. His dark hair was shorter than it had been in over a decade, though it still fell below his ears. The barber had slicked it back, though, keeping it out of Julian's eyes and leaving his face self-consciously visible.

Julian had purchased a dark, pine-green waistcoat shot through with gold thread that afternoon, to wear alongside a white shirt, beige trousers and ebony knee-high boots. An olive-coloured longcoat with gold buttons finished the entire ensemble. Looking at himself wearing such finely made clothes deeply unsettled Julian; he looked like his father in his heyday, though his blue eyes belonged to his mother.

She would be happy to see me finally dressed so appropriately, Julian mused as he took a swig from the tankard of ale he'd had ordered up to his room. It was his third since returning to the inn. Though he knew Evie had also returned by virtue of the magic in her hair Julian was yet to see or speak to her, namely because he dared not leave his room. He didn't know *what* to say. But the sun was low in the sky on what would likely be their final day together – an ever-present reminder that he was fast running out of time in which to be honest with her.

"I am a coward," Julian murmured, giving his outfit one final inspection before finishing his ale and leaving his room. He could sit inside it alone no longer, agonised by all his thoughts and actions over the past month. Either Julian would find solace in the tavern attached to the inn or by walking along the paved stone roads that followed the river which split Willow in two.

When he reached the tavern in question Julian was relieved to see that Evie wasn't there, though he already knew she was still in her room. But her very presence in the back of his mind kept Julian on edge at all times until he could scarcely bear to be conscious, so he decided going for a walk would perhaps give him enough distance to calm himself down.

"She's the princess," he said aloud, "she's the princess and she's nearly home. Your job is almost done." Julian made his way out into the lovely July evening, ignoring the looks of interest several young women threw his way. He'd forgotten what it was like to be admired like that, having spent so long hiding beneath his hair and beard and cloak.

Evie looked at me like that even when she couldn't see my face properly, Julian mused as he made his way towards the river. *But, then again, she'd spent most of her life locked up alone. Her standards are probably pretty low.*

He chuckled at the thought as he absorbed the last of the evening's warmth. If Evie had been with him her hair would be set alight by the sunset, garnering sighs of admiration and envy everywhere she went. It upset Julian to think he'd probably enchanted her hair for the final time that afternoon.

Don't think about that. Don't think about her. *Think about literally anything else.*

But how could Julian refrain from thinking about Evie when he was only in Willow because of her? When he was embroiled in the mess her family had created – the same mess that Julian's father had somehow been involved in before his death? Julian needed answers just as much as Evie herself did. He could only hope that bringing her back to the palace would not be the mistake Francis Saule was convinced it was.

I'm here to protect her if things go awry, Julian reminded himself. *The moment something seems wrong I'll whisk Evie away never to be seen again.*

He entertained himself with the idea of taking Evie to see the forests where the fair folk lived. She'd been interested in their magical, shape-shifting ways, after all. Perhaps Julian might even be able to find the creature trapped as a fox once more to prove to Evie that it existed. He almost laughed at his previous assertion that his thirteen years of travelling had been unremarkable; had Julian really believed such a thing? For now all he could think of were the places Evie would love to see, both the wonders of the modern world and the relics of the past.

A few right turns – and several wrong ones – later and Julian made it to the river. The low angle of the sun had turned it to shining, flashing silver, so blinding he had to half-close his eyes simply to look at it. He leant on the intricate iron railing that separated the paved road from the river and heaved out a sigh.

Willow is a beautiful city, Julian supposed, though he reckoned it had become more beautiful simply by virtue of him having spent so many years away from it. If there was enough time in the morning, and if he worked up the nerve to ask her, Julian decided he'd take Evie for a walk through the expansive parks in the very centre of the city before escorting her to the palace.

It would be a smart idea to do so, he realised. *The more people who see her in public looking so obviously like Princess Genevieve then the safer she'll be.* But the people of Willow hadn't seen their princess in twelve years; would they recognise her? Julian certainly hadn't believed Evie's story of her parentage at first, so why would complete strangers have reason to think she was their princess?

Because they aren't cynical like me, and she looks every part King Pierre's daughter. Even though she isn't. I suppose it's a good thing Francis looks so much like his brother.

"You really brought her here. You brought her to *Willow.*"

Julian scowled at the sound of the man's voice. "Are you kidding me? Just where did you come from?"

Francis Saule wasn't amused. "You're distracted; you didn't even notice me approaching. Where is Genevieve?"

"Safe."

"But where?"

"Telling you that will compromise her safety, don't you think?"

584

The older man leant on the railing beside Julian, casting his solemn gaze across the river. "You do not trust me."

"And why should I?" Julian laughed humourlessly. "You've followed, and spied on us, whilst only giving me information as you yourself deemed it pertinent. That doesn't provide me with many reasons to trust you."

"Yet you know enough not to trust my brother, or the people he's sent out to find you. So why are you in Willow?"

Julian hung his head. "Because Evie wants to go home. I'm not going to disregard her wishes."

He knew Francis was staring at him, disbelief plain on his face even though Julian wasn't looking at it. "Have you not told her *anything*, Julian? Is she still in the dark?"

"Of course she is!" he spat out, rounding on the man with barely-contained fury. Out of the corner of his eye he saw that they were gathering the attention of several curious bystanders, so Julian lowered his voice and forced himself to calm down. He glared at Francis. "Why should her worldview be destroyed after everything she's been through?"

The king's brother merely smiled sadly. "Because that's the only way to keep her safe. Why can't you just spirit her far from here, away from the drama of Willow and its king?"

"Because then I'd be no better than any of you, doing as you please without once thinking about what Evie herself wants."

"But you're not truly thinking of what she wants, either," Francis countered. "You haven't told her the truth about what's going on. How can Genevieve know what she wants when she's ignorant of so much?"

585

"She's been doing just fine until now," Julian snarled, before turning from the man and stalking away. If he stayed any longer in Francis' company then he'd probably use magic, and that would draw too much attention in such a public spot, and then Julian would be found. It was bad enough to have been seen viciously arguing with someone by the river in the first place.

At least I no longer fit the description of a scraggly, ragged-clothed wizard, Julian reasoned, trying desperately to look on the brighter side of things. *If anyone looking for me hears of my current appearance then they will not think that I am me.*

Julian made it back to the inn with a head full of stormy thoughts. It was so full, in fact, that he had forgotten to check where Evie currently was, and it was only upon entering the tavern that he realised she was at the bar, being served a cup of wine, surrounded by admirers.

She wasn't in as elaborate a dress as Julian would have expected, given that it was supposed to be for returning to the palace, though Julian numbly thought that perhaps Evie had bought more than one given how much money he'd handed over to her.

Regardless, Evie looked breathtaking. The dress was a powder blue colour reminiscent of the ill-fitting clothing Julian had first found her in. The sleeves sat off her shoulders, and were slashed with a cream fabric embroidered with hundreds of tiny flowers. The bodice was similarly embroidered, whilst the sweeping material of the skirt was about an inch or two longer than Evie's magically braided hair.

She was the epitome of the sky, with her golden hair the sun and her dress the endless blue of summer. *So what does that make her eyes?* Julian wondered. *Emeralds don't live in the sky. Perhaps they are the forest.*

It was in that moment Julian finally realised why he'd bought the clothes *he* was wearing. They were the colours of the trees that had marked his journey with Evie all the way to Willow – broad leaved and evergreen, pale-branched and dark.

Just what have I become? Julian thought, laughing softly at his own ineptitude as he watched Evie from a safe distance away; she had not yet realised he was there. *I need another drink. All I can think of is her.*

And if all he could think of was Evie...how was he supposed to let her go?

CHAPTER FIFTEEN

Genevieve

Genevieve had never embraced so much attention before – not since she was a child, at least, and even then her father had largely kept her within the palace, so her experience with people was limited. The attention of tavern-goers was certainly different to the aristocrats who used to politely amuse her when they came to visit her mother and father, though the inn Julian had chosen was markedly more high-class than the ones they'd stayed in before.

And though Evie had chosen to forgo the formal gown she'd procured for returning to the palace in place of the one she'd bought solely for herself, she stood out. *It's because of my hair,* she thought, though Evie wasn't unhappy about this. Imbued with magic or not it was a part of her, and there was no sense in Evie wondering whether the rest of her would ever look as good as the woven, golden crown Julian had braided around her head.

Evie hadn't realised he'd done such a thing until she looked in the mirror to admire his handiwork. The rest of her hair fell to her ankles in a multitude of interlaced braids of varying thicknesses, and it was beautiful, but the woven crown was something else entirely. It was heartbreakingly intricate; Evie couldn't imagine the amount of thought the wizard must have put into styling it in such a way. And Julian had deliberately kept a few wispy strands of Evie's hair loose around her face, softening the look just enough that it seemed as if she had been born with her hair sitting this way instead of it being the work of genius magic.

For the first time in twelve years, in her well-fitting blue gown, matching slippers and sun-coloured crown around her head, Evie genuinely felt like a princess.

It was more bittersweet that she could ever have imagined.

Well, that's nothing that some wine cannot fix, Evie decided as she began drinking her second cup of the stuff. It was light and sweet – much unlike the wine she'd accidentally drank on the first night of her journey to Willow – but heady enough that Evie could feel it burning inside of her already. She thought back to how she'd so quickly fallen asleep that first time, never truly getting to experience the effects the alcoholic drink.

But tonight was different. Tomorrow Evie would make her way to the palace, to her mother and father and brother, and her life would change completely. One way or another she'd never have the opportunity to drink in a tavern under the guise of anonymity again, even though the attention her hair was getting was a far cry from what Julian would consider to be 'anonymous'.

589

He would be so angry with this much attention, she thought, laughing a little in the process. *He'd walk away from everyone to sit in the corner in a huff, and ignore any questions and greetings thrown his way.*

It was only in thinking this that Evie remembered she hadn't actually *seen* Julian since she'd pushed him away that afternoon. She could only assume he was somewhere in the inn.

She was too prideful to go and find him.

"If he wants to see me then *he* can find me," Evie muttered, knowing deep in her heart that if Julian didn't seek her out at some point that night then she'd probably cry into her pillow instead of falling asleep in a few hours. She didn't want this to be the way they left things between them – awkward, painfully formal, and silent.

"What was that, my lovely?"

Evie smiled for the young man who had spoken. His name was John, and he had pushed through several of his friends to stand by her side. "Oh, nothing," she replied. She held up her cup. "I was just thinking that this wine is delicious."

"Then I must buy you another one!"

"I have only just started my second," she protested. Evie could feel her cheeks growing rosy and warm from the stuff and knew she had to be careful. *Julian would be furious if I let down my guard enough to allow these men to get me drunk. He would think I haven't learned anything at all.*

Another of the men elbowed John out of the way. "We've never seen you around here before. Are you visiting your fiancé perhaps?"

Evie shook her head. "Family. I've been away from the city for a long time."

The man grinned. "Then you definitely need more wine to celebrate your return! We can show you around; Willow changes year on year on year. You must scarcely recognise it."

"I – I'm not sure," Evie admitted, for it was never as if she'd known much of the city in the first place. She could recognise most every stone of the palace and its grounds, and a few of the grand buildings which many of the members of her father's court lived in, but that was it.

"You don't want to be wandering the city at night," John said, though the excited look on his face suggested he hadn't said as much out of actual concern for Evie. "It's better to stay here and let us all keep you company. Are you staying here? Upstairs?"

"You can't possibly be travelling alone."

"She must have a lover, for sure."

Evie held her hands up as if they could stop the barrage of remarks being thrown her way. "There's nobody like that," she said, though it pained her to say it out loud. "I must admit I don't have much experience in that department."

The second man stared at her as if he couldn't believe his luck. "A lady so lovely as yourself? Your lack of experience must be rectified! What is the point of living if you don't explore everything it has to offer?"

That had been Evie's reasoning the night she somehow managed to convince Julian to answer her inane, intrusive questions. The night he let her touch him and almost lost control entirely. But hearing a stranger use such reasoning to try and charm Evie into his bed made her squirm uncomfortably. He wasn't thinking of her wellbeing, only his own pleasure at her hands.

Is this what Julian thought in the tent? Evie wondered

miserably. *Did I put him in an awful, unwinnable position simply for my own amusement? But I didn't want to hold him to make him uncomfortable. I didn't want to do it to satisfy my curiosity for a night. I wanted...*

"And who might you be to 'rectify' the lady's lack of experience?" an achingly familiar voice demurred. "Something tells me I'm much more qualified to help her out than you, sir."

An arm snaked its way around Evie's waist, pulling her close before she had the chance to look up at the man she'd only just been thinking about. When she finally *did* look she froze.

The Julian beside her was not the Julian she knew.

His face was clean-shaven, revealing cheekbones Evie's mother might have said were chiselled by the gods had Julian appeared in one of her Greek mythology tomes. His black hair was slicked back to tuck around his ears, and there was a charming smile upon his lips that Evie had never seen him use before.

Julian's clothes were gorgeous and intricately designed, right down to the embossed patterns on the gold buttons of his longcoat. Evie had once asked him why he never dressed like the amber-eyed stranger who they'd seen weeks ago. Now she knew why.

Julian was beautiful, and he was gathering attention.

How he must hate that, Evie thought, when her brain finally kicked back into action. Julian tightened his grip on her waist and grinned at her, a twinkle in his blue eyes which for the life of her Evie could not work out if it was genuine or caused by magic. It might have been both. She almost thought her heart would stop. *If he keeps acting like this I might get the wrong idea.*

"Are these gentlemen bothering you, my lady?" Julian

asked, much to the chagrin of the men in question.

"I'd say that you're the one bothering her!" John said, though Evie could tell by the look on his face that he knew he could not compete against Julian.

I wonder if I can compete against the women who like him, Evie thought, glancing around to see many lovely, excited faces watching him. When she caught the eye of one such lady she scowled at Evie; Evie in turn had to admit that it felt good to be envied for such a thing as claiming Julian's attention.

"Are you drunk?" she murmured up to him, so quietly nobody else heard.

His hand slid further down Evie's waist – a deliberate move that was noted by every one of Evie's admirers. "A little," he admitted. "Is that a problem?"

"Not that I can see. Are you here to rescue me?"

"If that is what you wish."

Evie's heart was pounding so loudly in her chest she wouldn't have been surprised if Julian could hear it. She inclined her head politely to the men who were staring at the pair of them, agog. "Thank you for your company, kind sirs," Evie said, "but it appears I must be whisked away. I hope you enjoy the rest of your evening."

Julian's hand nudged her away from the bar, though Evie was sure to grab her cup of wine before stepping away. They barely made it to a table at the back of the tavern before she heard the men muttering about how unlucky they'd been for Julian to have shown up.

"Luck had nothing to do with it," he said, smiling in an entirely satisfactory way as he stole the cup of wine from Evie's hand and drank the lot of it.

"Hey, that was mine!" she protested. He merely

593

pushed her onto a softly padded bench that was built below a stained glass window before sliding in beside her. When he waved over at the bar the man behind it promptly brought over a flagon and another cup.

"And now we both have more," Julian replied, handing the man several coins before pouring Evie a new drink. "That's the beauty of having money."

Evie eyed him warily as she drank her wine. "Nobody would have been so quick to serve you had you looked the way you usually look."

"And yet that's still the beauty of money, for look how beautiful my money has made me."

She couldn't help but snort in disgusted amusement at the comment, narrowly avoiding spilling wine over her new dress. "I never knew you were so narcissistic, Julian."

"Only when I have the outfit to support it, and the alcohol in my blood to keep it up."

Evie quirked her lips into half a smile, then looked away. "What did you mean that luck had nothing to do with you showing up when you did?"

"I may or may not have been in the tavern for an hour already, watching to see what would happen."

"And what did you think would happen?" Evie asked, close to outrage. Had Julian assumed she'd end up falling into bed with a stranger?

"Nothing, I suppose." He watched Evie out of the corner of his eye; she blushed. "Though I do recall a certain someone telling me they wanted to experience more of the world, including particularly...private affairs."

If Evie thought she'd been blushing before it was nothing compared to how hot her cheeks were now. "I didn't - that wasn't - I only wanted to experience such things with *you*, Julian!"

He put down his cup just as Evie did the same. She could scarcely look at him, horrified by her admission. But then Julian bent his head low until his lips were right by her ear; his breath tickled her skin.

"I guess that means I truly *am* the only one qualified enough to help you out," he said, voice low and seductive in a way Evie had never heard before.

Her breathing hitched. "You're drunk, Julian. You're only saying this because you're drunk. You –"

He held a finger to Evie's lips to quieten her, then gently turned her face until her eyes were locked on his. They were dark in the dim light of the tavern – hardly blue at all – but around the rims of Julian's irises was the glow of ever-present magic Evie yearned to feel touch her.

Julian tucked a hand behind Evie's neck, edging her face so close to his own that she was sure he was going to kiss her. "Do you want to come up to my room?" he asked.

Evie nodded before he'd even finished the sentence, then Julian snapped his fingers and they were gone.

CHAPTER SIXTEEN

Julian

"You didn't - I thought you had to be careful with your magic right now?" Evie exclaimed when the two of them materialised inside Julian's room. "We could have used the stairs."

He laughed at the notion, cupping Evie's face between his hands before saying, "I don't think I could have waited that long." And then he kissed her, and kissed her, and kissed her, until Evie's lips grew swollen beneath his own and she let out an almost imperceptible moan in response.

Julian pushed her back towards the bed; when they reached it Evie curled her hands into his shirt and broke away from his bruising kiss. Her cheeks were so attractively flushed Julian reached to kiss her again almost immediately.

When did she get so beautiful? he thought, through a

haze of desire rapidly going unchecked. *She had always been a skinny, annoying brat. She –*

"Julian, slow down!" Evie bit out, breathing heavily as she once more pulled away from his lips. His hands were making quick work of the ribbons which laced up her bodice, hungry to feel the warmth of her skin beneath it.

He shook his head. "I can't. I don't want to."

"Those are two different things."

"Yes, and they both apply. Is there something wrong with that?"

It was Evie's turn to shake her head. She rubbed her fingers against the fabric of Julian's shirt, watching her hands as she did so. "No, there isn't. But what...what changed, Julian? Is it really the alcohol making you do all this?"

"Oh lord no," he said. He grazed his lips along Evie's jawline to her ear. "Nothing's changed. Not really. Unless you count the fact you turned my world upside down the moment I found you in the tower, in which case everything has changed."

Evie turned her head until her mouth found Julian's once more. "You said you couldn't do this. You said –"

"I know what I said. And it's...still true." He kissed her softly. "It's still true, but for one night all I want to do is ignore what I *should* do. I want to forget the responsibility I have towards getting you to the palace, unspoiled and in one piece."

To his surprise, Evie laughed. She reached up on her tiptoes to snake her arms around Julian's neck. "You've been *spoiling* me from day one, Julian. You and I both know you should have magicked me to Willow immediately and been done with me."

597

"You know precisely what I mean."

"Yes, but can I not make my own decisions on who I share my bed with...at least until I return to my parents?"

When Julian eased Evie's arms away from him and took a step back there was a fear in her eyes that he revelled in. It told Julian that she really wanted him. That the desire building up in Evie these past few weeks was very much as genuine as the desire Julian, in turn, felt for her.

He dropped to his knees in front of her, clasping her hands within his own. She looked down at him uncertainly even as he smiled at her.

"Spend your final night as 'Evie' with me, Princess Genevieve. Spend the night with me, so when the sun rises neither of us can regret a thing."

How the pair of them removed each other's clothes so quickly Julian could not fathom, but before he knew it all that was left to strip away were Evie's underdress and his shirt.

"Your new dress is beautiful, by the way," he said between kisses. The blue fabric was pooled on the floor around them, so Julian picked Evie up and deftly carried her over to the bed without stepping on it. She clung to him as he did so, trailing kisses along Julian's collarbone that left his skin blazing.

"Thank you," Evie replied, a genuine smile at the compliment lighting up her face. "It's my favourite colour. Your new clothes aren't too bad, either. I never knew you had such good taste."

He dropped Evie onto the bed and eagerly climbed on top of her. "There's a lot you don't know about me," he murmured, kissing the hollow of her throat as he did so. Julian was satisfied to feel her squirm at his touch.

She glanced down at him through heavy, golden eyelashes. "I thought you said there wasn't much to know about you?"

"*You* were the one who said that. I told you that you knew enough."

"So you were lying?"

When Julian felt one of Evie's legs slide against his own he grabbed hold of her knee and hitched it around his waist. Her eyes went wide as she felt a hardness against her navel that the loose folds of Julian's shirt had been concealing from her.

He smirked. "You knew enough for back then. Now you could do with learning some more."

Julian pulled his shirt up and over his head before making quick work of the buttons of Evie's underdress. He flung both garments to the floor. Though the young woman below him had spent much of their time together in various indecently ill-fitting clothes, Julian had somehow managed to avoid seeing Evie completely naked before now. For some reason he had imagined she would be small and skinny as she had been when he'd first saved her life, despite their night in the tent together and all other growing signs to the contrary.

But a month of eating as if Evie was afraid she'd be locked up once more with no food had done wonders for her body. Julian marvelled at the sight of her lying beneath him, face flushed with embarrassment as he continued to stare without uttering a word.

"I know, I'm still a brat," Evie muttered, but when she turned her face away from Julian he reached down, grabbed her chin to keep her in place and kissed her, hard.

"Clearly eating like a piglet for slaughter has been to

your benefit...and mine," Julian murmured. He bit her lower lip. His hands crawled over her chest. He watched as Evie's breathing accelerated with every slide of his fingertips across her skin; every gentle pinch of her flesh; every inch of friction between their two bodies.

Eventually she couldn't take it any longer. "Julian," she moaned. "This is torture."

"No; torture is listening to you talk all day with no escape or end in sight."

His mouth covered hers to swallow any retort she might have had, though Evie didn't seem to mind all that much. Julian's hands wound their way through her hair, though he had avoided touching it so far; the enchanted braids unravelled instantly, allowing him to properly slide his fingers against Evie's scalp. Though Julian knew the full length of her hair would get in the way of what the two of them were about to do next, he didn't care.

I can fix it in the morning, he thought, as Evie pushed her own fingers through Julian's hair in order to keep him as close to her lips as possible. *In the morning I'll be Julian Thorne, the wizard, and Evie will be Princess Genevieve. But not now.*

The next time Evie opened her mouth to beg Julian to stop teasing her he happily obliged. He was at his limit too, after all, and the desperate tug of his groin ached with every second he didn't do what his body demanded he do.

Evie cried in shock, though Julian held her close and resisted moving as much as possible until her kisses became hungry and insatiable once more. It wasn't long before her nails dug into his back, insisting that he go faster, and harder, and deeper, until Evie was a mess of gasps and tears and vicious pleasure beneath him.

I can't let her go, Julian thought, the realisation

slashing through his blind lust like a knife in the dark. *I don't know what's waiting for her in the palace. I don't want to find out. Tomorrow I'll –*

But then it was Julian's turn to moan, for Evie shifted her hips and in the process undid him completely. He loomed above her on shaking arms, simultaneously exhausted and exhilarated. Every inch of his skin was shining wtth sweat; with glazed eyes he saw that Evie's was, too.

Julian gulped down a much-needed mouthful of air. "Are you –"

"Fine," Evie panted, a small smile curling her lips when Julian flung himself down beside her with a thump. "I'm fine. Better than fine."

"Good."

"Would you like some water?"

He glanced at her. Evie's hair was plastered to her forehead; her cheeks were so red they looked feverish. "I should be asking *you* that, not the other way around."

"I'm capable of looking after you when you need someone to, you know," Evie huffed, though her annoyance was short-lived when Julian pulled her into the crook of his arm and began smoothing her hair back.

"It's a good thing I'm not the one who needs looking after, then."

Evie kissed his shoulder before looking up at him. Her eyes glittered in the darkness. "Are you sure about that?"

"Fairly sure. You should get some sleep, Evie. Tomorrow will be a long, long day."

"I thought we weren't thinking about tomorrow?" she asked, frowning in concern. Julian squeezed her tighter against his side.

"You're right. We won't. But sleeping in an actual bed instead of a tent sounds great, does it not?"

Based on the look on Evie's contented face she readily agreed. By the time Julian's breathing returned to a normal, even pace she was already halfway to unconsciousness. *How can I not think about tomorrow?* he thought as he stared down at her. *No matter what happens, tomorrow will change everything.*

But before he could agonise over whether he'd be lying in bed alone once more the following evening, or whether he'd miraculously still have Evie curled up beside him, the overwhelming urge to sleep took over Julian and he forgot all about his problems.

CHAPTER SEVENTEEN

Genevieve

When Genevieve awoke the sun was shining in her face and Julian was nowhere to be seen. She sat up stock straight, immediately alert, only for the man himself to enter through the door carrying a tray of food.

"Morning," Julian said, smiling slightly when he saw that Evie was no longer sleeping. She blushed and pulled up the bedsheets to cover her chest when she realised she was completely exposed. Julian merely laughed. "I saw a lot more of you last night. There's no need to be embarrassed."

Evie took the cup of water he handed her with a nod of thanks. "Everything is different in the light of day," she said, glancing out of the window to the morning bustle of Willow down below.

Julian stiffened. "Are you saying you regret what

happened?"

"No!" she exclaimed, quick to correct him. "No. Absolutely not. But, you know, in daylight people look different, and alcohol changes things, and –"

Evie's ramblings were cut off when Julian collapsed beside her on the bed and pressed his lips to hers. His blue eyes glittered in the sunlight. "Are you worried that *I* might have regretted what happened?"

She look away, blushing furiously. "Maybe."

"I don't do anything that I'll regret later. I might make mistakes, or have to do things I don't want to, but I never regret them. What's the point?"

"Oh, so what happened last night could still be considered a mistake?"

Julian gave her a level stare. "I don't think that. You don't think that either. I think your nerves are getting the better of you, you ridiculous woman."

"I'm *not* ridiculous."

"Any person whose hair is eight feet long is ridiculous. It's a known fact."

Evie snickered at the comment despite herself. When Julian proffered her a bread roll she took it, though she had no appetite. She *was* nervous, after all. Today was the day: the day she was to be reunited with her family, took her place as princess and finally found out what had happened that resulted in her being sent to live in isolation for twelve years.

She gulped. "Julian, I –"

"Don't talk," he said, before gently placing his fingertips to Evie's scalp and turning her head slightly away from him. "Just eat, and I'll fix your gigantic bird's nest of hair."

"It's not *my* fault it's such a mess," she muttered.

"I'd say we're jointly to blame. Now sit still."

And so Evie forced herself to eat whilst Julian reignited the enchantment on her hair he'd so eagerly unravelled the night before. She almost didn't want him to; it felt like he was eliminating the most obvious sign that, even if it was for but a few hours, Evie had been his.

She sighed, then frowned when she noticed there were no clothes lying on the floor. Julian was wearing his, looking just as heart-stoppingly handsome in the daylight as he had done in the darkness. "Where's my dress?" Evie asked, glancing behind her at Julian when he let go of her head.

"I folded it away," he explained. "I packed all of your belongings up for you an hour or so ago, since you're so inept at it."

"I don't have *magic* to make all my clothes neat and tidy!"

"Do you honestly believe I use my powers for something so frivolous?"

Evie hesitated. "...yes?"

"On this one and only occasion you would be correct," he chuckled. "That blue dress was too large to fit in your bag, so I worked a spell into it so it could carry more. Now go back to your room and get dressed."

"I...do we really have to rush so quickly to the palace?" Evie asked, eyes downcast. She wasn't ready for this, even though it was all she'd ever wanted from the moment she was locked in the tower. But after experiencing what it was like to be an adult – to be free and happy and together with people instead of alone – Evie had to wonder if what she wanted had changed.

Julian kissed the top of her head. "I thought we might take a walk through the park first, then find somewhere to have lunch. Unless you'd rather not?"

"No, I'd love that!"

Pleased by the way Evie lit up at the idea, Julian held her hands and helped her from the bed. His eyes roved down her naked body, and he frowned slightly before looking away.

"I'll go get your dress for you," he mumbled. Evie thought she could see Julian's cheeks beginning to flush as he stalked out of the room, and her heart leapt.

If I ever doubted he was attracted to me before, I don't now.

When Julian returned he was holding the elaborate cream gown embroidered with golden flowers that Evie had bought for today. The sleeves hung long and loose and translucent from her shoulders, and the skirt whispered along the floor. The tailor had wanted Evie to buy a hoop skirt but the sheer size of them, as well as the difficulty in wearing one, meant she had declined.

"You look like a princess," Julian said after he finished helping Evie button up the back of the dress. His tone was almost reverent; something about it unsettled her. But Evie waved away her concerns when he held out an arm, and she gladly took it. "Shall we pretend we're pompous aristocrats for the morning?"

Evie's lips quirked. "Isn't that technically what we both are?"

"Our *families* are. We're simply their no-good children benefiting from the wealth they amassed."

"Well if that's the case," she laughed, "then lead on, Julian."

Two hours later and Evie's stomach was rumbling loudly. Julian rolled his eyes as they wound their way through the park, though he stopped walking when they reached the midway point of a thick, ancient wooden bridge crossing the narrow point of a lake. Above them a massive, sweeping willow tree provided partial shade from the heat of the summer sun. Its leaves brushed across the top of Evie's hair, tickling her scalp.

"Are you wanting to eat?" Julian asked, sliding an arm around Evie's waist when a pair of well-dressed woman spied him from afar. It sent a small shiver of pleasure running down her spine to know that he was telling them he was hers, even if that would only remain true for another few hours.

She looked up at Julian, enthralled by the way the willow tree cast alternating strips of shadow and light rippling across his face. It was almost magical. "I can wait," Evie smiled, "if it means we get to spend a little longer here."

When Julian returned her smile it made her heart ache. Did she really have to say goodbye to him today? What was the protocol for princesses marrying wizards? Could she choose who she married?

Stop getting ahead of yourself, Evie, she scolded. Who was she to be thinking of marriage – least of all with Julian – when she didn't even know what kind of welcome awaited her at the palace?

"Evie, I have a confession to make," Julian said, starkly bringing her out of her thoughts. There was something about the expression on his face that both excited and scared her.

Evie brushed her fingers against his arm. "What kind of confession?"

"I –"

"Do not take her to the palace!"

Evie didn't immediately turn to see who had interrupted her conversation with Julian. Rather, she watched in growing concern as Julian's irises began to glow, and his hands clenched into fists by his sides.

"I told you to leave us alone, old man," he muttered.

"You think I can allow my daughter to walk right into a trap?!"

It was this comment that made Evie turn, and when she did her heart stopped for an achingly long moment.

"Uncle...?" she whispered, barely able to comprehend the sight of the man standing before her. He was greying at the temples where his hair had once been golden, and his face was far more lined that Evie remembered it being, but it was her uncle Francis nonetheless.

He called me his –

"Julian, what's going on?" she asked, alternating between glancing at him and her uncle. "You know my uncle? What's –"

"Genevieve, please," Francis pleaded. "There isn't time. You must get away from Willow as fast as you can."

"Why did you call me your daughter? What's going on? Why must I leave?"

Francis glared at Julian. "If you had taken her away when I asked you to there would be all the time in the world to explain everything to her!"

Evie frowned. "Julian, what is he saying? What do you know that I don't?"

608

The wizard was agitated and angry. He took hold of Evie's hand, insistently pulling her closer to him. "I'm not taking her to the palace but nor am I letting you or the rest of your family near her."

"Wait, what?!" Evie tried to yank her hand away from Julian's and failed; he was too strong. She turned to her uncle. "What's going on here? Someone explain it to me *now.*"

Francis took a step towards her. "Genevieve, the king is not your father. Your mother and I – we – we loved each other for a long time. We hadn't meant for things to end up like this. We –"

"No," Evie mouthed. She didn't want to believe what she was hearing. If the king was not her father, and the king had found out, then...

I was sent to the tower because I'm not his daughter. I thought he loved me, like I loved him.

"It's true," her uncle said, shaking his head miserably. "I wish you weren't finding out like this. But my brother is *looking* for you; he's been looking for you since you disappeared from the tower. If you go to him now nothing good will come of it."

Evie's eyes darted towards Julian, whose face bore an agonised expression. "And you...knew? You knew this whole time yet you didn't tell me? Even though it was about *me*? And now you're saying you were never going to take me to the palace anyway? So why are we here? Why –"

"Evie, let me explain –"

"No!" she cried, and this time she managed to wrench herself away from Julian. "No. I don't want to hear it." She looked at her uncle. "Both of you could have told me the truth whenever you wanted. You could have kept me involved so I didn't feel so in the dark about my own life." Evie laughed bitterly. "Here I was longing for answers and you had them. You just didn't want to give them to me."

"Evie –"

"Genevieve –"

She ran from both Julian and her uncle. Blinded by tears, barely comprehending where she was going, and not caring if they were following, she ran. Concerned bystanders held out their hands as if to help but Evie ran past them all, too. It was too much. She couldn't trust anyone.

Julian had lied to her for god knows how long, and yet she had trusted him anyway because she had nobody else *to* trust.

I was a fool. A hopeless, naïve fool.

When Evie crashed into the broad chest of a stranger she stumbled back and stuttered her apologies. She didn't expect him to grab her arm in a crushing grip. "Please, sir, I didn't mean to hit you," she babbled wildly. When Evie looked up she realised the man was a soldier.

"I'm here to escort you to the palace, Princess Genevieve," he said, face flat and impassive in a way only a soldier's could be.

"I – I don't want to –"

His grip tightened. "That wasn't a request."

Upon looking around Evie realised there were at least five additional soldiers of a lower rank than the one holding her, as well as a man in fine clothing who was looking around for something – or someone.

"Thorne is close by," he said. "I can feel his magic."

Evie felt her insides turn to ice. *Thorne? Wasn't that the name people called the wizard who worked for my father – the king? Just how involved is Julian in what happened to me?*

"Leave him for now," the man whose hand was crushing Evie's forearm ordered. "We have the princess; we don't need him."

Evie numbly allowed the soldiers to escort her to the palace, though it was now the last place on earth that she wanted to go to. All she could think about was what Julian had told her that night in the tent, when Evie realised she'd fallen for him.

She'd known him well enough, he'd said. Well enough.

For Julian, 'well enough' meant Evie had known him precisely not at all.

CHAPTER EIGHTEEN

Julian

"You just couldn't leave us alone, could you?" Julian seethed. "Everything was going fine until you showed up!"

Francis stared at him in disbelief. "Until *yesterday* it seemed as if you intended to take Genevieve to the king! What was I supposed to do?"

"You think I couldn't have protected Evie if something went awry at the palace? The last time I checked the only wizard in the country better at transportation magic than I am is my father, and he's *dead.*"

When the other man flinched Julian became certain that Francis had been keeping some hugely important secret from the beginning. He was furious. *If I'd had every piece of information then I could have made the right call much earlier than this!* Julian thought, though such a belief was tainted by the knowledge that he'd so easily done to Evie what Francis had done to him.

Julian closed the gap between them. To Francis' credit he didn't back away, though Julian's entire frame was rippling with magic. "Tell me what it is you don't want me to know. Tell me what it is, then I'll take Evie and get her away from all of this."

Francis shook his head. "No, find Genevieve first and -"

"She's fifty metres that way," Julian interrupted, pointing to his left. "There's no 'finding' necessary."

"...you cast a tracking spell on her?"

"Of course I did. Do you take me for a fool?"

Francis frowned. "Does she know?"

"What do *you* think? Now tell me what it is you're hiding from me before I blast your head off."

"You said something similar to me before," Francis murmured, "but I know you wouldn't do anything of the sort, Julian."

Julian's fury only grew. "And why do you *know* such a thing, old man?"

"Because your father told me. He said you had always been gentle - that combative magic hadn't come easy to you as a child, because you preferred not to fight. It's how I knew I could trust you with such dangerous powers around my daughter."

"I'm not who I was as a child," Julian laughed derisively. "Having my father mysteriously die changed things, unsurprisingly."

"Julian, he isn't dead."

"He - what?"

The two men stared at each other in silence for a few

613

moments, though the air crackled with sparks and bolts of magic. Julian could barely suppress it anymore; after everything that had transpired over the past month it threatened to consume him.

My father told me that's why one needed a strong mind to control it, he thought numbly. *He said I wasn't suited for such aggressive magic. Clearly he was right, though I've been desperate to prove him wrong. For the past twelve years all I've wanted to do is show a* dead man *that I can do all the things he could do.*

But now Francis Saule, the king's brother, was telling Julian his father was very much alive.

"If he's alive why haven't I heard from him?" Julian asked, voice clipped and very, very quiet. "If he's alive then why is it that only *you* know that he is?"

Francis shook his head. "I'm not the only one who knows – I'm merely the only one who isn't confined to the palace. Julian, I told you before that your father was the one who sent Genevieve to Thorne tower, but I didn't tell you the truth of *why* he did so."

"So tell me now, and I can be on my way."

The older man darted his eyes back and forth as if checking they weren't being listened to. At this point Julian couldn't care less if they were or not.

"Jacques knew about me and Mariette," Francis explained. "He didn't approve of what we were doing but the country was stable and safe only because we were around to temper my brother's selfishness. Jacques knew that too many would suffer if he said anything to the king, so he kept quiet."

"But then Pierre found out anyway," he continued, voice getting faster with every word as if he was expecting to be caught by an invisible hand at any moment. "He found out about what Mariette and I were doing – that we'd been together for years. He found out about Genevieve. And...he found out that your father had known about it, and hadn't told him."

"Pierre didn't want the country – or neighbouring kingdoms – to know of his humiliation. What did it say of a king when those closest to him all betrayed him? So instead of killing us for our treasons he punished us in different ways. He shamed me as a war criminal and exiled me from the country. He imprisoned Mariette in the palace, preventing her from going out and helping those most in need as she had always done. He sent Genevieve away, since he couldn't bear to look at her. And then, since *he* had lost a child, he forced the same fate upon your father."

Julian struggled to comprehend what he was being told. "I am still alive," he said. "There was never an attempt on my life. So what –"

"My brother reasoned that if he *actually* killed you then he could never force Jacques to continue working for him," Francis interrupted. "And so he imprisoned your father in the palace as he had done with Mariette, upon pain of death to his son if he didn't do everything he ordered."

"...did that include sending food and other supplies to Evie in the tower?" Julian asked, thinking about how half-starved she'd been when he first met her.

Francis nodded. "Going by how small Genevieve was a month ago I can only conclude that my brother didn't want her to grow strong. Another punishment for me and Mariette, I suppose, for us to suffer knowing our daughter wasn't being –"

"*Evie was the one who suffered,*" Julian corrected, his

615

fury rediscovered on her behalf. "You talk about how this person was punished and that person was punished but you were all guilty! You deserved to be punished! But Evie is innocent; so innocent, in fact, that the only thing she wanted to do was to be reunited with the family responsible for ruining her life!"

"Julian, I –"

"Why did you keep the information about my father to yourself?" he cut in, not interested in the man's apologies. All he needed was an answer to that one question, then Julian could be done. He'd grab Evie, disappear with her, then apologise to her until the end of time if need be.

Francis sighed. "Because you would have gone to the palace immediately to seek your father out, instead of keeping Evie safe. Jacques and I had been in contact all these years through a long-running channel he'd used his magic to set up back in the war, so when you appeared in the tower he informed me of your arrival immediately. As it happened, I'd spent months sneaking back into the country and working out how to breach the tower. I was surprised by my luck in having the solution to getting Evie out of the damn thing literally appearing out of thin air."

"When I met you on the road – when I watched as, instead of burning those men intent on harming my daughter, you stunned them – I saw with my own eyes what Jacques had always told me: that you were gentle at heart. But I also saw just how strong you were. Even the gentlest soul can break, Julian, and your weak point is your family just as it is Genevieve's. You would ignore her wellbeing in favour of saving your father, and –

"Don't talk as if you know me!" Julian yelled. He sent a wicked blade of heat out towards Francis, smothering the magic entirely the moment before it would have obliterated him. "You think I'd so easily put Evie in danger after saving her life? After looking after her? I *love* her, damn it!"

He didn't know where the words had come from but if Julian had spoken them then he knew they must be true. It was liberating in a bizarre, twisted way, to realise the extent of his affection for Evie mere moments after potentially ruining their relationship forever.

But Francis shook his head sadly. "You don't love her, Julian. You love that she relies on you, and that she gives your life purpose. After spending thirteen years aimlessly travelling all alone, how could you not?"

"Don't tell me –"

"If you loved her you wouldn't have kept her in the dark about why she was sent to the tower after I told you," Francis cut in. His eyes were hard; his mouth set in a tight line. "Even now, you're not doing what's best for Genevieve. You should have run after her and told her everything she wanted to know. Instead, you're so obsessed with getting the answers *you* need that you've thrown her wellbeing to the side."

Julian hated being called out on his behaviour like that. Who was this man – who was responsible for what happened to Evie in the first instance – to tell him whether his own feelings were genuine or not? But then he became aware of another feeling that turned his bones to ice.

Julian could no longer feel his connection to Evie.

With a snap of his fingers Julian transported to the last place she'd been before his magic was snuffed out. He found himself standing on a paved road that led out through the park towards the river, but Evie was nowhere to be seen. Out of the corner of his eye Julian saw a group of soldiers pointing and running towards him, so with a curse he once more clicked his fingers and disappeared right out of the city.

Back to Thorne tower.

He stared at his trembling hands with eyes gone blind with panic and horror.

"...what have I done?"

CHAPTER NINETEEN

Genevieve

When Evie was brought through the ornate palace gates, across the handsome paved courtyard and into the palace itself, all she could think of was how stupid she'd been to have ever believed her return to Willow would be a joyful one.

Never mind the fact Julian should have told me what he knew, she thought, *I should have been far more suspicious about the reason I was sent to the tower in the first place. I should have searched for answers before I came anywhere close to the palace.*

But it was too late now. Come hell or high water Evie had returned home. Alone. She could only hope her world wouldn't come crashing down around her more than it already had done.

It was only once she was escorted to the doors of the

throne room that the soldier holding her arm finally let go. She massaged the area immediately, wincing at the pain he'd caused. Evie knew that, in a few hours, there would be bruises where the man's fingers had been.

"Your father will see you now," he said, before unceremoniously pushing Evie through the doors once they'd been opened for her.

If everything miraculously works out okay then I'm going to strip him of his job, Evie decided, though she could have laughed at so ridiculous a notion as 'everything working out'. Nothing was going to work out the way she wanted it to, and she knew it.

"Genevieve."

As soon as she heard her name Evie stopped thinking at all. She slowed to a stop several feet from the throne she used to sit on as a child, back when she played at being queen when her father was busy. The marbled floor beneath her was polished to such a high shine Evie could vaguely see her reflection in it; her face was painted with fear and trepidation. But she couldn't look at the floor.

She had to look up.

"Father," she said, voice coming out as barely a whisper. Evie gulped, and tried again, this time bowing her head slightly as she spoke. "Father. I don't know what to – it's so good to see you."

The worst part was that, despite everything she'd learned today, Evie wasn't lying. The man sitting on the throne was older than he was in her memories, but time had not been as unkind to him as it had been his brother. King Pierre's hair was still sun-gold all the way through, and the lines on his handsome face made him look regal instead of worn and tired. Evie's heart hurt to see him in a powder blue jacket and waistcoat similar to the ones he'd so frequently worn when she was a child – the reason she loved the colour so much.

When he smiled Evie couldn't help but return it. "My love," he said. "My beautiful Genevieve. Look how much you've grown. You are my spitting image."

The words felt wrong to Evie's ears, perhaps because she was now aware that the man in front of her wasn't actually her father, and he knew he wasn't, too. But he did not necessarily know that *she* knew. Perhaps her fate might not be as bad as Francis feared.

"I've missed you," she said. "How I've missed you and mama. Where is she? Can I see her?"

"We've been reunited for less than one minute and you want to see *her*?" the king spat, his previous loveliness gone as if it had never existed. "That whore who spent more time travelling the country than looking after her own child? You want to see her so badly even after all that?"

Evie said nothing. The king was testing her, she realised, to see if she knew about her true parentage. But it was only in her silence that Evie worked out that she'd failed the test. She cursed silently at her own stupidity. *I should have defended her,* Evie thought, as she watched the king's mouth contort into an ugly, satisfied snarl.

"I see your *real father* found you before I did. Tell me, Genevieve, how did you escape the tower?"

Evie tried to think on her feet as fast as she could, for if the king was asking how she did it then it was possible that she might be able to protect Julian. Though the wizard had lied to her – had concealed the truth from her at every opportunity – he had still saved her life several times. She didn't want the king to catch him.

"I climbed out," she said, allowing a flash of pride to

621

cross her eyes. "I learned how to make a rope from a book in the tower, and turned every piece of clothing I was sent into another part of it. Eventually I made one long enough to escape."

The king raised a sceptical eyebrow. "You were strong enough to do such a thing?"

"I think desperation makes a person far stronger than they might otherwise be."

To Evie's complete surprise, he laughed. Her 'father' laughed, and it was loud and pleased and genuine. It left her feeling utterly confused.

He curled a finger towards her, motioning for Evie to come closer. She complied, walking onto the dais the throne sat on until she stood directly in front of her father. She kept her head held high. "Perhaps I should have listened to Thorne sooner," he said, casting a critical eye over her as he did so. "Clearly you are still my daughter in spirit if not in blood."

"So why send me away at all?" Evie demanded, realising that the best way to get answers was not to simper and fawn over the king but to instead face up to him directly, as he would have done. "Did you not love me? I didn't know what was going on. You are, and always will be, my father."

"Of course I loved you," he insisted. "You are the only one whom I *do* love. But what your mother did to me – what my own brother did to me – was inexcusable. They had to be punished. Knowing you were locked up because of their own vile natures was the least I could do to ensure justice was served."

That's not love. That's not –

"I can see from your face what you're thinking, Genevieve," the king said, frowning. "You think that if I

622

loved you I couldn't have done that. But some things are bigger than one person's love for another. But I'll demonstrate my love for you now: you can spend the night with your witch of a mother, then tomorrow I will gladly present you to the people of Willow as the princess and heir to the throne you truly are."

Evie hesitated before asking her next question. "And what of my brother? I heard I have a –"

"A brother of no consequence," he sniped back. "Whose ungodly sick blood demonstrates just how ruinous your mother truly is." The smile he plastered on his face did absolutely nothing to hide the hatred and malice lurking in his eyes. He motioned to a guard by the door. "Take her to her mother. Genevieve, I shall see you tomorrow. I have a lot to prepare before then."

Evie could do nothing but allow herself to be swept down corridors she had once known so well. They were meticulously clean, and immaculately furnished, but she realised there was no love in the grand building she used to adore. She wondered if there had ever been.

I hardly got any answers to my questions, Evie thought sadly. *Though seeing how bitter and angry my father is I can understand why my uncle wanted me to stay away.* Evie froze for a moment when she remembered that, technically, her father was her uncle and vice-versa.

None of that matters. Nothing matters at all. I should never have –

"Evie."

It was different from hearing the king say her name. It was different from hearing her uncle say her name. The voice belonged to the one person Evie had longed to see above anyone else.

"Mama," Evie cried, tripping over her own feet in her

623

haste to fall into the woman's arms. Her mother was sitting upright in her bed, supported by several pillows. When Evie bowled into her most of them fell to the floor, but neither of them cared.

"How I've missed you, Evie," her mother sobbed, tears falling from her eyes to land on Evie's forehead. They clung to each other desperately, as if at any moment either of them might be taken away forever.

"I love you," Evie said, over and over again until her mother must surely have grown tired of hearing the words. Instead she merely said them right back until, eventually, she placed a gentle finger below Evie's chin and lifted her face.

"How beautiful you have become," she said. "And your hair – what is in your hair? It's the loveliest thing I've ever seen."

"...magic," Evie said, though something had felt different about it ever since she'd been caught by the soldiers. Something off. "I think I might like to brush it out, though, if you wanted to help me?"

Her mother broke out into a fresh sob, voice cracking even as she smiled and said, "Yes. Yes, of course, my beautiful little girl."

But as Queen Mariette pulled out the golden comb and baby-soft brush that had been stored away for twelve years and began unravelling Evie's countless braids, part of her daughter sincerely wished to jerk away from her touch. For so long as magic remained within every strand Evie's hair belonged as much to someone else as it did to her.

Julian, she thought, though she didn't want to think of him at all. *You no-good, lying, heart-breaking wizard.* Evie wanted him to leave Willow and never come back, so that her father would never find him and Evie herself would never have to see him again. But it was hopeless to think such a thing, because of course she wanted to see Julian again, even just once.

We never got to say goodbye.

CHAPTER TWENTY

Julian

Evie is in the palace.

My father is in the palace.

Evie is a prisoner in the palace.

My father is a prisoner in the palace.

Evie is –

Julian loosed a blast of magic at the old, rickety bed that still smelled so much of her. It exploded into pieces, driving large wooden shards and splinters into books and walls and Julian's flesh alike, knocking him unconscious.

When he woke, hours later, the sky was dark outside the tower's window. Julian cursed as he struggled to sit up, groggily sending out a pulse of magic from within his very core to drive out the wooden stakes that had lodged themselves in him. He didn't want to stop the bleeding they'd caused even as he resigned himself to doing exactly that, feeling as if he deserved each and every wound he'd inflicted upon himself. He deserved so much worse.

Evie had been taken away and it was all his fault.

Julian knew he should never have stood there arguing with Francis for so long. Had he immediately gone after Evie and spirited her away with him he could easily have located the man at a later, much safer, time and gotten the answers from him that Julian badly needed. The problem was that Francis himself had been right: Julian should have been honest with Evie from the very moment he'd found out about her true parentage. Had he done so then the past few hours might never have happened.

"So why didn't he *tell her himself*?!" Julian demanded to the empty air of the tower. "Why did he leave it to me to tell Evie about *his* mistakes?"

He couldn't understand it. What had Francis hoped would happen by entrusting the fate of his daughter to Jacques Thorne's son? Why *had* he entrusted Evie to Julian? He'd said he was planning to help Evie escape himself.

Had he explained who he was on the road then Evie could have chosen to go with her uncle instead of me. Or her father. Whoever he is. Or we could have all travelled together.

Julian thought back over the past month he'd spent with Evie. Days and weeks of her incessant chatter and disgusting naïvety and insatiable curiosity, driving him to the point of madness on more than one occasion. But it was *Julian* she had bothered with everything she wanted to know, or wanted him to know. *Julian* whom she spoke to about the food she'd tried for the first time that day, or the heron she saw fishing in a river, or the shooting star she'd thought was falling from the sky.

If Francis had been there things would have been very, very different.

Was he right to say I don't truly love her? Who is he to deny my feelings when I've only just worked out what they are?

Julian kicked the windowsill. Nobody had the right to tell him what he did or didn't feel, or what he should or shouldn't do. He'd gotten by just fine acting on his own impulses; listening to his own morality. By and large Julian was a good man, even if he was grumpy and quick to irritate. He helped people. He saved princesses from towers and brigands and leering boys and guided them all the way back home.

"And bedded them in the process," he muttered, chuckling darkly. He really had messed everything up. But who else but Julian himself could fix things? He certainly wasn't going to rely on Francis, who up until this point had only made things worse.

With a grim smile Julian waved a hand at the floor. The wooden panelling opened up to reveal a helical stairway, which he promptly descended.

How Evie would cry in frustration if she knew this had been here all along, Julian thought, amused despite himself when he reached the bottom of the tower. There were several rooms and stores down here which contained a multitude of magical tomes and spells and both dangerous and wondrous elixirs. Julian ignored them all, choosing instead to venture into another room full of fabric.

"You really do have a flair for good clothes, father," Julian mused as he browsed through the man's expansive selection. "So what outfit would Evie like the most...?"

In the end Julian chose a deep red waistcoat with the suggestion of flames embroidered into the fabric with burgundy thread, and a pair of tan trousers with polished ebony buttons. They paired well with dark boots and a white shirt, which meant all Julian had left to select was an overcoat.

Or a cloak, he thought, grinning when he spied one made of a thick, lush fabric the colour of wine. It was so expansive that Julian imagined enveloping Evie within it, holding her against him as he kissed her until they both couldn't think of anything else but each other.

When he finished selecting clothes Julian headed back upstairs to the small bathroom Evie had used for twelve years. There was no water to be seen, so Julian focused his magic outdoors and redirected some from a stream through the tower's window into the old, rusted iron tub. He didn't bother heating it up, instead relishing in the nip of cold water on his skin as he washed his own blood from his skin. After that Julian shaved his face and cleaned his hair, smoothing it back the way his father had always worn it.

Julian glanced outside. His fire magic would be stronger when the sun was up. Though he was antsy and impatient to do something *now,* it was better to wait. Just another few hours and he could be on his way. So Julian set about cleaning the mess he'd left of the tower after he'd exploded the bed, then searched through some of his father's books until he found the transfiguration spells he'd need to conjure up a new one.

It kept him busy enough, though Julian's thoughts were constantly on Evie. What kind of bed would *she* like? Something grand? Something modest? Something made of beech or maple or cherry wood? Iron? In the end Julian made a sturdy oak four-poster bed with curtains

629

to keep out the morning sun, which at this point had flooded the tower.

Julian grinned as he felt it heat up his skin. He could do his best – or worst – magic now. He retrieved the clothes he'd chosen from his father's store then, with adrenaline-shaking hands, carefully put them on. When he was done Julian hardened a layer of air in front of him to turn it into a mirror to inspect his reflection.

He frowned at the person he saw. Just two days ago Julian had thought he looked like his father – except for his eyes. Blue eyes. His mother's eyes. Gentle eyes that meant Julian didn't have the heart to use the powerful, fiery magic within him to its fullest potential.

"We'll see about that," Julian announced in challenge, fastening his cloak with one final glance out through the tower window. A challenge to the king, who didn't know what he could do. A challenge to his father, who had always thought his gentleness a flaw. A challenge to Francis, who was convinced Julian would only use such devastating power for his blood-related family.

And a challenge to himself, to prove them all wrong.

"I'm coming for you, Evie," Julian said, and then he was gone.

CHAPTER TWENTY-ONE

Genevieve

If somebody had asked Genevieve what she thought she'd be doing that morning it was not having breakfast at a solemn dining table with her father, her mother, and a hunched-over, greying man she did not recognise.

"Did you sleep well, Genevieve?" her father asked, all sweet smiles and false politeness as he began eating. He deliberately avoided casting his gaze over anyone but her, which raised the question: why were her mother and the stranger there at all?

"I – well, father," Evie replied. "I slept well, thank you." She glanced to her left; her mother was picking away at her plate of food listlessly. In the bright morning light Evie could see how frail she'd gotten, as if a stiff wind might blow her away. Now, for all intents and purposes, it seemed as if the queen had been the one locked in a tower whilst Evie had been free to eat as she pleased.

Evie didn't like it. Though her mother had indeed betrayed the king alongside his brother, she had been the one to bear the worse fate of the two.

At least my uncle got to roam free, she thought, *though I suppose for him the worst part of his punishment was no longer being able to rule the country fairly in place of the king. Or maybe being separated from my mother was the worst part.*

Evie had to admit she didn't know the adults around her nearly as well as she needed to. When she was a child she'd loved them all regardless of their temperament, or the secrets they held, or the way they punished others. Dully she thought of Julian, whom she thought she *had* known.

And look where that got me. Clearly I'm not cut out for understanding people.

"Ah, if only my brother were here," the king opined, sighing dramatically. "Then we'd have the whole, happy family back together. Wouldn't that be wonderful, Mariette? You could continue fucking him behind my back and laughing at my ignorance, all the while handing me bastard children with a treacherous smile on your face!"

Mariette flinched at her husband's words, though she stayed silent. Evie didn't think she'd have been able to do the same if anybody spoke to *her* like that. She had to wonder where her mother's backbone had gone – had her imprisonment truly broken her? Evie had been locked up as long as she had, after all, and she certainly wasn't ready to give up on the life she wanted just yet.

It's simply a case of whether I can grab it, she thought, watching her father with careful eyes as she did so. *He*

632

says he's going to make me his heir. Do I even want that? Did I ever want the throne, aside from when I played games of make-believe as a child? Considering how poorly I have judged people thus far I somehow doubt I'd be any good at it. But then again...

"We'll have to get you some new clothes, Genevieve," her father said, pointing distastefully at her dress. "What you have on is much too common. It sickens me to see you debase yourself so."

Evie was wearing the dark green dress Julian had paid for the day they first slept in the tent together. She loved it dearly, despite the pain thinking of Julian caused her. Her father hated it because it was 'too common', though it was beautiful and well-made. He really didn't care for anyone living outside of Willow – anyone with real problems living on a pittance in villages in desperate need of help.

I could not be worse than my father at ruling, though that doesn't exactly set the bar very high.

"Forgive me, father; I did not have the resources to procure fine clothing on my journey home," Evie said, wording her sentence as carefully as possible. *Never mention Julian. Never mention getting help at all.*

Evie knew Julian had been worried someone was tracking his magic; he never told her why. If the king already knew about him and had someone tracking him Evie could do nothing to help him, though if she denied having any aid from him whatsoever regarding her escape from the tower then perhaps, even if he *was* caught, Julian would receive no punishment. It was the best outcome Evie could hope for.

"You'll need never have to worry about such things again, my daughter," the king said. He poured himself a cup of pale, golden wine, and then another for Evie, and

633

then – to her surprise – one for her mother and one for the unmoving, greying statue of a man sitting to the right of Evie. When the king indicated for them to pick up the drinks she watched the old man slowly reach a shaking hand out for his. She wondered if he was strong enough to hold it.

"A toast to the palace, and to our *family*," her father announced. "May we –"

"Mama?"

Evie turned her head to stare at the entrance to the dining hall. There stood a small, golden-haired boy around the age she'd been when she was sent to the tower. His large, green eyes stood out in stark contrast against his pale and sickly skin. He coughed several times into his hands; when he pulled them away there was blood on his fingers.

The king wrinkled his nose in distaste. "Get him away before he makes us all sick," he ordered the woman who frantically appeared in the doorway a second later. "I told you to keep him away from –"

"Louis? Are you Louis?" Evie asked, ignoring her father completely.

The boy's eyes grew even wider when they spied her. "That's my name. Who are you? You look like me."

"I'm your sister." She smiled gently. "I have been gone for a long time, but now I'm back. Won't you come in so I can greet you properly?"

"Genevieve, don't touch him," her father said. "He is full to the brim with disease. It won't be good for you to get close."

"If he's spent this long in the palace without getting anyone else sick I somehow doubt he's contagious," Evie fired back, remembering one of several books on

634

medicine she'd read back in the tower. "And I think I'd like to meet my brother, all things considered."

This time the king kept his opinions to himself. Evie knew she was treading a fine line right now, hoping that her father's wish to 'demonstrate his love' for her would last just a little while longer. She waved Louis over and, with small, uncertain steps, he made his way over to her. When he reached her chair Evie swept him up into her lap, and he laughed in surprise.

"Much better," Evie said happily. She reached for some toast. "Are you hungry, little brother? You look like you could eat a horse."

Louis nodded, immediately enamoured with this new sister of his who was unafraid to touch him, stood up to his father and offered him breakfast. He took the toast in his bloodied hands and eagerly wolfed it down.

Out of the corner of her eye Evie saw that her mother was watching the pair of them with the oddest expression on her face. It was torn between happiness and the deepest, darkest sadness, and it was only then that the extent of Louis' condition truly set in.

He is going to die soon, Evie realised with certainty. *His poor health has not been an exaggeration. He is doomed.* It was the worst situation imaginable in which to meet the other victim of the Saule family, and her only sibling.

"Your hair is very long," Louis said around a mouthful of toast, casting his eyes down to the floor where Evie's hair pooled beneath her.

She laughed. "Yes, well, I didn't have anything with which to cut it where I was staying."

"Do you want to cut it?"

"Maybe one day," she said. "One day. Some day.

We'll see."

The look her father gave her suggested he wanted it to be sooner rather than later.

"Louis, would you like some cheese?" she asked her brother, ignoring her father's looks as she reached out a hand to grab a platter full of the stuff. But her hand glanced against the edge of a sharp knife set beside it, slicing open her skin. Evie recoiled, wincing at the pain. "Guess I could cut my hair with that," she joked, to which her brother giggled.

The old, silent man to Evie's right held out a napkin to her. His trembling fingers touched the cut on her hand for but half a moment as she gratefully took it from him.

His trembling stopped.

"What is it, Thorne?" the king demanded, immediately aware that something was wrong. Evie stared at the man in horror – *this* was what remained of The Thorn Wizard? And then it hit her, though she should have worked it out a time ago.

The man was Julian's father.

Oh, Julian, she thought sadly. *Do you know he's here? You told me he was dead. Is this the reason you didn't want to tell me anything you knew? Is this –*

"Your Majesty," the man croaked. He finally looked up, pushing his hair out of his eyes in an achingly familiar gesture. And though his face was severely lined and gaunt from his imprisonment, and though his eyes were brown instead of blue, there was no doubt that this man was indeed Julian's father. "Princess Genevieve really *is* your daughter."

The king froze. "...what did you say?"

"Her blood," the wizard said, holding up his hand to

636

show where he'd grazed past Evie's cut, "her blood does not match your brother'. It matches yours."

Both Evie and her father darted their eyes towards the queen. Her face was ashen; she was shaking.

"You *lied* to me about my own daughter?" the king seethed. He stood up in order to tower over her. "You had me believe all this time that –"

But then a rumbling in the corridor gave them all pause; even the king forgot what he was about to say. The rumbling got louder, and closer, until by the time it reached the dining room it was a dull roar. There was a crackling to it, too.

Like fire.

"Julian," Evie whispered, a split second before the man himself appeared through the doorway, surrounded by flames and seemingly dressed in them, too. His eyes were murderous coals. He raised a hand to point at Evie.

"I'll be taking her with me."

CHAPTER TWENTY-TWO

Julian

"*Julian!*"

Evie's voice cut through the commotion all around him like an arrow to the heart. Julian locked eyes with her, the ghost of a grin upon his lips before he turned to snarl at the king.

"After sending her away you have no right to have her by your side. I'm leaving with her whether you like it or not."

It took the king a few moments to regain his composure. After all, a man enveloped in fire was not a common sight. But then he looked closer at who the man in question was, and smiled. "You must be Thorne's boy. Nice to see you following in his footsteps so perfectly. You even walked yourself right into the palace for me. So obedient."

"I'm here for *her* and to save my father," Julian said through gritted teeth. "Where is he?"

The king gestured to an old man on his left whom Julian had admittedly not taken notice of yet. But now the old man was staring at him, and –

"Father."

Jacques Thorne nodded, his eyes bright as they took in the sight of his fiery, furious son. Julian was horrified by how old and gaunt he was; clearly Evie hadn't been the only one who'd been starving for twelve years. Forcing his gaze away from his father Julian realised that the queen, too, was looking just as frail, and the boy Evie had clutched to her chest wasn't doing well either.

In contrast Evie herself looked healthier than she'd ever been, tearing Julian's heart up as he thought about each and every pastry and pie and apple he'd complained about having to pay for on her behalf.

And then there was the king, resplendent in his finery and looking younger than his years. He was vicious and golden as a lion, standing to face off against Julian as if he didn't have a care in the world. His eyes gleamed as they took in the sheer power emanating off his adversary.

"You don't scare me with your magic, wizard," he said. "If you meant to do me harm you'd have done it already. So you want my daughter and your father? Well, how about you stay and work for me instead? Lord knows your father is well past his prime. Let him enjoy his retirement. I think that's a more than fair deal."

"There's nothing *fair* about what you inflicted upon him."

"Oh, so the fact he kept my wife and brother's treachery from me for years didn't deserve punishment? He – quiet, Louis!" he screamed at the small child sitting

639

on Evie's lap, who had begun to sob. He only cried harder, so Evie wrapped her arms around him and stroked his hair until he quietened down.

For a moment Julian forgot to be angry, so enthralled as he was with the sight of Evie being gentle and kind in amongst the chaos surrounding her. *She is too good for them all,* he thought, casting his gaze around the room. *Her father, mother, uncle. All of them.*

Julian glared at the king. "I don't care for the transgressions of the past. I'm taking my father, and I'm taking Evie, and you aren't going to stop me."

"You're a confident one, aren't you?" he laughed. Pierre moved around the table, stopping by Julian's father. He put a hand on his shoulder. "But you are not the king, boy; *I* am. And as a subject of this country you must do as I say. And if you continue to refuse, well..."

The king left his threat hanging obvious and ominous in the air. Julian faltered for but half a moment, then sent a strike of magic towards the dining table, sending it up in flames. Mariette, Evie and Louis recoiled from the heat immediately; Julian's father did not. Their magic could never hurt each other.

But Pierre acted as if nothing was wrong. "You know, wizard, your father discovered something very interesting not one moment before you showed up. Did you know the beautiful Genevieve really *is* my daughter? In name and in blood, she is mine. Do you really think that, after finding this out, I would so easily hand her over to the likes of you?"

Julian glanced at Evie, who nodded silently. Her long hair was no longer imbued with magic, hanging all the way down like a coil of gold to the floor. Her brother clung to it desperately, as if it would protect him from the flames.

"I don't care about her parentage," Julian said. "I never have. She could be a peasant for all I care."

"Ah, but she's not, and it matters. Stay here and work for me, Julian Thorne, or face the consequences. This is your last chance to obey my orders."

The two men stared at each other for what felt like eternity. The table collapsed in on itself, smouldering to ashes upon the marble floor. Nobody dared say a word; all eyes were on Julian.

"I'm taking Evie," Julian finally said, just as the king pulled a blade from his sleeve and slashed his father's neck open from ear to ear.

"*Go,*" the dying man mouthed at his son, who stared in horror and disbelief as his father's life drained away before his very eyes. With no time left to think, Julian grabbed Evie's hair from the floor and snapped his fingers, barely aware of her cry of shock as his magic pulled them back to Thorne tower.

My father was right all along, Julian thought numbly. *I did not have it in me to kill a man, even one as deplorable as the king. Now both of us must suffer for it.*

CHAPTER TWENTY-THREE

Genevieve

It took Evie several moments of heaving oxygen into her lungs and struggling through tears before she realised Julian had transported her back to Thorne tower.

"I – Louis!" she cried out, grasping at air where her brother had been. "Where's Louis? And my mother! My –"

"He killed him," Julian bit out, though going by the look on his face he had not meant to interrupt Evie. Rather, he was speaking to nobody in particular, his eyes caught somewhere between blue and yellow, glowing magic. When Julian collapsed to the floor the angry flames surrounding him dissipated in puffs of smoke which filtered out the window.

Evie scrabbled to her feet to reach him, all concerns for her family momentarily forgotten in the face of Julian's desolation. But she tripped up on her hair in the process, falling gracelessly even as Julian held out an arm to catch her and pull her beneath his thick, billowing cloak.

He rested his chin on top of Evie's head; she could feel the erratic beating of Julian's heart against her right down to her bones. "He killed him, Evie," he muttered. "Your father killed mine. He –"

"You couldn't have done anything to save him," Evie cried, though the words felt hollow.

Julian's arms tightened around her. "I should have killed the king first. The moment I stepped foot inside that room I should have set his heart on fire, if he had one to set fire to at all."

"You could never do something so brutal," she replied, burying her head against Julian's chest to hide her tears. "Never in a hundred years could you do something like that."

"And look where 'couldn't' got me. I regained and lost my father in the space of twenty-four hours. What cruel world tells a son his father is alive only to rip him away moments later?"

"A world where princesses get put in towers for twelve years when they did nothing wrong."

The two of them were silent then, until finally Julian's heart rate slowed back down to normal. Evie's, however, continued to flutter as fast as a hummingbird, filling her stomach with nerves and foreboding.

"I have to go back, Julian," she said, very quietly.

"No."

"Julian –"

"I just lost my father, Evie. I'm not letting you go, too."

Evie struggled against him, though Julian only

643

tightened his grip on her until she could barely breathe. "I need to go back for my mother!" she barely managed to exclaim. "For my brother!"

"They're both as good as dead," he spat. "The king will murder them as he did my father, or he'll let them continue to waste away to nothing." Julian loosened his arms, allowing Evie to finally take a large gulp of much-needed air. He held her out in front of him, eyes wet with tears and blind to all reason. "Don't you see, Evie? It's all over for them. There's nothing for you to go back to the palace for. Stay here."

Evie shook her head. She clung to the front of Julian's waistcoat miserably even as his hands dropped from her shoulders. "I need to save them. I need to do *something*. I can't stay here."

"...you would leave me?"

"Julian, you lied to me!" Evie cried, forcing her eyes back to his. Her previous fury at the man in front of her reignited as if he'd set her on fire himself. "You could have told me what was going on so many times, but you didn't. Why should I stay with you?"

He frowned. "I was trying to protect you. You idolised your family; I didn't want to ruin that for you."

"I'm an adult. I could have handled it."

"Could you?"

"Why do you keep underestimating me?!" Evie raged, banging her fists against Julian's chest in the process. "Do you really think a young girl sent to live alone with no explanation as to why – who survived half-starved for twelve years, who actively tried to escape her fate – wouldn't be able to *handle* knowing that the people responsible for her misery were her family?"

Julian's expression hardened. He laughed bitterly.

"Well now you know. And what did it matter, anyway? Turns out your mother lied about who your father was all along! What a mess of a family. I hope the king is kicking himself for having sent you, his own daughter, away. I hope he –"

Evie slapped him. "You are grieving. You just lost what remained of your family. But that does *not* give you the right to say such things to me. Now let me go, Julian. Send me back to the palace."

"No."

"Julian!"

He ran a hand through Evie's hair, pulling her face closer to his. There was a shine to his eyes that had nothing to do with magic and everything to do with madness. "I'll get revenge against the king for both of us. Just let him come, and I'll obliterate him from the face of the planet. He'll never bother either of us again. We'll be free."

Julian kissed her, a desperate gesture that caused Evie to stumble backwards and fall to the floor. Julian followed her down; climbing on top of her and deepening the kiss even as she struggled against him.

"Julian," she cried, "stop it! Stop it!" Evie clawed at his clothes, trying to drag him off her, but it was only after she kicked him in the stomach that he recoiled enough for her to scramble free. Evie retreated to the other side of the room, clutching her arms around herself protectively.

Julian watched her from his position on the floor, expression all disbelief and incomprehension. It broke Evie's heart to see him so twisted. "Why are you refusing me?" he asked, genuinely hurt.

"Because so long as you forbid me from leaving then you're no different from my father," Evie told him. She ran to the bathroom and locked the door behind her, for all the good it would do.

I can't believe I ever thought for a moment I'd go to bed happy tonight, she thought miserably, crying for everything she had lost. Her mother. Her brother.

Julian.

CHAPTER TWENTY-FOUR

Julian

Almost a week had passed and Genevieve hadn't spoken aloud even once. Not once since she pushed Julian away from her and locked herself away in the bathroom. Evie had since resurfaced, of course, but she resolutely refused to look at or talk to or listen to Julian.

It didn't matter what he did – what food he brought to her, what baths he ran her, what blankets he wove out of thin air to accompany the bed he'd made with her in mind – Evie did not respond. And so Julian slept on the floor night after night, keeping a respectful distance away, believing that eventually Evie would see the folly of her silence and come back to him.

For though Julian was sorry for the way he'd acted towards her he could not be sorry for refusing to let her leave the tower. Evie was blinded by her longing for a brother who was doomed to die, and a mother who would soon follow. A mother who lied about her affair, and Evie's true parentage, and was the reason Evie had suffered so much in the first place. Perhaps Julian *should* have told her about why she'd been sent to the tower weeks ago; that way, her annoyingly-insistent, naïve love for the woman might have died already.

Died like my father, with a knife through his throat, Julian thought darkly, once more returning to mull over the precise moment all life drained from the man's eyes entirely.

It was sunset outside, and the sky was bloody and brutal. Julian revelled in it, so he sat on the windowsill to watch the horizon grow darker and darker in parallel to his mood. *I should have killed the king where he stood. I shouldn't have listened to a word he said. That way my father would be alive and Evie would not hate me so.*

He glanced behind him; Evie lay unresponsive on the bed, the gauzy curtains partially obscuring her from view. Julian could just barely spy the ends of her golden hair splayed in a mess across the floor at the foot of the bed. Evie hadn't let him enchant it to keep it clean and out of the way.

She hadn't let him touch her at all.

A familiar twist of longing mixed with frustrated, unruly desire consumed Julian as he watched her. He wanted Evie. He wanted to hold her and have her cling to him, like she had done before. To beg Julian for more; more touches, more kisses, more pleasure. More of him. *All* of him.

Instead Evie wanted nothing, leaving Julian wanting everything.

She'll come around, he thought, shielding his eyes

from the glare of the sun's dying rays. *She has to. Soon I'll correct my mistake and kill the king. For the first time in her life Evie will truly be free. She'll thank me then.*

Perhaps, had Julian not been so incandescent with rage on his father's behalf, he'd have been able to see just how wretchedly he was treating Evie. He'd see what he was doing to her, and let her go. But Julian *needed* the rage. He needed to cling to the belief that getting his revenge would make everything right once more, just as he wished to cling to Evie herself.

If he didn't have his rage then all he had was grief, and Julian didn't know how to deal with it. So he hid it away beneath layers and layers of fire, never to be felt again.

"Julian, let her go!"

Julian's ears pricked up at the voice. It was infuriatingly familiar.

"Go away, you bastard," he threw down to Francis, who stood at the base of Thorne tower looking exhausted beyond belief. To have reached the tower from Willow in seven days meant the king's brother had likely not slept much at all since he set out.

Julian didn't care.

"The king and part of his army are on their way, you fool!" Francis yelled. "What did you think would happen by kidnapping Genevieve?"

"He killed my father!"

"Because you stormed into the palace *on fire.*"

"He meant to imprison me there in place of him!" Julian screamed back. "Do you really think I was going to let that happen?"

Francis shook his head in frustration. "Look at the mess you've caused, Julian. Stop trying to fight like you're

649

the only one who's on your side. Had you told me your intention to take back your father and Genevieve I'd –"

"What? Snuck me in through a back door?" Julian sneered. "My plan would have worked, had I only killed the king in time."

"But you didn't." Francis' eyes were hard. "You didn't, and now your father is dead."

"You don't get to berate me for what I did wrong! Not when you and the queen are the reason all of this happened in the first place. Although, at this point I'd say it's largely the queen at fault."

"...what do you mean by that?" the man called out, though the wind took most of the volume away from his voice. When the words reached Julian's ears they were more like a whisper.

He bent low over the windowsill to grin like a madman; if he leant out any further then he would fall. "All this time Queen Mariette played everyone for a fool. You. My father. The king. Evie was *his* child the entire time, not yours! She was locked in this godforsaken tower for absolutely no reason at all!"

The look on Francis' face was terrible; Julian relished it. He wanted to inflict as much pain as possible on all those responsible for what happened to his father until everyone felt as wretched as him.

"You're lying," the man said.

"I'm not. It was the last thing my father found out before he was murdered. One wonders why the queen lied about such a thing. Do you have any ideas?"

There was a darkness to Francis' expression that had nothing to do with the murky blues and purples pervading the sunset sky. "You are trying to rile me up because you are angry. You're upset. You have every right to be. But

_"

"I'm not lying about Evie's parents," Julian cut in. "And I think you know that."

Francis hesitated before saying, "It doesn't matter who her father is."

"It sure as hell matters to Evie."

"Julian, let me up there," the man insisted, knocking upon the stone tower as if a door would somehow open in front of him. "We need to come up with a plan to combat my brother. You cannot face him alone."

"I can and I will!" Julian screamed back, though he knew he sounded like a petulant child. "I made the mistake of staying my hand before. I won't do the same next time."

And then he turned from the windowsill, though Francis called for Julian to come back. Then he called for Evie, begging for her to listen to him, but she did not rouse from the bed. Julian knew she was listening going by how still was; when Evie was actually asleep she tossed and turned, full of fitful nightmares.

Eventually Francis quietened down and, when Julian moved back over to the window, saw that he had retreated into the forest. Julian discovered he didn't feel particularly victorious about sending the man on his way.

I can't think of him now. The king is on his way. I have to be ready.

He took a few quiet steps over to the foot of the bed, watching Evie through the curtains. Julian wondered if she'd try to stop him, regardless of what the king had done to her and everyone else she loved. But he couldn't let such doubts stop him; it was much too late for that.

One way or another Julian Thorne was going to kill a

king. He'd face the consequences of what came after when they happened. But as he watched Evie his resolve faltered. He'd done so much to her. Too much. She would hate him until the end of time, and Julian would deserve it.

He sat on the end of the bed.

"Evie."

CHAPTER TWENTY-FIVE

Genevieve

Of course Evie had heard Julian's conversation with Francis. The king and an entourage of soldiers were on their way to Thorne tower to defeat the wizard and rescue the princess.

I don't want rescued, Evie thought. *Not like this. But I don't want to stay trapped in the tower either. I want to save my mother and little Louis. I want –*

"Evie."

She didn't respond. Julian had tried to get her to talk for a week now, though not one of his attempts had worked. Her self-imposed silence made Evie feel like she was living in the tower alone, as she had done for most of her life. It didn't matter that the bed was large and comfortable now, or that she had hot water and all the food she could eat.

Evie was trapped. She was a prisoner and didn't know what to do to free herself.

"Evie, please. I know you heard your uncle."

When she felt Julian's weight on the bottom of the bed she just barely glanced over at him. He sat by her hair, twisting strands of it around his fingers. Enveloped by the curtains hanging around them, Evie felt very much like she and Julian were the only people left in the world.

"I'm going to kill your father," Julian said quietly, still twirling Evie's hair. "I have to."

"I know."

His eyes darted to hers in surprise; clearly Julian hadn't thought Evie would actually reply. He reached a hand out a few inches before bringing it back to his lap, as if he meant to touch her but thought better of it.

"You don't approve?"

"I know it must be done."

"But you wish it didn't?"

Evie buried her head in the pillow beneath her, then sat up to face Julian. He ventured a little closer towards her.

"He means to allow my brother to die," she began, very slowly. "And my mother, too. He killed your father because you wouldn't bow down to his threats. He is callous and cruel and doesn't care for anyone who doesn't live outside of Willow. If he could be imprisoned then I'd want to go down that route, but he's marching to meet you with an army. I don't see what other choice you have but to kill him."

"Evie –"

"Would you send me back to the palace *now,* Julian?" she cut in. "My father isn't there. We could easily save my mother and Louis now. You know we could."

Julian's eyes shone in the darkness. He shook his head. "They are safer there for now. If we were to remove them from the palace word would reach the king about it. And then what would he do? At least we know what to expect if we remain here and wait for him."

Evie stayed silent. Julian had a point, but that didn't mean she had to like it. Especially not when his entire frame of mind was still bent and angry and riddled with grief. He wasn't himself when she needed him to be.

But then what did that say of *her?* Julian had needed her all week, and she had ignored him. He didn't know how to cope with the death of his father. He had nobody to help him, even though Evie was right there.

She reached out a hand, brushing her fingertips against Julian's arm. He watched her do so with an agonised expression.

"Do you remember the nightmare that woke you from your sleep at the inn?" he asked. All around them the air became just as oppressive as it had done on the night in question to which Julian was referring, and though the evening was hot Evie shuddered.

"What about it?" she replied. Julian closed the gap between them, sliding a careful hand through Evie's hair as his lips grazed her collarbone. He kissed the skin there, whisper-soft, then moved up her neck to her jawline, trailing kisses as he went. Evie drew in a breath and closed her eyes. "What about it, Julian?" she asked again.

When he pushed her down with the full weight of his body on hers Evie did not resist. "You didn't know the name of the tower," he said, while his hands made quick work of the buttons on Evie's underdress and his trousers. "You didn't know my family name, and yet you dreamed of thorns trapping you in here, digging into your skin and consuming you."

Julian's mouth found Evie's; she desperately reciprocated the kiss. She cupped her left hand to Julian's face, feeling the unmistakable dampness of tears upon her fingertips.

"Let me help you," she begged. "Don't go through all of this alone. Talk to me, Julian." When Evie locked eyes with him she saw that his were burning. She reached up and kissed them, one after the other, feeling Julian's wet lashes against her lips. "Let me help."

"I'm going to destroy you," he said, miserable even as his hands continued to rove across Evie's body. He didn't seem to realise she was responding in kind. "See what I've done to you already. I have to let you go."

"I won't go now."

"...why not?"

"Because you need me," Evie told him. She pushed Julian's hair out of his face and smiled. "You told me once that I'd forgotten what it was like to be looked after, and I said I sometimes thought the same about you. Now I believe that more than ever. So let me look after you, Julian, as you've looked after me."

Julian looked at her uncertainly. "Evie –"

"You won't destroy me," she assured, "and I think we both know you won't trap me anymore, either. So just...let me help you."

There were no words for a long time after that. The desperation in Julian's body as he touched and kissed and clung to Evie was all she needed to know what he was feeling. It filled every stolen breath of air he forced into his lungs, even as that desperation seamlessly turned into wild, fervent desire that left Evie gasping for more.

It was only when the pair of them had been reduced to an exhausted entanglement of limbs that Julian finally sobbed. He broke down against Evie's shoulder, his sweat-soaked skin shuddering alongside his cries.

"What do I do?" he whispered. "What do we do, Evie?"

"We end this," she said, before kissing Julian's forehead and wiping his tears away. "We end this, and move on."

CHAPTER TWENTY-SIX

Julian

"Did we really have to involve him, Evie?"

"To help us construct a plan to overthrow the king? Yes, Julian, I'd say it serves us well to have my uncle here."

Julian glared at the man in question, who was sitting cross-legged on the floor and glaring right back at him. "He has been less than useless so far. All he's done is make things worse."

"So you keep saying," Francis fired back, "yet it appears that *you* are the only one with a body count to your name."

"You –"

"Both of you, stop!" Evie begged. "Uncle, you said my father wasn't far behind you. When might we expect him?"

"By sunrise for sure," he said, still glaring at Julian. "Which is good for Julian's magic, I suppose. If he has the *heart* to use it."

"Julian being unable to kill a man is not a flaw, uncle."

"It is in this particular situation," Julian and Francis said in unison, which only served to further their dislike of each other.

Evie sighed. When she dragged her hand across her face in exasperation Julian burst out laughing; it was a gesture he was very familiar with, considering the numerous times he had done it in Evie's presence.

She frowned. "What is it?"

"I think you're beginning to understand what it's like to look after a brat," Julian explained, before sliding an arm around her and pulling her closer towards him. Evie blushed even as she rolled her eyes at Julian's insinuation.

Francis watched their interaction with disapproval. It only served to make Julian want to show off how close he and Evie were even more, but for her sake he resisted.

"It doesn't matter if Julian can't kill Pierre, anyway," Francis said, after a moment of crackling tension between the two of them.

Julian's eyes narrowed. "And why is that?"

"Because I'm going to take care of my brother personally. All you have to do is incapacitate his army so it'll be a fair fight."

"*You* will kill him?" Julian asked incredulously. To his left Evie let out a small gasp of surprise. "You're old and tired, Francis."

"Not so old and not so tired that I can't pierce my brother's heart with a sword or shoot him with a pistol,"

Francis said, smiling grimly. "I was a better swordsman than he was in the war, and he's grown slow and spoiled in the palace. He will not be able to beat me."

"And if he does?"

"Then I guess, for everyone's sake, you better set him alight this time."

Nobody said a word in response to Francis' jibe.

Hours later, after the sun had long since dipped below the forest, Julian and Evie lay huddled together, enjoying the breeze that came through the window to flutter at the curtains surrounding them. Francis had insisted on spending the night in the forest, where his supplies were, so he could be ready on the ground for his brother's arrival. Julian had, unsurprisingly, not bothered to convince him to stay.

"Why do you hate my uncle so?" Evie asked, when all they could hear was silence. Owls and songbirds alike were both resting; soon the sky would lighten and everything would change. The air would be full with the sounds of a midsummer morning.

And gunfire.

Julian sighed, rolling onto his front and propping himself up on his elbows before answering. "Because he followed us for so long. Because he thinks he knows me, but he doesn't. Because he thinks he knows *you* –"

"He is only trying to help," Evie said. She smiled softly. "Nobody knows me better than you, Julian. Certainly not as an adult. But my uncle isn't a bad man; far from it. He and your father were the only reason the country functioned for the first ten years of *my* father's rule."

Julian grumbled incoherently. He knew Evie was right, though he didn't want to admit it. He tucked a lock of

Evie's hair behind her ear, allowing his fingertips to linger around it long enough to send a small wave of magic pulsing through her. The resultant flush of pleasure that crept up Evie's neck and cheeks had Julian kissing her before he could stop himself, though he knew that what the two of them had would eventually have to end.

He'd done something unforgivable to Evie, after all. Julian had imprisoned her for his own selfish reasons, never mind the fact that he'd also lied to her and made decisions on her behalf without considering what she thought of them. Julian didn't deserve her.

But he couldn't break away from Evie *now,* not with the king approaching and with her nestled into the crook of his arm, yawning herself to sleep. When the sun rose, and her father was dealt with, Julian would say his goodbyes.

"I love you," he murmured, just as Evie slipped into unconsciousness.

He wondered if she heard him.

CHAPTER TWENTY-SEVEN

Genevieve

When Evie awoke it was to the sound of cannon fire. She leapt out of bed; Julian was already awake, standing close enough to the window to see what was going on but not so close as to be seen himself.

She stalked over to his side. "Why didn't you wake me?"

Julian glanced at her for a moment before returning his gaze to the window. "I didn't want to disturb your sleep when all the king was doing was crossing the meadow. You should probably get dressed; he'll be at the foot of the tower soon."

Evie peered through the window somewhat nervously. "What was the cannon fire all about?"

"Intimidation, I guess," Julian chuckled, suggesting he

wasn't scared in the slightest. "It makes no difference, anyway. Cannons run on gunpowder, and gunpowder is lit with fire."

Despite the dangerous situation they were in, there was something about the gleam in Julian's eyes that Evie loved. He was enthralling to watch when he was caught in the throes of the magic dwelling deep within him. Evie felt an inkling of what it must be like to be a human who possessed such power whenever he'd enchanted her hair. It was frightening and lovely in equal measure.

And he can wield it with minute control just as he can let it loose to devastating effect, she thought as she moved through to the bathroom to pull on a dress. It was a deep, sunset purple, transformed from a cloak Julian found in his father's stores. When he showed Evie the lower part of the tower she'd kicked a wall in frustration. To think that there had been so much more to the tower just below her feet – and for her not to have known of it – would eat away at her until the end of time.

Evie struggled to manoeuvre around her hair as she rejoined Julian. She wished she'd asked him to enchant it the night before; now it was too late. He needed every ounce of magic he could get, and her hair was the least of his problems.

"Wizard!" came the voice of her father hollering through the window, above the sounds of horses whinnying and men yelling to each other. "Show me that my daughter is unharmed or I will destroy your tower here and now!"

Julian smiled grimly, waving towards the window. "We'd be off to a bad start if he blasted us into the sky before I managed to work any magic," he joked. His hand lingered on Evie's when she walked past him; she squeezed it before reaching the window.

663

"I'll be fine," she murmured, then turned from Julian to address her father. He was resplendent in gold finery, sitting upon a large horse whose ebony hair shone in the sun. It pawed at the ground impatiently.

The king smiled up at her. "My lovely daughter. You are not hurt, I hope?"

Evie knew her father would try to sweet-talk her out of the tower the moment he opened his mouth. She supposed she couldn't blame him – she *had* been kidnapped, after all, and Evie had made no indication to him that she'd wanted to leave the palace.

"I am alive and well, father," she said. She gestured over the small battalion of cavalry her father had brought with him; in the rear were two deadly-looking cannons aimed directly at the tower. "Did you really need all this just to seek me out?"

He laughed bitterly. "You and I both know that Thorne's son is not to be taken lightly. Tell me, Genevieve, can you convince him to let you go? I will have mercy on him, for his father's sake, if he does."

"And what mercy is that?" Julian yelled, stepping forwards to stand beside Evie. The cannons swung to aim directly at him, though the king held up a hand to steady them.

"You will hit my daughter," he said. "Stand down." To Julian he called, "You brought your father's death upon you, boy. You defied your king, and now you have kidnapped a princess. The greatest mercy you can hope to receive now is a quick and painless death."

Evie knew her face had paled at the thought. All the blood in her seemed to rush out of her, leaving only cold. *It really will come down to my father's death or Julian's.*

Evie knew which of those options she couldn't bear to

664

live with.

Down below it seemed as if the soldiers had grown uncomfortable, as had their horses. Their whinnying increased, and they hopped upon the grass as if it was burning them. When one of the soldiers cursed and threw his helmet to the floor Evie heard Julian cackle.

"Idiots," he muttered. "Did they really think I hadn't begun attacking already?"

Evie watched the king as he, in turn, watched his soldiers with a frown. He hadn't been personally affected, but as the seconds stretched out it became apparent that Julian was slowly but surely cooking the men outside the tower.

"Don't kill them!" Evie told him, horrified.

He squeezed her hand in reassurance. "They'll have the worst sunburn of their life, and clothing will be unbearable to wear for a while, but they'll recover. The point is to drive them to distraction with the pain."

Evie supposed it was clever – the soldiers were certainly in disarray, no longer listening to their captain nor the king. The men controlling the cannons had to back away from them, for the metal sizzled and scorched their skin. On closer inspection Evie realised the cannons themselves were melting.

All the while Julian smiled pleasantly, as if slowly cooking a field of soldiers alive was no big deal whatsoever. But Evie could see his fingers beginning to twitch, and knew that even for him trying to control such a large quantity of magic must be tremendously difficult.

The king laughed up at him. "You think you can best me with that, Thorne? I thought you – ah!" He recoiled, almost thrown from his horse in the process, for Julian had shot out a barely-visible flare of magic which burst into flames inches from the king's face.

"I think you shouldn't underestimate me, *Your Majesty*," Julian chided, though the trembling in his fingers was beginning to creep along his forearms. Evie resisted the urge to hold on to one of them to keep him stable; she didn't want her father to know how much Julian's wide-ranged attack was costing him.

How much energy is required to burn one hundred soldiers, their horses and two cannons? A lot, I imagine. For though Evie had witnessed Julian stun five men before, and set a table alight, and surround himself in fire, most of that magic had involved igniting a flame and setting it loose. Julian was a catalyst in those situations.

What he was doing now was much, much different.

"Y-your Majesty," one of the soldiers called out. Evie could scarcely look at him; his face had reddened and blistered and was beginning to weep. She felt sorry for him – she felt sorry for all of them – but she knew she couldn't stop Julian. Many of the soldiers had fainted from the pain his attack had inflicted, though a few still stood or knelt on the grass, moaning and screaming. Horses were bucking their riders off their backs, crying out in pain as they fled the meadow. She winced away at the sight before she knew what she was doing.

"See how my daughter turns away from what you're doing in horror, wizard!" the king cried, eyes shining triumphantly when he caught Evie's expression. "This is your last chance. Let her go."

Julian glanced at Evie; a bead of sweat rolled down his forehead. "Ask her if she would like to go," he said, in lieu of a proper answer.

Her father cocked his head to one side. "Genevieve, of course you want to go. You're the heir to the throne.

You're my daughter."

"You locked me up in here, father," she said, forcing herself to keep her voice hard and dispassionate.

"I did not know you were –"

"You told me some things were bigger than your love for me."

"Genevieve –"

"The pain you've caused to the people I love – to your entire country – is bigger than my love for *you*," Evie finished. She turned from the window so that she wouldn't have to see her father's face.

"You – you will come down here," her father spluttered, furious, "or I will force you to!"

"I can't hold this spell up for much longer," Julian admitted to her through gritted teeth. "I'm going to send out a final blast to knock them out, then – *get down*!"

Evie was thrown to the floor before she knew what had happened; Julian was hunched protectively over her. The bed was on fire. A few seconds later part of the wooden floor was, too, and then the door to the bathroom. Flaming arrows were streaming in through the window, catching hold of anything that could be set alight.

"Time's up, wizard," she heard her father yell. "Send her down or you shall both perish!"

Julian stared at Evie with wide eyes. They reflected the flames consuming the room, though his irises were still full of magic. His skin was shining with sweat.

"Let go of your spell, Julian," Evie begged. "Let's get out of here. Let's –"

"Evie, your hair!"

Evie yelped when she spied a lick of flame crawling up

667

the length of her hair, heading towards her at a sickening rate. She looked around frantically for water or a heavy blanket – anything to put it out. There was nothing.

But there *was* a knife.

"Evie, let me put it out for you," Julian heaved, barely conscious, but she pushed him aside, grabbed the blade and cut off her hair where it hit her shoulders. She barely made it in time; when the golden mass she'd cut off thumped to the floor it was engulfed in flame.

Evie grabbed Julian's trembling hand. "Drop the spell outside and get us out of here."

"I –"

"*Do it!*"

With a frown of concentration, and one final look at the flames consuming the tower all around them, Julian grabbed hold of Evie and snapped his fingers.

She hoped he'd stay conscious long enough to complete the spell.

CHAPTER TWENTY-EIGHT

Julian

All around was fire and chaos. Julian could smell the damage his and the king's flames had wrought upon the air – burning flesh, seared metal, a meadow turned to ash. He felt sick with it. Dimly he became away that he'd transported Evie and himself to the outskirts of the forest, where he knew Francis to be.

The trees are burning, he thought, looking up above him and seeing only fire. *So much destruction. Was that the king or was that me?* For the days had been long and dry for weeks now; the heat Julian had forced upon every living thing in front of the tower was more than capable of turning the entire area into a blaze.

"I should have simply killed the king," Julian coughed. His throat was raw and seared from smoke and flames and magic, and his eyes were stinging and blurred.

"You gave him a chance to stand down and he didn't take it," Evie insisted. Julian became aware that his arm was slung over her shoulders – Evie was supporting most of his weight as they walked as far from the burning tree line as possible. But there was nowhere they could go quickly enough to be of any use. Julian was exhausted. He knew he couldn't transport the two of them anywhere, and behind them he could hear the king on his horse, looking for them.

"You really thought that would work, wizard?" the king hollered. "Did you think I'd surrender because you burned my men? Even if you turned them to ash I wouldn't give up! Now hand me my daughter!"

Julian tripped on a fallen tree trunk and whined in pain – he didn't even have the strength to curse. Evie merely shifted more of his weight onto her.

"Come on, Julian," she panted. She was covered in sweat and soot and ash, her newly-shortened hair dull and uneven from the filthy blade she'd used to cut it. "We can do it. Just a little further. We just have to find my uncle. We just have to –"

"No," Julian sighed, and he dropped to the forest floor. "No, I can't go any further, Evie. I don't have the strength."

There were furious tears in Evie's eyes as she tried to force him back up. "Come on, you idiot! Don't give up now! What was the point of taking a stand against the king if you don't survive it? Get up!"

Julian merely shook his head. With aching, trembling fingers he ran a hand through Evie's hair. He laughed noiselessly when he reached the end of it so quickly. "You cut your hair."

"Yes; it was either that or burn alive."

"The former sounds like a much better idea."

Evie let out a garbled sob at the ridiculous joke. "My hair will grow back. The rest of me would not." She ran the back of her hand across Julian's brow, and although he knew her skin must have been burning hot it felt cool against the inferno raging inside of him.

"Evie, you have to let me send you somewhere safe," Julian insisted, as loudly as he could. "I don't know where Francis is, and your father is almost upon us. Let me –"

"I am *not* leaving you behind," Evie cried. "If he finds us, he finds us, but I won't let him touch you! He'll have to kill me first!"

"Evie, he'll use you as a puppet to the people and keep you prisoner to his will if he thinks he has leverage against you," Julian reminded her. He coughed and hacked on the smoke rapidly filling the forest. Neither of them could see much further past the other one's face. "He already has your mother and brother. Don't allow him to use me against you, too. Let me send you away."

"Julian –"

The air was split by the cracking of a bullet. Julian stilled, and Evie too. It was close by. When they heard another Evie dug her nails into Julian's arm; it kept him clinging to consciousness even though his mind so eagerly wanted to slip away.

"Who goes there?" the king demanded. Through the sounds of burning and screaming Julian could just barely make out the sound of the man's horse upon the forest floor, several feet to his left.

"A stranger," Francis growled, and then the king's horse screamed in fright; Julian heard it topple to the ground, so close he could smell its singed mane.

"You bastard!" Pierre exclaimed between grunts and

shouts. Clearly the two of them were fighting, though neither Julian nor Evie could see what was going on.

She squeezed his hand. "How much magic would it take to clear the air?" she asked, very quietly.

"I would not want to risk Francis' advantage."

"We will choke to death on this smoke before long."

"Then let me –"

"*Don't* say you want to send me away. I'm staying with you, Julian."

He sighed, before sending just enough magic out into the air to clear the smoke in the immediate vicinity. The relief on his and Evie's lungs was immediate; Julian's head felt altogether clearer the moment he took a clean breath.

Evie's eyes darted to her father's horse. The beast hadn't been hurt from what Julian could see, though it was struggling to get back to its feet. Evie crawled over to it, whispering reassurances as she urged it upright.

"Do you think you can get on him?" she asked Julian.

"If I said no, what would you do?"

"Force you onto him somehow."

"You're a weak, skinny brat."

"So it will make *you* look even more pathetic when I manage it."

Julian chuckled despite himself and then, with a tremendous amount of effort, hauled himself to his feet. Evie brought the horse over to him, allowing him to use her arm in order to help him up onto the animal. Then she jumped up in front of him, took hold of the reins and urged the horse forwards.

"Let's get out of here before my father finds –"

Just as Evie spoke both the king and his brother

appeared in front of them. They were smeared with blood and grime and ash; for a moment Julian could not tell which was which. But then the king turned his head to stare at them, furious.

"You would dare attempt to escape on *my* horse!" he raged, but then Francis slashed a knife across his cheek and he focused back on their fight.

"Get out of here!" Francis urged. He dodged out of the way when Pierre sent a punch his way, then fired back with one of his own.

Evie and Julian didn't have to be told twice. They wound their way through the burning trees, the horse beneath them following its own instincts to escape the fire more than paying attention to where Evie directed him. Julian took a deep breath, fought back the urge to throw up, then sent out several tendrils of magic to find the stream than ran through the forest.

"What are you doing, Julian?!" Evie screamed back at him when she felt his head droop down to her shoulder. "Stop using magic!"

"Just a little bit," he mumbled, closing his eyes in order to focus on dowsing the fire around them. He sent water to the meadow, too, to sooth the agonised soldiers, and then when he was sure the blaze itself was extinguished he added a little healing magic to the water to relieve them of their wounds.

"Julian, that's enough," Evie said, her voice trembling. "Whatever you're doing, it's enough. You're going to kill yourself."

By the time they made their way back to the meadow most of the soldiers were lying on the burned grass. Their horses were huddled some distance away from the dirty steam filling the air around their riders. Nobody had died.

673

Good, Julian thought dully. *Good. No deaths.*

"Princess," the captain said when he spied the pair of them. He frowned at the king's horse. "What is going on? What is –"

"My brother is dead."

They all turned; Francis appeared from the forest, limping heavily. He dragged the king's body behind him, though he dropped him as soon as he reached the meadow.

"General Francis!" the captain exclaimed, alarmed, and he drew his sword. "You have killed the –"

"Stand down," Evie ordered. She sat up straighter on her father's horse, though she kept her hands on Julian's arms wound around her waist to keep him upright behind her. He was grateful, for without her support he'd have likely fallen.

The captain faltered.

"Stand down," she repeated. "You heard yourself that my father named me heir to the throne, did you not? And even if you argue that the title remains my brother's, I am still your princess, and I am telling you to stand down. Do you defy me?"

"I wouldn't dare to," Julian muttered into her ear. He felt Evie's lips quirk into a smile more than he saw it, for in a moment it was gone.

"My father was not a good man," she called out to the soldiers. "He painted my uncle as a war criminal and exiled him for a personal slight. He imprisoned The Thorn Wizard and murdered him in cold blood to enrage his son. The queen and my little brother are also held prisoner in the palace. Do you truly wish to follow my father's orders, or will you instead follow mine?"

674

The captain surveyed his soldiers, who were watching both Evie and Julian in awed terror. He inclined his head. "And what are your orders, Princess Genevieve?"

She squeezed Julian's arm. "Take us to the nearest inn where we all can recover, then escort us back to Willow."

It was then, and only then, that Julian passed out, and did not wake for a long, long time.

675

CHAPTER TWENTY-NINE

Genevieve

"How long do you think he'll sleep for, mama?"

"For as long as he needs, I imagine."

"If Julian had his way then that would mean three months," Evie muttered. Julian was so still upon the bed he lay in that a stranger might have believed he was no longer alive. "He's been asleep for ten days, mama. By anyone's measure that's a long, long time."

Queen Mariette smiled softly at her daughter. "Perhaps he needs to heal more than just his injuries, my love. He's been through a lot."

Evie, Francis and Julian had arrived at the palace the day before. They'd headed back on horses as quickly as they were able to after the debacle at the tower, though word had been sent ahead to the queen of what had transpired. Knowing that her husband was dead, and that herself, her children and Francis were free seemed to have added years to the woman's life; already she looked much better than she had done when Evie was first reunited with her.

But Evie had a burning question for her mother that would no doubt bring up bad memories. She didn't want to burden her after everything she'd been through, but Evie *needed* answers. She couldn't rest until she did.

"...mama," she said, before leaving Julian's bedside to stand in front of a mirror. Evie had washed and washed her hair until no trace of fire and destruction lay within it, and her mother had brought someone in to cut the ends evenly so that it sat nicely around her shoulders, but the lack of weight on her head unsettled her deeply. Evie felt like she'd lost a limb – some integral part of her very being that made her who she was.

"What is it, Evie?" her mother asked, following her to the mirror with a brush in hand. They sat in front of it, and Evie allowed her to brush through her hair as she had done when she was a child. But it wasn't enough.

It was Julian's hands she wanted to feel on her scalp, weaving golden crowns into her hair.

"Why did you lie about who my father was?" Evie asked. She fidgeted with her fingers in her lap. Was she ready for the answer to her question?

"I didn't – I never knew if you were Pierre or Francis' child," her mother replied. She sighed heavily. "I could have asked Jacques to check for me when you were born, but that would have raised suspicion. He didn't find out about me and Francis until you were around six, you see, and by then it seemed inconsequential whose chose child you really were."

"But then why did you say that uncle was my father, when you were found out?"

"Because I knew Pierre would send you away if you were. I hoped you would escape; I was so happy when I discovered you *had.* I wanted you to live a normal life free from the reach of your father. Had he known you were his daughter he'd never have let you go, and he would stop me from seeing you in order to punish me."

Evie stayed silent as she digested all of this information. Her mother's plan had been flawed, for sure, but Evie saw the sense in it. Twelve years locked in a tower was far better than a lifetime of indentured servitude to her father, especially if she had been raised not to know what it was that he was doing.

"The last time your hair was this length, you were five," her mother said, working out a tug as gently as possible as she spoke. "Louis' hair got as long as yours did when he reached that age, but Pierre made me cut it. Your brother cried for days about it."

Evie laughed softly. "I'd have loved to see it. How is he?"

Her mother didn't respond, instead gesturing in the mirror towards the half-open door. Evie could just barely see the boy in question standing there, watching them.

"Louis, don't you want to come in?" Evie asked, turning from the mirror to smile at him directly. He returned it with an anxious one of his own as he padded across the carpet to join them.

"I can? I really can?"

"But of course! Why would you think I'd say no?"

He looked at the floor. "Papa always –"

"Papa isn't here to tell you no," Evie said firmly, "but

678

I'm here to tell you yes."

Louis perked up upon hearing his sister's answer, though that wasn't saying much. In contrast to his mother, he looked even sicker than the last time Evie had seen him.

So frail and small, she thought. *And no amount of eating like a piglet can save him.* Reaching out her arms for Louis, the boy gladly climbed onto her lap and lay against her chest. Evie rested her chin on his head, which caused Louis to giggle.

"Your hair tickles," he said, wrinkling his nose when several strands of it swept across his face. "I thought you said you wouldn't cut it yet?"

"I said I'd cut it *some day.* I guess that day came."

"I'd say cutting it under threat of fiery oblivion doesn't count as you doing it willingly."

Evie froze. She stared at the mirror, past herself and her little brother, only to realise that her mother was no longer sitting right behind them. She was standing over by the bedside, giving a very grumpy, very groggy wizard a glass of water.

"Julian!" Evie cried. She carried Louis straight over with her to Julian's bedside, excited as she was. "I can't believe you're awake! You've been asleep for ten days. *Ten days.* Can you believe –"

"Will you shut up?" Julian muttered. Both the queen and Louis looked horrified that he would say such a thing to Evie, but when they saw her smile they relaxed. He glanced at her brother. "So this is Louis. Huh. He looks just like you."

"Because I'm a brat," Evie said. "I get it."

Julian quirked an eyebrow. "I was going to say you

679

share the same hair and eyes, but that'll do." He held out his hand to the boy. "How do you do, Your Majesty? He *is* the king now, isn't he? Or did you – Evie, you didn't actually take up the throne, did you?"

"No need to sound so terrified of such a prospect," she laughed. "But no. I'm not...I'm not ready to be the queen of anything. I have so much to learn. My uncle will act as regent until Louis comes of age, or..."

Evie didn't finish her sentence. They all knew what she meant, even Louis himself.

Julian stretched his arms over his head and cracked his neck to one side. "That reminds me. Queen Mariette, what is it exactly that ails your son?"

"A disease of the blood," she said sadly, drooping her head as she did so. "It's afflicted Louis for years. Nobody can find a cure."

"I can see one with my own eyes."

Evie frowned. "What are you talking about – ah!"

Julian had snatched her hand and pricked the meat of her thumb open with a pin; she didn't even know where he got it from. *It was probably stashed up his sleeve,* she thought. *He always kept god knows what inside that old cloak of his, after all.*

"May I have your hand, Your Majesty?" he asked Louis, though the boy seemed a little frightened after watching what had happened to his sister.

"It doesn't hurt, Louis, I swear," Evie reassured him. "Julian just surprised me."

"Okay..." the boy said, still uncertain as he gave his tiny hand over to Julian. The wizard grinned at him and, before Louis had a chance to realise what had happened, Julian pricked his thumb.

"Well isn't this a lucky turn of events," he muttered, rubbing the two drops of blood he'd obtained from the siblings between his fingers.

"It's a match?!" the queen exclaimed. "Is it a – it's a match?"

Julian nodded. "Completely. It will take a while, but regular transfusions from Evie to her brother will clean up his blood and cure his disease. I'd say once every three weeks for four months, then every two months thereafter for a year or so. Evie will need to get plenty of bed rest and lots of food to regain her blood quickly...which shouldn't be a problem." He gave her a wry smile, but Evie was too emotional to return it. She knew she was crying but she didn't care.

She looked from Julian to her mother to Louis then back again. "And that will fix him? That will actually cure him?"

"Would I be telling you to do this if it wouldn't?"

"I – no. Thank you, Julian. Thank you!"

Evie would have thrown her arms around him, had her mother not done so first. Her body was wracked with silent sobs. Evie instead wrapped her arms around her brother, who looked up at her with disbelieving eyes.

"I'm going to be okay?"

"Just so long as you keep me company when I'm growing more blood, then yes!"

He giggled when Evie planted a kiss on his forehead. "Do you think we'll look even more alike if I have your blood in me?"

"Who knows? I guess we'll have to find out."

The room was full of excited chatter and thanks for Julian for another few minutes, then the queen lifted Louis into her arms and made for the door. "I shall give the two of you some privacy," she said, smiling. "I will arrange for a doctor to arrive first thing in the morning if that suits you, Evie."

She nodded, and then her mother was gone.

Julian did not say anything for a while. Evie couldn't bring herself to break the silence, either, though before she knew it her hand had found itself intertwined with Julian's.

Eventually he drew in a deep breath. "Evie –"

"I know."

He frowned. "You –"

"You have to leave. I know, so don't say it." She stared at him miserably. "I don't blame you for what you did. You were in pain. You didn't mean to do it."

"Yet I did it all the same." Julian squeezed her hand. "I need to be by myself for a while, Evie, to clear my head. To work through my grief and anger. What happened to me...I cannot afford for that to happen again. I don't want to ever hurt you."

"But it isn't fair!" Evie cried. "Julian, I love –"

"No," he interrupted. Though he was smiling, Julian's eyes were too tight, and his grip on Evie's hand reflected that. "Don't say it. Not now."

She pushed against his chest. "You got to say it when you thought I was sleeping."

He chuckled. "Then I suppose I really *am* being unfair. Goodbye, Princess Genevieve."

And then Julian clicked his fingers, and he was gone.

"Not now, he said," Evie mumbled as she forced herself to dry her tears and get to her feet. She had to keep all her strength for Louis; now was not the time for crying. "I won't tell you *now,* then, Julian."

Evie could wait. After all, she'd spent twelve years of her life waiting in his tower to meet him.

EPILOGUE

Julian

Julian was nursing a tankard of ale in the corner of a tavern, hating himself.

Fourteen months had passed since Francis Saule had become regent. Louis had made a remarkable recovery from his illness, thanks to Evie's blood, and with her imprisonment finally over Mariette's health was much improved, too. Between them all they were working to fix everything King Pierre had destroyed, ignored or otherwise made a mess of. Julian had heard in several towns and villages that the queen was restarting her tours of the country, too. People were excited to have her back.

And where am I over a year later? Julian wondered. *Drinking in the inn where Evie and I first stayed the night after I saved her life. She drank a cup of wine believing it to be water.* He snorted in amusement, drawing the gazes of several curious bar-goers in the process.

Despite his promise to himself that he would not let his hair grow as long as it had been before, Julian had failed miserably at keeping said promise. It was currently tied back to keep it away from his face. It properly fell to his shoulders now – the length Evie's hair had been when she cut it free from the flames rapidly engulfing it.

I wonder if I should let it grow longer and longer, just to annoy her, Julian thought, amused by such a notion. *At least I've been shaving my face. Well...most of the time.* He ran a hand over his jaw, where several days' worth of stubble grew. He grimaced. *I'm certainly better dressed than I was when I first met Evie.*

Julian hated that he had to think of such trivial improvements to mark that he'd done anything of worth in the last fourteen months. Evie was in Willow, learning how to rule a country alongside her brother – a brother she was directly responsible for saving the life of. She was flourishing. The people adored her. For how could they not?

She could not have done all of that if I was with her, Julian knew, for he would never have wished to stay in Willow long enough for Evie to enact any kind of positive change. And he couldn't bear the thought of staying in the palace, where his father had died. The expansive, beautiful building felt like far worse a prison to Julian than his father's tower ever had.

Though Evie might object to me saying as much. The tower was burned to rubble, anyway, though Jacques Thorne's stores of elixirs, spell books, curses and clothing had remained untouched. Julian had since paid for a house to be rebuilt there, using stones from the original tower wherever possible. Many of them had been scorched beyond repair in the fire, but there had been enough to build one of the walls and a chimney of the new house. Julian hadn't moved into it yet, though it had been completed weeks ago.

He wasn't sure he ever could.

"Mister Thorne, there's a visitor for you up in your room."

Julian stilled, fingers tensing on his tankard just a little too much. He hadn't told the innkeeper his name.

"Ah, Mister Thorne," the man repeated, nervously this time. "Forgive me, but the lady really was insistent about letting you know she was here. She told me I should call you Mister Thorne. My apologies."

Julian frowned. "The lady?"

He nodded. "Beautiful woman. Gold hair like you rarely see in these parts. Something really special -"

Julian was out of his seat and flying up the stairs before the innkeeper could finish his sentence. *Don't be ridiculous,* he thought, barely daring to believe what - or who - might be waiting for him inside his room. *I told her to stay away. I told her.*

"Evie," he breathed, the moment he slammed open the door. Her hair was woven down her back; it reached below her shoulder blades now.

She smiled when she saw the look on his face, and took a few steps towards him. "*Not now,* you said a year ago. Not now. Have I waited enough time?"

"What are you talking about?" Julian asked, dizzy from his sprint up the stairs and the sight of the woman before him. "What are you -"

"I love you, Julian," Evie said, closing the distance between them just as he reached out for her. "Am I allowed to say that now?"

686

"You're – you were in Willow."

"I'm taking over my mother's tours of the country," Evie explained. She crawled her hands up Julian's chest as if she barely believed him to be real. "But not for another year or two."

"So what are you doing so far away from the city?"

She slid her hands down until they found Julian's. He held them tightly, though he hated that he was shaking. Evie looked down at them, interlacing her fingers through Julian's and squeezing his hands until the shaking stopped.

"I thought I might...see some of the world first. You know, to combat my wilful ignorance. Do you know of anyone who might act as my willing guide? I hear there's a faerie trapped as a fox that I'd quite like to see with my own eyes."

Julian bent his head down until his nose touched Evie's. "You are...so annoying. This trip sounds so annoying. One or two years of you never shutting up, and eating all of my money, and complaining about being *cold*, and –"

"Is that a yes?"

"I guess it must be," he said, and he kissed her. Evie let go of his hands to guide her own through his hair, untying it in the process. When she saw it fell to Julian's shoulders she gasped.

"Your hair is so long! Why haven't you cut it?"

His lips quirked into a smile. "I'll cut it if you cut yours."

EXTRA CHAPTER

Genevieve

"Remind me *never* to travel by boat again, Julian."

Evie's face was pale and sallow. She stood hunched over the wooden railing of the ship they'd boarded to get them across the channel, having spent the last half an hour heaving into the sea. There was nothing left in her stomach anymore.

"You're the one who wanted to see the fair folk," Julian pointed out, rubbing Evie's back before he eased her over to a wooden bench bolted onto the deck.

She made a face. "I thought you might have, oh, I don't know, *clicked your fingers* and we'd be there already."

"Using transportation magic across a single country is one thing – over multiple lands is another entirely."

"Does it take too much energy?" Evie asked, releasing

all the air from her lungs as she leaned against the bench. Julian smoothed her hair away from her face - the ends of it reached the small of her back now.

"Yes and no," Julian replied, frowning at the horizon. "It does take more energy, but not so much that I couldn't do it. The problem is that I don't know the British Isles the way I do our home. If I don't know exactly where I'm transporting to - a pinpoint location - then the magic is likely to go...awry. I think you'd like that far less than being sick over the deck of a ship."

"Please don't talk about being sick." Julian smirked in response; Evie didn't like the mischievous look on his face at all. "What?" she demanded, crossing her arms over her chest until she realised that it made her feel worse. Evie bowed her head instead, breathing shallow and laboured as she fought the urge to retch.

The wizard laughed. "I can stop you feeling nauseous, you know. I must admit I'm beginning to feel genuinely sorry for you."

Evie froze for a moment. She looked up at Julian very, very slowly. "You could have stopped me feeling like this and you're only mentioning it *now*?"

He shrugged. "You're the one who wanted to experience the world. I figured that meant even the bad stuff."

"I'd have been more than happy to skip over sea sickness!"

"You might not have been affected by it, though," Julian reasoned. "There's no point wasting magic until I know it's needed."

Evie glared at him. "It. *Is*. Needed."

Julian laughed once more, then splayed his fingertips across her forehead. "You might have been alright had you not pigged out at lunch," he murmured, but upon seeing Evie grit her teeth he grew silent.

A few seconds later and Julian's magic had snaked its way through Evie's entire body, easing her nausea, relaxing the spasms in her stomach and eliminating the pain in her skull. She became aware that he had also woven magic into her hair, though it wasn't long enough to warrant needing it for practicality's sake.

Show off, was all Evie thought as she felt the braids Julian enchanted her hair into forming. When he removed his fingers Evie closed her eyes and breathed deeply.

When she opened them she felt completely fine, all traces of her previous sickness gone.

"Thank you," she muttered, "though I'd say this was all your fault in the first place, Julian."

He rolled his eyes before planting a kiss on her forehead. "At least now you know what sea sickness feels like, so you need never experience it again."

"Wonderful. I think I need something to eat." The subsequent rumble from Evie's stomach backed up her claim.

Julian smiled as he stood up and stretched. "I guess we better head below deck, then."

The two of them crossed the deck towards the stairs, Evie stumbling a little on her feet as she fought to regain her balance, when she became aware of an oddly familiar couple standing by the bow of the ship.

She frowned. "Julian, aren't they the ones who were watching us in that town, back when you were taking me to Willow?"

"We are indeed!" called the woman by the bow, which

caught both Evie and Julian by surprise. She turned her head, lustrous hair shining in the sunlight, and smiled at them. "My name's Scarlett Duke. Won't you join us for a while?"

Evie raised an uncertain eyebrow at Julian. "Should we...?"

"You were the one who wanted to eat."

"I think I can hold off for a few minutes for curiosity's sake."

Julian made a non-committal noise in the back of his throat, slipped an arm around Evie's waist to stop her from stumbling against the rolling waves beneath them, then led her over to where Scarlett and her mysterious companion were waiting.

This close up Evie could see that the woman was even more beautiful than she'd thought the first time she'd seen her. Scarlett's blue eyes were rich and dark against her pale skin, and her hair was wound over one shoulder in a thick, heavy braid all the way to her waist.

It won't be long until my hair is longer than that again, Evie thought as she fingered the ends of her own hair.

Scarlett's lips quirked in amusement. "Your hair is certainly much shorter than it was last time I saw you, Princess Genevieve."

Evie took half a step away from her, discomfited. "How do you know who I am?"

Scarlett inclined her head towards the man standing beside her, who was looking out towards the horizon. "Adrian worked it out. Well, he used magic to work it out, which isn't the same as using your brain, so –"

"Charming," the man named Adrian interrupted, casting a sidelong glance at Evie in the process. His amber

691

eyes were alarming to behold at such close-range; Julian's arm tightened around Evie.

"You're a magician," Julian said, narrowing his eyes at Adrian. "I should have known."

"And you're a wizard, going by the princess' hair," Adrian replied. "Impressive work, though I'm loathe to admit it."

Scarlett clucked her tongue. "That wasn't very nice, Adrian."

"Wizards are always full of themselves," he countered, as if a very powerful wizard who could most certainly burn him to ashes if he was offended by such a comment wasn't standing right in front of him. "They're born with the smallest affinity for magic and they think they're so much better than –"

"Most of us *are* better at our craft than you, magician," Julian said. "That's the point of being born into it. Talent for a subject very rarely trumps a natural-born magic-user."

Evie pulled away from Julian, confused. "Didn't you once tell me that the line between the two was getting blurred, and soon there would be no need for two separate terms...?"

Adrian laughed even as Julian ran an exasperated hand over his face. "Is that so, wizard?" he asked. "Are we not so dissimilar, after all?"

Julian glared at him. "I'd like to see *you* weave an enchantment like the one in Evie's hair."

"Oh, I'd never be able to do it," Adrian replied without a shred of disappointment. "My expertise lies in curses."

"Of course it does."

"And what is that supposed to mean?"

"It means," Scarlett interrupted, holding an arm out in front of Adrian to push him back just as Evie did the same to Julian, "that the two of you are very clearly talented men, and there's no use getting into a fight to see who's better with magic than the other."

"Especially not when I know at least one of you could set the entire ship on fire," Evie muttered, digging her fingernails into Julian's arm when he still didn't back down. His eyes were beginning to glow. "I'd rather that didn't happen."

Julian glanced at her, then at Scarlett and Adrian, then back to Evie. He took a few steps back and shook his head. "You're right. Miss Duke, my apologies. I didn't mean to lose my temper."

Evie frowned. "Do *I* not get an apology?"

Julian bent down until his lips were by her ear. "I'll apologise to you later," he murmured, in a tone that suggested very few words were likely to be spoken during said apology. Evie's cheeks flushed slightly at the insinuation.

Adrian bowed his head politely. "I'm sorry, Princess Genevieve. It's very unbecoming of me to act in such a manner. I should know better."

Scarlett chuckled. "Yes, you should. I haven't seen you this competitive since Sam asked me to marry him."

"That was justified!"

"Is that so?"

Evie stared at the two of them in wonder. "The two of you are...interesting," she blurted out loud, without thinking about how the statement actually sounded.

Adrian raised an eyebrow; a scar ran through it,

splitting it in two. "Is that an insult, or a compliment?"

"Compliment, of course!" Evie insisted, though out of the corner of her eye she saw Julian mouth the word *insult* very clearly. She elbowed him in the ribs before returning her attention to Scarlett and Adrian. "Where are you from?"

"Germany," Scarlett said. "We're your next door neighbours, as it were."

"I've never been there before," Evie admitted, "though you have, haven't you, Julian?"

"Once. It's pretty enough, I suppose."

Evie had to fight the urge to shout at him. She'd never seen Julian so disgruntled by a human being that wasn't her uncle before.

Scarlett ignored the back-handed compliment. "Where are the two of you headed now? We're visiting London for the time being."

"Scotland," Julian answered. The hint of a smile played across his lips – he was looking forward to reaching the country just as much as Evie herself was. "We're on the hunt for a fox."

"I take it this is no ordinary fox," Adrian murmured, cocking his head to one side in interest. "I've avoided the fair folk myself, given their propensity to turn people into animals."

Scarlett laughed before kissing him on the cheek. "You have so much experience in that area, though. You'd probably thrive in Scotland."

"Perhaps...if wolves hadn't become extinct there last century."

When Evie's stomach rumbled insistently everyone looked at her. She flushed with embarrassment. "Sorry," she mumbled, staring at the floor, "I might be a little hungry."

"Well how about we all head below deck for something to eat?" Scarlett suggested, much to the horror of both Adrian and Julian. She moved forward and linked an arm with Evie. "Or the two of us could go and leave these sorry men to fend for themselves. I'm fascinated to know your story, Princess Genevieve."

"Call me Evie," she replied, giggling when she realised the men in question were watching them walk away with shocked expressions upon both their faces. "Though I must admit I think Adrian and your story seems far more interesting than my own."

"I suppose it might be, but it's a story I know, whereas I don't know yours."

"I guess that means both our stories may be just as interesting as the other."

Scarlett beamed. "Exactly."

They barely made it to the stairs before Julian and Adrian caught up with them. "Don't you dare leave me with him, Evie," Julian muttered under his breath when he reached her side. "Otherwise I might burn his other eyebrow clean off."

"I heard that, wizard," Adrian said.

"Good."

"*Julian!*"

Evie and Scarlett both let out equally resigned sighs, then laughed at each other. It was clear from Julian's face that he didn't understand how the two of them could have become friends quite as quickly as they had done.

"I think the rest of the journey should pass rather pleasantly," Scarlett said as they all sat down at a large table. Julian sat as far from Adrian as was physically possible, much to Evie's amusement. Scarlett wound her arm through Adrian's just as he nuzzled his nose against her face.

"Yes, so very pleasant," Adrian said, firing a glare at Julian before returning his attention to Scarlett.

Evie interlaced her hand with Julian's below the table, then leant her head against his shoulder. "Consider this part of your apology," she murmured, "though I still expect one in private."

Julian kissed her hair and smiled softly.

"I guess, if it's for you, I can deal with that."

PRINCE OF FOXES EXCERPT

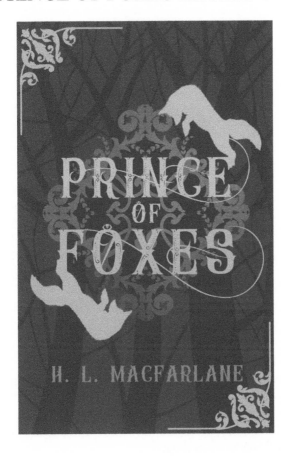

PROLOGUE

Names were important. They always had been, from the moment man first developed language to understand the world around him. They were important, but the intense popularity of a particular playwright's work in the South of England suggested otherwise. When hoards of Londoners leeched into Scotland in search of good hunting grounds, golfing estates and other leisurely pursuits that they could not find at home Sorcha became unwillingly familiar with Shakespeare's plays.

But Sorcha and her family knew better than to take his words to heart. A rose by any other name would *not* smell as sweet, for once it lost its name it was no longer a rose as one knew it. And names weren't important simply for their superficial usage in eliminating the need to wordlessly point at things.

All her life Sorcha had the rules of names drilled into her. Do not call a person by their first name if you are not familiar with them. Take your husband's surname when you marry and leave your own behind. Bear a son to pass on his father's name. Give your children names full of luck, strength, wisdom and beauty, for they would need such traits when they grew up.

But these mantras all paled in comparison to the one rule the infuriating English tourists liked to laugh at most. They would not laugh so loudly if they knew the truth. Nobody who knew the truth laughed about it. This rule was the very reason Sorcha often went by Clara, an anglicised version of her first name that she despised but eagerly used nonetheless.

She had witnessed first-hand, as a child, what happened when you did not follow this one, most important rule. You disappeared – sometimes forever, sometimes for no time at all – but if you returned you were changed, and almost never in a good way. Sorcha had seen calm and even-tempered folk go mad, and the loudest, brashest of her father's friends retreat into their own minds, never to speak another word.

Tourists often thought the locals were crazy when they came to visit the little town of Darach. It was nestled between large, sweeping forests and breathtakingly beautiful lochs, so it was a popular place to visit away from the hustle and bustle of Glasgow and Edinburgh. Locals warned them against conversing with anyone they might meet roaming beneath the trees, or wandering along the shores of the lochs, especially at twilight. The tourists, without fail, never heeded their advice.

So they disappeared, in one fashion or another, and they only had themselves to blame. They had been warned, after all, and they didn't listen.

Never, ever give your real name to a faerie.

CHAPTER ONE

Lachlan

Today was the queen's funeral and Lachlan, her only child and heir to the throne, was deliberately avoiding the ceremony.

His mother would understand, he was sure. He'd never been one for mournful occasions; most of the Seelie folk weren't. Their lives were long enough to be considered immortal by the humans who largely lived, unknowing and unseeing, beside them. If Lachlan allowed himself to be truly sad he'd spend centuries feeling that way.

It was the last thing he wanted.

So Lachlan was currently whiling away his morning

following a human girl who was collecting early autumn brambles on the outskirts of the forest. She lived in Darach, the closest human settlement to the central realm of the Scots fair folk. The people who lived there were, in general, respectful and wary of Lachlan and his kind. They saw what members of the Seelie Court could do fairly regularly, after all. The rest of the British Isles was another story entirely, though it hadn't always been that way.

Everybody in the forest knew things were changing.

The advancements made in human medicine, and human technology, and human ingenuity, meant that humans were beginning to forget what it felt like to fear 'otherness'. They believed themselves above tales of faeries, and magic in general, though Lachlan knew there were humans capable of magic, too.

Not here, though, he thought, creeping from one tall bow of an oak tree to another to trail silently after the girl. She was happily eating one bramble for every two she placed in her basket, seemingly without a care in the world. *Not on this island. Not for centuries.* Lachlan knew this was largely because his mother, Queen Evanna – as well as King Eirian of the Unseelie Court far down south, in England – spirited all such magically-inclined British children away to the faerie realm, to live for all intents and purposes as faeries themselves.

That's certainly better than being an ordinary human, especially now, when they've forgotten about us.

A stiff breeze tearing through the oak tree caused Lachlan's solitary earring to jingle like a bell. Adorned with delicate chains and tiny sapphires, and spanning the entire length of his long, pointed ear as a cuff of beaten silver, the beautiful piece of jewellery had been a gift from his mother from a time long since passed. Back then Lachlan had been enamoured with the blue-eyed faerie, Ailith, and had been convinced the two of them would marry. The earring was ultimately meant as a gift for Ailith, he'd decided. His mother would never be so direct as to give it to Lachlan's beloved herself. It wasn't in her nature.

But then Queen Evanna had married the half-Unseelie faerie, Innis, who was the Unseelie king's brother. He had himself a grown son, Fergus, who came with his father to live in the Seelie realm. The two were silver where Lachlan and his mother were gold, and Ailith had become betrothed to his new-found stepbrother instead of him.

So Lachlan lost his love and, now, he'd lost his mother. The earring was all he had left of both.

I should go to the funeral, he decided, turning from the girl as he did so. *I am to be king, after all. I should –*

Lachlan paused. He could hear something. More chime-like than his earring in the wind, and clearer than the sound of the nearby stream flowing over centuries-smooth stone.

The human girl was singing.

"*The winds were laid, the air was still,*

The stars they shot alang the sky;

The fox was howling on the hill,

And the distant echoing glens reply."

Lachlan was enamoured with the sound of her voice. The words were Burns; the melody unfamiliar. He thought perhaps she'd invented the tune herself and, if so, she was a talented girl indeed. He peered through the yellowing leaves of the oak tree, intent on seeing what the human with the lovely voice truly looked like.

She was not so much a girl as a young woman – perhaps not quite twenty – though since Lachlan himself had lived for almost five times that long she was, for all intents and purposes, still simply a girl. Her skin was pale and lightly freckled, though her cheeks held onto some colour from the fast-fading summer. Her hair was a little darker than the oak trunk Lachlan was currently leaning against. It flashed like deep copper when it caught the sunlight and hung long and wild down her back, which was a sight rarely seen on a young, human woman.

A cream dress fell to her ankles and sat low on her shoulders. Small leather boots, made for wandering through forests and across meadows, were laced across her feet. A cloak of pine-coloured fabric was slung over the handle of her almost-full wicker basket. *Well-made clothes,* he concluded, *but nothing elaborate or expensive. Just an ordinary girl.* She dithered over the correct words of the next verse of her Burns poem as Lachlan merrily watched on. *Fair to look at, for a human. But it is her voice that is special. Special enough to ask her name.*

He delighted over thinking how his stepfather and stepbrother would react when he brought back a human girl, enchanted to sing for him until the end of time. *I wonder what Ailith would think. Would she be jealous? Would she mourn for the loss of my attention?*

Lachlan was excited to find out.

He stretched his arms above his head, causing his earring to jingle once more. Below him the girl stilled. She stopped singing, dark brows knitted together in confusion.

"Is somebody there?" she asked, carefully placing her basket down by her feet as she spoke.

"You have a lovely voice," Lachlan announced. He was satisfied to see the girl jump in fright, eyes swinging wildly around before she realised the voice she'd heard came from above. When she spied Lachlan standing high up on the boughs of the oak tree she gasped.

"You are – it is early to see one of your kind so far out of the forest," she said. She struggled to maintain a blank face, to appear as if she wasn't surprised in the slightest to see a faerie standing in a tree.

Lachlan laughed. "I suppose it is. Today is a special occasion; we are all very much wide awake."

The girl seemed to hesitate before responding. Lachlan figured she was trying to decide if it was wise to continue such a conversation with him. "What occasion would be so special to have you all awake before noon?"

"The funeral of the queen. My mother."

"Oh."

That was all she said. Lachan had to wonder what kind of reaction he'd expected. Certainly not sympathy; he had no use for such a thing.

"You are not at the funeral?" the girl asked after a moment of silence. "If you are her son –"

"I shall get there eventually," Lachlan replied. He sat down upon the branch he'd been standing on. "Tell me your name, lass. Your voice is too beautiful to not have a name attached to it."

To his surprise, she smiled. "I do not think so, Prince of Faeries."

Clever girl.

"You wound me," he said, holding a hand over his heart in mock dismay. "An admirer asks only for a name and you will not oblige his lowly request? How cruel you are."

"How about a name for a name, then?" she suggested. "That seems fair."

Lachlan nodded in agreement. The girl could do nothing with his name. She was only human.

"Lachlan," he replied, with a flourish of his hand in place of a bow. "And you?"

"Clara."

"A pretty name for a pretty girl. Is there a family name to go with –"

"I am not so much a fool as to give you my family name," Clara said, "and I think you know that."

He found himself grinning. "Maybe so. Come closer, Clara. You stand so far away."

He was somewhat surprised when she boldly took a step forwards, half expecting her to decide enough was enough and run away.

Even careful humans give in to the allure of faeries, he thought, altogether rather smug. *It won't be long until I have Clara's full name.*

When Clara took another step towards him Lachlan noticed that her eyes were green.

No, blue, he decided. *No, they're –*

"Your eyes," he said, deftly swinging backwards until he was hanging upside down from the branch. Lachlan's face was now level with Clara's, though the wrong way round. She took a shocked half-step backwards at their new-found proximity. "They are strange."

"I do not think my eyes are as strange as yours, Lachlan of the forest," she replied. "Yours are gold."

"Not so uncommon a colour for a Seelie around these parts. Yours, on the other hand...we do not see mismatched eyes often."

Clara shrugged. "One blue, one green. They are not

707

so odd. Most folk hardly notice a difference unless they stand close to me."

"Do many human boys get as close to you as I am now?" Lachlan asked, a smile playing across his lips at the blush that crossed Clara's cheeks.

She looked away. "I cannot say they have."

"Finish your song for me, Clara. I'll give you something in return."

"And what would that be?" she asked, glancing back at Lachlan. Her suspicion over the sudden change of subject was written plainly on her face.

He swung himself forwards just a little until their lips were almost touching. "A kiss, of course."

"That's...and what if I do not want that?"

"Then I guess I leave with a broken heart."

Clara's eyebrow quirked.

"You do not believe me," he complained.

"With good reason."

"You really are a cruel girl."

The two stared at each other for a while, though Lachlan was beginning to grow dizzy from his upside down view. But just as he was about to right himself, Clara took a deep breath and began to sing once more.

There were four verses left of her Burns poem, about a ghost who appeared in front of the poet to lament over what happened to him in the final years of his life, and it was both haunting and splendid to hear. Lachlan mourned for the spirit as if it had been real, and wished there was more to the poem for Clara to sing.

But eventually she sang her last, keening note, leaving only the sound of the wind to break their silence. When

Lachlan crept a hand behind her neck and urged her lips to his Clara fluttered her eyes closed. The kiss was soft and chaste - hardly a kiss at all - but just as it ended Lachlan bit her lip.

The promise of something more, if Clara wanted it.

The girl was breathless and rosy-cheeked when Lachlan pulled away. A rush ran through him at the sight of her.

"Tell me your last name," he breathed, the order barely audible over the breeze ruffling Clara's hair around her face.

She opened her eyes, parting her lips as if to speak and -

The sound of bells clamoured through the air.

Clara took a step away from Lachlan immediately, eyes bright and wide and entirely lucid once more.

"I have to go," she said, stumbling backwards to pick up her forgotten basket and cloak before darting away from the forest.

No matter, Lachlan thought, as he dropped from the branch to the forest floor. *I shall see her again. I will have her name next time.*

But he was disappointed.

Now he had to go to his mother's funeral alone, with no entertainment to distract him from his grief when evening came.

CHAPTER TWO

Sorcha

"Have I lost my senses entirely?" Sorcha cried. "Singing for a faerie. Their *prince*! I must have gone mad!"

She passed Old Man MacPherson's farm in a haze of scurried footsteps, dropping brambles from the basket clutched to her chest as she went. The man's son was up on the roof; he waved to Sorcha when he noticed her, and she nodded in response. He was replacing a slate tile which had come loose and smashed upon the ground in the middle of the night. Soon the mild weather would turn and the farm would need to be as watertight as possible to avoid the coming rain, which arrived hand-in-hand with the darkest months of the year.

But Sorcha was happy with the promise of wet, cold days and wetter, colder nights. For though the creeping autumn weather and the inevitable winter that followed caused damage to roofs and fields and sometimes livestock, it also signalled a blessed end to the slew of tourists that had bombarded the tiny town of Darach since April.

Good riddance to them, Sorcha thought with vicious pleasure. *Let them return to their cities and their pollution.*

She paused by the loch-side to pick up a pair of empty glass bottles and a filthy handkerchief. Sorcha scowled; only a city-dweller would leave behind such a mess on the shore of the most beautiful loch in the country.

I'm biased, of course, she thought. *All lochs are beautiful. But Loch Lomond is...special.*

Sorcha skipped a stone across the water's surface, watching as it leapt once, twice, three times. On its fourth skip it fell beneath the dark, shimmering surface of the loch, never to be seen again.

She rearranged the basket and cloak in her arms to make room for the rubbish she had picked up, tossing the offending items into a large receptacle behind her parents' house when she finally reached it. The house was handsome to look at, and finer made than the nearby farmhouses. Red stone and slate, with painted windowsills and a sweeping garden that circled all around the building. Sorcha loved it; it had been in the Darrow family for as long as anybody could remember. Now it was almost all that remained of their wealth.

Generations ago the Darrows had been far richer than they were now. They were the landlords for the area, owning the very ground Sorcha walked upon right up through the forest and along the shore of the loch. The farmers in the area were all tenants of her father, and nobody could so much as cut down a tree or keep a boat on the loch without his permission.

But Sorcha's father was a kind man, and an understanding one. Despite outside pressure from the cities and an increased cost of living, he never raised the rent for the people who lived on his land. It was part of the reason the Darrows were much poorer now, but Sorcha was happy for it.

She could never forgive her father if he sold his principles for a more comfortable life.

Though I have to wonder why he's agreed to meet this Londoner for the third time in as many months, Sorcha thought as she crept into the kitchen as quietly as possible. She dumped her basket of brambles on the table, hung up her cloak, then used the large window overlooking the back garden to check her reflection. She looked just about as windswept and bothered as she felt, with wild hair, red cheeks and a dishevelled dress.

Sorcha knew she really should have put her hair up before going outside. She knew this, but it hadn't stopped her keeping it long and loose down her back instead. She ran her fingers through it in an attempt to tidy her appearance, wincing when she met tangle after tangle. She smoothed out her dress, splashed cold water on her face from a basin by the sink, then left the kitchen to walk down the corridor towards the parlour room.

She could hear both of her parents inside, as well as the stranger they had insisted upon Sorcha meeting today. Of course she hadn't wanted to; she had no interest in Londoners. But she was an obedient daughter, and she knew she was lucky to have parents that had not once pressured her into marriage, though Sorcha would turn

712

twenty at the end of the month. She could be polite and lovely for this *one* Englishman.

The very notion of being lovely caused Sorcha's thoughts to return to Lachlan. It had seemed like a dream, to meet the Prince of Faeries. Sorcha had met her share of his kind before, though they tended to slip from her vision just as easily as she had laid eyes on them. On the occasions they had spoken to her they quickly gave up trying to charm her once they realised she would not give them her name.

I nearly gave it to Lachlan, though. This wasn't quite true, of course; Sorcha hadn't given him her real first name. Had she told him her surname was Darrow he could have done nothing with it. And, even then, if he knew her first name was Sorcha, he did not know her middle name.

Her father was a smart man. He had raised a clever daughter. Sorcha would not be caught be a faerie so easily.

I wanted to be caught even just for a moment, she thought despite herself, dwelling longingly on the memory of Lachlan's warm, golden skin and molten eyes. Even his braided, bronze-coloured hair had seemed to be spun of gold when the sunlight shone upon it. The silver cuff adorning one of his inhumanly pointed ears had seemed mismatched against it all, though the sapphire-encrusted piece of jewellery had been so beautiful Sorcha thought she might well have died to possess it for but a minute.

She brought her fingertips up to her lips, committing the feeling of Lachlan's mouth on hers to memory. *He kissed me like it was nothing at all. Does he go around kissing every young woman he sees whilst hanging upside down from a tree?*

It struck Sorcha that she had not taken notice of

Lachlan's clothes even once, though he had said he was going to a funeral. *Were they black?* she wondered. *I do not think so. Would faeries wear black to a funeral? What are faerie funerals like? And this was their queen. Lachlan's mother. He did not seem all that sad. Just how did she –*

"Sorcha Margaret Darrow, if you do not get in here this instant I will lock you in your room until the end of the year!"

Sorcha flinched at her mother's voice reverberating through the door. The woman had the uncanny ability to know when her daughter was lurking where she shouldn't be – which was often – and was quick to scold her. She sighed heavily, forced all thoughts of Lachlan away for another time, then fixed a smile to her face before swinging the door open.

"I'm sorry, mama, I was cleaning up by the loch-side," Sorcha apologised. Her mother clucked her tongue.

"It is not befitting a young lady to go around cleaning up filthy bottles and – look at your hair! That is no way to appear in front of a guest! Go and –"

"It's quite alright, Mrs Darrow," interrupted a low, gravelly voice. Though it was largely smoothed over with the typical accent of upper-class London that Sorcha had come to resentfully recognise from tourists, there still existed a trace of local, melodic Scots that she liked the sound of.

Out of the corner of her eye she saw her father, a mild expression on his face that suggested he did not care what Sorcha looked like. He was simply glad she had shown up at all. He inclined towards his guest with a hand.

"Sorcha, this is Murdoch Buchanan, a gentleman who grew up not ten miles from here before moving down to

London when he was twelve. Mr Buchanan, this is my lovely daughter, Sorcha."

She withheld a wince; Sorcha did not like her real name revealed to anyone but her closest friends, despite the fact her mother thought this silly. But the lessons her father had instilled in her from a young age – to be wary of strangers, for they might be faeries – very much filtered into her attitude towards tourists. And this man, Murdoch Buchanan, had already heard her full name.

Thanks, mama, she thought dully as she turned towards the man with an apologetic smile on her face, curtsying as she did so. "I am truly sorry for my appearance and my lateness, Mr Buchanan. It was an accident."

"No need to be sorry for wishing to keep the loch-side clean. It is a truly beautiful place; those responsible for sullying it ought to be ashamed of themselves."

Maybe this Londoner isn't so bad. He was born around here, after all. He might not be detestable.

Sorcha allowed herself to look at the man properly for the first time. Murdoch was tall and dressed impeccably in a white shirt, dark grey tail coat with matching waistcoat, ebony trousers and shiny leather boots. His black hair grew in loose curls around his head, and his face was clean-shaven. His eyes were dark.

Not just dark, Sorcha thought. *They are as black as his hair.* They were the most striking thing about him, though Murdoch was, by anyone's measure, a very handsome man.

His impossibly dark eyes watched Sorcha intently as she watched him. She did not know what to say; she had the most unsettling feeling that something bad was about to happen.

715

"Mr Buchanan is going to be staying with us for a few days, Sorcha," her mother said, dragging her daughter out of her own head.

"Why?" she asked, though she knew she could have worded the question a little more politely.

"You know things have been getting harder for us around here," her father said. "Something has to be done to preserve the area so that nothing bad can happen to us, or to the farmers. I don't want what's happening in the Highlands to occur here."

Sorcha nodded. Everyone knew about the Clearances. An icy chill ran down her spine.

"What does this have to do with Mr Buchanan staying with us?"

It was her mother who answered. She sounded excited, which was a bad thing. Margaret Darrow being excited was a very, very bad thing indeed. "Why, Sorcha," she began, standing up to envelop her daughter's hands within her own. She smiled brightly. "You are going to marry him!"

Sorcha's mind went blank. She could only stare at Murdoch Buchanan in horror. He was a Londoner. A stranger. She did not know him, nor did he know her.

Yet he had already agreed to marry her.

She took a step towards the door, then another and another.

"No," was all she said, before fleeing for her bedroom.

No, no, no.

CHAPTER THREE

Lachlan

"Lachlan, where have you been?! The ceremony ended five minutes ago!"

Ailith came rushing towards Lachlan just as he pushed open the heavy, ornate wooden doors to his bedroom, her breathtaking face full of genuine concern. When she touched his shoulder he shrugged her off.

"I consider it a blessing to have missed it," he told her. "We both know my mother herself hated funerals. Who do you think I learned to loathe them from? But she looked forward to the feasts that followed them and I'm here for that, at least."

"You didn't answer my question."

Lachlan rolled his eyes, pouring a goblet of wine from the bronze pitcher on his bedside table when he reached it. Wordlessly he handed it over to Ailith before pouring another for himself. "Here and there," he finally replied. "Nowhere of consequence."

"Lachlan –"

"The outskirts of the forest. I sat in a tree and watched the world go by. Are you happy now?"

Lachlan didn't look at the beautiful faerie as he lied. Well, it wasn't exactly a lie. Faeries could never truly lie. The human girl Clara *was* part of the world, but he hadn't simply watched her. That was a secret he had no desire whatsoever to divulge to Ailith.

I want Clara's full name, he thought longingly. *I want it now.*

"You don't seem affected by Queen Evanna's death at all."

Lachlan was struck by the sadness in Ailith's voice. Most faeries didn't wear such negative emotions on their sleeves for everyone else to see; the blue-eyed creature in front of him was different. Perhaps it was because her father died almost a decade ago, and she was yet to get over it. Perhaps she was just as emotionally impulsive as humans were. Perhaps it was something else entirely.

Either way, it was one of the reasons Lachlan had loved her so. Now, because he couldn't have her, it was one of the things he could stand least of all.

"I shall deal with my grief however I like," he said before swallowing a large mouthful of wine. He glanced at Ailith out of the corner of his eye. "Shouldn't you be consoling my beloved stepbrother, anyway? Or your future father-in-law? I'm quite certain they are both missing your company."

Ailith grimaced. "Lachlan, don't talk about your family like –"

"Those two? My family? Don't make me laugh, Ailith. Innis and Fergus are no more my family than you are."

"You don't mean that."

Lachlan lay back onto his bed, careful not to spill his wine as he did so. Ailith *wasn't* his family, but it was a cruel thing to say nonetheless. She stood in front of him, close to tears, though even in her misery she was beautiful. It was as if her pale, elegant face had been carved to display such an emotion.

His own expression softened. "You're right. I apologise. You're all I have left in the world. You know that. I'm merely...handling my grief in my own way. I didn't mean to snap at you."

Being polite was the only way the two of them managed to deal with their intimate past, though ultimately all that meant was that they ignored how they'd felt towards each other before Fergus stole her away. But that suited Lachlan just fine.

Give it a few decades and I'll forget I loved Ailith altogether.

"Speaking of Fergus," Ailith said, though her tone suggested she was bringing him up reluctantly, "he and his father were looking for you. There's a lot that needs prepared before your coronation ceremony."

He made a face. "It is still two weeks away. If they wish to speak to me they can find me themselves."

"Lachlan –"

"Alright, alright," he sighed, swinging up from his bed and waltzing over to the large, gilded mirror hanging on the opposite wall. Lachlan fiddled with his hair, inspecting the braid that crawled across the left-hand side of his scalp. After hours spent climbing in the forest he knew he could do with unravelling the braid to comb it out, but he resisted. He liked having his hair styled this way; it ensured his mother's earring was on full display. Despite this, Ailith seemed determined never to notice it, as if she knew exactly for whom it had been intended.

In the mirror Lachlan could see Ailith walking towards the door. She sighed when she saw Lachlan watching her. "You do not have to be king if you don't want to, remember."

Lachlan scoffed at such a notion. "Where did you get that idea? If I'm not king then my half-Unseelie step family will have the crown. That's almost as bad as allowing the creatures lurking deep in the lochs to take over our court."

Ailith laughed softly into her hand. "That your mother named you after the thing you so hate never fails to amuse me."

"You and me both. Though it's not the *lochs* I mislike," Lachlan corrected, fitting on a chestnut-coloured tailcoat over his loose white shirt and dark breeches. "Merely what lives in them. You know every dark thing in there hates Seelies."

"And we hate them right back," Ailith said. "Perhaps it's time to reassess such feelings. After all, both the forests and the lochs are having to fight humans nowadays."

Lachlan said nothing. He knew Ailith was right, of course, but that didn't mean he wanted to let her know she was right. Humans really were becoming a growing problem with every tree they felled, every badly-extinguished bonfire they left behind and every broken bottle abandoned upon the forest floor.

"Come find me after you've spoken with your stepfather," Ailith murmured when Lachlan joined her by the door, brushing her elegant fingers along his sleeve before leaving his room. He touched the fabric where her fingers had been.

Another few decades, Lachlan reminded himself. *Another twenty or thirty years and Ailith will not matter to me at all.* And so Lachlan left his room, once more alone, to venture down the palace corridor with his wine goblet in hand. He veered in the general direction of his mother's old chambers, where Lachlan knew he'd find both his stepfather and stepbrother.

The building wasn't so much a traditional palace as it was a network of connected rooms carved into the very forest itself. The fair folk were a vain and prideful race, so the labyrinthine home of the royal family was painfully exquisite to look upon. The very walls were aglow, lighting the way to Queen Evanna's chambers in soft, golden tones the colour of Lachlan's skin. The tunnels and hallways were perfectly curved; not a single sharp angle existed anywhere within the palace. Some days Lachlan adored this – it was beautiful, after all. Other days he detested it, for there was nowhere to hide.

Nowhere to cry, or scream, or keep secrets from one another.

"Lachlan, there you are!"

Lachlan resisted grimacing at Innis' voice. It wasn't that he hated the faerie – he hardly bothered to hate any faeries at all – but rather that Lachlan simply did not have the patience to deal with him. Innis and his son were always scheming and plotting, their silver skin and hair stark and obvious against the gold of the Seelie Court. When his mother first announced her engagement to Innis, Lachlan had been convinced the marriage was somehow a scheme concocted by the faerie himself.

But my mother would never have been so stupid to fall for an Unseelie plot. Lachlan knew this. He *knew* it, but it didn't stop him indulging in his paranoid beliefs, either.

"We didn't see you at the funeral," Fergus said, smiling slightly as he patted Lachlan on the shoulder. Lachlan hated the way he tried to act brotherly towards him. It was all a lie, that much he was sure of. After all, had Fergus ever felt even vaguely brotherly towards him then he'd never have orchestrated a betrothal to Ailith.

Lachlan was still unsure how the faerie had managed it. Ailith certainly never told him.

Perhaps she was enamoured by his silver countenance, Lachlan supposed. *It certainly looks better against her fair skin than mine does.*

"I was grieving in my own way," Lachlan replied, giving both faeries the same answer he'd given Ailith.

Innis nodded in understanding. "Whatever you need to do, I support you. We all do. In two weeks you are meant to be king, after all."

Lachlan said nothing. Fergus' hand was still on his shoulder; when he tried to shove it off his stepbrother instead moved his hand to the silver cuff on Lachlan's ear.

"This was meant for Ailith, wasn't it?" he asked, removing the piece of jewellery before Lachlan had a chance to protest. "It truly would look beautiful on her. Have you ever considered giving it to her as a betrothal gift? Or a wedding gift, perhaps?"

"I'd rather keep it to remember my mother by," Lachlan replied, on-edge from the drastic change in subject. Something was off. Wrong. He didn't know what.

Fergus held the earring up to the light, his mercurial eyes transfixed by the way the sapphires shone. "A shame," he muttered. "It really doesn't suit you. Neither does being king."

Lachlan froze. A terrible shiver ran down his spine. "Excuse me?"

"Now, now, Fergus," his father said, shaking his head in disapproval, "you can afford to be more delicate with the boy. He just lost his mother."

Lachlan bristled. "I'm not a *boy*. Fergus is barely two decades older than me."

"And it shows." Innis' face grew stony, all previous sympathies gone. "Lachlan, you must know that you are not fit to rule. You despise the Unseelie Court –"

"I do not *despise* it," Lachlan interrupted. He made to snatch his mother's earring from Fergus but he easily glided out of the way. "I merely disagree with the Unseelie King's brother being married to the Seelie Queen."

"Come now. My mother was Seelie, or have you forgotten? I spent most of my life growing up off the coast of your own land! I have always been closer to your kind than I have been to Eirian or our father."

"And that's beside the point, anyway," Fergus added on, smiling widely at Lachlan to show his vaguely pointed teeth. "Ailith and I are to be married before the month's end. The two of us would make far greater rulers than you, Lachlan."

And then it clicked. Fergus was marrying Ailith because the court adored her. He and Innis had been plotting his ascension to the throne for months.

"You killed my mother," Lachlan said, staring at Innis with all the hatred he could muster.

But the faerie shook his head. "That I did not do, nor did my son. It was Evanna's time. That Fergus would be better on the throne than you has nothing to do with your mother's death."

"So you mean to kill *me,* instead."

His stepfather shook his head once more. "Others would ask what had happened to you, and we could not lie about it. No, Lachlan, you must disappear."

He bristled at the suggestion. "As if I would leave of my own volition!"

"Oh, that we already knew and had prepared for," Fergus said. He wrapped his hand around the silver earring; Lachlan clutched at his stomach and dropped his wine glass, sending it clattering to the floor. He watched with unfocused eyes as the dark liquid within it spilled across the cream-and-gold carpet, soaking the fibres as if it were blood. Lachlan fell to his knees, then collapsed on his side; the shiver from before had become full-on convulsions, rending his insides into tiny little pieces.

He glared at the two of them, though his eyes were watering and he could barely see. "What have you - what is this? What have you done to me?!"

"Just a little magic," Fergus said, grinning. "You know, I think I'll give Ailith your earring myself. I'll tell her it's all you left behind before you ran from the forest to escape your mother's shadow. She would believe that. I think she'd even cry for you. Would you like that, Lachlan? To know she's crying for you?"

"I -" But Lachlan couldn't verbalise the rest of his sentence through the pain. His body was changing - shimmering and twisting and cracking into something else entirely. When the convulsions finally stopped Lachlan felt altogether much smaller that he had been before, and

Innis and Fergus much taller by comparison.

Innis stared down at him with a grave expression on his face. "I'd suggest you run while you can. Nobody will ask if we killed a stray fox, so we will not need to lie about it."

"A fox?!" Lachlan cried out, though the words were strange in his new throat. He bolted for the closest mirror, dismayed beyond reckoning to see russet fur, dark, pointed ears and a white underbelly. His eyes were small and beady, though his golden irises remained. There were no two ways about it; his new appearance wasn't a glamour or an illusion or a trick of the light. Lachlan really was a fox. "How did you –"

"You underestimate the power of Unseelie magic, you fool," Fergus sneered. "Now run off or we really will kill you. But who knows? Maybe an owl will do the job for me."

Lachan swung his head from Innis to Fergus then back again, too shocked to feel anger or disgust. But then fear began to creep in – the kind of deep-set instinct all animals had for anything bigger or more predatory than themselves.

He ran.

Lachlan fled the palace, winding through the corridors so quickly that even the spare passers-by who weren't yet at Queen Evanna's funeral feast did not know what to make of him. He ran out through the forest, stumbling over rabbit holes and fallen branches and loose stones until he reached the very outskirts of the trees. And then he ran some more, for good measure.

When finally Lachlan slowed to a halt to fill his lungs with much-needed air he found himself in a garden to the back of a handsome red-stoned house. Though it was by the tree line it was so close to the loch that Lachlan had never ventured near it before. When he saw the shape of a human shifting behind a window he crept closer to see what they looked like, despite the fact that he was a fox and they might throw a rock his way if they saw him.

But then the figure turned to look out the window, and Lachlan felt his heart stop.

It was Clara.

CHAPTER FOUR

Sorcha

"For the last time, Sorcha, open the door!"

"Come on, dove, I know this is a surprise. Just let us explain."

"Explain what?" Sorcha demanded from her position slumped against the door. Her parents had spent the last fifteen minutes attempting to coax her out of her room; she didn't want to budge. "You've never brought up marriage before. Why now? Why so suddenly?"

There was a pause. Sorcha heard her father sigh.

"Please, Sorcha," he said, very quietly. "Let us in. This isn't a conversation to be had shouting through a door with a guest sitting two rooms away."

Sorcha bristled at the reminder. Murdoch Buchanan was indeed a *guest,* not a family friend or a man she had fancied from afar for years. So why did her parents wish for him to marry her? Realising that her curiosity was ultimately getting the better of her Sorcha dolefully got to her feet, unbolted the heavy iron lock on the door and swung it open.

Her mother's angry face greeted her; behind her mother stood her father, who looked resigned. He gave Sorcha a small smile as the two of them trailed into her room, Sorcha closing the door behind them.

"Thank you," he said. He sat on the well-made fir wood rocking chair by the window; like their dining table and the chairs that matched it, the piece of furniture had been carved by Sorcha's great-grandfather. She loved the chair dearly, though it was beginning to creak in protest whenever someone sat upon it.

Her mother fussed for Sorcha to sit on the bed, then located a brush and began untangling the knots in her daughter's hair. Sorcha knew better than to protest, so she sat in dull compliance whilst her mother went to work.

"Why now, then?" Sorcha asked again. "And why... him? Why Mr Buchanan?"

"Do you not like the look of him?" her mother cried, offended on the man's behalf. "He is so handsome, and so gentle and well-spoken! London has been very good to him. And he's *wealthy,* Sorcha –"

"So I am to be bought, then?"

Her father shook his head. "You know it isn't like that, dove. Mr Buchanan is an investor. He informed me that there are many people in the same position as him who are interested in acquiring our land and moving the farmers off it. Mr Buchanan is from here, Sorcha. He doesn't wish for that to happen. But I didn't want him to outright buy our land, either. I want to keep it in the family."

Sorcha rolled her eyes. "That *does* sound like I'm being bought, papa. You won't sell him the land but you'll give him it by selling me to him."

"Don't speak to your father like that!" her mother chastised, dragging the brush through a tangle in Sorcha's hair far harsher than necessary to drive home her complaint. "He is doing the best he can!"

"But what about what's best for me, mama? I don't want to get married! You only wish for me to marry him because you're besotted by every city-dwelling tourist who plagues –"

"Sorcha, don't speak to your mother like that."

She winced; it was rare for both her parents to admonish her in the same conversation. But Sorcha was *angry*; how could she not be? She was to be married to a stranger.

Her father looked out of the window at the dazzling afternoon sun. "Sorcha, my health isn't what it used to be. Everyone knows that. I was always planning to pass over the land to you upon your twenty-first birthday. I would feel much better if you were financially secure and in a position to look after the farmers for many years to come."

"Papa –"

"We will not force you to marry Mr Buchanan," he interrupted, voice firm. He stood up and moved to the door. "But you can at least put in the effort to get to know the man over the next few days. Your union may not be one of love, but it could be. You have to give it a chance. He is a kind one, dove. I would not wish for you to marry

729

him if he was not."

Her father left her room then, leaving Sorcha with her uncharacteristically quiet mother. Though her hair was smooth, shiny and tangle-free once more, her mother was still brushing through it. It was only after several more minutes of silence that she put down the brush and turned Sorcha round to face her.

"Sorcha –"

"I know," her daughter said, though her tone was miserable. "I know papa is right. I will get to know Mr Buchanan, if that is what you both wish."

Her mother smiled approvingly; she stroked the side of Sorcha's face with the back of her hand. "I know you disapprove of city folk, especially Londoners. But remember – I grew up in Edinburgh! And I didn't turn out so bad, did I?"

Sorcha averted her eyes. "Debatable."

"Such a rude daughter!"

"I wasn't aware that honesty was considered rudeness."

The two of them giggled softly. Though Sorcha and her mother were often at each other's throats they still loved each other dearly. She ultimately trusted the older woman's judgement, even if at times she did not like it.

"Come on, then," her mother said, taking hold of Sorcha's hands to pull her up from the bed and out of the room. "Mr Buchanan will be wondering what happened! I do believe that you will rather like him, once you get to know him."

"Again: debatable. But I shall at least try to act civil."

She smiled at the look her mother gave her, and kept that same smile on her face when she was brought back through to the parlour room and left alone with Murdoch.

He was sitting by the large bay window overlooking the loch, and did not notice Sorcha's presence until she nervously sat in the armchair opposite him.

"Miss Darrow," he said, eyebrow raised in surprise when he looked at her. "You brushed your hair."

Sorcha couldn't help but laugh at the comment. She ran her fingers through a lock of it, causing it to shine like burnished copper in the sunlight. "My mother did. I apologise for my reaction earlier. The news of our engagement was...unexpected, to say the least."

The hint of a smirk crossed Murdoch's lips. Sorcha thought he almost looked amused, though it could just as easily have been the man making fun of her.

Don't think like that, she thought. *Be nice. Papa likes him. He can't be that bad.*

She fidgeted with her hands in her lap, fishing for something to say. "You're from close by, then? Where did you grow up? How old are you?"

"Twenty-seven," Murdoch replied. He pointed out through the window towards the northern point of the shimmering loch outside. "I'm from further up the loch shore, where it gets narrow and deep. I used to spend all my days swimming – even when winter was approaching – but that all stopped when I moved to London."

"Why did you move?"

"My mother died, and my father took up a new position at a bank down there. He insisted I learn his trade, so it wasn't all that surprising when I ended up as an investor."

"And now you're looking to, what? Save the loch-side from other Londoners like you?"

Murdoch straightened in his chair, expression serious

as he replied, "I do not think I am as similar to them as you think, Miss Darrow. If I were I'd have simply forced your father off the land, like what is happening in the Highlands as we speak."

Sorcha said nothing. It was a sobering thought, and not one she wished to dwell upon.

She looked at her hands. "So why marry me? That seems like an awful lot of effort to go to just to procure some land."

To her surprise Murdoch laughed, his voice rough and low and very much entertained by Sorcha's take on things. Sorcha still couldn't tell if he was making fun of her, which she did not like at all. "Are you implying that you mean to be difficult, Miss Darrow?" he asked, voice full of mirth. "That you will *be* a lot of effort? Because it is most certainly effort that I'm willing to put in, having now finally met you."

Sorcha darted her eyes up to the man's face, suspicious. He only laughed harder.

"You do not believe me," Murdoch said. He clasped his hands together and rested them in his lap; Sorcha watched him do so to give her an excuse not to look into his eyes. "Are you always so sceptical of compliments? You are of good birth, and bonnie to look at. You aren't afraid to speak your mind, which I like, and you clearly care deeply for the land on which you live, which I like even more."

Sorcha didn't know what to say. She'd had local lads attempt to woo her with sweet words before; it had been easy to ignore them. But she was supposed to *marry* Murdoch Buchanan. She could not ignore him, nor what he said.

"You are kind to speak of me in that way," she ended

up saying, inclining her head politely. "But I must profess that I remain dutifully suspicious. I think, after a few more days of truly getting to know me, you will realise what a horrible mistake you have made."

Sorcha half expected Murdoch to laugh at the comment as he had laughed at her previous assertions. When he remained silent she raised her head to look at him. All traces of amusement had left his face, leaving only his dark, bottomless eyes staring at her with unknowable intent.

"I do not think so," he said, so quietly Sorcha wasn't sure if she had been meant to hear it. But the words unnerved her, as did Murdoch's gaze; she shot up from her seat.

"I am tired," she mumbled, averting her eyes as she curtsied slightly. "Today has been full of surprises. If you would excuse me."

Sorcha didn't give Murdoch an opportunity to respond before she marched back to her bedroom and closed the door firmly shut behind her. She began pacing upon the wooden floor, a frown of worry creasing her brow.

"He is not bad, but I don't want to marry *anyone*," she said aloud, not caring if anybody heard her. The afternoon sunshine filtered through her window, lighting dust motes on fire and warming Sorcha's skin when she passed through it.

He is not bad, but there is something wrong with him.

That she didn't dare say aloud.

Several hours later, when the sun was low in the sky and her parents had both come and gone to see if she was hungry, Sorcha was still pacing around her room. Something felt off. Awry. She felt like she was being watched.

733

Is Murdoch behind the door? she wondered. She wouldn't put it past the man, despite the fact she knew very little about him. *Or is he outside, spying on me through the window somehow?*

But when she moved over to look into the garden all she could see was the russet fur of a fox where the garden met the forest. The creature was quick to hide when it spied her.

"Strange to see a fox so far out of the forest," Sorcha yawned. She felt suddenly and inexplicably exhausted, as if she had ran for days on an empty stomach. She needed to lie down. She needed to rest. She needed sleep to help her sort through everything she had learned today. But Sorcha slipped on the flat-woven rug that lay beneath the end of her bed, tumbling over her feet with a panicked cry lodged firmly in her throat.

She was unconscious before her head hit the floor.

***

ACKNOWLEDGEMENTS

I can't believe I've released my first box set! That means I actually have enough content in a single series to make one, which is baffling. I guess I must be doing okay at this whole writing thing, after all...

I hope you've enjoyed Chronicles of Curses so far. As you can see from the extra chapters, as well as Scarlett and Adrian's appearances in both Snowstorm King and The Tower Without a Door, I enjoy having characters from one book show up in another. Julian and Evie will definitely be appearing in the fourth book, Prince of Foxes! I'm very excited for all of you to read it.

Will I write books featuring these characters again? Definitely! I have plans for Scarlett and Adrian to feature in a story loosely based on Snow White/Sleeping Beauty, and for Julian and Evie to feature in a Thumbelina-based one. As for Elina and Kilian, they'll be showing up in a story based on Greek mythology, where they find Elina's father.

And that's not to mention all of the other fairy tale ideas I have! And my Assassin and Monsters trilogies, and my sci-fi plots I want to write. So many books, so little time...

Here's to the next one,

Hayley

ABOUT THE AUTHOR

Hayley Louise Macfarlane hails from the very tiny hamlet of Balmaha on the shores of Loch Lomond in Scotland. Having spent eight years studying at the University of Glasgow and graduating with a BSc (hons) in Genetics and then a PhD in Synthetic Biology, Hayley quickly realised that her long-term passion for writing trumped her desire to work in a laboratory.

Now Hayley spends her time writing across a whole host of genres, particularly fairy tales and psychological horror. During 2019, Hayley set herself the ambitious goal of publishing one thing every month. Seven books, two novellas, two short stories and one box set later, she made it. She recommends that anyone who values their sanity and a sensible sleep cycle does not try this.

Lightning Source UK Ltd.
Milton Keynes UK
UKHW010805070521
383312UK00003B/524